"I name my enemy William Allen Hillman Fitzclarence, Steadholder Burdette," Honor said in a voice colder than the heart of space. "I accuse him of murder, of treason, of my own attempted assassination, and of the deaths of children.

"Your Grace, by your oath to me and the proofs I have offered, I claim the life of William Allen Hillman Fitzclarence as forfeit for his crimes, for his cruelty, and for his violation of his sacred oaths to you, to this Conclave, to the People of Grayson, and to God Himself."

"My Lady," Benjamin Mayhew said softly, "by my oath to you, you shall have it."

"Wait!" Fitzclarence lunged to his feet. "My Lords," he cried, "I do not dispute the facts this harlot claims, nor do I regret any of my acts! I did each thing this foreign-born whore claims, and I would do them again—a thousand times again!—before I let an infidel fornicator and this traitor who calls himself Protector pollute and poison a world sacred to God!

"I reject your right to condemn me to death in order to silence God's voice of opposition to your corrupt abuse of power! As is my ancient right, I challenge your decree! Let your Champion stand forth and prove the true will of God sword-to-sword, in the ancient way of our fathers, and may God preserve the righteous!"

Exulation filled him as he saw Mayhew's astonishment, and he snarled in triumph, for he trapped the bastard in his own snare: his so-called "Champion" was the bitch Harrington, who stood bleeding on the Conclave floor. God had brought her openly within reach of Burdette's own sword at last.

Baen Books by David Weber

HONOR HARRINGTON
Flag In Exile

DAVID WEBER

BAEN

> To Roger Zelazny—
> A gentleman, a scholar, a story-teller,
> and a friend I didn't know long enough

FLAG IN EXILE

Copyright © 1995 by David M. Weber

A Baen Book

Baen Publishing Enterprises
P.O. Box 1403
Riverdale NY 10471

ISBN 0-671-87681-3

Cover art by Larry Ruddell

First printing, September 1995
Third printing, November, 1998

Distributed by Simon & Schuster
1230 Avenue of the Americas
New York, NY 10020

Typeset by Windhaven Press, Auburn, N.H.
Printed in the United States of America

• PROLOGUE

Admiral of the Green Hamish Alexander, Thirteenth Earl of White Haven, sat on HMS *Queen Caitrin*'s flag deck and gazed into his display. The Nightingale System's G3 primary was a white speck of fire, and its single habitable planet, too distant to be seen on visuals, showed as a tiny, blue-green light deep in the plot.

So did the angry red rash of enemy warships between it and *Queen Caitrin*, and White Haven studied that crimson wall of light with care. The People's Navy's sensors had detected him hours ago, but the Peeps hadn't tried anything fancy; they'd simply formed a wall between his task force and its objective and steered to meet him well inside the system's hyper limit. That left him the initiative, yet there was only so much he could do with it. They knew why he was here, and they were inside him and able to stay there. Worse, they were staying together, without the erratic maneuvering he'd seen so often. They outnumbered him by four to three, and he'd abandoned any thought of tactical sleight of hand in the face of their steadiness, but he was confident in his ships' qualitative superiority. If he could neither split them up nor outmaneuver them, he was willing enough to meet them head-on.

He checked the range once more, then looked into the com screen to *Queen Caitrin*'s command deck.

"Very well, Captain Goldstein. You may open fire."

"Aye, aye, My Lord!" Captain Frederick Goldstein rapped, and the first, massive salvo spat from *Queen Caitrin*'s port broadside.

The rest of Battle Squadron Twenty-One fired with

her, and all eight superdreadnoughts simultaneously flushed the missile pods towing astern of them. BatRon Eight and BatRon Seventeen's dreadnoughts followed suit, and thirty-two hundred impeller drive missiles lanced out across five and a half million kilometers of vacuum.

White Haven watched their outgoing tracks, and his frown deepened. The opening phase was almost classic, straight out of the tac manuals, yet he felt a nagging, unformed uneasiness. He had nothing overt to justify it, but there were more targets over there than there should have been. Peep resistance had been spotty for months, based on whatever frontier formations had held together long enough to be redeployed against Manticore's drive on Trevor's Star. But this formation's unit strength looked far more like a proper task force, and the difference between its steady, unswerving course and the confusion which had plagued Peep fleet commanders since the war's start was too marked. It roused an instinctive wariness, and that instinct jabbed at him like a sharp stick. It was why he'd fired at such long range rather than closing before he unleashed his first and heaviest salvo, and he made himself sit motionless, fighting an urge to fidget, as return fire stippled his plot.

That fire was lighter than the deluge his own ships had spawned, for the Peeps had no equivalent of Manticore's missile pods, but there were four full battle squadrons—thirty-two ships of the wall, all of them superdreadnoughts—over there. The Peep wall of battle spat twelve hundred birds back at him, and White Haven swallowed a stillborn curse as he realized they'd concentrated solely on BatRon Twenty-One's eight units.

The deadly fireflies streaked towards one another. *Queen Caitrin* twitched as she expelled her second broadside, and her third, and then the green dots of defensive fire spewed out to meet the destruction roaring down on White Haven's lead squadron. Peep missiles began to die, ripped apart by charging counter missiles, but there were simply too many targets. The Peeps were catching on; their tightly concentrated fire was an unmistakable bid to saturate BatRon Twenty-One's point defense, and despite Manticore's superior technology, at least some of that massive salvo would get through.

White Haven's opening broadsides reached attack range first and drove in through the desperate lattice of last ditch defenses. Lasers swiveled and spat coherent light, fighting to kill the incoming missiles at least twenty-five thousand kilometers out, but probability theory plays no favorites. White Haven had spread his fire over three squadrons, not one, yet his salvo density was actually greater, and bomb-pumped lasers gouged at their targets as laser heads began to detonate.

Impeller wedge sidewalls twisted and attenuated the beams, but scores of them got through, and battle steel hulls spat glowing splinters. Atmosphere streamed from the Peep leviathans' lacerated flanks, men and women died, weapons were smashed away, and energy signatures fluctuated as drive nodes blew apart. Yet even as White Haven's missiles pounded his enemies, the remnants of the first massive Havenite salvo broke past his own counter missiles. It was *his* laser clusters' turn to spit fire, but BatRon Eight's lasers were too far astern to range effectively. It was all up to BatRon Twenty-One and BatRon Seventeen, and they simply had too few clusters. Sheer weight of numbers swamped them, and the green lights of friendly ships flashed the spiteful sparkle of battle damage.

Fresh salvos scorched out, battle chatter and the beep of priority signals washed about White Haven, and his eyes narrowed. His squadron commanders and captains knew their business, and their first broadsides had hurt the Peeps badly. CIC's estimates of enemy damage danced across the bottom of his display, and three times as many Peep ships had taken hits. One or two looked to have been half-wrecked, but they kept coming, and *Queen Caitrin* lurched as something got through to her. She bucked again to a second hit, and his plot flickered. It steadied almost instantly, and a corner of his mind noted the damage control side-bar. *Queen Caitrin's* wounds were light, but the two walls of battle angled together, missiles streaking back and forth with mounting fury as the range fell, and he knew it was going to be ugly.

"There goes the first one, My Lord!" his chief of staff announced as a crippled superdreadnought pulled out of the enemy wall and rolled up to interpose the belly of its wedge against the Manticoran fire.

"I see it, Byron," White Haven replied, but his flat voice lacked Captain Hunter's exultation, for his sense of this engagement's new and dangerous rhythm only grew as the wounded vessel withdrew. Mounting damage might have driven that ship out of formation, but its consorts held their course, missile tubes belching back at his wall, and his jaw clenched as he realized the Peeps had finally gotten themselves back together. Their initial, concentrated targeting had been a far cry from the dispersal of the earlier battles, and so was their steadiness under fire. By now, that wall should have been shedding ships by twos and threes. It was being hit far harder than his own, and the fresh proof of Manticore's technical superiority should have taken the heart out of the demoralized Peeps. But it hadn't, and that was frightening to any admiral who knew how the People's Navy still outnumbered the RMN. These people knew Manticore's superior missiles and electronics gave White Haven every advantage in a missile engagement, and they were coming in anyway, taking their losses in ships and lives to get to energy weapon range.

A green light in the plot suddenly flashed the red critical damage icon as half a dozen Peep lasers blasted into HMS *King Michael*, and White Haven's hands clenched on his command chair's arms. The superdreadnought's wedge faltered, then came back up, and for a moment he thought that was the extent of it—until the entire ship simply blew apart. Eight-and-a-third-million tons of warship and six thousand human beings vanished in a sun-bright boil of plasma, and someone behind him gasped in horror.

"Starboard fifteen, Captain Goldstein." White Haven's voice was cold as his eyes while his flag captain acknowledged the order. His vector edged away from the Peeps—not in flight, but simply to hold the range open and exploit Manticore's missile advantage—and his lips tightened as the Havenite force matched his maneuver. More than matched it; they were coming in even more sharply, despite the marginally better angle that gave his fire. More of his missiles were detonating in front of their ships now, sending lasers lashing down their wedges' open throats, and the first Havenite ship suddenly exploded. The range was down to a bare four million kilometers, and more of White Haven's ships were taking hits, but so were the Peeps. Another enemy ship blew apart, then a third. CIC's projections flickered and changed, the odds against his command falling as still more Peep weapons were destroyed, and he bared his teeth as he felt them shifting in his favor.

"Port ten, Captain Goldstein. If they want to close, let's oblige them."

"Aye, aye, My Lord. Coming ten degrees to port," Goldstein replied, and the task force stopped trying to hold the range open. The missile exchange redoubled, but the weight of fire favored Manticore more and more heavily as Peep launchers fell silent. Another Havenite fell out of the wall, covering herself with her impeller wedge as best she could, and something stirred in the back of White Haven's mind. That was five Peep SDs destroyed or out of action to only one of his. At this rate, he'd have a decisive edge, even at energy range, when the two fleets finally came together. Whoever was in command over there had to know that, so why in hell was he still coming in this way? Nightingale was an important outwork for Trevor's Star, but hardly worth the destruction of a force this size! There had to be a reason—

"New contact! Multiple contacts—multiple capital ship impeller sources at zero-four-six zero-three-niner! Range one-eight million klicks and closing! Designate this force Bogey Two!"

White Haven's head snapped around to the main plot as the passionless computers updated it. Two dozen fresh lights glowed crimson off *Queen Caitrin's* starboard bow as a *second* force of Peep superdreadnoughts lit off their drives, and his nostrils flared in sudden understanding.

No wonder that wall had closed so steadily! White Haven extended his enemies a single moment of ungrudging respect as he recognized the trap into which that unflinching Peep formation was herding his own. Another fifteen minutes, and he would have been hopelessly boxed, committed to close action against Bogey One even as Bogey Two came boring into his flank from above, and he'd walked straight into it.

But they didn't have him boxed yet, he thought grimly. The new Peep government's purges of its officer corps had cost them dearly in experience, and it showed. Bogey Two's commander had jumped the gun, possibly out of panic at the losses Bogey One was taking, and lit off his drives too soon. A more experienced CO would have waited, whatever happened to Bogey One, until he had the Manticoran wall at point-blank, trapped between both enemy walls and with its long-range advantages negated in an energy weapon engagement.

White Haven studied the projected vectors, and his blue eyes hardened in concentration. He couldn't fight a force that size and live. He had to break back across the hyper limit before they trapped him, and he couldn't simply reverse course to do it. The Peeps' vectors converged twelve million kilometers ahead of him on his present track, and his velocity was too high to kill before he reached that point. His only chance was to break to port, away from Bogey Two, but that would take him right into Bogey One's teeth, and for all its damage, Bogey One still had the energy weapons to kill too many of his ships.

He made himself accept it. It was going to be even uglier than he'd thought, but at least his people would give as good as they got as they broke past Bogey One's wall. His fingers flew as he punched a new course into his auxiliary astrogation display. Numbers flickered, and a core of fire flashed in his eyes as vector projections changed. He was ahead of Bogey One. Not by much, but by enough that he could cross its track without turning straight into its broadsides and letting them rake his entire wall. The Peeps would have to alter course, curving inside him, or let him cross *their* wall's bows. They could stay with him, if they chose, draw out the pounding match to cost him more ships, but it would cost *them* more ships, too.

"Come to two-seven-zero zero-zero-zero! Maximum military power! All units roll ship against Bogey Two and continue engagement against Bogey One!"

Acknowledgments crackled, and his wall turned sharply towards Bogey One. Its units rolled, presenting the roofs of their impeller wedges to Bogey Two—still far beyond the powered missile envelope—while their own missiles ripped into Bogey One across the dwindling light-seconds between them, and White Haven glared at his plot as he ran for it.

And he *was* running. He knew it, just as he knew how much the approaching beam engagement was going to cost, and so did everyone else, the Peeps as well as his own people. For the first time, the People's Republic of Haven had stopped a Manticoran offensive cold, and he watched numbers dance across the bottom of his plot as both Peep forces changed course and CIC worked the new numbers to tell him just how bad it was going to be.

It would be close, even if he made it out, but the problem with this sort of trap was that the timing had to be exactly right. Space was big enough to hide whole fleets as long as they radiated no betraying emissions, yet for an ambush to succeed, the ambushers had to be on the right vector when they *did* bring their drives up, and even when the intended victim cooperated as he had—

The numbers froze, and Hamish Alexander breathed a silent, heartfelt prayer of thanks. They'd missed. Bogey

Two had lit off its drives just too soon to catch him. That meant it was all up to Bogey One, and—

Another green light flashed scarlet in his plot, and he tasted blood from a bitten lip as HMS *Thunderer* broke in half. Life pod beacons flashed in the display as her survivors bailed out, but he could do nothing for them. If he slowed to pick them up, Bogey Two *would* overhaul his wall, and any light units he detached for search and rescue purposes would be overtaken and destroyed.

Thunderer's broken halves vanished in a brilliant flash as her scuttling charges blew. A sixth Peep superdreadnought joined her in death moments later, and Hamish Alexander clenched his jaw and shoved himself firmly back in his command chair. At least Bogey Two would have plenty of ships available for SAR. No doubt they'd pick up his people as well as their own, and he tried to soothe his guilt with that cold comfort. A prisoner of war camp—even a Peep POW camp—was better than death, he told himself bitterly.

"Energy range in thirty-seven minutes, My Lord," Captain Hunter said quietly. "CIC estimates Bogey One can stay with us clear to the hyper limit if it wants to."

"Understood." White Haven made himself sound calm and unworried. He knew he wasn't fooling Hunter, but the rules required them both to pretend.

He watched a seventh SD withdraw from Bogey One's wall and tried to be glad. It was only twenty-two to twenty-five, now, and his missile crews would make those odds still better before they reached beam range, yet Bogey One maintained its unwavering course. The People's Navy was larger than the RMN, able to accept heavier losses, and Bogey One's obvious intention to do just that sent a fresh chill through White Haven.

The war had just changed, he thought distantly, watching the exchange of fire grow still more furious. The Peeps were back on balance. They were initiating, no longer reacting with clumsy panic to Manticoran attacks. He'd known it was coming, that the People's Republic was simply too vast to be toppled in a rush, but he'd prayed for it to take longer. Now he knew it hadn't, and he drew a deep breath.

"We'll go with Delta-Three, Byron," he said quietly, formally committing himself to hyper out and run for it as quickly as possible. "Put everything we've got on their central squadron. That's probably where their flagship is; maybe we can take it out before we get to energy range."

"Aye, aye, My Lord," Captain Hunter replied.

The Earl of White Haven listened to his chief of staff passing orders over the task force command net and leaned back in his chair, watching the flash of warheads pock the visual display. He'd done all he could.

Now it only remained to see how many of his people would survive.

• CHAPTER ONE

Like all public buildings on Grayson, Protector's Palace lay under a controlled-environment dome, but a corner of the grounds held another, smaller dome, as well. It was a greenhouse, and High Admiral Wesley Matthews braced himself as an armsman in the House of Mayhew's maroon and gold opened its door for him. An almost visible wave of humid heat swirled out, and he sighed and unhooked his tunic collar, but that was as far as he intended to go. *This* time he was going to stay in proper uniform if it killed him.

"Hello, Wesley." Benjamin Mayhew IX, Protector of Grayson, greeted his senior military officer without looking up from whatever he was doing.

"Good morning, Your Grace." Matthews' respectful reply sounded curiously stifled, for the climate in here was even worse than he'd expected. The Protector was in shirtsleeves, his forehead beaded with perspiration, and the high admiral mopped at his own suddenly streaming face, looked at the enviro display, and winced. Resolution was no defense against a temperature of forty degrees centigrade and a ninety-six percent humidity, and he grimaced and stripped off his uniform tunic to emulate his ruler.

The rustle of fabric wasn't loud, but it was very quiet in the greenhouse. The soft sound carried well, and Benjamin looked up with a grin.

"Did you turn the thermostat up just for me, Your Grace?" Matthews inquired, and Benjamin looked innocent.

"Of course not, Wesley. Why would I do such a thing?"

Matthews arched a polite eyebrow, and the Protector chuckled. Wesley Matthews was extraordinarily young for his rank, even for a world like Grayson, where the prolong anti-aging treatments were only just becoming available. He'd jumped from commodore to commander-in-chief of the Grayson Space Navy less than four T-years ago, and like Bernard Yanakov, the man he'd succeeded, he was baffled by his Protector's taste in hobbies. Floriculture and flower arrangement were high art forms on Grayson, but they were traditionally female ones. Matthews willingly admitted that his ruler produced breathtaking arrangements, yet it still seemed an . . . odd avocation for a head of state. Bernard Yanakov, however, had been Benjamin Mayhew's older cousin, as well as his senior admiral, which had given him certain advantages Matthews lacked. He'd known the Protector literally since birth and twitted him about his hobby for years; Matthews couldn't do that—which hadn't kept Benjamin from guessing how he felt.

Matthews had been vastly relieved when the Protector chose to be amused rather than offended, yet sometimes he wondered if things had worked out so well after all. Benjamin took a positive glee in summoning him for meetings during which he puttered about with vases and cut flowers or which just *happened* to take place in spots like this greenhouse furnace. It had become a sort of shared joke, and Tester knew they both needed any relaxation they could find these days, but this time the heat and humidity were almost overwhelming.

"Actually," Benjamin said after a moment, "I hadn't intended to inflict anything quite this, ah, energetic upon you, Wesley, but I didn't have much choice." His voice was genuinely contrite, yet he also returned his attention to the blossom before him, and Matthews stepped closer, fascinated despite himself, as the Protector manipulated a collecting probe with surgical precision and continued his apology, if such it was.

"This is a specimen of Hibson's Orchid from Indus, in the Mithra System. Beautiful, isn't it?"

"Yes, it is, Your Grace," Matthews murmured. The bell-shaped flower was an incredibly subtle blend of blues and dark purples with a deep-throated, golden core shot with scarlet, and the admiral felt an odd, drifting sensation, as if he were falling into its perfumed depths. The feeling was so strong he had to shake himself, and Benjamin laughed softly.

"Indeed it is, but it's extremely difficult to propagate off-planet, and the male flower only blossoms for a single day once every three T-years. I've been fascinated by it since I first saw it in a conservatory on Old Earth, and I think I'm on the brink of developing a hybrid that will bloom about twice as frequently. Unfortunately, timing is everything in a project like this, and reproducing its natural environment is critical. I'm afraid I didn't expect it to flower today, and I hadn't actually expected to drag you out here when you asked to drop by, but if I don't jump on it right now—"

He shrugged, and Matthews nodded, forgetting for once to assume his proper attitude of martyred tolerance as the orchid's beauty worked upon him. He stood in respectful silence while Benjamin finished collecting the pollen and examined his treasure under a magnifier with intense satisfaction.

"Now we just have to wait for *these* to open," he said more briskly, waving to the tight-furled buds on another vine.

"And how long will that take, Your Grace?" Matthews asked politely, and Benjamin chuckled again.

"At least another forty hours, so I don't expect you to stand around and wait." The Protector slid his pollen into a storage unit, wiped sweat from his forehead, and gestured to the door, and Matthews sighed in relief.

He followed his ruler from the greenhouse, and Benjamin's armsman fell in at their heels while they crossed to a comfortable nook beside a splashing fountain. The Protector took a seat and waved Matthews into a facing chair, then leaned back as a servant appeared with towels and iced drinks. The admiral scrubbed his soaking hair briskly, then mopped his face and sipped gratefully, and Benjamin crossed his legs.

"Now, Wesley. What was it you wanted to see me about?"

"Lady Harrington, Your Grace," Matthews replied promptly. Benjamin sighed, and the admiral leaned forward persuasively. "I know you still think it's too soon, Your Grace, but we *need* her. We need her very badly, indeed."

"I understand that," Benjamin said patiently, "but I'm not going to push her. She's still recovering, Wesley. She needs time."

"It's been over nine *months*, Your Grace." Matthews' tone was respectful but stubborn.

"I realize that, and I also realize how valuable she could be to you, but her life's hardly been what you could call easy, now has it?" Benjamin held the admiral's eyes, and Matthews shook his head. "She deserves however long she needs to heal," the Protector went on, "and I intend to see she has it. Wait till she's ready, Wesley."

"But how will we know when she *is* ready if you won't even let me ask her about it?"

Benjamin frowned, then nodded as if against his will.

"A point," he admitted. "Definitely a point, but—" He broke off with an angry little shrug and sipped his own drink before he continued. "The problem is that I don't think she's gotten herself put back together again. I can't be certain—she's not the sort to cry on people's shoulders—but Katherine's gotten more out of her than I think she realizes, and it was bad, Wesley. Really bad. I was afraid we were going to lose her completely for a few months, and the way certain elements have reacted to her hasn't helped."

Matthews grunted in understanding, and a look of something very like guilt crossed Benjamin's face.

"I knew some of the reactionaries would come into the open once they got over the initial shock, but I didn't expect them to be quite this blatant, and I should have." The Protector's free hand fisted and pounded his knee while he grimaced in distaste. "I still think it was the right move," he went on, as if to himself. "We *need* her as a steadholder, but if I'd realized what it was going to cost her, I never would have done it. And when you add the protesters to Captain Tankersley's death—"

"Your Grace," Matthews said firmly, "this isn't something for you to blame yourself over. *We* didn't have anything to do with Captain Tankersley's murder, and Lady Harrington knows it. Even if she didn't, you were right; we *do* need her as a steadholder if the reforms are going to stand, and whatever the lunatic fringe thinks, most of our people respect her deeply. I'm quite sure she knows *that*, too, and she's a very strong person. We both know that, because we've both seen her in action. She'll get through this."

"I hope so, Wesley. I hope to God she will," Benjamin murmured.

"She will. But that brings me back to my point. We need her naval experience just as badly as we need her as a steadholder, and with all due respect, Your Grace, I think we're doing her a disservice by not telling her so."

It was the admiral's strongest statement of disagreement with his own view Benjamin had heard yet, and he frowned. Not angrily, but in consideration. Matthews recognized his expression and sat waiting while Grayson's ruler ran back through the arguments and counter arguments.

"I don't know," he said finally. "You may be right, but I still want to give her as much time as we can."

"Again with all due respect, Your Grace, I think that's a mistake. You're the one who insists we have to learn to treat women with full equality. I believe you're right about that, and I think most of our people are coming around to the same view, whether they like it or not. But I also think you haven't quite learned to do it yourself yet." Benjamin stiffened, and Matthews went on in a calm, measured tone. "I mean no disrespect, but you're trying to protect her. That's a very fine thing, exactly what I would expect from any decent Grayson . . . but would you try quite so hard if she were a man?"

The Protector's eyes narrowed, his expression arrested, and then he shook his head in chagrin. Unlike most Graysons, he'd been educated off-world, on Old Terra herself. The traditional Grayson view held that asking women to bear the same responsibilities as men was a perversion of nature, but he'd been exposed to a society in which the notion that men and women might possibly be considered *un*equal would have been regarded as equally grotesque, and he'd accepted that view. Yet at the bottom of all his genuine commitment to it, he was a Grayson, and one who owed his entire family's lives to Honor Harrington. How much *had* his auto-reflex instinct to protect her affected his judgment?

"You may be right," he said at last. "I don't think I want you to be, but that's beside the point." He rubbed his chin for another long moment, then met Matthews' eyes once more. "I'm not saying I agree or disagree with you, but what makes it so urgent to press the point right this minute?"

"The Manticorans will have to pull their last capital units out of Yeltsin within two months, Your Grace," the admiral said quietly.

"They will?" Benjamin sat up, and Matthews nodded. "No one's said anything about it to me or Chancellor Prestwick—not yet, at least."

"I didn't say the decision had been made, Your Grace. Nor did I say they wanted to. I said they'd *have* to do it. They won't have any choice."

"Why not?"

"Because the momentum is shifting." Matthews laid his tunic across his lap, extracted an old-fashioned hardcopy note pad from one pocket, and opened it to double-check the figures he'd jotted in it.

"In the war's first six months," he said, "Manticore captured nineteen Havenite star systems, including two major fleet bases. Their total capital ship losses during that time were two superdreadnoughts and five dreadnoughts, against which they destroyed forty Havenite ships of the wall. They also added thirty-one capital ships to their own order of battle—twenty-six captured units, exclusive of the eleven Admiral White Haven gave us after Third Yeltsin, and five more from new construction. That put them within roughly ninety percent of the Peeps' remaining ships of the wall, and they had the advantage of the initiative, not to mention the edge the People's Navy's confusion and shattered morale gave them.

"In the last three months, however, the RMN's captured only *two* systems and lost nineteen capital ships doing it—including the ten they lost at Nightingale, where they *didn't* take the system. The Peeps are still taking heavier losses, but remember that they have all those battleships. They may be too small for proper ships of the wall, but they provide a rear area coverage the Manties can't match without diverting dreadnoughts or superdreadnoughts, which frees a higher percentage of the Peeps' ships of the wall for front-line use. Put simply, the Peeps still have more ships to lose than Manticore does, and the war is slowing down, Your Grace. Peep resistance is stiffening, and the Manties are transferring more and more of their own strength to the front in an effort to hang onto their momentum."

"How bad is it?" Benjamin asked intently.

"As I say, their losses are climbing. They've already reduced their Home Fleet to barely a third of its pre-war strength, and it's not enough. I think they know it, too, but they also know the Peeps are going to bring them more or less to a halt in another few months. They're trying to push as hard as they can before that happens—to get as deep into the People's Republic as possible before the Peeps can start thinking about counterattacks. That means they're going to start calling in every ship they can spare—maybe even a few *more* than they can withdraw with complete safety. Given that the last of our own SDs recommissions in January, Yeltsin's Star is certainly one place they can trust to look after itself. In light of that, I'm astonished they haven't already pulled out the last of their capital units. Certainly no strategist worth his salt will leave them here much longer, Your Grace. They can't."

Benjamin rubbed his chin again. "I knew things were slowing down, but I hadn't realized how drastically. What's changed, Wesley?"

"That's hard to say, Your Grace, but I've been in correspondence with Admiral Caparelli, and Admiral Givens at the Manties' ONI confirms that this Committee of Public Safety that's running the PRH has consolidated all previous security organs under one new, monster umbrella. You'd have to look back to Old Earth's Totalitarian Age for a parallel to how ruthlessly they've purged their officer corps, and there are rumors they're sending out 'political officers' to watchdog their fleet commanders. Their purges cost them virtually all their senior—and experienced—flag officers, and the officers they *haven't* killed off are competing out of their class against the RMN, but the ones who survive are learning . . . and they know what'll happen if they fail the new regime. Add in some sort of political commissars to *remind* them of that, and you get a navy with a powerful will to fight. They're far clumsier than the Manties, but their navy's still bigger, and once some of their new admirals start lasting long enough to gain the experience their predecessors had—"

Matthews shrugged, and the Protector nodded unhappily.

"Do you expect Manticore to totally lose the initiative?"

"Not totally, Your Grace. What I *do* expect is a period of balance . . . and then for things to get really nasty. I imagine the Peeps will try a few counterattacks, but I also expect the Manties to chew them up when they do. I can't predict events with any certainty, but I can give you my personal estimate of what's going to happen, if you want to hear it."

Benjamin nodded, and Matthews raised his hand, extending one finger at a time as he made his points.

"First, there'll be a period of stalemate, with both sides skirmishing for advantage but with neither daring to withdraw too many ships of the wall from the main combat area. Second, the Alliance will get its industry fully cranked up. The Manties are already there. They had eighteen of the wall under construction in the Star Kingdom itself from prewar programs; those units are now proceeding on a crash priority basis to commission over the next six months, and their new war program will start delivering additional units within ten months. Our own yards will complete our first home-built SD about the same time, and the Manty yards in Grendelsbane and Talbot will do the same. Once we hit our stride, we'll be turning out four or five of the wall a month.

"On the Peeps' side, they've already effectively lost their advantage in ships of the wall, and the Manties have taken out a half dozen of their major forward service bases. That means simply repairing battle damage will put a greater strain on their building yards and, in turn, slow construction rates. Despite its size, their industrial plant's less efficient than the Alliance's, and I don't think they can outbuild us. On the other hand, *we* can't outbuild *them*, either, certainly not by a decisive margin, and they still have the battleships I already mentioned. Which means, three, that this is going to be a long, long war unless one side or the other completely screws up.

"In the long run, the decisive factor will probably be the relative strengths of our political systems. At the moment, Pierre and his Committee have instituted what amounts to a reign of terror. Whether or not they can sustain that, or find something more stable to replace it, is the critical question in my own view, because this war isn't about territory anymore. It's become a war for *survival*; someone—either the Kingdom of Manticore and its allies, including us, or the People's Republic of Haven—is going down this time, Your Grace. For good."

Protector Benjamin nodded slowly. Matthews' assessment of the war's political dimensions dovetailed exactly with his own, and he'd developed a powerful respect for the high admiral's military judgment.

"And that, Your Grace," Matthews said quietly, "is why we need Lady Harrington. Virtually our entire cadre of senior officers was wiped out in the Masadan War, and we're promoting men who've never skippered anything heavier than a light attack craft to command destroyers and cruisers—even *battle*cruisers. My own experience is limited enough by Manticoran standards, and when the Manties pull out, I'll be the most experienced officer we've got . . . except for Lady Harrington."

"But she's a Manticoran officer. Would they even let us have her?"

"I think their Admiralty would be happy to," Matthews replied. "It wasn't *their* idea to put her on half-pay, and, historically, the Star Kingdom often 'loans' half-pay officers to allies. They've already loaned us a lot of other officers and enlisted people, for that matter. I don't know what political impact commissioning Lady Harrington in our Navy would have, of course. Given her expulsion from their House of Lords, I suppose it might be viewed pretty negatively, but my impression is that Queen Elizabeth is firmly in Lady Harrington's corner."

"She is, and so is most of the House of Commons," Benjamin murmured. He leaned back and closed his eyes in thought, then sighed. "Let me think about it. I agree with your assessment, and I agree we need her, but whether it's parochial and protective of me or not, I refuse to place fresh demands on her until I'm certain she's ready to bear them. It won't do her or us any good to drive her too hard too soon."

"No, Your Grace," Wesley Matthews said respectfully, but deep inside he knew he'd won. Benjamin Mayhew was a good man, one who cared deeply for the woman who'd saved his world from Masada forty-two T-months ago, but he was also the planetary ruler of Grayson. In the end, the overriding responsibility of that position would force him to put Honor Harrington into Grayson uniform . . . whatever it cost her.

• CHAPTER TWO

Lady Dame Honor Harrington, Countess and Stead-holder Harrington, took three quick steps and bounced on her toes. The diving board flexed sharply, and she arced through the air to enter the water with scarcely a splash. Ripples turned the surface to wavy glass, but the pool was crystal clear, and Senior Chief Steward James MacGuiness watched her glide over its tiled bottom with a dolphin's grace. She planed up to the surface, then rolled and backstroked towards the far end of the fifty-meter pool on the final leg of her regular morning swim.

Harrington House's crystoplast dome muted the strength of Grayson's F6 primary, and a sleek, six-limbed treecat opened grass-green eyes in a puddle of filtered sunlight atop a poolside table as MacGuiness draped a towel over his arm and crossed to the pool steps. The 'cat rose and stretched his sinuous, sixty-centimeter body luxuriously, then sat upright on his four rearmost limbs. He curled his fluffy, prehensile tail about his true-feet and hand-paws, and a lazy yawn bared needle fangs in an unmistakable grin of amused tolerance as he watched his dripping person emerge from the pool. She wrung out her shoulder-length braid before she accepted MacGuiness' towel with a murmured thanks, and the 'cat shook his head. Treecats hated getting wet, but Nimitz had adopted Honor Harrington forty T-years before. He'd had plenty of time to get used to her sometimes peculiar notions of enjoyment.

Major Andrew LaFollet of the Harrington Stead-holder's Guard hadn't, and he did his best not to look

20

uncomfortable as the Steadholder wrapped the towel about herself. Despite his youth, the major was the HSG's second ranking officer and very, very good at his job. He was also Lady Harrington's personal armsman and the head of her permanent security team, and Grayson law required that a steadholder be accompanied by his—or, in Lady Harrington's very special case, *her*—bodyguards at all times. It was a requirement LaFollet knew she'd found less than easy to accept, yet there were times he and his fellows found the arrangement even less comfortable than she did.

The major had been horrified when he learned his Steadholder intended to *deliberately* immerse herself in over three meters of water. Swimming was a lost art on Grayson; LaFollet hadn't known a single person who'd ever acquired it, and he'd been unable to imagine why any sane individual would want to. Grayson's high concentration of heavy metals meant even its "fresh" water was dangerously contaminated. In all his thirty-three T-years before entering Lady Harrington's service, Andrew LaFollet had never drunk or even bathed in water which hadn't been distilled and purified, and the notion of putting thousands of liters of precious water into a hole in the ground and then jumping into it was . . . well, "bizarre" was the kindest word which had sprung to mind when Lady Harrington ordered her "swimming pool."

Of course, any steadholder—and especially this one— was entitled to his or her foibles, yet LaFollet had nursed one deep concern over the project. Well, two concerns actually, but only one he'd cared to voice to Lady Harrington. She and Chief MacGuiness were the only two people in the entire Steading of Harrington who could swim, so what were her armsmen supposed to do if she got into trouble out in the middle of all that wet stuff?

He'd felt like a blushing, untutored yokel as he put that gruff-voiced question to her, but she'd simply considered it gravely, and his blush had turned darker when she didn't laugh. Of course, she seldom laughed anymore. Her huge eyes seemed perpetually dark and shadowed, but this time they'd held a small gleam of humor, too, and, despite his embarrassment, he'd been glad. It was far better than other things he'd seen in them, yet that amusement had also underscored the very thing that made it so hard to do his job properly.

The Steadholder had problems with the concept that protecting her was the most important task in her armsmen's universe, and the things she enjoyed doing were enough to turn any bodyguard's hair white. LaFollet had been able to accept her naval career, when she'd had one. Though he hadn't really *liked* it, the risks that came with commanding a warship were fitting for a steadholder and far less . . . frivolous than certain others she insisted upon running.

Swimming was bad enough, but at least she did that on a nice, flat piece of Harrington House's protectively domed grounds—which made it infinitely preferable to her *other* pursuits. Hang-gliding was a planetary passion on her home world, and LaFollet cringed every time he thought of it. He knew she'd been an expert glider before *he* learned to walk, yet her refusal to so much as consider taking along an emergency counter-grav unit was less than reassuring to the man charged with keeping her alive.

Fortunately, hang-gliding was as out of the question on Grayson as skinny dipping. Over the course of their thousand-year history, Graysons had developed higher tolerances for heavy metals than most humans. Lady Harrington hadn't, and—praise God fasting!—her career as a naval officer had given her a healthy respect for environmental hazards. Which, unfortunately, wasn't much help on her rare visits to her parents. LaFollet and Corporal Mattingly had spent an absolutely horrifying afternoon following her fragile glider around Sphinx's craggy-peaked Copper Wall Mountains and far out over the Tannerman Ocean in a tractor-equipped air car, and thoughts of what an ill-intentioned person with a pulse rifle might have done to such a sitting target were not calculated to help a bodyguard sleep soundly.

Her passion for mountain climbing was even worse, in a way. He was willing to accept her assurances that other people did "real" rock climbing, but scrambling up and down steep slopes and along the brinks of towering precipices with her—and on a 1.35-gravity world, at that—was quite enough of an adventure. Then there was the ten-meter sloop she kept in her parents' enormous boathouse. Even counter-grav life jackets had seemed dreadfully frail props to people who hadn't had the least idea how to swim as she sent it skimming over the waves and they clung white-knuckled to stays or cleats.

She'd done it on purpose, and LaFollet even knew why. It was her way of announcing her refusal to abandon the life she'd spent forty-seven T-years learning to live just because she'd become a steadholder. She was willing to accept her armsmen's insistence on guarding her as their oaths required, but she was who she was. Her refusal to be anyone else might set her at infinitely polite loggerheads with her chief armsman on occasion, yet he knew it was also one of the traits which won her people's devotion, not simply the obedience to which any steadholder was entitled. And despite all the worry it caused him, it eased his heart to know there were things she could still enjoy doing.

Still, there *were* times he wished she were just a *little* like a traditional Grayson woman. His own concepts of propriety had been—"expanded" was the best word for it—as her armsman, but he was still a Grayson. He'd tackled the task of learning to swim and completed a life-saving course out of grim devotion to duty and, to his own surprise, found he enjoyed it. Most of her security detail did, though Jamie Candless still harbored pronounced reservations. They'd even taken to spending many of their own off-duty hours in the Steadholder's pool, but Lady Harrington's swimsuit was an armed assault on Grayson mores. LaFollet's standards had

become progressively less "proper" over the past year—
which he was prepared to admit, intellectually, was probably a good thing—yet he was guiltily aware of the
ingrained criteria of his rearing whenever he watched
his Steadholder swim.

He knew she'd made concessions. Her one-piece suit
was positively dowdy by Manticoran standards, but the
corner of his mind where the most basic elements of
socialization lived insisted she might as well be naked.
Worse, she'd received the newest, most efficient prolong treatment in early childhood. She looked absurdly
youthful, and her exotic, almond-eyed, strongly carved
beauty and athletic grace threatened to provoke a highly
improper response in the major. She was thirteen T-years
older than he, yet she looked like someone's younger
sister, and he had no business at all thinking of his
Steadholder as the most attractive woman he knew—
especially not while her soaked swimsuit clung to every
supple curve.

Now he stood with his back to her while she finished
drying, then heaved a mental sigh of relief as she
accepted a robe from MacGuiness and belted its sash.
She settled into the poolside chair, and he turned back
to take his proper place at her shoulder and felt his lips
twitch as she looked up with one of her small, crooked
smiles. It wasn't much of a smile, and the tiny hesitation as the left corner of her mouth obeyed its rebuilt,
artificial nerves pulled it off center, but it showed she
knew what he was thinking, and her amusement was far
too gentle to resent. There was nothing taunting or con-
descending about it. It was a wry, shared awareness of
the differences in their birth societies—nothing more—
and just seeing it warmed his heart. Darkness lurked
behind it even now, and he knew how quickly and unexpectedly it could be quenched, yet the grief and loss
which had weighed upon her for far too long had begun to ease at last. It was a slow and painful process,
but he was profoundly grateful it had begun. He could
stand a little embarrassment if it made Lady Harrington

smile, and he shrugged to acknowledge their shared awareness of his harassed cultural parochialism.

Honor Harrington's smile broadened at her armsman's acknowledgment of his own sense of the absurd, and then she looked away as MacGuiness uncovered a tray and set it on the table with a flourish. Nimitz leapt up into his own chair with a happy "Bleek!" and Honor's smile became a grin. She preferred a light luncheon, and MacGuiness had prepared one of salad and cheese for her, but Nimitz's whiskers twitched in delight as the steward placed a dish of roasted rabbit before him.

"You spoil us, Mac," she said, and MacGuiness shook his head fondly. He poured rich, dark beer into her stein, and she selected a cheese wedge and nibbled it appreciatively. She still had to approach Grayson foods with care—the Diaspora's two millennia had taken Terran vegetables to very different environments, and subtle variations between nominally identical species could have unfortunate consequences—but the local cheeses were delicious.

"Ummmmmm!" she sighed, and reached for her beer. She sipped and looked back up at LaFollet. "Are we on schedule for the dedication, Andrew?"

"Yes, My Lady. Colonel Hill and I are going over the arrangements this afternoon. I should have the finalized schedule for you this evening."

"Good." She sipped more beer, but her eyes were thoughtful, and she cocked an eyebrow as she lowered the stein. "Why do I have the feeling you're not entirely satisfied about something?"

"Not satisfied, My Lady?" LaFollet gave a slight frown and shook his head. "I wouldn't say that." Her other eyebrow rose. He met her gaze levelly for a second, then sighed. "I suppose I *am* still just a bit unhappy about the crowd control planning, My Lady," he confessed, and she frowned.

"Andrew, we've been over this. I know it bothers you, but we can't go around arresting people for exercising their right of assembly."

"No, My Lady," LaFollet replied with deferential obstinacy, resisting the temptation to point out that some steadholders could—and would—do just that. "But we certainly *can* exclude anyone we think is a security risk."

It was Honor's turn to sigh, and she leaned back with a small, fond grimace. Her empathic link to Nimitz was far stronger than the normal human-'cat bond. So far as she knew, no other human had ever been able to sense a 'cat's emotions, much less sense those of others *through* the 'cat, and she'd tried, at first, to discourage Nimitz from sharing the feelings of those about her with her. But it was like trying to remember not to breathe, and, she admitted, she'd clung to Nimitz with such near desperation over the last T-year that it had become almost impossible not to know what people around her felt. She told herself—or tried to—that it was little different from being exceptionally good at reading expressions, but either way, she'd finally accepted that Nimitz wasn't going to let her *not* use her newfound abilities.

Like now. Nimitz liked LaFollet, and he saw no reason not to convey the major's emotions to her—or to hide his own approval of him. Both of them knew how devoted to her LaFollet was, and she was perfectly well aware the true reason he wanted to crack down on demonstrators was only peripherally connected to security risks. Oh, there was a trace of that, but his real motives were far simpler: outrage and a determination to protect her from fresh wounds.

Her smile faded, and her long fingers toyed with her stein. She was the first female steadholder ever, the symbol and, many would say, the *cause* of the upheavals echoing through the bedrock of Grayson society. Worse, she was not only female, but a foreigner who wasn't even a communicant of the Church of Humanity Unchained! The Church might have accepted her as Harrington Steading's liege lady, just as the Conclave of Steadholders had accepted her into its membership, but not everyone supported those decisions.

She supposed she couldn't blame the dissenters,

though it was sometimes hard to remember that. Their attacks could hurt—badly—yet a part of her actually welcomed them. Not because she liked being vilified, but because her desperate, back-to-the-wall defense of Grayson against the fanatics of Masada gave her a stature with the majority of Graysons which she still found an uncomfortable fit. The honors with which they'd heaped her, including her steadholdership, sometimes left her feeling uneasily as if she were playing a part, and the proof that not all Graysons saw her as some sort of holo-drama heroine could be almost reassuring.

It was unpleasant, to put it mildly, to be called "the Handmaiden of Satan," but at least the street preachers' ranting cut through the deference others showed her. She remembered reading that one of Old Earth's empires—she couldn't recall whether it had been the Roman or the French—had placed a slave in the chariot of a victorious general as he paraded triumphantly through the streets. While the crowds screamed his praises, it was the slave's function to remind him, again and again, that he was only mortal. At the time she'd read it, she'd thought it a quaint custom; now she'd come to appreciate its fundamental wisdom, for she suspected it would be seductively easy to accept the endless cheers at face value. After all, who *didn't* want to be a hero?

That thought flicked her unexpectedly on the raw, and her eyes darkened with the sudden stab of cold, familiar pain. She gazed down into her stein, mouth tightening, and fought the darkness, but it was hard. So hard. It came without warning, perpetually waiting to ambush her. It was a weakness deep within which she knew had diminished her, and the complexity of its components only made its attacks harder to anticipate. She never knew what would set them off, for there were too many still bleeding edges, too many wounds to be ripped open yet again by some unexpected word or thought.

None of her Grayson subjects knew about her night-mares. No one but Nimitz knew, and she was grateful. The 'cat understood her pain, the grinding, hopeless guilt of those horrible nights—becoming blessedly, if slowly, less frequent—when she remembered how she'd become Grayson's heroine . . . and the nine hundred people who'd died aboard the ships of her squadron in the process. The people a *real* hero would have kept alive somehow. Nor were they all the deaths she had to mourn. She'd always known commanding a warship meant people might live or die by her judgment. It was only in stupid stories written by idiots that good triumphed unscathed and only the evil died. She'd *known* that, but where did it say *her* people must always be the ones to pay for victory?

Her hand tightened on her beer stein, and her eyes burned at the universe's uncaring callousness. She'd had to face her dead before, yet this time was different. This time the pain sucked her under like a Sphinx tidal bore, for this time she'd lost her certitude. "Duty." "Honor." Such important words, yet the bitter, wounded part of her wondered why she'd ever devoted her life to such thankless concepts. They'd seemed so clear, once, so easy to define, but they'd become less so with every death. With every medal and title heaped upon her while the cost to others grew and grew. And under the pain of all those deaths was the knowledge of how fiercely another part of her clung to those honors—not for their own sakes, but in the despairing hope that they proved it had *meant* something. That the one thing she did better than anything else had some meaning beyond the pointless extinction of people who'd followed her orders to their deaths.

She drew a deep breath and held it, and she knew— didn't simply think, *knew*—that her people's deaths *had* meant something, and that no one else blamed her for not dying with them. Nimitz's ability to share others' feelings with her proved it, and she knew about "survivor's guilt." She knew *she* hadn't created the terrible odds which had killed so many, and she'd done her best.

There'd been a time after the Masadan War and even after the Battle of Hancock when she'd been able to accept that. Not happily or easily, but without the terrible dreams when she heard and saw her people die once more. She'd faced the same doubts then and fought them down and gone on with her life, but this time she couldn't, for something had broken inside her.

She knew, in the dark hours of the night when she faced her soul with desolate honesty, what that something was, and knowing made her feel small and contemptible, for the loss she *hadn't* learned to live with— the one that had destroyed her ability to cope—was personal. Paul Tankersley had been but one man; the fact that she'd loved him more than life itself shouldn't make his death so much more terrible than those of all the men and women who'd died under her command. Yet it did. Oh, *God*, it did! They'd had less than a single T-year together, and even now, ten months after she'd lost him, she still woke in the night, reaching out to the emptiness beside her, and felt the terrible weight of her aloneness once more.

And it was that loss—*her* loss—which had truly stolen her certainty. It was her own selfish grief that weakened her and made all the other deaths so much more terrible, and a part of her loathed herself for it. Not because she was uncertain, but because it was unspeakably weak and wrong to grieve for all those others only as an echo of her anguish over Paul's death.

She'd wondered—sometimes, when she let herself— what would have become of her without Nimitz. No one else knew how she'd longed for extinction, how much part of her had hungered simply to quit. To end. She'd once intended, coldly and logically, to do just that as soon as she'd destroyed the men who'd killed Paul. She'd sacrificed her naval career to bring them down, and a corner of her mind suspected she'd actually *wanted* to sacrifice it—that she'd planned to use the loss of the vocation she loved so much as one more reason to end her dreary existence. It had seemed only reasonable then; now the memory was one more coal of contempt for her own weakness, her willingness to surrender to her own pain when she'd always refused to surrender to anyone else.

A soft, warm weight flowed into her lap. Delicate true-hands rested on her shoulders, a cold nose nuzzled her right cheek, a feather-light mental kiss brushed the wounded surfaces of her soul, and she folded her arms about the treecat. She hugged him to her, clinging to him with heart and mind as well as arms, and the soft, deep buzz of his purr leached into her bones. He offered his love and strength without stint, fighting her quicksand sorrow with the promise that whatever happened, she would never truly be alone, and there were no doubts in Nimitz. He rejected her cruel moments of self-judgment, and he knew her better than any other living creature. Perhaps his love for her made him less than impartial, but he also knew how deeply she'd been hurt and chided her for judging herself so much more harshly than she would have judged someone *else*, and she drew a deep breath and reopened her eyes as she once more made herself accept his support and put the pain aside.

She looked up and smiled wanly at the worry in MacGuiness' and LaFollet's eyes. Their concern for her flowed through Nimitz's link, and they deserved better than someone who floundered in the depths of her own grief and loss. She made her smile turn genuine and felt their relief.

"Sorry." Her soprano was rusty, and she cleared her throat. "I guess I was wool-gathering," she said more briskly, her voice determinedly normal. "But be that as it may, Andrew, it doesn't change facts. As long as they don't break any laws, people have a right to say whatever they want."

"But they're not even from the steading, My Lady," LaFollet began stubbornly, "and—"

She laughed softly and interrupted him with a gentle poke in the ribs.

"Don't worry so much! My skin's thick enough to put up with honestly expressed opinions, even from outsiders, however little I may care for them. And if I started using my security people to break heads or quash dissent, I'd only prove I was exactly what they say I am, now wouldn't I?"

The major looked mulish, but he closed his mouth, unable to dispute her argument. It was just that it was so cursed unfair. He wasn't supposed to know the Steadholder's treecat let her sense the emotions of others. He hadn't quite figured out why she was so intent on hiding that from everyone, though he had more than sufficient reasons of his own to agree with her. Even on Grayson, whose people had reason to know better, humans persistently underestimated Nimitz's intelligence. They thought of him as some exceptionally clever pet, not as a person, and his ability to warn the Steadholder of hostile intent had already proved a life-saving secret weapon.

As far as Andrew LaFollet was concerned, that was ample reason to keep it secret, yet no one could serve her as closely as he did without realizing the truth. But he'd also realized she could sense *only* emotions . . . and that she thought no one knew how badly she'd been hurt. That none of her armsmen—or even MacGuiness— knew about the nights she wept with quiet desperation. But all Harrington House's security systems reported to Andrew LaFollet, and he knew. He was sworn to protect her, to die for her if that was what it took, yet there were things no one could protect her from, unless that someone was Nimitz, and to hear bigoted pigs, deliberately shipped into Harrington Steading to harass her, rail at her and denounce her when she'd given so much, *lost* so much, filled him with rage.

Yet she was not only his Steadholder, she was right. And even if she hadn't been those things, he refused to add disputes with her own armsmen to all the things already weighing down upon her, so he closed his mouth on counter-arguments and simply nodded.

Her small smile thanked him, and he smiled back, grateful once again that Nimitz wasn't a telepath. After all, what the Steadholder didn't know wouldn't upset her, and Colonel Hill's intelligence net had identified the agitators most likely to inveigh against her for the "lechery" of her unmarried affair with Paul Tankersley. They were the truly dangerous ones, he thought, for the sanctity of marriage—and the sinfulness of unmarried sex—were part of Grayson's religious bedrock. Most (though certainly not all) Graysons reserved their contempt for the man when such things occurred, for female births outnumbered male on Grayson by three to one, and Grayson was a hard world, where survival and religion alike had evolved an iron code of responsibility. A man who engaged in casual dalliance violated his overriding obligation to provide for and protect a woman who gave him her love and might bear his children. But it wasn't entirely one-sided, and even the Graysons who most respected the Steadholder were often uncomfortable over her relationship with Tankersley. The majority of them seemed to accept the self-evident fact that Manticorans had different standards and that, by those standards, neither she nor Tankersley had done wrong, but LaFollet suspected most of them did their best not to think about it at all. And he more than suspected that the handful of fanatics who hated her for simply being what she was knew it, too. Sooner or later one of them would use it against her where *she* could hear it, and the major knew how cruelly that would wound her. Not just politically, but inside, where the loss of the man she loved had cut so deep into her soul.

And so he didn't argue with her. Instead, he made a mental note to double-check the agitator files with Hill for the names of the true scumbags. No doubt Lady Harrington would be furious with him for . . . reasoning with those individuals, but he was prepared to risk much more than that to shut the mouths of the only filth who might truly hurt her.

Honor's eyebrows lowered for just a moment as her chief armsman met her gaze. There was something going on behind those innocent gray eyes, but she couldn't quite figure out what it was. She made a mental note to keep an eye on him, then put the thought aside and set Nimitz back in his own chair so she could return her attention to her lunch.

Her afternoon's schedule was crowded, and she'd wasted enough time feeling sorry for herself. The sooner she finished eating, the sooner she could be about it, she told herself firmly, and picked up her fork.

• CHAPTER THREE

Honor stopped dead on the path as Nimitz catapulted
abruptly from her shoulder. She watched him vanish into
the formal garden's shrubbery like a streak of cream-
and-gray smoke, then closed her eyes and twitched a
smile as she followed him through flowering masses of
Terran azalea and Sphinxian spike-blossom via their link.

Andrew LaFollet stopped when his Steadholder did,
and his eyebrows rose as he noted Nimitz's absence.
Then he shook his head in wry understanding, gave their
peaceful surroundings a careful scan out of sheer,
instinct-level habit, and folded his arms in patient silence.

On most worlds, a garden such as this would have
included at least some local flora, but no native plants,
however beautiful, were allowed on Harrington House's
grounds. Grayson's vegetation was dangerous to humans,
especially to those who'd grown up on safer worlds, and
none of the Manticore Binary System's three habitable
worlds had toxic-level concentrations of heavy metals.
That meant Honor lacked even the limited tolerance for
them which adaptive evolution had given Grayson's
natives, and the people who'd planned Harrington House
had declined to expose her—or Nimitz—to them.
Instead, they'd gone to the expensive (and clandestine)
effort of discovering which of her home world's flowering plants she most loved and imported them, but most
of the garden's contents were pure Old Earth species.

As with flora, so with fauna. The grounds were a
botanical and zoological garden of Terran and Sphinxian
species, crafted specifically for her pleasure, and she'd
been both touched by the gesture and shocked by its

cost. If she'd known what was planned, she would have fought the entire project, but she'd found out too late and Protector Benjamin himself had ordered its construction. Under the circumstances, she could only be grateful, and not just for her own sake. Nimitz was smarter than most two-footed people, and, despite his inability to utter anything like human speech, he understood more Standard English than the majority of Manticoran adolescents, but concepts like "arsenic poisoning" and "cadmium" were a bit much to expect him to grasp. She was confident she'd convinced him danger lurked beyond Harrington House's dome, yet whether or not he truly understood the nature of the risk was far more problematical, and the garden was his playground even more than hers.

Now she located a bench by touch and sank down onto it. LaFollet moved to stand beside her, but she hardly noticed as she sat, eyes still closed, and tracked Nimitz through the undergrowth. Treecats were deadly hunters, the top of Sphinx's arboreal food chain, and she felt his happy sparkle of predatory pleasure. He had no need to catch his own food, yet he liked to keep his skills sharp, and she shared his zest as he slunk silently through the shadows.

The mental image of a Sphinxian chipmunk (which looked nothing at *all* like the Old Earth animal of the same name) came to her suddenly. The 'cat projected it with astonishing clarity, obviously by intent, and she watched as if through his eyes as the chipmunk sat near its hole, gnawing at a near-pine pod's heavy husk. A gentle, artificially induced breeze stirred the foliage, but the chipmunk was upwind, and Nimitz slithered noiselessly closer. He crept right up to it and hovered, sixty centimeters of needle-fanged predator perched at the small, oblivious animal's shoulder, and Honor felt his uncomplicated delight at his own success. Then he stretched out a wiry forelimb, extended one true-hand's long, delicate finger, and jabbed the chipmunk with a lancet claw.

The near-pine pod went flying as the little beast leapt straight up into the air. It whirled in astonishment, then squeaked, paralyzed by terror as it found itself face-to-face with its most terrible natural enemy. It quivered, trembling in every muscle, and then Nimitz bleeked cheerfully and batted it nose-over-tail with the same true-hand. The blow was far gentler than it seemed, but the chipmunk wailed as shock broke the spell of terror. It rolled madly to its feet, and all six limbs blurred as it darted for its hole. It vanished down its burrow with another wailing squeak, and Nimitz sat up on his haunches with a chitter of amused satisfaction.

He padded over to the hole and sniffed at it, but he had no more intention of digging his quivering victim out than he'd ever had of killing it. The object—*this* time—had been to make sure he still could, not to deplete the garden's livestock, and he flirted his prehensile tail as he sauntered back to rejoin his person.

"You're a pretty terrible person, aren't you, Stinker?" Honor greeted him as he emerged.

"Bleek!" he replied cheerfully, and hopped up into her lap. LaFollet snorted, but the 'cat ignored the armsman's amusement as unworthy of notice. He examined his claws and flicked away a stray clot of earth, then sat up and groomed his whiskers at Honor with insufferable smugness.

"That chipmunk never did anything to you," she pointed out, and he shrugged. Treecats killed only out of necessity, but they *were* hunters who took an undeniable pleasure in the stalk, and Honor often wondered if that was why they got along so well with humans. But however that might have been, Nimitz clearly cataloged his hapless prey as "edible, chipmunk, one," and any trauma it might have suffered was a matter of supreme indifference to him.

Honor shook her head at him, then grimaced as her chrono beeped. She glanced at it and grimaced again, harder, before she picked Nimitz up and set him back on her shoulder. He rested one strong, delicate true-hand on her head for balance and chittered a question at her, and she shrugged.

"We're late, and Howard will kill me if I miss this meeting."

"Oh, I doubt the Regent would do anything *quite* that extreme, My Lady." Honor chuckled at LaFollet's reassurance, but Nimitz only sniffed his disdain for the importance humanity in general—and his person in particular—attached to the concepts of "time" and "punctuality." He recognized the futility of protest, however, and settled down, sinking the claws of his true-feet and hand-paws securely into her vest as she moved off.

Honor wore reasonably traditional Grayson costume, and her long-legged stride swirled her skirts as she strode towards the East Portico. LaFollet, like most Graysons, was shorter than she, and he had to trot to keep up. She supposed it made him look undignified and spared him a silent apology for making him scurry, but she didn't slow down. She truly was running late, and they had a long way to go.

Harrington House was entirely too large, luxurious, and expensive for her own taste, but she hadn't been consulted when it was built. The Graysons had intended it as a gift to the woman who'd saved their planet, which meant she couldn't complain, and she'd come to a slightly guilty acceptance of its magnificence. Besides, as Howard Clinkscales was fond of pointing out, it hadn't been built *solely* for her. Indeed, most of its imposing space was given up to the administrative facilities of Harrington Steading, and she had to admit that there seemed to be precious little room to spare.

They emerged from the garden, and she dropped to a more decorous pace as the permanent sentry at the East Portico—Harrington House's main public entrance—snapped to attention and saluted. Honor suppressed a naval officer's automatic reflex to return the salute and settled for a nodded reply, then swept up the steps with LaFollet just as a fierce-faced, white-haired man emerged from the guarded door and gave his own

chrono a harassed glance. He looked up at the sound
of her foot on the steps of native stone, and his scowl
vanished into a smile as he came down them to meet
her.

"I'm sorry I'm late, Howard," she said contritely. "We
were on our way when Nimitz spotted a chipmunk."

Howard Clinkscales' smile turned into a grin any
urchin might have envied, and he shook a finger at the
'cat. Nimitz flicked his ears in impudent reply, and the
Regent chuckled. Once upon a time Clinkscales would
have been far less at ease with an alien creature—not
to mention horrified by the very notion of a woman's
wearing the steadholder's key—but those days were gone,
and his eyes gleamed as he looked at Honor.

"Well, of course, My Lady, if it was *important* no
apologies are necessary. On the other hand, we *are* supposed to have the paperwork ready when Chancellor
Prestwick coms to confirm Council's approval."

"But it's also supposed to be a 'surprise announcement,'" Honor said plaintively. "Doesn't that mean you
can cut me some slack?"

"It's supposed to be a surprise to your steaders and
the other Keys, My Lady—not to *you*. So don't try to
wiggle out of it by wheedling me. You haven't acquired
the proper knack for it, anyway."

"But you keep telling me to learn to compromise. How
am I supposed to do that if you won't compromise with
me?"

"Hah!" Clinkscales snorted, yet they both knew her
whimsical plaint had its serious side. She was uncomfortable with the autocratic power she exercised as a
steadholder, yet she'd often thought it was fortunate
things were set up as they were. It might be alien to
the traditions under which she'd been reared, but, then,
she would have been supremely unsuited to a government career back in the Star Kingdom, even without
the unpleasant experiences the rough and tumble of
Manticore's partisan strife had inflicted upon her.

She'd never really considered it before she was

pitchforked into the steadholdership, but once she'd come face-to-face with her role as one of Grayson's autocratic Keys she'd recognized the true reason she'd always disliked politics. She'd been trained all her life to seek decision, to identify objectives and do whatever it took to attain them, knowing that any hesitation would only cost more lives in the end. The politician's constant need to rethink positions and seek compromise was foreign to her, and she suspected it would be to most military officers. Politicos were trained to think in those terms, to cultivate less-than-perfect consensuses and accept partial victories, and it was more than mere pragmatism. It also precluded despotism, but people who fought wars preferred direct, decisive solutions to problems, and a Queen's officer dared settle only for victory. Gray issues made warriors uncomfortable, and half-victories usually meant they'd let people die for too little, which undoubtedly explained their taste for autocratic systems under which people did what they were told to do without argument.

And, she thought wryly, it *also* explained why military people, however noble their motives, made such a botch of things when they seized political power in a society with *non*autocratic traditions. They didn't know how to make the machine work properly, which meant, all too often, that they wound up smashing it in pure frustration.

She shook free of her own thoughts and gave Clinkscales a smile.

"All right, *be* that way. But watch yourself, Howard! *Someone* has to make that speech to the Ladies' Gardening Guild next week."

Clinkscales blanched, and his expression was so horrified Honor surprised herself with a gurgle of laughter. Even LaFollet chuckled, though his face went instantly blank when Clinkscales glanced at him.

"I'll, ah, bear that in mind, My Lady," the Regent said after a moment. "In the meantime, however—?"

He waved at the steps, and Honor nodded. They

climbed the last few meters to the portico together, with
LaFollet at their heels, and she started to say something
else to Clinkscales, then froze. Her eyes narrowed and
took on the hardness of brown flint, and Nimitz gave
an ear-flattened, sibilant hiss. The Regent blinked in surprise, then grunted like an irate boar as he followed the
direction of her gaze.

"I'm sorry, My Lady. I'll have them removed immediately," he said harshly, but Honor shook her head. It
was a sharp, angry gesture, and her nostrils flared, but
her fists unclenched. She reached up to stroke Nimitz,
her gaze never moving from the fifty or so men gathered just beyond the East Gate, and her soprano was
toneless when she spoke.

"No, Howard. Leave them alone."

"But, My Lady—!" Clinkscales exclaimed.

"No," she repeated more naturally. She glared at the
demonstrators a moment longer, then shook herself and
managed a crooked smile. "At least their artwork's
improving," she observed almost lightly.

Andrew LaFollet's teeth ground as he glowered at the
demonstrators marching stolidly back and forth beyond
the dome gate. Most of their placards bore biblical
quotations or passages from *The Book of the New Way*,
the collected teachings of Austin Grayson, founder of
the Church of Humanity Unchained, who'd led the
Church from Old Earth to the world which bore his
name. Those were bad enough, for the sign-makers had
dredged up every citation they could think of to
denounce the notion that any woman could be a man's
equal, but half the other posters were crude political
caricatures that turned Lady Harrington into some sort
of leering gargoyle intent on leading society to ruin. The
least offensive of them would have been a deadly insult
to any Grayson woman, but even they were less infuriating to the major than the signs which bore only two
words: "INFIDEL HARLOT."

"*Please*, My Lady!" His voice was far harsher than
Clinkscales. "You can't just let them—!"

"I can't do anything else," Honor said. He made an inarticulate sound of fury, and she laid a hand on his shoulder. "You know I can't, Andrew. They're not on the grounds, and they're not breaking any of our laws. We can't touch law-abiding demonstrators without breaking the law ourselves."

"Law-abiding *scum*, you mean, My Lady." The cold venom in Clinkscales' voice was frightening, but he shrugged unhappily when she looked at him. "Oh, you're right. We *can't* touch them."

"But none of them are *our* people! They're all outsiders!" LaFollet protested, and Honor knew he was right. Those men had come to Harrington—been sent, really—from outside, the expense of their journey and their support here paid by contributions from others who felt as they did. It was a crude effort beside what the professional opinion-shapers of Manticore might have managed, but, then, they were handicapped by their sincerity.

"I know they are, Andrew," she said, "and also that they represent a minority opinion. Unfortunately, I can't do anything about it without playing their game for them." She gazed at them a moment longer, then turned her back deliberately upon them. "I believe you mentioned some paperwork that needs attention, Howard?"

"I did, My Lady." Clinkscales sounded far less calm than she did, but he nodded in acceptance and turned to lead the way indoors.

LaFollet followed them down the hall to Honor's office without another word, yet Nimitz carried the major's emotional turmoil to her. The 'cat's own outrage seethed in their link, melding with LaFollet's to snarl in the back of her brain, and she paused at the door to squeeze the major's shoulder once more. She said nothing. She only met his eyes with a small, sad smile and released him, and then the door closed behind her and Clinkscales.

LaFollet glared at the closed panel for a long, fulminating moment. Then he drew a deep breath, nodded to himself, and activated his com.

"Simon?"

"Yes, Sir?" Corporal Mattingly's voice came back instantly, and the major grimaced.

"There are some . . . people with signs at the East Gate," he said.

"Are there, Sir?" Mattingly said slowly.

"Indeed there are. Of course, the Steadholder says we can't touch them, so . . ." LaFollet let his voice trail off, and he could almost see the corporal nod in comprehension of what he *hadn't* said.

"I understand, Sir. I'll warn all the boys to leave them alone before I go off duty."

"Good idea, Simon. We wouldn't want them involved if anything untoward were to happen. Ah, by the way, perhaps you should let me know where to find you if I need you before you're due to report back."

"Of course, Sir. I thought I'd go see how the Sky Domes construction crews are coming. They're finishing up this week, and you know how much I love watching them work. Besides, they're all devoted to the Steadholder, so I try to sort of keep them up to date on how things are going for her."

"That's very kind of you, Simon. I'm sure they appreciate it," LaFollet said, and broke the connection. He leaned back against the wall, guarding his Steadholder's privacy, and his thin smile was hard.

• CHAPTER FOUR

The woman in her mirror was still a stranger, but she was becoming gradually more familiar. Honor ran the brush over her shoulder-length hair once more, then handed it to Miranda LaFollet and stood. She turned before her reflection, running her hands down her hip-length vest to smooth a tiny wrinkle from its rich, jade-green suede, and studied the drape of her white gown. She'd actually grown accustomed to her skirts, and while she still considered them utterly impractical, she'd come to the grudging conclusion she actually liked the way they looked.

She cocked her head, inspecting her image as if it were a junior officer reporting to her command for the first time, and Miranda watched, poised to repair any real or imagined flaws in her appearance.

Honor's refusal to surround herself with the army of servants steadholder tradition required irritated some members of the Harrington House staff, who felt it reduced their own consequence. That view left Honor unmoved, yet she'd capitulated—unwillingly—to the demand that she retain at least one female servant. None of her household dared comment on the fact that MacGuiness was a man, which automatically made him totally unacceptable as a woman's personal attendant, but it had offered her public critics ready-made ammunition. Besides, Mac was fully occupied as her major-domo, and he'd been no more familiar with Grayson notions of style than she when they arrived.

She'd expected it to be hard to find a maid she could stand, but then Andrew LaFollet had somewhat diffidently suggested his sister Miranda. The fact that she was the major's sister automatically recommended her to Honor, and if Miranda wasn't the woman to storm the bastions of male supremacy, she *was* a sturdy-minded, independent sort.

Honor had feared Miranda might feel her official title of "maid" was somehow slighting, but the occupation had a far higher social status on Grayson than the word might imply to an off-worlder. An upper-class Grayson woman's maid was a well paid, highly respected professional, not a menial, and Miranda suited Honor very well. She needed a companion and cultural guide far more than she did a servant, and Miranda had slipped into the role with ease. She could flutter a bit too anxiously over Honor's appearance, but that seemed an inescapable part of any Grayson woman's cultural baggage. Which, Honor conceded, made sense on a planet where women outnumbered men three to one and the only fully acceptable female career for almost a millennium had been that of wife and mother. And while she might wish Miranda would hover a little less, she knew her new role required her to master the skills Miranda had to teach her. It wasn't really all that different from a naval officer's need always to present the best possible appearance; all that had changed were the rules which defined what the proper appearance *was*.

Now she took her hat from Miranda with a nod of thanks and set it on her head with a small smile. She preferred a uniform beret or the style which once had been called a fedora, yet a sort of impish delight chased the sadness from her eyes as she adjusted this one and admired herself in the mirror.

Like most Grayson women's hats, this one was broad-brimmed, but its right side turned sharply up. The rolled brim resembled a Sphinx Forestry Commission ranger's bush hat, and she'd insisted upon it largely for the same reason the SFC had: treecats rode their people's shoulders, and a normal brim would have gotten in Nimitz's way. But it also gave the hat a certain dashing elegance, which was only emphasized by its almost stark simplicity. It was white, and it rejected the usual bright-colored, multi-plumed adornments of traditional women's hats in favor of a simple band, exactly the same dark jade green as her vest, that split into a waist-length, twin-tailed ribbon train. Like her gown's long, elegant sweep, it emphasized her height and flowed with her movements, and it was part of the image she'd deliberately cultivated.

Upper-class Grayson women reminded Honor irresistibly of Old Earth peacocks. They were gorgeous, colorful, lively . . . and too baroque for her tastes. Their jewels were ornate, their loose-fitting vests rich with brocade and embroidery, their gowns a billow of body-shrouding skirts and pleats and lace. Honor's were none of those things, and not by happenstance. Such styles would have made someone her height look as huge as a house, she thought, and she hadn't needed Miranda's painfully tactful expression to tell her she lacked the native Grayson's ability to manage such costumes gracefully. She was working on it, but those skills were harder to acquire than they appeared, especially for someone who'd spent a lifetime in uniform, so she'd reminded herself that a good tactician overcame disadvantages by maximizing her *ad*vantages. If she couldn't cope with local fashion, then it was time to trade ruthlessly on her steadholder's status to *set* fashion, instead, and Miranda had dived into the project with enthusiasm.

Honor's sharply carved beauty was the sort which blossomed only with maturity, and the prolong process had stretched that maturation out over more than twenty T-years. As a consequence, she understood exactly how the ugly duckling had felt, and she suspected that was one reason she'd always loved athletics—it was a sort of compensation prize for her face that not only kept her in peak condition but maximized the assets she did have. Yet whatever her subconscious reasoning might have been, she knew she was both fit and trim and that she moved well, and her uncluttered yet flowing garments emphasized the graceful lines of her body and carriage with a frankness which once would have horrified Grayson society.

She gave the mirror one of the curtsies she'd practiced so hard to master and chuckled as the stately lady in the mirror returned it with aristocratic hauteur. That reflection was a far cry from her childhood as a yeoman's daughter on Sphinx, and anything less like Captain Honor Harrington, Royal Manticoran Navy, was impossible to imagine.

Which was probably a good thing, she told herself with a spurt of familiar bitterness, for she no longer *was* Captain Harrington. Oh, she was still entitled to the uniform she'd worn for three decades, but she refused to wear it. It wasn't the Navy's fault she'd been stripped of her command and placed on inactive, half-pay status. If it was anyone's "fault," it was hers, for she'd known the politicians would leave the Navy no choice when she shot a peer of the realm in a duel. But however it had happened, Honor Harrington would not cling to the symbolic crutch of a uniform whose responsibilities had been denied her. When the time came to assume those responsibilities once more, *if* it ever came, then—

She heard a scolding *bleek* and turned to open her arms to Nimitz, and he leapt into her embrace and flowed up onto her shoulder. He was careful to avoid her hat's streamers as he sank his hand-feet's claws into her vest just above her right collarbone, and she felt the familiar pressure against her shoulder blade as his true-feet's matching claws dug in further down her back to support his normal, half-standing perch. Those murderous claws were just over a half-centimeter long, but what looked like natural suede was nothing of the sort, and she wondered who was happiest about that, Nimitz, or Andrew LaFollet? The tabbard-like vest was made of the same material that was sewn into her uniform tunics to protect them from Nimitz's claws; the fact that it would also stop light-caliber pulser darts was simply a welcome plus from the viewpoint of her chief armsman.

She grinned at the thought and reached up to scratch

Nimitz's chin, then made one last, finicky adjustment to the only two items of "jewelry" she wore. The golden Star of Grayson gleamed on its blood-red ribbon about her throat, and the equally golden patriarch's key of a steadholder hung just below it on its heavy, intricately worked chain. They were required dress on formal occasions, which today certainly was. Besides, she thought with a lurking glint of humor, she supposed she might as well admit she liked the way they looked.

"Well?" she said to Miranda, and her maid gave her an equally intense scrutiny, then nodded.

"You look lovely, My Lady," she said, and Honor chuckled.

"I'll take that in the spirit it was intended, but you really shouldn't fib to your Steadholder, Miranda."

"Of course not, My Lady. That's why I don't." Miranda's gray eyes, so like her brother's, gleamed with mischief, and Honor shook her head.

"Have you ever considered a diplomatic career?" she asked. "You'd be a natural."

Miranda grinned, Nimitz bleeked his own soft laugh into her ear, and Honor drew one last, deep breath, nodded a passing grade to her reflection, and turned to the door and her waiting armsmen.

• CHAPTER FIVE

Harrington City would have been only a large town on Manticore, but it seemed much bigger, for Grayson architecture reflected the limits of Grayson's pre-Alliance tech base, with none of the mighty towers of most counter-grav civilizations. Its buildings were low-growing and close to the ground—thirty stories was considered a monster—and that meant the same amount of housing spread out over a far wider stretch of ground.

Honor still found that a bit odd as her ground car purred down Courvosier Avenue and she gazed out at her capital. She'd gotten over her discomfort (not without a struggle) at learning any steading's capital always bore the steading's name, but watching the buildings pass reminded her yet again of the vast differences between Graysons and Manticorans. It would have been far more efficient to use the newly acquired technologies to build proper towers—one tower would have held Harrington City's total population with ease, and it would have been easy to seal it against the hostile environment, as well—but Grayson didn't do things that way.

Honor's subjects were a baffling mix of obstinate tradition and inventiveness. They'd used the new technology with impressive innovation to build this entire city from the ground up in barely three T-years, which had to be a record for a project of such size, but they'd built it the way *they* thought it should be, and she'd been wise enough not to argue the point. After all, it was to be their home. They had a right to make it one they were comfortable in, and as she gazed down broad cross streets and green swathes threaded through the city grid,

48

she had to admit it felt right. Different from any city she'd ever before known, but curiously and completely *right*.

She pressed the button to lower the armorplast window and inhaled the sweet scents of dogwood and cherry as the car entered Bernard Yanakov Park. A thousand years, she thought. The struggle the first few Grayson generations had waged to keep just themselves alive had been more terrible than most people could imagine, yet a thousand years of Graysons had preserved the trees of Old Earth, as well. The sheer labor involved in preserving dogwoods, not because they were useful but simply because they were beautiful, was daunting, yet they'd done it. These trees might no longer be identical to the Old Earth originals, but they were close, and Grayson cherries were still edible—by Graysons, at least. Honor herself would never dare eat them, unless they came from one of the orbital farms, where the original Terrestrial strains *had* been maintained unchanged or imported anew once Yeltsin's Star regained interstellar capability, yet the natives had adapted sufficiently to handle them. They'd had to, for it was physically impossible to completely decontaminate planetary farmland and keep it that way.

Or it *had* been, she reminded herself, glancing up at the towering crystoplast dome that covered the entire city and several thousand hectares of as yet empty ground. People on Grayson lived more like the denizens of an orbital habitat than a normal planetary population, and their homes were sealed enclaves of filtered air and distilled water, but Harrington City was different. For the first time, Grayson architects had been able to design a city as a living, breathing unity—one whose people could walk its streets without emergency breath masks—and the same technology would soon be extended to the agricultural sector, as well.

Food production had always been a major limiting factor on Grayson's population. Not even its natives could survive on vegetables grown in unreclaimed soil, and keeping farmland decontaminated was a nightmare task, so over two-thirds of their food was grown in space. The orbital farms were far more productive, on a volume-for-volume basis, than any dirt-side farm, but building them had been hideously expensive, especially with pre-Alliance technology. Historically, simply feeding its people had soaked up something like seventy percent of Yeltsin's gross system product, but that was about to change. Sky Domes' projections indicated that food could be produced in domed farms—essentially nothing more than vast, self-contained greenhouses—for little more than two-thirds of the orbital habitats' ongoing production costs and with far smaller startup investments.

The consequences, both economically and for the population the system could support, would be stupendous. Sky Domes wasn't merely going to make Grayson cities nicer; it was going to eliminate factors which had forced Grayson to practice draconian population control throughout its history, and only the influx of Manticoran technology and Honor's own financial backing had made it possible.

She felt a deep, uncomplicated sense of triumph at the thought and smiled up at the dome, but then the ground car turned a last corner, and her smile vanished. A line of demonstrators ringed Yountz Center, the heart of Yanakov Park, like stony-faced vultures, ignoring the taunts and jibes flung at them by a small crowd of native Harringtons. An expressionless cordon of the Harrington Guard in their jade tunics and lighter green trousers guarded the protesters against anything more physical than taunts, and Honor felt LaFollet's anger beside her. The major hated the Guard's responsibility to protect people who despised his Steadholder, but she managed to keep her own expression serene. It was hardly a surprise, after all. The agitators had pulled in their horns of late, yet she'd known they'd be here today.

She sighed and told herself she should be grateful for the general drop in demonstrations. The pickets who'd besieged Harrington House on a daily basis had abandoned their posts entirely in the last week, and Honor still felt a guilty sense of delight over the reason they'd decamped. The first counter-demonstration had apparently been staged on the spur of the moment by a hundred or so of Sky Domes' construction workers. They'd arrived spoiling for trouble, and the two groups of pickets had indulged in a lively exchange of personal opinions which had given way to an even more lively exchange of blows and ended with the construction workers pursuing their foes down Courvosier Avenue with obviously fell intent. The same thing, except for the appearance of several dozen Harringtons who *weren't* Sky Domes employees, had happened the next day, and the next. By the fourth day, there were no hostile placards at her gates.

Honor had been enormously relieved, both by their absence and by the Harrington City Police's scrupulous neutrality. She suspected the HCP had deliberately waited until the anti-Steadholder groups were in full flight before moving in to quell the various riots, but that wasn't the same thing as Honor's having used them to suppress dissent. Best of all, her stern injunctions to Andrew LaFollet had kept her personal armsmen completely out of it, and the riots had given her a legitimate excuse to exclude *any* demonstrators from today's ceremonies.

But even so, today was too important an event—and too positive an occasion—for her enemies to let pass without attempting to ruin it, and they raised their voices in a denouncing chant as they saw her car. Her jaw clenched as some of the words came to her, but she maintained her calm expression somehow, and then the car swept past them and a sudden surf of cheers drowned their chant as the vehicle passed through the Center's gates.

"The Center" was a small complex that included the Yountz Pavilion and half a dozen other buildings surrounding a small lake, and its grounds were packed. Colored banners waved overhead, a band took up the

swelling strains of the Steadholders' Anthem, scores of
police—some borrowed from Mayhew Steading to make
up the needed numbers for the occasion—lined the
access road to restrain the shouting crowd, and Honor
felt herself relax as a jubilant roar of genuine welcome
swept over her. She raised a hand to acknowledge it,
and Nimitz rose in her lap. The 'cat preened as the
cheers redoubled, and she laughed as he poked his
muzzle out the window and twitched his whiskers at his
admirers.

The car pulled up at the foot of the platform work
crews had erected before Yountz Pavilion. The facing
temporary bleachers were crowded to the bursting point,
and Honor climbed out into the tumult of music and
shouting voices while picked guardsmen snapped to
attention in a double row. Her cheeks heated as the
waves of sound rolled over her. Even now, she found
it hard to accept that she was these people's direct,
personal ruler, and she fought the urge to explain that
they'd mistaken her for someone truly important.

She set Nimitz on her shoulder as Howard Clinkscales
stepped forward to greet her. Her burly, white-haired
regent leaned on his silver-headed staff of office as he
bowed deeply, then extended his arm to her and escorted
her between the lines of guardsmen to the platform's
stairs. The band reached the end of the Steadholder's
Anthem with perfect timing as they stepped out onto
the platform, and the cheers faded into silence as Honor
released Clinkscales' arm and crossed to the flag-draped
podium.

Another white-haired man, this one frail with pre-
prolong age and dressed all in black, relieved only by
the white of an antique clerical collar, waited there for
her. She dropped one of her newly mastered curtsies
to him, and the Reverend Julius Hanks, spiritual head
of the Church of Humanity Unchained, extended his
hand to her with a smile, then turned to face the crowd
and cleared his throat as she took her place at his side.

"Let us pray, Brothers and Sisters," he said simply,

and the crowd fell instantly silent as his amplified voice floated over them. "Oh God, Father and Tester of Mankind, we thank You for this day and for the bounty with which You have rewarded us in this, the fruits of our labor. We beseech Your blessing on us always as we face the Great Test of life. Strengthen us as we rise to its challenges, and help us to know and to do Your will always, that we may come to You at the end of all labor with the sweat of Your work upon our brows and Your love in our hearts. And we most humbly beseech You to bestow Your wisdom always upon our leaders, and especially upon this Steadholder, that her people may prosper under her rule and walk always in the sunshine of Your favor. In the Name of the Tester, the Intercessor, and the Comforter, Amen."

A deep, reverberating "amen" echoed from the crowd, and Honor joined it. She hadn't converted to the Church of Humanity—that was one of the things which most infuriated the street preachers—yet she respected both the Church and the personal faith of people like Reverend Hanks. She was uncomfortable with some elements of Church doctrine, yet for all its lingering sexism, the Church was a vital, living organism, a central part of Grayson life, and its beliefs were far less rigid and fixed than some.

Honor's interest in military history meant she knew only too well how often the intolerance of religious bigotry had exacted its price in blood and atrocity, how seldom a single faith had enjoyed universal acceptance without becoming an instrument of repression. And she knew how fanatical the original Church of Humanity had been when it shook the dust of Old Earth from its sandals to found its own perfect society on this beautiful, deadly planet. Yet somehow the Church had avoided repression here. There had been times, in its past, when that was not true. She knew that, too, for she'd applied herself to the study of Grayson history with even more intensity than she had to that of Manticore. She had to, for she must learn to know and understand the people accident had called her to rule. So, yes, she knew of the periods when the Church *had* ossified, when doctrine *had* hardened into dogma. But those periods seldom lasted, which was all the more surprising in such a deeply traditional people as those of Grayson.

Perhaps it was because the Church had learned from the horrors of Grayson's Civil War, when over half the planet's total population had perished. Surely that terrible lesson had cut deep, yet she thought it was only half the answer—and that the very world on which they lived was the other half.

Grayson was its own people's worst enemy, the invisible threat perpetually waiting to destroy the unwary. That wasn't unique to Yeltsin's Star, of course. Any orbital habitat offered its inhabitants countless ways to do themselves in, and many another planet was equally, if less insidiously, dangerous. But most people in such environments either became slaves to the traditions they knew spelled survival or else developed an almost automatic, instinctive *rejection* of tradition in eternal search for better ways to survive. What made the Graysons different was that, somehow, they'd done both. They did cling to the traditions they'd tested and found good, yet they were simultaneously willing to consider the new in ways even Manticorans were not, for the Manticore System's three inhabited worlds were friendly to Man.

She raised her head as the silence of prayer eased into the rustle and stir of bodies, and once again she felt the dynamism which imbued these strange, determined people who had become hers. The balance of tradition and its sense of identity set against the need to conquer their environment and the drive to experiment that created. It was an oddly heady brew, one she envied, and as she turned to face her subjects and a fresh ovation rolled up to meet her, she wondered yet again how her own infusion into it would ultimately affect it.

She gazed out over the faces. Thousands of intent, expectant faces, all turned towards her, and spoke sternly to the butterflies in her middle. The soft, almost chirping sound of amusement Nimitz made in her ear helped, and she smiled out at the enormous crowd.

"Thank you for that kind, if somewhat overwhelming, welcome." The sound system carried her soprano clearly, and a ripple of laughter greeted her wry tone. "There are a few more of you than I'm used to speaking to at one time," she went on, "and I'm afraid I'm still a bit new at making speeches, so I'll keep this simple. And—" she waved at the heavily laden tables dotted across the grass "—since I see the caterers are waiting, I'll keep it short, as well."

That woke fresh laughter and a spatter of applause, and her smile became a grin.

"I suppose that shows me *your* priorities," she teased, and shook her head. "Well, since you're all so hungry, let's not waste any more time.

"We're here," she went on more seriously, "to dedicate the city dome. This is a new steading, and, for the moment, at least, a poor one. You all know how stretched our fiscal structure is right now, and you know, even better than I, how expensive it is to build a new steading from the unreclaimed ground up. You know how hard you've worked, how much each of you, and all the people still out on the projects, who can't join us here today, have sweated and labored to create this beautiful city." She waved at the park around them, the buildings looming beyond its trees, and the sparkling, half-invisible dome above them and let her voice fall silent for a moment, then cleared her throat.

"Yes, you all know that," she said quietly. "But what you may not know is how proud of each and every one of you *I* am. How deeply honored I am that you chose to give up places in older, established steadings to come here, to this place where there was *nothing*, and create such beauty for us all. Yours is an ancient world, one to which I am a newcomer, but surely none of your ancestors have done more, or done it better, and I thank you all."

A pleased, embarrassed hush answered her quiet

sincerity, and she turned to beckon for a young man to join her from among the other dignitaries on the platform. Adam Gerrick still looked as if he felt out of costume in his formal attire, but the crowd recognized him and applauded loudly as the chief engineer of Grayson Sky Domes, Ltd., stepped up beside his Steadholder.

"I think you all know Mr. Gerrick," Honor rested one hand lightly on his shoulder as she made the redundant introduction, "and I'm sure you all know the role he played in designing and executing our city's dome. What you may not know, since *he* hasn't heard it yet, is that the success of this project," she waved her free hand at the overhead dome, "and of our demonstration farm projects, has been followed very closely elsewhere on Grayson. As I said, we're a new steading, with a strained fiscal structure, but Mr. Gerrick is about to change that. I have been officially informed by Protector Benjamin that his Council has approved a funds-matching appropriation for any city which wishes to follow our example and invest in city or agricultural domes." Several people in the crowd stiffened, looking at her with sudden, intent speculation, and she nodded. "As of this morning, Sky Domes has received definite construction commitments worth over two hundred million austins, with more to follow."

The dome itself seemed to quiver with the volume of the shout that awoke. The entire Sky Domes project had been a risky venture for a fledgling steading, and only Honor's off-world wealth had made it possible. She'd used her prize money and the income from its investment to bankroll the company to the tune of twelve million Manticoran dollars—over sixteen million austins—and Sky Domes had built Harrington City's dome at cost, expressly as a demonstration project, but the gamble had paid off. Sky Domes, Ltd., had a lock on the new dome technology, which meant income and investment and jobs for all of Harrington Steading's people.

Gerrick stood beside her, face fiery as the crowd

cheered him as loudly as their Steadholder. He hadn't really considered his idea's financial implications when he first proposed it to Honor. He'd thought purely in terms of efficiency and the engineering challenge it represented, and she wondered if he realized even now how wealthy he was about to become. But whether he did or not, he deserved every penny of it, and so did Howard Clinkscales, who served as Sky Domes' CEO.

She waited for the jubilant cheers to ease, then raised her hands overhead and grinned hugely at the crowd.

"And on that note, ladies and gentlemen, let's eat!" she shouted, and shouts of laughter answered her as the spectators headed for the food. HCP officers and Guardsmen acted as traffic controllers, but her Harringtons showed more discipline than she would have expected from Manticorans. There was remarkably little confusion as they began falling into lines, and she stood watching them while she chatted with Clinkscales and Reverend Hanks. It had gone well, she thought. Much better than she'd expected, really—which only made the sudden, jarring interruption even more shocking.

"*Repent!*" The amplified voice blared from the top row of the emptying bleachers, and Honor turned involuntarily to face it. A single man stood there, garbed in funeral black, one hand brandishing a battered black book while the other held a microphone before his lips. "Repent and renounce your sins, Honor Harrington, lest you lead the people of God to sorrow and damnation!"

Honor flinched, and her stomach knotted. His amplifier was nowhere near as powerful as those of the speaker's stand—there were limits to the size of any speaker which could be smuggled past her security people—but he had it cranked all the way up. Feedback whined, yet his voice thundered out to every ear, and she felt her wounded, fragile center quail from the confrontation. She couldn't handle this, she thought despairingly. Not now. It was too much to expect of her, and she started to step back from the podium. Perhaps she could simply ignore him, she told herself. If she pretended he was so inconsequential he didn't even matter, perhaps—

"Repent, I say!" the black-clad man thundered. "Down on your knees, Honor Harrington, and beg the forgiveness of the God you so grossly offend by your damnable transgressions against His will!"

His contemptuous words burned like acid, and something happened inside her. Something she'd thought lost forever snapped back into place like the resocketing of a dislocated limb . . . or the click of a missile tube loading hatch. Her chocolate-dark eyes hardened, and Nimitz reared high on her shoulder. He hissed an echo of her sudden rage, flattening his ears and baring his fangs, and she felt Julius Hanks stiffen beside her as the happy crowd noise faltered and people looked back. One or two Harringtons started angrily towards the speaker, only to stop as they saw his clerical collar, and she sensed Andrew LaFollet reaching for his com. She reached out and intercepted his wrist without even looking.

"No, Andrew," she said. His arm tensed as if to jerk free, and her link to Nimitz carried her his seething fury, but then his muscles relaxed. She turned her head to give him a level glance, one eyebrow arched, and he nodded in unhappy obedience.

"Thank you," she said, and moved back to her own microphone. Silence hovered as she adjusted it minutely. Her people had come to Harrington Steading, by and large, because they were among the most open-minded of Grayson's people. They'd *wanted* to come here, and they respected their foreign-born Steadholder deeply. Their indignation at the jarring interruption matched LaFollet's, but they also had a Grayson's ingrained respect for a man of God. That clerical collar held even the most irate at bay, and it gave the angry words far more weight, as well.

"Let me deal with him, My Lady," Hanks whispered. She glanced at the old man, and his eyes burned with anger. "That's Brother Marchant," Hanks explained. "He's an ignorant, opinionated, intolerant, closed-minded bigot, and he has no business here. His congregation is up in Burdette Steading. In fact, he's Lord Burdette's personal chaplain."

"Ah." Honor nodded. She understood Hanks' anger now, and she clamped down an iron control as her own stirred. So that *was* how all those demonstrators had gotten here, she thought coldly.

William Fitzclarence, Lord Burdette, was probably the most prejudiced of all Grayson's steadholders. Some of the others might be in two minds about accepting a woman steadholder; Burdette wasn't. Only Protector Benjamin's personal warning had kept his mouth shut during her formal investment, and he ignored her with icy contempt whenever he couldn't completely avoid her. There was no way Marchant had come here without his patron's permission, which suggested Burdette and those of like mind had decided to openly support the opposition and probably explained the source of the funds which had brought so many outside protesters to Harrington.

But that was for future consideration. At the moment, she faced Marchant's challenge, and she couldn't ask Hanks to answer it. Technically, he held authority over all the Church's clergy, but Grayson religious tradition enshrined freedom of conscience. If she let him slap Marchant down, it might provoke a crisis within the Church which would be bound to spill over onto her and make the political situation still worse.

Besides, she thought, Marchant's challenge was to *her*, and she could taste his gloating delight. The small-minded pleasure of a bigot, feeding his desire to hurt and denigrate with the sanctimonious assurance that he was simply doing God's will. His attack was too direct, too public, for her to let anyone else deal with it. *She* had to meet it if she was to retain her own moral authority as Steadholder Harrington, and even if she hadn't had to, she *wanted* to. She faced an open confrontation at last, one that had broken through to the part of her which had lain too long dormant and lost, and she shook her head at Hanks.

"No. Thank you, Reverend, but this gentlemen seems to want to speak to me." The sound system carried her voice clearly, exactly as she'd intended. Her clear, quiet soprano was an elegant contrast to Marchant's belligerent bellow, and she brought up the telescopic function of her artificial left eye, watching his expression closely, as she inclined her head towards him. "You had something you wished to say, Sir?" she invited, and the clergyman flushed as she goaded him with her very courtesy.

"You are a stranger to God, Honor Harrington!" he proclaimed, waving his book once more, and Honor felt LaFollet bristle afresh at his repeated use of her first name. As his omission of her title, it was a calculated insult from a man who'd never even been introduced to her, but she simply reached up to soothe Nimitz once more and waited. "You are infidel and heretic, by your own admission before the Conclave of Steadholders when you refused to embrace the Faith, and one not of Father Church is no fit protector for God's people!"

"Forgive me, Sir," Honor said quietly, "but it seemed to me more fitting to state openly, before God and the Conclave, that I had not been raised in the Church of Humanity. Should I have pretended otherwise?"

"You should never have profaned by seeking worldly power!" Marchant shouted. "Woe be unto Grayson that a heretic and woman should claim the steadholder's key as God's steward! For a thousand years, this world has been God's—now those who have forgotten His law profane it by turning to foreign ways and leading His people into the wars of infidel powers, and it was you, Honor Harrington, who brought these things to us! You corrupt the Faith by your very presence, by the unclean example and ideas you carry like pestilence! 'Beware those who would seduce you, my brothers. Heed not those who would defile the temple of your soul with promises of material things and worldly power, but hold fast to the way of God and be free!'"

Honor heard Hanks inhale between clenched teeth

as Marchant quoted from *The Book of the New Way*. It was the second most sacred of all Grayson texts, and she felt the Reverend's fury as Marchant twisted it to his purpose. But Honor had spent hours poring over *The New Way* herself in an effort to understand her people, and now she blessed the sharpness of her own memory.

"Perhaps you should finish your citation, Sir," she said to Marchant, and her prosthetic eye showed her the shock on his face. "I believe," she continued calmly and clearly, "that Saint Austin ended that passage with 'Shut not your minds to the new because the chains of the past bind you tight, for it is those who cling most desperately to the old who will turn you from the New Way and lead you once more into the paths of the unclean.' "

"*Blasphemy!*" Marchant shrieked. "How *dare* you set your tongue to the words of the Book, heretic?!"

"Why should I not?" Honor returned in a tone of deadly reason. "Saint Austin wrote not simply for those who had already accepted the Church, but for those he sought to bring to it. You call me heretic, but surely a heretic is one who claims to accept your Faith and then twists it to his own liking. I make no such claim, for I was reared in another faith, but should that prevent me from reading and respecting the teachings of yours?"

"What do *you* know of the Faith?!" Marchant spat. "You parrot the words, but their meaning is not in you! The very key about your neck proclaims it, for woman was never meant to rule. 'Gather your sons to build the world God ordains, and guard your wives and daughters well. Protect them and teach them, that they may know God's will through you.' *Through you!*" Marchant repeated, glaring furiously at her. "God Himself tells us Woman is to be governed by Man, as a father governs his children, not to violate His law by setting herself against His will! You and your accursed Star Kingdom infect us all with your poisons! You lead our young men into godless war and our young women into the sins of pride and debauchery, turning wife against husband and daughter against father!"

"I think not, Sir." Honor allowed an edge of ice into her own voice as she met the clergyman's glare and chose another passage from *The New Way.* "'Fathers, do not close your minds to the words of your children, for they are less fixed in the old ways. Nor should there be strife between a man and his wives. Love them and heed their council. We are all the Sons and Daughters of God, Who created us Man and Woman that we might comfort and aid one another, and a day will come when Man will need Woman's strength as well as his own.'"

Marchant went purple as murmurs of agreement rippled through the crowd. Honor felt Reverend Hanks' approval and sensed his own surprise at her command of the Church's teachings, but she kept her eyes on Marchant and awaited his next attack.

"How *dare* you speak of a man and his wives?" the clergyman hissed. "The union of holy marriage is a sacrament, ordained and blessed by God, while you, who fornicate in the pleasures of the flesh, spit upon all it means!"

Nimitz's snarl burned in Honor's right ear. A deep, angry growl went up from the crowd, and Andrew LaFollet cursed savagely under his breath, but her own mind was cold and clear and her eyes were deadly.

"I do not spit upon the sacrament of marriage, nor upon any other sacrament," she said, and more than one listener quailed before her icy tone, "but your own Book says, 'Without love, there can be no true marriage; with love, there can be nothing else.' And again, Sir, Saint Austin wrote, 'Yet I say to you, do not rush to marriage, for it is a deep and perfect thing. Test first, that you may be certain you are called to it by love, and not simply by the pleasures of the flesh which will consume themselves and leave only ashes and misery.'" Her dangerous brown eyes stabbed Marchant like paired lasers, and her voice was very, very quiet. "I loved Paul Tankersley with all my heart. Had he lived, I would have married him and borne his children. But I am *not* of your Church, however much I respect it, and I followed the customs to which I was born, as I would expect you to follow yours."

"And so you proved your unclean nature!" Marchant shouted. "You and all your sin-filled people who worship at the shrine of sensuality have no place among God's chosen!"

"No, Sir. So I proved only that I loved a man as God intended and shared his love in a way different from your own." Honor's voice was as cold and level as ever, but tears streaked her cheeks as the anguish of Paul's death twisted within her like a knife, and Nimitz's harsh, angry snarl rippled over the sound system once more. She stood like a tall, slim statue, facing her enemy with her pain plain on her face, and the mutters from the crowd turned darker and angrier as they saw it.

"*Lies!*" Marchant screamed. "God struck down the man with whom you rutted like some beast of the fields as punishment for *your* sins! It was His judgment upon you, harlot!" Honor went bone-white, and vicious satisfaction twisted Marchant's expression as he realized he'd hurt her at last. "Woe be unto you, Harlot of Satan, and to the people of this steading when God's sword smites them through you! God knows the truth of your whore's heart, and—"

A sudden, bass-throated roar boiled up from Honor's subjects. It buried Marchant's voice like an ocean, and he stopped abruptly, mouth hanging open, fury-congested face suddenly pale as he realized he'd gone too far at last. He'd violated a bone-deep, thousand-year code of conduct when he publicly attacked a woman, and only the deep, instinctive respect for his collar and Honor's readiness to answer his diatribe with reasoned argument had balanced his shocking breach of all decent behavior. That balance vanished now. Every citizen of Harrington Steading knew the story of her love for Paul Tankersley and how it had ended. Now they saw her agony as Marchant ripped open her wounds, and a dozen men surged towards the clergyman.

He shouted something, but the ugly crowd bellow swamped his amplified voice, and he scrambled frantically up the bleachers. His feet slipped as he reached the uppermost tier, but he regained his balance and scurried desperately along the empty seats while the crowd thundered in pursuit, and Honor fought free of her pain and turned to grab LaFollet's shoulder.

"Stop them, Andrew!" He stared at her, as if unable to believe his own ears, and she shook him fiercely. "They'll kill him if we don't stop them!"

"Uh, yes, My Lady!" LaFollet jerked out his com and started barking orders, and Honor wheeled back to the podium mike.

"*Stop!*" she shouted. "Stop it! Think what you're doing! *Don't make yourselves like him!*"

Her amplified voice carried even through the roar, and a handful of men stopped, but her subjects' fury was out of control. Other Harringtons charged on, and they were gaining. Marchant fled madly, running for his very life while a knot of green tunics battled through the crowd towards him, and Honor clung to the podium, willing her guardsmen to reach him first.

They didn't. A shout of triumph went up as a flying tackle brought Marchant down, and he and the man who'd caught him rolled down the bleachers, bouncing from seat to seat. The pack converged like hungry hounds, and someone jerked him to his feet. He cowered down, covering his head with his arms and hands while fists and feet battered him, and then, miraculously, the Guard was there. They closed in, knocking his attackers aside, enclosing him in a ring of green-on-green uniforms and hustling him from the bleachers amid a hurricane of catcalls and shouted threats, and Honor sagged in relief.

"Thank God," she breathed, covering her face with one hand as her Guard dragged the battered, bleeding, half-conscious clergyman to safety while Nimitz hissed with fury on her shoulder. "Thank God!" she whispered again, and then lowered her hand, blinking on tears, as an age-frail arm went about her.

Reverend Hanks drew her close, and she needed his support. Nor did she feel any patronization in the fierce, furious disgust for Marchant's cruel bigotry flowing from him through Nimitz, and she leaned against him, trembling with the residual anguish Marchant's words had waked and her awareness of how close he'd come to death.

"Yes, My Lady, thank God, indeed." Hanks' resonant voice quivered with anger, and he turned her away from the crowd and produced a handkerchief. She took it and dried her eyes, still leaning against him, and he continued in that same harsh voice. "And thank you, too. If you hadn't reacted so quickly—" He broke off and shook himself, then drew a deep breath.

"Thank you," he repeated, "and I beg you to accept my apologies on behalf of Father Church. I assure you," he said, and if his voice was calmer, it was also harder—and more implacable—than she'd ever thought the gentle Reverend could be, "that Brother Marchant will be . . . dealt with."

• **CHAPTER SIX**

"*Hai!*"

Honor's right foot came down on the polished floor,
quickly and neatly, her weight centered, and her wooden
practice sword flashed. Master Thomas' blade caught the
head cut, and her left foot swept around behind her,
carrying her to his left. She shifted her weight, driving
his sword back to gain a split-second's freedom, then
slid her own weapon down his, twisted her wrists, and
feinted a cut to his left arm in a single blur of movement.

"*Hai!*" she shouted again, diverting her stroke into a
whistling torso cut as he moved to parry, but his parry
had *also* been a feint.

"*Ho!*" He floated aside, graceful as a dancer or a cloud
of smoke, and Honor grunted as his blade cracked down
on her padded right forearm just before her own strike
went home. She lowered her sword instantly and bent
her head to acknowledge the touch which had preempted
her own attack, then stood back and took her right hand
from her hilt. She shook it for a moment, grimacing at
the tingle in her fingers, and Master Thomas raised his
mask with a smile.

"The best offense, My Lady, is sometimes to offer your
opponent a juicy target in order to turn her attack against
her."

"Especially when you can read her like a book," Honor
agreed. She removed her own mask and mopped her face
on the sleeve of her fencing tunic. It was similar in cut
to the gi she wore for her *coup de vitesse* workouts, but
stiffer and heavier. Grayson had long ago adopted high

tech substitutes for more traditional fencing armors, and the tunic was designed to let her move easily yet absorb blows which could easily break unprotected limbs.

Unfortunately, it was *not* so well designed as to prevent bruising, for Grayson's swordmasters subscribed to the theory that bruises taught best.

"Oh, I wouldn't say you were quite that obvious, My Lady," Master Thomas disagreed, "but you might cultivate a more, ah, subtle approach."

"I thought I was *being* subtle!" Honor objected, but her fencing master shook his head with another smile.

"Perhaps against someone else, My Lady, but I know you too well. You forget this isn't a real battle, and you think in terms of decision. Given an opportunity to achieve outright victory, your instinct is to seize it even at the expense of taking damage yourself, and in a real fight, I'd probably be dead now, while you would simply be wounded. But in the salle, you must always remember that it's the *first* touch which counts."

"You did it on purpose, didn't you? Just to make your point."

"Perhaps." Master Thomas smiled serenely. "Yet it also gave me the victory, didn't it?" Honor nodded, and his smile broadened. "And whether I did it as an object lesson or simply to win is really beside the point. I was *able* to do it by taking advantage of the way you think, because I knew your arm cut would be only a feint when I offered you the opening to the body."

"Did you, now?" Honor cocked an eyebrow at him.

"Of course, My Lady. Did you really think my guard could be that weak by accident?" Master Thomas shook his head sadly, and Nimitz bleeked a laugh from his perch on the uneven parallel bars.

"*You*," Honor said, wagging a finger at the 'cat, "can just be quiet, Stinker!" She turned back to Master Thomas and tugged at the end of her nose while her eyes crinkled in amusement. "Would you have tried something like that against someone you didn't know as well as you know me?"

"Probably not, My Lady—but I *do* know you, don't I?"

"True." Honor shook her arm again. "It *is* a bit hard to surprise someone who's taught you everything you know, isn't it?"

Master Thomas grinned and raised one hand in the referee's gesture that signified a touch, and she chuckled. Thomas Dunlevy was the second ranking Swordmaster on Grayson, and she felt honored by his agreement to train her. Unlike Grand Swordmaster Eric Tobin, who'd out-pointed him by only the tiniest margin for the grand mastery, Master Thomas had no problem with the fact that she was a woman. Tobin had been horrified by the very notion of training a mere female; Master Thomas' only concern had been whether or not the mere female in question could master the sword, and, like virtually all Graysons, he'd seen the video Palace Security's cameras had shot the night Honor saved Protector Benjamin's family from assassination. Indeed, he'd agreed to teach her the sword without charge if she agreed to teach him *coup de vitesse*, and *he* was as vulnerable to surprises there as she was here.

Honor had accepted willingly, and not just because she loved teaching the *coup*. For most Graysons, the sword was simply another form of athletic competition, and that, in great part, was how Honor saw it, too. Yet it was more than that for her, as well. She was the only living holder of the Star of Grayson, which, by law, made her Protector's Champion, and the Protector's symbol was not a crown, but a sword. It had been a bit difficult for Honor to learn the trick of substituting "the Sword" where a subject of Queen Elizabeth would have said "the Crown," but she was getting the hang of it, just as she'd learned that Graysons used "the Keys" to refer to the Conclave of Steadholders.

But the point was that Benjamin Mayhew's symbol *was* a sword, and that archaic weapon had a very special significance here. Any Grayson could learn the sword, but the law allowed only those who'd attained at least the rank of Swordmaster—or those who were stead-holders—to carry a live blade. And while Grayson had no equivalent of Manticore's code duello, its fundamental law still enshrined any steadholder's right to trial by combat against the Protector's decrees. No one had resorted to it in over three T-centuries, yet the right remained, and such challenges could be settled only with cold steel.

Honor had no expectation of ever being called upon to fulfill her obligation as Benjamin IX's champion, but she didn't believe in surprises, either. Besides, it was fun. Her own training had never included weapon work, for the *coup* was strictly an unarmed style, but it had given her a firm basis for Master Thomas' lessons, and she'd found the elegance of steel suited her, though it wasn't a bit like the sports of foil and épée fencing still prac-ticed in the Star Kingdom of Manticore.

Grayson's original colonists had fled Old Earth to escape its "soul-destroying" technology, and the first few generations had renounced technological weapons. But they'd still been products of an industrial society, with absolutely no background in the use of primitive weap-ons, so when the sword reemerged among them, they'd had no basis on which to build the techniques for its use. They'd had to start from scratch, and, according to Master Thomas, tradition held that they'd based their entire approach on something called a "movie" about someone called "The Seven Samurai."

No one could really be certain after so long, since the "movie" (if there'd ever truly been such a thing) no longer existed, but Honor suspected the tradition was accurate. She'd done some research of her own after beginning her lessons and discovered that "*samurai*" referred to the warrior caste of the preindustrial King-dom of Japan on Old Earth. Grayson's library data base contained virtually no information on them, but her request to King's College on Manticore had produced quite a bit of background, and Master Thomas had joined her study of it with intense interest.

She still hadn't tracked down the word "movie," but the connotations suggested some form of visual entertainment medium. If so, and if the Graysons *had* based their own swordplay on such a thing, its creators seemed to have done their research more thoroughly than modern HD writers did theirs. King's College had sent along a description of the traditional swords of ancient Japan, and the Grayson weapon bore a pronounced resemblance to the *katana*, the longer of the two swords which had identified the *samurai*. It was a bit longer—about the same length as something the records called a *tachi*—with a more "Western-style" guard and a spine that was sharpened for a third of its length, which the *katana's* hadn't been, yet its ancestry was evident.

Master Thomas had been fascinated to learn the *samurai* had actually carried two swords, and he was experimenting with adding the shorter of them—the *wakizashi*—to his own repertoire, evolving his own techniques for fighting with both of them. He had visions of introducing them as an entirely new school, but he'd also been delighted by the university librarians' inclusion of background on a fencing style called "*kendo.*" *Kendo* was similar to existing Grayson styles, but he'd licked his chops as he identified differences between them. He was already developing a brand-new series of moves by combining them, and he looked forward to next year's planetary finals and an overdue settlement with Grand Master Eric.

"Well," she said now, working her fingers as the last tingles drained out of them, "I suppose I should be grateful practice swords don't have edges. On the other hand, you realize you've just motivated me to land at least one touch of my own, don't you?"

"A man's—or woman's—reach should always exceed her grasp, My Lady," Master Thomas agreed with a gleam of humor, and Honor snorted.

"My reach, indeed! All right, Master Thomas," she lowered her mask and stepped back into the guard position, "let's be about it."

"Of course, My Lady." Master Thomas took his own position and they exchanged salutes, but the soft, insistent tone of the salle's door buzzer sounded before either of them could make another move.

"Darn!" Honor lowered her blade. "Looks like you've been saved by the bell, Master Thomas."

"*One* of us has, My Lady," he replied, and she chuckled again, then turned her head as James Candless crossed to the door. He touched a button and listened for a moment, then straightened with an expression of surprise.

"Well, Jamie?" Honor asked.

"You have a visitor, My Lady." There was something a bit odd in her armsman's tone, and Honor cocked her head.

"A visitor?" she prompted.

"Yes, My Lady. High Admiral Matthews asks if it would be convenient for you to receive him."

Honor's eyebrows rose in astonishment. High Admiral Matthews here to see *her*? She had enormous respect for him, and they'd come to know one another well during and after their fight to defeat Masada's attack on Grayson, but why was he here? And why—her eyebrows lowered, furrowing in thought—hadn't he warned her he was coming?

She shook herself. Whatever it was, it was probably too important to waste time changing to receive him.

"Please ask him to come in, Jamie."

"Of course, My Lady." Candless opened the salle door and stepped through it, and Honor turned to her instructor.

"Master Thomas—" she began, but the swordmaster simply bowed and headed for the dressing rooms.

"I'll leave you to your meeting, My Lady. We can reschedule the rest of today's session later this week, if you like."

"Thank you. I'd like that very much," she said, and he nodded and vanished just as Wesley Matthews entered the salle behind Candless.

"My Lady, High Admiral Matthews," the armsman said

with a bow, and stepped into his proper place behind his Steadholder. Nimitz slithered down from his perch on the bars, and Honor handed her practice sword and protective headgear to Candless, then stooped to gather the 'cat in her arms.

"High Admiral." She held Nimitz in the crook of her left arm and extended her right hand, and Matthews gripped it firmly.

"Lady Harrington. Thank you for seeing me on such short notice. I hope it's not an imposition."

"Of course not." Honor studied his expression for a moment, then glanced at Candless. "Thank you for showing the Admiral in, Jamie."

"Of course, My Lady." It wasn't quite proper for an armsman to leave his Steadholder unguarded, but Honor's bodyguards had learned to adjust to her foibles. "High Admiral, My Lady." Candless braced to attention and left, and Honor turned back to Matthews.

"And now, High Admiral, what can I do for you?"

"I've come to you with a proposal, My Lady. One I'd like you to consider very carefully."

"A proposal?" Honor's right eyebrow crept back up.

"Yes, My Lady. I'd like you to accept a commission in the Grayson Navy."

Honor's eyes opened wide, and Nimitz pricked his ears. She started to speak, then closed her mouth and bought a few seconds to think by lifting the 'cat to her shoulder. He sat higher than usual atop it, his spine straight, and his fluffy tail curled about her throat in a protective gesture as both of them looked intently into Matthew's face.

"I'm not certain that would be a good idea," she said finally.

"May I ask why not, My Lady?"

"For several reasons," Honor replied. "First and foremost, I'm a steadholder. That's a full-time job, High Admiral, especially in a steading as new as this one, and particularly when there's been as much, ah, public discussion of whether or not I even ought to *be* one."

"I—" Matthews paused and rubbed an eyebrow. "May I speak frankly?"

"Of course you may."

"Thank you." Matthews rubbed his eyebrow a moment longer, then lowered his hand. "I've discussed my desire to offer you a commission with Protector Benjamin, My Lady, and he gave me permission to do so. I'm sure he considered your responsibilities as Steadholder Harrington before he did so."

"No doubt he did, but *I* have to consider them, as well. And they're only one consideration. There are others."

"May I ask what they are?"

"I'm an officer in the Royal Manticoran Navy, for one." Honor's mouth twitched with an edge of bitterness as she said it. "I realize I'm on half-pay now, but that could change. What if they recall me to active duty?"

"If they do, you would, of course, be free to leave Grayson service, My Lady. And, if I may anticipate a part of your point, I should point out that Manticore has a tradition of detaching officers to assist allied powers, and they've already lent us a large number of personnel. Under the circumstances, I feel confident First Space Lord Caparelli would agree to any request we might make to offer you a Grayson commission."

Honor grimaced and chewed her lower lip. The offer had completely surprised her, and her own reaction to it puzzled her. A part of her had leapt in instant excitement, eager to get back into the one job she truly understood. But another part of her had responded with an instant stab of panic, an instinctive backing away in something uncomfortably like terror. She gazed deep into Matthews' eyes, as if what he saw when he looked at her could somehow tell her what she truly felt, but there was no help there. He simply returned her gaze, politely but directly, and she turned away from him.

She took a quick turn about the salle, arms folded, and tried to think. What was *wrong* with her? This man was offering her the one thing she'd always wanted most in the universe—in the Grayson Navy, not the Manticoran, perhaps, but she was a Grayson herself, as well as a Manticoran. And he was undoubtedly correct. Political pressure might make it impossible for the Admiralty to find her a ship, but the Navy would certainly be willing to "loan" her to the Graysons. In fact, it would be an ideal solution, so why did her throat feel so tight and her heart race so hard?

She stopped, facing out the salle's windows across her mansion's manicured grounds, and realized what it was. She was afraid. Afraid she couldn't do it anymore.

Nimitz made a soft sound, and his tail tightened about her throat. She felt his support flow into her, but her eyes were bitter as she stared out the windows. It wasn't like other times, when she'd been nervous at the thought of assuming new duties, greater responsibilities, in her Queen's service. There was always a lurking anxiety when the push of seniority thrust her into some fresh, more demanding assignment. A tiny fear that *this* time she might prove unequal to those demands. But this was darker than that, and it cut far deeper.

She closed her eyes and faced herself, and dull shame burned deep inside as she admitted the truth. She'd been . . . damaged. Memories of all her uncertainties, of her nightmares and unpredictable bouts of paralyzing grief and depression, flashed through her, and she shied away from the half-crippled portrait they painted. An officer who couldn't control her own emotions had no business commanding a ship of war. A captain wallowing in self-pity couldn't offer people who must live or die by her judgment her very best. That made her more dangerous than the enemy to them, and even if that hadn't been true—it was, but even if it weren't—did she have enough left inside to lay herself open to still greater damage? Could she live with herself if still more people died under her command? And perhaps more dangerous even than that, could she make herself *let* them die if the mission required it? People were killed in wars. If anyone in the universe knew that, *she* did. But could she live with sentencing her own people to death yet again if she had to? Or would she flinch away, fall short of her duty because she was too terrified of bearing more blood on her conscience to do what must be done?

She opened her eyes and gritted her teeth, taut and trembling, and a seething uncertainty not even Nimitz could ease filled her. She fought it as she might a monster, but it refused to yield, and her reflected face looked back from the window before her, white and strained, with no answer to the questions that lashed her mind.

"I'm . . . not certain I should *be* an officer anymore, High Admiral," she made herself say at last. It was one of the hardest things she'd ever done, but she knew it must be said.

"Why?" he asked simply, and the wounded part of her flinched at the lack of judgment in his quiet voice.

"I . . . haven't been exactly—" She broke off and inhaled deeply, then turned to face him. "An officer has to be in command of herself before she can command others." She felt as if she were quivering like a leaf, yet her voice was level, and she made the words come out firm and clear. "She has to be able to *do* the job before she accepts it, and I'm not sure I can."

Wesley Matthews nodded, and his hazel eyes were intent as he studied her face. She'd learned, over the years, to wear the mask of command, he thought, but today the anguish showed, and he felt ashamed for inflicting it upon her. This woman wasn't the cold, focused warrior who'd defended his home world against religious fanatics with five times her firepower. She'd been afraid then, too; he'd known it, even though the rules of the game had required them both to pretend he hadn't. But she hadn't feared what she feared today. She'd been afraid only of dying, of failing in the near hopeless mission she'd accepted, not that the job was one she lacked the courage to do.

She gazed back at him, meeting his eyes, admitting that she knew what he was thinking, refusing to pretend, and he wondered if she'd ever faced this particular

fear before. She was three years older than he, despite
her youthful appearance, but three years either way
mattered very little, and in this moment he felt suddenly
as if she were truly as young as she looked. It was her
eyes, he thought; the pleading look in them, the honesty
that admitted she no longer knew the answers and
begged him to help her find them. She was ashamed
of her indecision, her "weakness," as if she didn't even
realize how much strength it took to admit she *was*
uncertain rather than pretend she wasn't.

He bit his lip and realized how right the Protector
had been to stop him from offering her a commission
months ago. Not because she couldn't do the job, but
because she was *afraid* she couldn't. Because she would
have refused it, and that refusal would have ended her
career forever. Inability, real or imagined, could never
truly be overcome once an officer accepted deep inside
that he could no longer hack it. That damage was almost
always permanent, for it was self-inflicted and no one
else could heal it for him.

Yet Lady Harrington's inner jury was still out, its
verdict as yet undecided, and as her haunted eyes met
his without flinching, he knew the final judgment lay
as much in his hands as in hers. He was the one who'd
pushed it to the decision point, brought it out into the
open where she had to decide, and he wished, suddenly,
that he hadn't.

But he had.

"My Lady," he said quietly, "I can only respect the
courage it takes for an officer of your caliber to admit
to uncertainty, but I believe you've been too harsh on
yourself. Of course you 'haven't been yourself.' How
could you have been? You've seen your entire personal
and professional world torn apart and been pitchforked
into a totally different society and forced to become not
simply a tourist there but one of its rulers. You know
our beliefs—that God tests His people, that it's by rising
to the Test of Life that we nurture and develop all
we can be. Your Test has been far harsher and more

demanding than most, My Lady, but you've risen to it as you always have, with a courage any Grayson not poisoned by bigotry and blind fear of change can only admire. It may not seem that way to *you* at this moment in your life, but just this once, trust our judgment more than your own, please."

Honor said nothing, only stared into his eyes, every cell of her brain focused on his quiet words while she weighed them through her link to Nimitz. The 'cat sat very still on her shoulder, body rumbling with the pulse of his faint, barely audible purr, and she sensed the intensity with which he strained to convey Matthews' emotions with absolute fidelity.

"You say you doubt your ability to 'command yourself,'" the admiral continued. "My Lady, the manner in which you've discharged your duties as Steadholder Harrington is the clearest possible proof that you can. You've brought this steading further in a shorter time than any other steading in our history. I fully realize that you've had help, that Lord Clinkscales is an outstanding regent and that the influx of new technology has given you opportunities few other new steadholders have had, but you've *seized* those opportunities. And when hate-filled, frightened men attacked you simply for being what you are, you neither let them stop you from doing your duty nor lashed out at them. You've acted, always and in every way, *responsibly*, however badly you may have been hurt. I see absolutely no reason to believe you'll act—that you even know *how* to act—in any other way in the future."

Still Honor said nothing, but his sincerity washed into her through Nimitz. He truly believed his own words. He might be wrong, but he wasn't saying them simply to win a point or because courtesy demanded he pretend she was still a whole person.

"I—" She stopped and cleared her throat, then looked away, breaking the intensity of the moment. "You may be right, High Admiral," she went on after a pause. "I'd like to believe you are. Perhaps I even *do* believe it, and there's certainly something to be said for getting back up on the horse." She paused again, and surprised herself with a small, genuine smile. "'Back up on the horse,'" she repeated softly. "Do you know, I've used that cliché all my life, and I've never even been within a hundred kilometers of a horse?" She shook herself, and her voice was brisker, closer to normal when she continued.

"However, the fact remains that I *am* Steadholder Harrington. Is it really more important for you to have one more captain—especially one who may or may not, whatever either of us thinks, be up to doing her duty— than for me to continue with my responsibilities here?"

"My Lady, Lord Clinkscales has proven he can govern Harrington in your complete absence if he must, and you'll never be more than a few hours com time from him at any point in the Yeltsin System. You can continue to discharge your duties to your steading, but you may not realize just how desperately the Navy needs you."

"Desperately?" Honor's eyebrows rose once more, and the admiral smiled without humor at the genuine surprise in her voice.

"Desperately, My Lady. Think about it. You know how tiny our Navy was before we joined the Alliance, and you were here when Masada attacked us. Only three of our starship captains survived, and we never had the experience with modern weapons and tactics the Manticoran Navy takes for granted to start with. I think we've done well, but aside from those officers like Captain Brentworth with limited experience in antipiracy operations, *none* of our new captains have ever commanded in action, and all of them are very, very new to their duties. More than that, we've suddenly found ourselves with a fleet more huge than any Grayson officer ever dreamed of commanding. We're stretched to the breaking point, My Lady, and not one of my officers—not even me, their commander-in-chief—has a fraction of the experience *you* have. I don't believe for a moment that the RMN will leave you dirt-side long. Their

Admiralty's not that stupid, whatever the political situation in the Star Kingdom. But it's absolutely imperative that, while we have you, you pass on as much as possible of that experience to us."

His stark sincerity sank into Honor's mind, and she frowned. She'd never considered it in that light. She'd seen only the determined way the GSN had tackled the task of expanding its forces and mastering its new weapons, and she suddenly wondered why she hadn't realized what an enormous leap into the unknown that must be. She herself had been trained and groomed in a fleet with a five-hundred-T-year tradition as a first-rank interstellar navy. It had shaped and formed her, infused its views and confidence into her, given her its heroes and failures as metersticks and a rich body of tactical and strategic thought on which to base her own. The Grayson Navy lacked those advantages. It was barely two centuries old, and before the Alliance, it had never been more than a system defense fleet, with no access to the reservoirs of institutional memory and experience the Royal Manticoran Navy took for granted.

And now, in less than four T-years, it had been thrust into a war for survival that raged across a volume measured in hundreds of light-years. It had expanded a hundred fold and more in those same four years, but its officers must be agonizingly aware of how thinly stretched they were, how new they were to the duties and challenges they faced.

"I . . . never thought of it that way, High Admiral," she said after a long pause. "I'm only a captain. I've always been concerned with just my own ship, or possibly a single squadron."

"I realize that, My Lady, but you *have* commanded a squadron. Aside from myself and Admiral Garret, there's not a single surviving Grayson officer who'd ever done that before we joined the Alliance, and we've got eleven *superdreadnoughts* to command, not to mention our lighter units."

"I understand." Honor hesitated a moment longer,

then sighed. "You know the buttons to punch, don't you, High Admiral?" Her voice was amused, not accusing, and Matthews shrugged and smiled back at her, acknowledging the truth of her statement. "All right. If you really need one somewhat less than mint-condition captain, I suppose you've got her. What were you planning to do with her?"

"Well," Matthews tried to hide his exultation at her response, but it was hard, especially when her treecat flipped its ears and wrinkled its muzzle at him in an unmistakable grin. "The yard will finish refitting the *Terrible* next month. She's the last of the prizes Admiral White Haven turned over to us, so I thought it would be fitting to give you her."

"A superdreadnought?" Honor cocked her head, then chuckled. "That's quite an inducement, High Admiral. I've never skippered anything bigger than a battlecruiser. Talk about a jump in seniority!"

"I don't think you quite understand, My Lady. I don't intend to put you in command of *Terrible*. Or perhaps I should say, not *directly* in command of her."

"I beg your pardon?" Honor blinked. "I thought you said—"

"I said I was giving you *Terrible*," Matthews said, "but not as her CO. That will be up to your flag captain, *Admiral* Harrington; I'm giving *you* the entire First Battle Squadron."

• CHAPTER SEVEN

The man behind the outsized desk was of medium height, thin-faced and dark-haired, and touches of white at his temples marked him as a first- or second-generation prolong recipient. There was nothing imposing about him—he might have been a businessman, or perhaps an academic—until one saw his eyes. Dark eyes, intense and focused and just a bit dangerous, as was only fitting in the most powerful single man in the People's Republic of Haven.

His name was Robert Stanton Pierre, and he was chairman of the Committee of Public Safety which had been formed after the assassination of Hereditary President Sidney Harris, his cabinet, and the heads of virtually every important Legislaturalist family. The Navy had killed them in an attempted military coup—everyone knew that . . . except for less than thirty people (still living, that was) who knew *Pierre* had arranged it all himself.

Now he leaned back in his chair, gazing out across the city of Nouveau Paris through the floor to ceiling window of his three-hundredth-floor office, and his narrowed eyes took on the cast of flint as he contemplated his achievements. He fully appreciated both the complexity and the staggering scope of the operation he'd carried off, yet something a bit more anxious, with a hint of what could almost have been desperation, flawed the flint in his gaze, and there was a reason for that. One he disliked admitting, even to himself.

Pierre couldn't have accomplished all he had without the rot spreading from the Legislaturalists' policies, yet the very thing which had made their overthrow possible also made it all but impossible to fundamentally change the system they'd spent two centuries building. They'd created a vast, permanently unemployed underclass, dependent upon the Republic's stupendous welfare machine for its very existence, and in so doing, they'd sown the seeds of their own destruction. No one could place two-thirds of a world's population on the Dole and keep them there forever without the entire system crashing . . . but how in *hell* did one get them *off* the Dole?

He sighed and walked over to the windows as darkness closed in on the capital and its lights blinked to life, and wondered yet again what had possessed the Dolist system's creators to birth such a monster. The enormous towers blazed alight, flaming against the gold and crimson of Haven's sunset, and a sense of his own mortality warred with his fierce determination. The system was so vast, the forces which drove it almost beyond calculation, and he was a product of the old regime, as well as its executioner. He was ninety-two T-years old, and he yearned for the days of his youthful certainty, when the system had worked—superficially, at least— even as a part of him knew it had been doomed long before his birth. That younger Pierre had bought into the lie that said the state could provide every citizen a guaranteed, ever higher standard of living, regardless of his own productivity or lack thereof, and that was what had so enraged him when he recognized its hollowness. It was rage which had fueled his ambition, driven him to claw his own way off the Dole and become the most powerful of Haven's Dolist managers, and he knew it. Just as he knew that same rage—that need to punish the system for its lies—was what had fused with the death of his only child to make him the hammer that smashed the system to splinters.

He laughed bitterly, without mirth. *Smash the system.* Oh, that was a good one! He'd done just that, wiped away the Legislaturalists in a thunderbolt of precision-guided bombs and colder, bloodier pogroms. He'd destroyed the old officer corps, Navy and Marine alike, crushed every source of organized opposition. The Legislaturalists' hydra-headed security organs had been ambushed, dissolved, merged into one, all-powerful Office of State Security responsible only to him. He'd achieved all that in less than a single T-year, at the cost of more thousands of lives than he dared remember . . . and "the system" sneered at his efforts.

There'd been a time when the Republic of Haven—not "the People's Republic," but simply "the Republic"—had inspired an entire quadrant. It had been a bright, burning beacon, a wealthy, vastly productive renaissance which had rivaled Old Earth herself as the cultural and intellectual touchstone of humanity. Yet that glorious promise had died. Not at the hands of foreign conquerors or barbarians from the marches, but in its sleep, victim of the best of motives. It had sacrificed itself upon the altar of equality. Not the equality of opportunity, but of *outcomes*. It had looked upon its own wealth and the inevitable inequities of any human society and decided to rectify them, and somehow the lunatics had taken over the asylum. They'd transformed the Republic into the People's Republic—a vast, crazed machine that promised everyone more and better of everything, regardless of their own contributions to the system. And, in the process, they'd built a bureaucratic Titan locked into a headlong voyage to self-destruction and capable of swallowing reformers like gnats.

Rob Pierre had challenged that Titan. He'd poured out the blood of the men and women who'd been supposed to run the machine like water, concentrated more power in his person than any Legislaturalist had ever dreamed of possessing, and it meant nothing, for, in truth, the machine had run *them*, and the machine remained. He was a fly, buzzing about the maggot-ridden corpse of a once great star nation. Oh, he had a sting, yet he could sting but one maggot at a time, and for each he destroyed, a dozen more hatched in its place.

He swore softly and raised his fists above his head,

planting them against the window, and leaned into the tough plastic. He pressed his face to it and closed his eyes and swore again, more viciously. The rot had gone too far. The Legislaturalists' parents and grandparents had taken too many workers out of the labor force in the name of "equality," debased the educational system too terribly in the name of "democratization." They'd taught the Dolists that their only responsibilities were to be born, to breathe, and to draw their Basic Living Stipends, and that the function of their schools was to offer students "validation"—whatever the hell *that* was— rather than *education*. And when the rulers realized they'd gutted their own economy, that its total collapse was only a few, inevitable decades away unless they could somehow undo their "reforms," they'd lacked the courage to face the consequences.

Perhaps *they*, unlike Pierre, actually could have repaired the damage, but they hadn't. Rather than face the political consequences of dismantling their vote-buying system of bread and circuses, they'd looked for another way to fill the welfare coffers, and so the People's Republic had turned conquistador. The Legislaturalists had engulfed their interstellar neighbors, looting other economies to transfuse life back into the corpse of the old Republic of Haven, and, for a time, it had seemed to work.

But appearances had been misleading, for they'd exported their own system to the worlds they conquered. They'd had no choice—it was the only one they knew— yet it had poisoned the captive economies as inexorably as their own. The need to squeeze those economies to prop up their own had only made them collapse sooner, and as the revenue sources dried up, they'd been forced to conquer still more worlds, and still more. Each victim provided a brief, illusory spurt of prosperity, but only until it, too, failed and became yet another burden rather than an asset. It had been like trying to outrun entropy, yet they'd left themselves no other option, and as conquest bloated the People's Republic, the forces needed to safeguard those conquests and add still more to them had grown, as well.

The galaxy at large had seen only the Republic's stupendous size, the massive power of its war machine, and Haven's neighbors had shivered in terror as the juggernaut bore down upon them. But how many of those neighbors, Pierre wondered, had seen the weakness at the juggernaut's heart? The ramshackle economy stumbling towards collapse, dragged down by the dead weight of the Dole and the crushing cost of its war machine? The Republic had become little more than an appetite, a parasite which must devour more and more hosts to survive. Yet there were only so many hosts to *be* devoured, and when all of them were drained, the parasite itself must perish.

Rob Pierre had looked below the surface. He'd seen the inevitable and tried to stop it, and he couldn't. He, too, was caught, like a blind aerialist forced to run along a high-wire while he juggled a dozen hand grenades. He controlled the machine, yet the machine had him in its jaws, as well, and he turned away from the window and returned to his desk while the dreadfully familiar cycle of his options churned through his brain.

At least he'd managed one thing no Legislaturalist ever had, he told himself bitterly. He'd actually awakened the Dolists from their apathy, but they'd waked ignorant. They'd been drones too long. They'd been taught that that was the way things were supposed to be, and their fury was directed not towards scrapping the old system and building anew, but to punishing those who had "betrayed" them by robbing them of their "economic birthright."

Perhaps it was his own fault for clutching at the familiar catchwords when he found himself straddling the vast, hungry beast that was the People's Republic. He'd punched the buttons of expediency in the name of survival, embracing the rhetoric of people like Cordelia Ransom because it was the language the mob understood and he'd feared the mob. He admitted it to himself. For all his contempt for the people who'd let things reach this pass, he, too, had been afraid. Afraid of failure. Of admitting to the mob that there were no quick fixes. Afraid the beast would turn upon him and devour him.

He'd meant to introduce genuine reforms, he thought wearily. He truly had. But the mob wanted simple solutions, uncomplicated answers, and it didn't care that the real world wasn't like that. Worse, it had tasted blood and discovered the pleasure of smashing its enemies, and it sensed—dimly, perhaps, yet sensed—its own immense, latent power. It was like a homicidal adolescent driven by urges it didn't understand, without the self-discipline that might have controlled those urges and unconcerned with consequences, and the only way to avoid becoming its target was to give it other targets.

And so he had. He'd pointed at the Legislaturalists as traitors who'd battened on the wealth that should have gone to the Dolists, denounced them as profiteers and grafters, and the undeniable wealth of the great Legislaturalist families had made it work, for they *had* siphoned off immense fortunes. But what he hadn't told the mob—what the mob hadn't wanted to hear—was that all the wealth of all the Legislaturalists of the PRH was meaningless against its debts. Nationalizing their fortunes had provided a temporary relief, a fleeting illusion of improvement, yet it could be no more than that, and so he'd given the mob the Legislaturalists themselves. He'd loosed Oscar Saint-Just's new Office of State Security upon them and watched the "People's Courts" condemn family after family to death for "treason against the people." And as the execution totals rose, he'd learned a terrible truth: bloodletting simply begat more bloodletting. The conviction that the mob had a right to vengeance upon its "betrayers" only fanned the frenzy with which that vengeance was demanded, and when the supply of victims ran short, new ones were required.

And when Pierre realized the impossibility of fulfilling even the modest promises of reform he'd made upon seizing power, he'd also realized that sooner or later, as the latest savior to fail the mob, *he* must become its victim unless, somehow, he could find someone else upon whom to fix the blame. And so, in desperation, he'd turned to Cordelia Ransom, the third member of the triumvirate which now ran the Republic.

Pierre was firmly placed as that triumvirate's senior member and master. He'd taken steps to stay that way and seen to it that both his associates knew it, yet he needed them, as well. He needed Ransom's ability as the new regime's propagandist . . . and he needed Saint-Just not simply to control the security forces but to watch Ransom, for there were times the golden-haired, blue-eyed Secretary of Public Information frightened Pierre almost more than the mob did.

She wasn't brilliant, but she had a quick, iron-nerved cleverness and an innate talent for intrigue which had made her invaluable when it came to staging the coup. But she was also utterly ruthless and a brilliant demagogue who actually *enjoyed* the bloodshed, as if it were some sort of drug. A proof of the power she wielded. Something dark and hungry at her core seemed to crave destruction for its own sake, however it might cloak itself in the rhetoric of "reform" and "rights" and "the service of the people."

Yet however much he might fear her, he'd seen no choice but to call on her ability to sway the mob. Not even she had been able to calm it—assuming she'd ever actually tried—but she spoke its language, and she understood the need to outrun its passions. To stay ahead of it by anticipating its next furious demand. And because she did, she'd been able to redirect its frenzy to an external target for its hate.

The Legislaturalists had been the people's enemies, elitist conspirators who'd stolen the people's birthright and squandered it in imperialist wars of aggrandizement. Never mind that those wars had been fought to shore up a collapsing economy and preserve the Dolists' own parasitic lifestyle. Never mind that expansion, once embraced, was part of a feeding cycle which couldn't be renounced. The mob didn't want to hear that, so Cordelia hadn't told it.

Instead, she'd offered it what it *did* want to hear. Her argument was so riddled with gaping inconsistencies that Pierre hadn't been able to believe anyone could accept it, but she'd sold it to the mob by pandering to its belief in its own rectitude. The mob wanted—*needed*—to believe it was more than a parasite, that it truly was entitled to all the "rights" it claimed by some sort of natural law, and it followed from that belief that only some vast conspiracy could deny it those rights. Cordelia had recognized its need to see itself as the victim of enemies working perpetually for its downfall rather than admit the system it demanded work *couldn't* work, and she'd given it those enemies.

Of course the people wanted only peace, asked no more than to be left alone in the enjoyment of the prosperity which was their basic right, for wasn't that peace and prosperity the natural order of things? But the traitors who'd filched away their rights had also committed them to a course of war from which the people could not turn aside. After all, the Manticoran Alliance had attacked *them*—hadn't the Office of Public Information told them so? Never mind that an attack by the Alliance was totally at odds with the notion of the Legislaturalists as warmongers. The Alliance was part of the same corrupt order of imperialist militarists. Its member systems were no more than puppets, controlled by the Star Kingdom of Manticore, which hungered for the Republic's destruction because it recognized the inevitable, natural enmity between itself and the people. The Star Kingdom wasn't even a republic, but a monarchy, ruled by a Queen and an overt aristocracy, and it didn't even pretend to respect the People's Republic's rights. It denied the Republic's citizens their prosperity by hoarding its vast wealth for the selfish ends of its own hereditary ruling class. That alone would have made it the people's mortal foe, but it also knew what would happen if its own subjects should realize the people were right, recognize how *they* had been victimized, as well. No wonder Manticore had attacked the Republic; it must destroy the PRH root and branch before the inexorable spread of the people's rightful demands brought about its own destruction.

The people had arisen in their just and terrible wrath to overthrow their plutocratic overlords only to find that it faced a still more heinous foe. A *foreign* foe whose overlords must be smashed in turn if the people were to be safe and secure. And so the mob had mobilized, with a fierce devotion to purpose which could have achieved almost anything if only there'd been a way to convert it to some constructive purpose.

But there wasn't. Insane as it seemed, the coup Rob Pierre had staged in no small part to stem the military's drain on the economy had become a crusade. He'd meant only to use the immediate crisis of the Manticoran War to distract the mob and stifle dissent until he was firmly in control, but Cordelia's rhetoric had imbued that war with a life of its own. After half a T-century of total apathy and disinterest in whoever the Republic was conquering this month, the mob was willing—even eager—to defer demands for a higher BLS in order to finance the destruction of Manticore and all its works. The Committee of Public Safety couldn't renounce the war, lest the Dolists it had awakened turn upon it for its apostasy. Its only salvation, and the only hope for the reforms of which Pierre once had dreamed, was to *win* the war, for that and that alone might give it the moral authority to make genuine reforms.

And for now, at least, the mob *was* willing to sacrifice. It was actually willing to set aside its comfortable, nonproductive lifestyle and report for military training, even to learn useful skills and labor in the shipyards to replace the ships which had been destroyed. It was even possible it would reacquire the *habit* of working, that there would be enough skilled workers when the war ended to turn their hands to rebuilding the PRH's threadbare infrastructure. Stranger things had happened, Pierre told himself, and tried to pretend he was doing something more than clutching at straws.

But for any of that to happen, the war must be won, and in return for its own sacrifices, the mob demanded that the Navy—and the Committee of Public Safety—do just that. The extremism that possessed the Republic like a blood fever demanded proof of its leaders' commitment, and since the Navy had been branded with responsibility for the Harris Assassination, the Navy must prove its worthiness by winning victories. Any who failed the people in their time of trial must be punished, both for their own crimes and as a warning to others, and so Pierre had embraced a public policy of collective responsibility. The officers of the Navy were all on trial; any who failed in their duties must know that not just they but their entire families would suffer for it, for somehow this had become a war of extermination, and no quarter could be given to enemies—foreign or internal—when the stakes were victory or annihilation.

It wasn't the revolution Pierre had wanted, but it was the one he had. And at least the reign of terror he'd unleashed had stiffened the Navy's spine, so perhaps the mob had a point. Perhaps it *was* possible to find at least some simple solutions if a man was willing to kill enough people in the search.

He scrubbed his face with his hands, then keyed his terminal to view the top secret file once more. The old Naval Intelligence Branch had been merged with the Office of State Security along with every other intelligence organ of the PRH. The bulk of the precoup Navy's strategists had vanished in the purges, yet the core of analysts who'd served them had not only survived but learned what would happen if they failed to produce. Their analyses contained too many qualifiers and reservations, no doubt in an effort to cover their own backs, but they were generating an immense amount of raw data, and a handful of new strategists were emerging to use that data. They were ambitious, those strategists. They sensed the opportunities for personal power that hid in the Republic's barely restrained chaos. Too many were loyal to the Committee of Public Safety only because they dared not be anything else—yet—and Pierre suspected Admiral Thurston, the author of the plan on his terminal, was one of those. But for now, at least, the men and women like Thurston knew their own success—and survival—depended upon the Committee's survival.

They also knew the Navy needed a victory. As an absolute minimum, it had to stop the Manties' advance into the People's Republic, yet that would be the least desirable option. No doubt Cordelia's ministry could turn that into a decisive triumph, but how much better if it could win an *offensive* victory. And, from a strategic viewpoint, the People's Navy desperately needed something to divert Manty strength from the front-line systems. That front *was* stabilizing, but it was far from certain that it would stay stabilized . . . unless the RMN's strategists could somehow be distracted from fresh offensives.

It was the purpose of the operations outlined on Pierre's terminal to provide that distraction, and despite his weariness, he felt his own interest rousing as he reread the file. It could work, he thought, and even if it failed, it would cost little that truly mattered. The People's Navy had immense reserves of battleships, units that were too weak to face the shock of combat in the wall of battle but which, properly utilized, could nonetheless exert a tremendous influence on the course of the war.

He sat back, gazing at the data on his terminal, and nodded slowly. The time had come to put those battleships to use, and Thurston's plan was not only the most audacious suggestion of how to do that but also offered the richest prize if it succeeded.

He nodded once more and picked up an electronic stylus. He dashed it across the scanner pad and watched a brief, handwritten memo blink into life on the display.

"Operation Stalking Horse and Operation Dagger approved, by order of Rob S. Pierre, Chairman, Committee of Public Safety. Activate immediately," it said.

• CHAPTER EIGHT

The entire east end of Harrington Cathedral was a single, enormous wall of stained glass. The morning light pouring through it drenched the cathedral in gorgeous, luminous color, and Honor sat at its heart, enveloped in the swirl of incense.

The choir's glorious harmony swept through her, and she closed her eyes to savor it. The choir sang without accompaniment, for its superbly trained voices needed none, and the artificiality of instruments, however magnificent, could only have detracted from their beauty. Honor had always loved music, though she'd never learned to play and her subjects would have greeted her singing voice with pained politeness. Classical Grayson music was based on an Old Earth tradition called "Country and Western" and took some getting used to, but she was developing a taste even for it, and she was delighted by Grayson's popular music, while its sacred music was breathtaking.

The choir completed its selection, and Honor heard Nimitz mirror her own sigh of pleasure from his cushion in the pew beside her. Andrew LaFollet stood behind them, head uncovered but still on duty, even here, and she felt a familiar, wry amusement as she glanced to the left and saw the other two armsmen standing before the unoccupied Steadholder's Box. As someone who was not a communicant of the Church of Humanity, she was required by Church law to sit in the Stranger's Aisle, even in Harrington Cathedral, which had posed a problem for Harrington Steading's architects.

Honor made a point of attending services regularly.

Member of the Church or not, she was obligated to protect and defend it, and there were other, equally pressing reasons to be here. Her public respect for the Faith was an answer to her critics' charges that she disdained it, and her willingness to take her place in the Stranger's Aisle rather than insist upon occupying the box set aside for the steadholder in any steading capital's cathedral had won her even more acceptance. Her subjects' native Grayson stubbornness respected the honesty of a ruler who accepted the stigma of the Aisle rather than pretend to embrace their Faith. And the fact that she, who *wasn't* a member of the Church, was a regular attendant underscored the fact that she, in turn, truly respected the Faith which was not hers.

Those were the political reasons. On a personal level, she was here because she *had* learned to respect the Church and because it was so central to the lives of her people. She needed to share it, even at one remove, to understand them. And even if that hadn't been true, she found the solemn majesty of the Church's liturgy and music compellingly beautiful.

Honor had been raised in the Third Stellar Missionary Communion (Reformed), but her family, like most Sphinx yeomen, had always been low church. The Third Stellars emphasized each individual's direct, personal relationship with God, with a minimum of structure. The high church had become more formal over the last few T-centuries, but low church services tended to be quiet, introspective affairs, and Honor had been unprepared for the sheer pageantry of the Church of Humanity. She supposed Mother Helen, the priest who'd confirmed her so many years ago, would have sniffed at all the "unnecessary fol-de-rol." She'd certainly regarded the formalism of her own denomination's high churchmen with enough reservations! But Honor suspected even Mother Helen would admit the beauty of Grayson's liturgy, and no one could doubt the personal faith of the people who followed it.

Still, Honor's decision to attend regularly *had* put the

architects in something of a quandary. The Stranger's Aisle was always to the left of the nave and immediately adjacent to the sanctuary. Traditionally, this was to make the people who sat in it feel welcome by placing them in the very heart of the congregation rather than isolating them like pariahs, but it had the effect of putting them under everyone's eye, as well. It was also clear across the church from the traditional location of the Steadholder's Box, and the architects had decided that having Lady Harrington so obviously separated from her "proper" position would invite invidious comment. Honor wasn't too sure about that, but it was scarcely a decision in which she'd had a voice, so she'd let them work it out to suit themselves, and they'd compromised by making two changes in the accepted layout of every other cathedral on the planet.

Instead of placing the pulpit in its usual position at the sanctuary's extreme right, they'd swapped it with the choir loft. That put the *pulpit* to the left, which, in turn, required them to move the Steadholder's Box to the same side to maintain its proximity to the pulpit. All of which just happened to put the box directly adjacent to the Stranger's Aisle and meant Honor could sit right beside the seat which was nominally hers.

Honor would never have requested the changes, but she was touched by the way her Harringtons accepted them. They could have chosen to be affronted; instead, they went out of their way to compare their church to other cathedrals—always to the detriment of the more "traditional" churches. Besides, they claimed, the acoustics were better.

Honor smiled in memory, but her smile faded as Reverend Hanks genuflected before the altar and crossed to the pulpit. Each of Grayson's eighty steadings had its own capital cathedral, and by ancient tradition, the Reverend celebrated service in a different one each Sunday, working his way through every steading in turn. It must, Honor thought, have been an incredibly wearing cycle once, though modern transport had made it much easier. But Reverend Hanks had rearranged his entire schedule to be here today, and she—like everyone else in the cathedral—wondered why he had.

Hanks stepped up into the tall pulpit and looked out over the congregation. His white surplice seemed to glow in the light spilling through the stained glass, and the scarlet stole of his high office was a slash of color as he opened the immense, leather-bound book before him, then bent his head.

"Hear us, oh God," he prayed, his voice carrying clearly even without amplification, "that our words and thoughts may be always acceptable to You. Amen."

"Amen," the congregation replied, and he raised his head once more.

"Today's scripture," he said quietly, "is taken from Meditations Six, chapter three, verses nineteen through twenty-two, of *The New Way*." He cleared his throat, then recited the passage from memory without glancing at the book before him. "'We shall be known both by our works and by the words of our mouths, which are the echoes of our thoughts. Let us therefore speak the truth always, fearing not to show forth our inner selves. But let us also forget not charity, nor that all people are God's children, even as we. No man is without error; therefore let him not assail his brother or sister with intemperate words, but reason with them, remembering always that whatever our words may show forth, God knows the thought behind them. Think not to deceive Him or to preach divisiveness or hatred cloaked in His word, for all who are clean of spirit—yea, even those who remain strangers to the New Way—are His children, and he who seeks with malice or hatred to wound any child of God is the servant of corruption and abhorrent in the eyes of He Who is Father to us all.'"

The Reverend paused. Absolute silence enveloped the congregation, and Honor felt eyes turning towards her from every corner of the cathedral. No one who'd heard or seen the demonstrations against her could possibly misinterpret the challenge of Hanks' chosen text or doubt the Reverend had selected it deliberately, and she realized she was actually holding her breath.

"Brothers and Sisters," Hanks said after a moment, "four days ago, in this city, a man of God forgot the duty laid upon us by this passage. Filled with his own anger, he forgot to assail not his brothers and sisters and that *all* of us were created the children of God. He chose not to reason, but to attack, and he forgot that Saint Austin himself tells us that men—and women—may be godly even if they know Him in a way different from our own. Remembering that can be difficult for anyone filled with the Faith, for we know our own way to God, and unlike God, we are neither infinite nor omniscient. We forget, all too easily, that there *are* other ways. Nor do we always remember how limited our perceptions are compared to His, and that He, unlike us, sees to the hearts of all people and knows His own, however strange and different they may appear to us."

The Reverend paused once more, lips pursed as if in thought, then nodded slowly.

"Yes, it's difficult not to equate 'different' with 'wrong.' Difficult for any of us. But we who have felt God's call to serve Him as His clergy have a special responsibility. We, too, are fallible. We, too, can—and do—make mistakes, even with the best of intentions. We turn to Him in prayer and meditation, yet there are times when our fears can become intolerance, even hatred, for even in the stillness of prayer, we may mistake our own distrust of the new or different for God's.

"And that, Brothers and Sisters, is precisely what happened in your city. A priest of Father Church looked into his heart and took council not of God, but of his own fears. His own hatred. He saw changes about him which he feared, which challenged his own preconceptions and prejudices, and he mistook his fear of those changes for the voice of God and let that fear lead him into the service of corruption. In his own hatred, he closed his mind to the most fundamental of all Saint Austin's teachings: that God is greater than the mind of Man can comprehend, and that the New Way has no end. That there will always be more of God and His will for us to learn. We must test any new lesson against the truths God has already taught us, yet we must *test* it, not simply say 'No! This is strange to me, and therefore against the law of God!'

"Brother Marchant," Hanks said quietly, and a soft sigh went up as he spoke the name at last, "looked upon the immense changes our world faces, and those changes frightened him. I can understand that, for change is always frightening. But as Saint Austin also said, 'A little change from time to time is God's way of reminding us we have not yet learned everything,' Brothers and Sisters. Brother Marchant forgot that, and in his fear he set up his own will and judgment as those of God. He sought not to test the changes, but to forbid them without test, and when he was unable to forbid them, he fell into still more dangerous sin. The sin of hate. And that hate led him to attack a good and godly woman, one who showed forth her thoughts by her works four years past, when she confronted armed assassins with her bare hands to defend our Protector against murder. When she placed herself between our entire world and its destruction. She is not of the Faith, yet no one in the history of Grayson has more valiantly defended it or our people from those who would destroy us."

Honor's cheeks burned brilliant scarlet, but a vast, soft rumble endorsed Reverend Hanks' words, and its sincerity suffused her link to Nimitz.

"Your Steadholder, Brothers and Sisters, is a woman, which is new and strange to us. She is foreign born, which is also strange to us. She was raised in a Faith which is not ours, and she has not changed that Faith to embrace Father Church. For all those reasons, she seems a threat to some of us, yet how much more of a threat is it to forget the Test? To turn away from change simply because it *is* change, without first considering if, perhaps, this foreign-born woman might not be God's way of telling us change is required? Shall we ask her to *pretend* to embrace Father Church? To pervert her own Faith to deceive us into accepting her? Or shall we respect her for refusing to pretend? For revealing to us what she truly is and thinks and feels?"

Another, deeper rumble of agreement filled the cathedral, and the Reverend nodded slowly.

"As you, Brothers and Sisters, and as Brother Marchant, I, too, am fallible. I, too, feared the changes which might come upon us if we allied with foreign worlds, with planets whose faiths and beliefs differ radically from our own. Yet now I have seen those changes coming to pass, and I believe they are good ones. Not always pleasant and comfortable, no, but God never promised the Test would be easy. I may be in error to believe the changes we face are good, yet if I am, surely God will show me that as I continue to test them. And until he does, I must continue to serve Him as I swore to do when I first accepted His call, and again, when the Sacristy elevated me to Reverend. Not in the assurance that I will always be right, but in the assurance that I will always *try* to be right . . . and that I will always oppose evil, whenever I perceive it and wherever I find it."

The Reverend paused yet again. His face hardened, and his voice was deeper and more deliberate when he continued once more.

"It is never an easy thing, Brothers and Sisters, to tax a priest with error. None of us likes to believe a servant of Father Church *can* be in error, and for those of the clergy there is an added dimension. We flinch from opening the door to schism. We are tempted to take the easy road, to avoid the Test and conceal our divisions lest we weaken our authority in your eyes. Yet our authority is not ours to protect. The authority of Father Church springs only from God, and Father Church deserves that authority only so long as we strive earnestly and without flinching to know and to do His will. As such, it is our solemn duty to put aside such fears, to set the temple of the Lord in order when we see disorder, and to do our best, trusting in God's guidance, to distinguish between those who truly serve His will and those who but think they do. And because that is our duty, I have come among you this Sunday to publish to you a decree of Father Church."

An acolyte laid a sealed scroll in his hand, and the quiet crackle of parchment was ear shattering as he broke the seal, unrolled it, and read aloud.

"'Let it be published among all the body of the Faithful that we, the Sacristy of the Church of Humanity Unchained, being assembled to know and to do God's will as He shall give us to understand it, have, by our solemn vote, petitioned Benjamin IX, by God's Grace Protector of the Faith and of Grayson, to remove Brother Edmond Augustus Marchant from the rectory of Burdette Cathedral, and from the office of Chaplain to William Fitzclarence, Lord Burdette, pursuant to the findings of the High Chancery of Father Church that the said Edmond Augustus Marchant has turned aside from the Test of Life into error. Let it also be published that the former Brother Edmond Augustus Marchant is, by the High Chancery of Father Church, suspended from and deprived of all offices of Father Church until such time as he may satisfy this Sacristy of his true repentance and his return to that spirit of godly charity and tolerance beloved of God.'"

Not a breath disturbed the quiet as Reverend Hanks looked out over the hushed cathedral, and his deep, quiet voice was tinged with ineffable sorrow yet measured and stern.

"Brothers and Sisters, this is a grave step, and one not taken lightly. To cast out any child of God wounds all children of God, and the Sacristy knows well that to condemn error in another is always to risk error in oneself. Yet we can but act as we believe God calls us to act, acknowledging always that we may act wrongly yet refusing to turn aside from the Test God sets before us. I, as every member of the Sacristy, pray that he who was Brother Marchant will return to us, that we may welcome him once more into Father Church's arms and

rejoice, as any family must rejoice when one who was
lost is found once more. But until he chooses to return,
he is as a stranger to us. A child who by his own will
becomes a stranger is a stranger still, however deeply
our hearts may ache to see him estranged from us, and
the choice to return, as all choices God sets before us
in the Test of Life, must be his own. Brothers and Sisters in God, I humbly beseech your prayers for Edmond
Augustus Marchant, that he, as we, may know God's will
and love and be sustained in this, the hour of his Test."

Honor gazed pensively out the window as her ground
car rolled away from the cathedral. She'd been as
stunned as any native-born Grayson at the speed of the
Church's actions, and deep inside, she feared the consequences. The Sacristy, as the Church's highest gov-
erning body, had every legal right to act as it had, yet
the defrocking of a priest could not but be the gravest
of steps. And, she thought, one which would goad every
reactionary on the planet to fury. Few of them would
believe she hadn't had a thing to do with the decision
. . . and *none* of them would care. They would see only
that the off-world corruption they feared had reached
even into the Sacristy, and the potential for a violent
reaction from fanatics who already viewed themselves
as a persecuted minority was terrifying.

She sighed and leaned back in the luxurious seat. The
timing was another problem, she reflected while Nimitz
purred reassuringly in her lap. This had been the last
service she would be able to attend for the foreseeable
future, for she was due to report aboard GNS *Terrible*
tomorrow. No doubt there were arguments in favor of
getting her off-planet while the Church dealt with the
furor the Sacristy's actions were bound to provoke, yet
there were counter-arguments, too. Her enemies could
see it as a sign of cowardice on her part, as flight from
the just anger of God's true servants at the part she'd
played in the martyrdom of a priest. Conversely, they
might choose to see it as a sign of contempt for them—

a sort of swaggering insolence that no longer saw a reason to pretend to respect the Church now that Brother Marchant had been struck down.

And even if she left those possibilities out of the equation, how would Steadholder Burdette react? She had no idea how many of Grayson's other steadholders sympathized with him to one extent or another, but that Burdette himself would be livid was a given, and if other steadholders had shared his views in silence, the Church's declaration of war on the forces of reactionism might bring them out into the open. Even if it didn't, Burdette Steading was one of the five original steadings. It was densely populated and immensely wealthy, by Grayson standards, and the Fitzclarence family had held steading there for over seven centuries. That gave the current Lord Burdette immense authority and prestige, whereas Harrington was Grayson's newest and, so far, least populous and poorest steading. Honor was realist enough to admit that whatever authority she possessed sprang from who *she* was and the way mainstream Grayson opinion regarded her. That was a much more fragile thing than the dynastic prestige Burdette was heir to, and with her off-planet and out of mind, there was no telling how public opinion might be swayed. And whatever the public might think, she had no doubt Burdette's previous, behind-the-scenes opposition to her had just been transformed into implacable hatred.

She closed her eyes, caressing Nimitz, and a small, self-pitying inner voice railed against the universe's unfairness. She'd never wanted political power, never asked for it. She'd done her best to avoid it when it was thrust upon her, for whatever anyone else thought, she knew only too well how unfitted for politics she was. Yet it seemed no matter what she did or where she went, she took a vortex of political strife with her like a curse, and she wondered despairingly if there would ever be an end to it.

She hadn't meant to infuriate the Liberal and Progressive Parties back home when she was sent to Basilisk Station. She'd simply done her best to do her duty; surely it wasn't *her* fault that doing so had made the Liberal and Progressive leadership look like fools?

But it had, and the hatred that had earned her had only intensified when her grieving guilt over Admiral Courvosier's death had combined with disgust for Reginald Houseman's order to withdraw her forces and abandon Grayson to Masada. No doubt his powerful Liberal family would have been furious enough with her for simply ignoring his orders and underscoring his cowardice, but, no—she'd had to lose her temper and *strike* him! He'd had it coming, but a Queen's officer had no business giving it to a Crown envoy, and her actions had cast the Opposition's fury with her in ceramacrete.

Then there'd been Pavel Young. His court-martial for abandoning her in the Battle of Hancock had created the bitterest political fight in the memory of the House of Lords, yet that paled beside what had followed. Paul's murder and Young's death at her hands had almost brought Duke Cromarty's Government down—not to mention getting her exiled to Grayson.

And now this. The demonstrations had been bad enough, but God alone knew where this latest twist would end. She tried and tried to do her best, to recognize where her duty lay and meet her responsibilities, and every time she did, the galaxy blew up in her face, and she was sick unto death of it. Not even the knowledge that the people whose respect she valued supported her seemed to balance the exhausting strain of fighting political battles for which she was supremely unsuited. She was a *naval officer*, for God's sake! Why couldn't they just let her *be* one without all these endless, bickering attacks? Without the unending pressure of making *her* somehow responsible for the political and religious turmoil of two entire star systems?

She sighed again, opened her eyes, and gave herself a stern mental shake. They were about to let her be an officer again, and Reverend Hanks and Protector

Benjamin were eminently capable of fighting their own battles. Besides, it wasn't as if the universe were truly out to get her, however it felt from time to time, and she had no business losing her perspective this way. All she could do was the best she could, and as long as she did, she could face whatever came with the knowledge that she had. That, as her Grayson subjects would say, she'd risen to her own Test.

Her lips twitched at the thought, and the bleakness faded in her eyes. No wonder she and her Harringtons got along so well. Whether she shared their Faith or not, they were too much alike *not* to get along. The Church of Humanity didn't demand an individual triumph in the tests God sent her; it demanded only that she *try*. That she give it her very best shot, whatever the cost or outcome, and that was a code any warrior could appreciate.

She straightened her shoulders and glanced back out the window as the car moved past the entrance to Yanakov Park. She let her gaze rest on the soothing green welcome of the park, savoring the beauty of the sight, but then her eyes narrowed and she paled. Good God—was it starting *already?*

Nimitz's head shot up, ears pricked and whiskers quivering as he sensed her sudden alarm. Both of them stared for one more instant at the group of men moving purposefully through the park gates, and then she whirled to LaFollet.

"Get Colonel Hill on the com! *Now*, Andrew!"

"My Lady?" LaFollet stared at her for a heartbeat, then whipped his head around to peer quickly through all the car's windows. He was reaching for his portable com in reflex obedience to her barked order, but his face was a study in confusion. "What is it, My Lady?" he demanded as he keyed the com.

"Tell him to get hold of HCP and then get a platoon of the Guard to the park!" The major gaped at her, and Honor slapped an open palm on her armrest. It wasn't like Andrew to be slow on the uptake, she thought furiously, so why had he chosen today, of all days, for his brain to go to mush on her?!

"Uh, of course, My Lady," LaFollet said after a moment, so soothingly she wanted to scream. "May I tell the Colonel why?"

"*Why?*" Honor repeated incredulously. She stabbed an index finger at the men just vanishing through the gate. "Because of *them*, of course!"

"What about them, My Lady?" LaFollet asked cautiously, and she stared at him. His confused perplexity flowed to her over Nimitz's empathic link, and she was stunned by his obtuseness.

"We've had enough people banged up in riots without their taking *clubs* with them, Andrew!"

"Clubs?" LaFollet's confusion was complete, and he darted another look out her window just as a *second* group of men headed into the park. Like the first, they, too, carried long, slender clubs over their shoulders, and the major's eyes narrowed. Honor began to relax at the evidence that he finally recognized the threat, but then, impossibly, he began to *laugh!*

It started with an incredulous chuckle, and his face worked with his desperate effort to stifle it, but he couldn't. It got away from him, erupting in a choked bubble of relieved hilarity that filled the car's interior. Honor and Nimitz stared at him in disbelief, and their expressions only made him laugh harder. No, not laugh—they made him *howl*, and Honor reached out and shook him hard.

"*C-c-c-clubs*, My Lady?" The major gasped for breath, holding his aching ribs with both hands, and tears of mirth gleamed in his eyes. "Those . . . those aren't clubs, My Lady—they're *baseball bats!*"

"Baseball bats?" Honor repeated blankly, and LaFollet nodded as he freed one hand from his ribs to wipe his eyes. "What's a baseball bat?" she demanded.

"My Lady?" He was plainly astonished by the question, but then he shook himself. He wiped his eyes again and sucked in a deep breath, trying to force the echoes of laughter from his voice. "Baseball bats are what the batter uses in a baseball game, My Lady," he said, as if that explained something.

"And what," Honor asked through gritted teeth, "might a baseball game be?"

"You mean people don't play baseball on Manticore, My Lady?" LaFollet seemed as confused as Honor was.

"Not only do they not play baseball—whatever it is—on Manticore, they don't play it on Gryphon or Sphinx, either. And I'm still waiting for you to tell me what it *is*, Andrew!"

"Ah, of course, My Lady." LaFollet cleared his throat and nodded. "Baseball is a game. Everyone plays it, My Lady."

"With *clubs*?" Honor blinked. She'd always thought rugby was a violent sport, but if these people went about whaling away at one another with clubs—!

"No, My Lady, with *bats*." LaFollet frowned at her, but then his expression cleared. "Oh! They don't use them on each *other*, My Lady. They use them to hit the ball—the baseball."

"Oh." Honor blinked again, then smiled sheepishly. "I take it, then, that they aren't planning to go out and stage a riot after all?"

"No, My Lady. Although," the major grinned, "I've seen a few games where the losing side did just that. We take baseball seriously on Grayson. It's our planetary sport. That's just a pickup game," he jabbed a thumb at the gate through which the . . . baseball players had disappeared, "but you should see one of the professional teams. Every steading has a franchise. Do you mean they really don't play it at all in the Star Kingdom?" The notion seemed to be beyond his grasp, and Honor shook her head.

"I never even heard of it. Is it anything like golf?" It didn't seem very likely. Golf was hardly a team sport, and the thought of trying to tee off with one of those bat things appalled her.

"Golf?" LaFollet repeated cautiously. "I don't know, My Lady. I've never heard of 'golf.'"

"Never heard of it?" Honor frowned, but then her brow cleared. Of course Graysons didn't play golf any more than they swam. The mere thought of trying to maintain a proper golf course on a planet like this was enough to make her dizzy. None of which brought her any closer to understanding what in heaven's name Andrew was talking about.

"All right, Andrew," she said after a moment. "We're not going to get anywhere swapping the names of sports neither of us ever heard of, so suppose you explain just what baseball is, how it's played, and what the object is?"

"Are you serious, My Lady?"

"Of course I am. If 'everyone' plays it, then I should at least know what it is! And, speaking of that, if 'every' steading has a professional team, why don't *we*?"

"Well, teams are expensive, My Lady. A club's payroll can run fifteen or twenty million austins a year, and then there's the equipment, the stadium, the travel expenses—" The major shook his head in turn. "Even if the league were prepared to accept an expansion team, just paying for it would be impossible for Harrington, I'm afraid."

"It would, would it?" Honor murmured.

"Yes, My Lady. But as to what baseball is, it's a game between two teams of nine men each." LaFollet leaned back beside his Steadholder and slid his com back into his pocket, and his face glowed with the enthusiasm of the true aficionado. "There are four bases, arranged in a diamond pattern with home plate and second base at the top and bottom, and the object—"

The ground car rolled steadily onward, leaving the park behind, and Lady Dame Honor Harrington actually managed to forget about defrocked priests, political crises, and even her approaching return to space while she listened to her personal armsman begin her initiation.

• CHAPTER NINE

A soft tone alerted the passengers in the VIP lounge to their transportation's arrival, and Admiral Lady Dame Honor Harrington, Grayson Space Navy, glanced at the ETA board, drew an inconspicuous breath, and climbed out of her chair. She tried not to grimace as she adjusted her unfamiliar cap, but she'd served her entire military career wearing the simple, comfortable beret of the RMN. The high-peaked, visored cap of Grayson uniform seemed to weigh at least three kilos, and it would be utterly impossible inside a helmet. Of course, the GSN didn't *wear* headgear under its helmets, but that didn't prevent her from feeling that it ought to.

She snorted at her own perverse ability to worry about such minor points, yet the truth was that she felt like some sort of actress in the strange uniform. No doubt she'd grow accustomed, but so far she'd worn it for less than three hours, aside from fitting sessions, and Grayson had some peculiar notions of military tailoring.

The uniform was *blue*, for one thing, which could only strike any professional spacer as an unnatural color for naval uniform. The short-waisted tunic was a lighter blue than the trousers, as well, which seemed an equally unnatural reversal of the way things ought to be, and the gold leaves on her cap's visor made her feel like some comic-opera costumer's idea of a prespace military dictator. And what had possessed the GSN to use *buttoned* collars instead of the comfortable practicality of the RMN's turtlenecks or at least a simple pressure seal? And if they simply *had* to inflict buttons on people, couldn't they at least spare her this never-to-be-sufficiently accursed "necktie"? Not only did it serve absolutely no practical purpose, but they insisted that it be *hand-tied*, which made it an unmitigated pain in the posterior. Why anyone should put a noose around her own neck just to suit some centuries-out-of-date concept of military fashion surpassed Honor's understanding, and after trying for ten solid minutes to get its knot properly adjusted, she'd finally given up and had MacGuiness tie it for her. From his expression, Mac found it as ridiculous as she did, but he'd had the free time to practice with the thing, and she hadn't.

She snorted again, running a finger around her collar (which couldn't possibly be as tight as it felt), and reflected that women might actually have gotten the better of the Grayson fashion wars. She'd thought skirts were ridiculous when she first arrived, but she hadn't paid much attention to what Grayson *men* wore. Now she had to, since the Navy's uniform conformed to male fashion, and what she'd accepted simply as quaint local costumes appeared in a different light when *she* had to put up with them.

She glanced over her shoulder at the two armsmen guarding the lounge entrance, then at Andrew LaFollet, standing in his proper position to watch her back. Grayson law required her to take her security detail even into space with her, but none of her bodyguards had so much as commented to her about her new assignment or its impact on them. LaFollet had sent Simon Mattingly and nine of her twelve-man team ahead to *Terrible* to set things up while he, Jamie Candless, and Eddy Howard—her usual "travel party"—kept an eye on her. Each of those men was a silent, competent presence who seemed perfectly content to go wherever his duty to his Steadholder took him, yet Honor felt a stab of guilt at dragging them away from their homes and families. As a general rule, steadholders never left Grayson, which meant their armsmen didn't, either, but *her* armsmen would be stuck off-planet whenever she was. It wasn't her idea, and the law's requirements weren't her fault, but she'd already made a mental note to do something to show her appreciation, and now she knew what it would be. The Harrington Steadholder's Guard's uniforms also followed Grayson patterns, and if she couldn't save herself from this ridiculous monkey suit, she could at least have the HSG's uniform redesigned into something rational!

Nimitz bleeked a laugh from the chair beside the one she'd just left, and her crooked smile admitted he was right. RMN mess dress was almost as uncomfortable as her current outfit, and she was fretting over unfamiliar styles mostly in an effort to ignore the one part of her new uniform which was utterly familiar yet seemed more unnatural in her eyes than any of the rest of it. A Manticoran uniform would have had only three nine-pointed stars on its collar, not the four six-pointed ones she wore, but the four broad gold cuff rings were the same in both navies, and the notion of Honor Harrington in an *admiral's* uniform was still so ridiculous she half-expected to wake up any second.

She didn't. The tone sounded again, and the Navy pinnace drifted down to kiss the pad with gentle precision. It touched down exactly on schedule, and a fresh tremor of uncertainty ran through her as she folded her hands behind her and gazed through the crystoplast window at it.

Throughout her career, she'd made a point of familiarizing herself with any new command before she took it over. The one time she hadn't—when she'd assumed command of the light cruiser *Fearless* literally on an hour's notice—the nasty surprises, hardware and otherwise, she'd wound up facing had only confirmed the wisdom of her usual practice. But this time there'd simply been no way to do it. She knew, in general terms, what Grayson had done in the way of refitting their ex-Havenite prize ships, but that was only because she'd been interested enough to keep track as a more-or-less private citizen. She'd had no expectation of ever commanding one of them, so she'd seen no reason to push for anything specific, and the last week's mad administrative whirl as she prepared to turn the daily affairs of Harrington Steading back over to Howard Clinkscales had left no time to bone up on the details. Now she was about to assume command of a six-ship superdreadnought squadron, and she didn't even know her own flag captain's name or who her chief of staff might be!

Honor didn't like that. It was her job to know what she was doing, and the fact that she'd been "too busy" to prepare properly was a weak excuse. She should have *made* the time, she told herself as the pinnace powered down its turbines and the pad ramp extended itself to the midships hatch. She had no idea how she could have done it, but she ought to have found a way, and—

A louder bleek interrupted her thoughts, and she turned to look at Nimitz. He sat up in his chair, head cocked with an air of martyred patience, and made a sharp scolding sound when he was certain he had her attention. There was a limit to the amount of self-criticism he was willing to put up with in his person, and the look in his green eyes told Honor she'd just reached it. What with political decisions, religious crises, and ten thousand administrative details, there'd been no way she *could* have made time for anything else. She and Nimitz both knew that, and she felt her lips quirk as the 'cat's stern injunction to stop fretting flowed into her.

Nimitz, she thought, might not be the best—or most impartial—judge of naval officers, but this time he was probably right. The entire First Battle Squadron was still in the process of formation. She'd have time to familiarize herself with the hardware, and it wasn't as if there'd be a lot of preexisting SOP for her to fall over, since any operating procedures would be hers to create. As for personnel, she was confident High Admiral Matthews had picked a strong team for her, though the one person she'd specifically requested had been unavailable. She'd wanted Mark Brentworth as her flag captain, but he'd just been "frocked" to commodore and given GNS *Raoul Courvosier* and the First Battlecruiser Squadron.

She could still have had him, and part of her wished she'd insisted, but there was no way she was going to pull him from *that* command. Besides, it wasn't as if the Brentworth clan would be unrepresented in BatRon One. Mark's father, Rear Admiral Walter Brentworth, commanded its First Division, and no one could have deserved it more.

She was glad to know she'd have him, but aside from Mark and a handful of very senior officers—like his father or High Admiral Matthews himself—Honor didn't know anyone in the GSN well enough to have an opinion of them, and she'd had no desire to pick names for a squadron command team at random. Better to rely on the judgment of someone who did know them. It was entirely possible she and that someone else might differ on the qualities they found ideal in an officer, but some basis for evaluation was better than none, and she could always make changes later if she had to.

The pad ramp locked in place, and she lifted Nimitz to her right shoulder. Despite Matthews' undoubtedly correct reading of the strategic situation, Yeltsin's Star was almost two light-centuries behind the front, and it would take far more audacity than the Peeps had yet demonstrated to try any sort of operation that far in the Alliance's rear. No, unless the situation changed radically, the probability of anything major happening here was negligible—which was just as well, since the entire Grayson Navy would be basically one huge training command while it figured out what to do with its new wall of battle. If there *were* any problems, she told herself firmly, there'd be plenty of time to sort things out.

Nimitz made a soft sound and rubbed his head against the top of her preposterous cap. She felt his relief at the more positive trend of her thoughts and reached up to scratch his chin, then headed for the lounge door with MacGuiness and her armsmen at her heels.

The pinnace hatch was open, and Honor felt an eyebrow rise as two uniformed figures stepped out onto the ramp. She hadn't requested an escort, nor had anyone mentioned that there'd be one. Even if she *had* asked for one, she would have expected a junior officer, but the golden reflections flashing from their cap visors told her both those people were at least full commanders, and just to make matters more interesting, one was obviously a woman. There were few female officers—and no native-born ones—in Grayson service, so the woman on the ramp must be one of those the GSN had recruited from the Star Kingdom, and Honor wondered if they'd ever met. She brought up the telescopic function on her prosthetic eye, but the angle was bad; the woman was more than half-concealed behind her male companion and impossible to make out, so Honor flicked her curious glance to the man—and, for the first time in her life, literally stumbled over her own feet.

LaFollet's darting hand caught her elbow as she fought for balance, and Nimitz chittered in surprise as the bolt of shocked recognition exploded through her. She managed to stay upright and even keep walking almost normally, but she couldn't tear her eyes from the man beside her pinnace's hatch. It couldn't be! What in the name of all that was holy was *he* doing here?!

"My Lady?" LaFollet's low voice was sharp with concern, and Honor shook her head like a boxer throwing off a left jab.

"Nothing, Andrew." She reached across to pat the hand on her elbow with absent reassurance, then looked deliberately away from the hatch as they neared the ramp steps. "Just a sudden thought."

LaFollet murmured something, yet she knew she hadn't fooled him—especially when he turned his own gaze towards the waiting officers and frowned in speculation. But at least he knew when she wanted him to drop something, and he said nothing as she led the way up the steps and the slender man at their top saluted her.

"Good morning, Lady Harrington," he said, with an

accent which had never come from Grayson. He looked far more natural in the uniform of a GSN captain than Honor felt in that of an admiral, and his deep voice was steady, but wariness flickered in his eyes. Her own emotions were in too much turmoil for her to reach out through Nimitz and sample his, but she refused to show it. She hid her shock behind the calm mask of thirty years of naval service as she returned his salute, then extended her hand to him.

"Good morning, Captain Yu," she replied. His handclasp was firm, and something that wasn't quite a smile flitted across his lips as she cocked her head.

"I thought it would be a good idea to come dirt-side to meet you, My Lady," he said, answering the unspoken question. "I'm your new flag captain."

"Are you?" Honor was surprised she sounded so *un*surprised.

"Yes, My Lady." Yu's dark, steady eyes met hers for another moment, then he released her hand and waved to the sturdy, blue-uniformed junior-grade captain beside him. "And this, My Lady, is your chief of staff. I believe you've met," he said, and Honor's eyes widened again, this time in delight.

"Mercedes!" She stepped quickly forward and caught the captain's hand in both of her own. "I had no idea you were in Grayson service!"

"I guess I'm just the bad penny, Milady," Mercedes Brigham replied. "On the other hand, lieutenant commander to captain jay-gee in one fell swoop is nothing to sneer at for an old lady who figured she'd retire a lieutenant."

"I suppose not," Honor agreed, and released Brigham's hand to gesture at the rings on her own cuffs. "And speaking of unexpected promotions—!"

"They look good on you, Milady," Brigham said quietly. "I heard about all the crap back home, but it's good to see you back where you belong."

"Thank you," Honor said, equally quietly, then shook herself and turned back to her new flag captain. "Well,

Captain Yu, it seems we've all come up in the world since last we met, doesn't it?"

"Yes, it does, My Lady." Yu's reply acknowledged the slight barb in her tone with neither irony nor apology, and he stood back from the hatch. The Manticoran tradition was that the senior officer was last to board and first to exit from any small craft, but in Grayson service she both boarded and disembarked first, and Yu beckoned politely for Honor to precede him. "My officers and your staff await your pleasure aboard *Terrible*, My Lady," he said.

"Then let's not keep them waiting, Captain," she replied.

The two captains fell in at her heels, followed by James MacGuiness and Honor's armsmen. It was a ridiculously large entourage, she thought, but the reflection was sheer reflex, no more than a deliberate attempt to divert herself from the shock of learning who High Admiral Matthews had selected as her flag captain. She settled into the comfortable seat at the head of the compartment and lifted Nimitz back down into her lap, then turned her head to gaze out the view port as Yu sat beside her. LaFollet took his proper place directly behind her, but Mercedes Brigham politely but deliberately blocked anyone else out of the three rows of seats behind the major. Nimitz gazed speculatively at Brigham, but MacGuiness and the rest of Honor's armsmen took the hint and filled the after end of the cabin.

Honor glanced up, and Brigham gave her a small smile, then followed the others aft, leaving Honor, LaFollet, and Yu in the small island of privacy she'd created. Honor watched her go, then turned to give her flag captain a steady, measuring look.

Alfredo Yu was the last person she would have expected to see commanding a Grayson ship of the wall. She understood the GSN's desperate need for experienced officers, but it was unusual, to say the least, for a navy to hand one of its most powerful units to a man who less than four years before had done his best to conquer its home world for its mortal enemies.

Of course, Operation Jericho hadn't been Yu's idea. He'd simply been following his orders as an officer of the People's Navy, and if the religious fanatics who'd run Masada had let him do it without interference he *would* have conquered Grayson for them. There was no doubt in Honor's mind on that point, for Alfredo Yu was a dangerously competent man, and he'd had a modern, eight-hundred-and-fifty-kiloton battlecruiser to do it with.

But the Masadans hadn't let Yu use his ship properly. They'd had their chance—Honor had given it to them herself, when she pulled all but one unit of her own squadron out of Yeltsin—but they'd rejected his advice on how to proceed before she returned. And when she had returned and wrecked their own plans, he'd refused to let them use his command to brush her ships aside and bombard Grayson in one last, hopeless bid to force its surrender before a Manticoran relief force could arrive. But they'd refused to take no for an answer. Instead, they'd slipped enough men aboard his ship to seize control, put their own officers in command of her, and pressed on in a do-or-die effort.

Honor wished they'd listened to Yu and abandoned operations, but if they'd insisted on attacking, she was profoundly grateful they'd done it without him. *Thunder of God* had battered her heavy cruiser into a wreck in Masadan hands; what she would have done under *Yu's* command scarcely bore thinking on.

Unfortunately for Captain Yu, the PRH had been an unforgiving master even before Pierre and his lunatics took over. He'd known what would happen if he returned home after letting his Masadan "allies" seize his ship, especially when that ship and two-thirds of its crew had subsequently been lost in action. The fact that he'd managed, against near-impossible odds, to get a third of his crew off before her final action would have cut no ice with a naval staff determined to put the blame on something—or someone—other than its own plans. So Yu had requested political asylum in Manticore, and

Honor's last responsibility in Yeltsin had been to take him aboard her ship for the trip home.

She'd been prepared to feel contempt for a man who abandoned his birth nation, but she hadn't. The People's Republic wasn't the sort of nation that engendered loyalty, and Yu was better than Haven had deserved. She'd studied his record in some detail following the trip, and she still wondered how someone with his cool, independent intelligence had ever made captain in the PN. The man was a thinker, not a blind fighter, exactly the sort of officer whose independence of thought made a bureaucracy like Haven's uncomfortable, and his loss had hurt the People's Republic badly. Not only had it cost the PN one of its most competent commanders, but he'd been a priceless treasure for the Office of Naval Intelligence, as well. In fact, she'd assumed he was still tucked away in the Star Kingdom where ONI and the Admiralty would have immediate access to his in-depth knowledge of the People's Navy.

But he wasn't, and she chewed her lower lip and wondered if she was glad. A man like Alfredo Yu could be invaluable to her, if he could be trusted . . . and if she could forget how many reasons she had to hate him.

She sighed, and Nimitz made a soft, uncomfortable sound and shifted in her lap as she rebuked herself for that last thought. It wasn't Yu's fault he'd been ordered to help Masada conquer Grayson, and he'd done his duty just as she hoped she would have done hers. Intellectually, she could accept that; emotionally, she wondered if she could ever truly forgive him for planning and executing the ambush which had killed Admiral Raoul Courvosier and blown HMS *Madrigal* out of space.

A hot, familiar pain prickled behind her eyes, and she knew part of her hatred for Yu sprang from her conviction that *her* actions had led directly to Courvosier's death. Neither she nor the Admiral had been given any reason to suspect the imminence of a Havenite operation against Grayson. ONI hadn't had a clue, and neither had Grayson intelligence. Her decision to pull most of her squadron out of Yeltsin, leaving only *Madrigal* to support him, had made sense in the context of the diplomatic situation, and no one had known there was any other context to consider. There was no *reason* she should blame herself for what had happened . . . but she did, and she always would, for Raoul Courvosier had been more than simply her senior officer. He'd been the mentor who'd taken a shy, socially awkward midshipman with a glaring weakness in math and turned her into a Queen's officer. Along the way, he'd imbued that officer with his own standards of professionalism and responsibility, and she'd never fully realized until he died how much she'd loved, as well as respected, him.

And Alfredo Yu had killed him. She shivered inside with the memory of her sick hate for Yu when he'd first come aboard her ship. She'd made herself show him the courtesy his rank was due, even in exile, but it had been hard. Hard. And he'd sensed her hatred, if not all the reasons for it. The voyage to Manticore had been strained for them both, and Honor had never in her wildest dreams expected to serve in the same navy with him— and certainly not to find him commanding her first superdreadnought flagship!

Yu returned her gaze levelly, almost as if he shared Nimitz's ability to read her emotions. Turbines whined as the pinnace rose on its counter-grav, but a pocket of silence hovered between them, and then Yu sighed, clasped his hands loosely in his lap, and cleared his throat.

"Lady Harrington, I didn't realize until yesterday that no one had told you I'd been given command of *Terrible*," he said. "I apologize for the oversight—if that's what it really was—and also for not screening you in person to inform you. I *did* consider comming you, but . . ." He paused and inhaled. "But I chickened out," he admitted. "I knew when we first met that Admiral Courvosier had been killed in Yeltsin." Her eyes hardened, but he met them unflinchingly and continued in a voice which was tinged with genuine regret yet refused

to apologize for doing his duty, "But I didn't know—
then—how close to the Admiral you'd been, My Lady.
When I found out, I realized how difficult it must have
been for you to have me as a passenger in your ship.
More than that, I can appreciate now that you might
not want me aboard *Terrible*." He drew another breath
and squared his shoulders. "If you'd care to request my
relief, Admiral," he said quietly, "I'm certain High
Admiral Matthews can find you a suitable replacement."

Honor gazed at him in masklike silence, but she felt
her own surprise at his offer. He had to know how
tempted she'd be to replace him, just as he knew she
could, whatever *he* might want. Yet rather than try to
avoid the issue or finesse his way around it, he'd brought
it out into the open and all but offered to go if that was
what she wanted. He was a man who'd lost everything,
one who'd somehow overcome almost unimaginable odds
to find his way into a starship command once more, but
his eyes were steady, and the quiet sincerity behind them
flowed to her through Nimitz.

It would be so easy to do it, she thought. To have
him replaced rather than deal with her own ambiguous
emotions. And there was another factor. As her flag captain, Yu would be her tactical deputy, the individual
charged with executing her orders and maneuvers. If
by some chance her squadron *was* called to action, he'd
be positioned to do incalculable harm if some fragment
of loyalty to the People's Republic still lived deep inside
him, and could even he know with certainty whether
or not one did? If it came time to fire on the ships of
his birth nation, possibly on officers and men he'd helped
train, could he do it? More to the point, could *she* take
the risk that he couldn't?

"I was surprised to see you, Captain," she said, spar-
ring for time as thought and counter-thought warred in
her mind. "I assumed you were still assigned to ONI
back in the Star Kingdom."

"No, My Lady. Your Admiralty, ah, loaned me to
Grayson two years ago at High Admiral Matthews'

request. The Office of Shipbuilding wanted to pick my brains about Havenite design and tactical doctrine before it wrote the specifications for Grayson's first locally built ships of the wall."

"I see. And now?" Honor made a small gesture at the blue-on-blue uniforms they both wore, and Yu smiled faintly.

"And now I'm an officer of the GSN, My Lady—and a Grayson citizen."

"You are?" Honor couldn't keep the surprise out of her voice, and Yu gave another thin smile.

"I'd never met a Grayson before Operation Jericho, Lady Harrington. When I did meet some of them, I was . . . impressed. I suppose I'd assumed one religious fanatic was very like another, that there was nothing to choose between Masada and Grayson, but I was wrong. Wrong to think Graysons were fanatics, and wrong to equate them with Masadans."

"So you just moved out here? Just like that?"

"Hardly 'just like that,' My Lady," Yu said wryly. "I know I'm still paying my dues. They need people with my qualifications, but there were—and are—people out here who haven't forgiven me for Jericho." He shrugged. "I can accept that. In fact, the thing that amazed me was how many of them *were* willing to if not forgive at least accept that there'd never been anything personal in it. That I was simply following my orders."

He looked straight into her eyes with the last sentence, and Honor nodded, acknowledging the implications.

"But I also found, My Lady, that I *like* Graysons. They can be the most stubborn, infuriating people I've ever met, but I can't quite imagine anyone who wasn't those things accomplishing as much as they have so quickly. Lady Harrington, I couldn't go 'home' to the People's Republic if I wanted to. I didn't—and don't—want to, but even if I did, the People's Republic I served doesn't exist anymore. I accepted that I could never go home when I requested asylum from Manticore; what's happened since only makes that more true. I suppose I could even tell myself that taking service with Grayson against Pierre's people is an act of loyalty to the old regime, but, frankly, what happens to the Republic isn't very important to me anymore."

"No? Then what *is* important, Captain?"

"Following my own conscience, My Lady," Yu said quietly. "That's not something the People's Navy ever gave its officers much opportunity to do. I knew it at the time, but it never occurred to me that anything else was possible. It was simply the way it *was* . . . until, suddenly, I wasn't *in* the PN anymore. I don't know if a Manticoran can truly understand just how big a shock to my system that was. And then I was sent back here, given a chance to get to know the people I almost helped Masada conquer, and—"

He paused, then gave a tiny shrug. "I don't suppose I'll ever be a 'real' Grayson in their eyes—not the way you are—but I'm not a Peep anymore, either, and this is my home now. I came back here originally because Manticore told me to and, perhaps, because I saw it as a sort of apology. Now that I'm here, I want to help defend it, and I imagine—" he smiled again, this time with an edge of true humor "—that one reason High Admiral Matthews made me your flag captain was to have someone he trusted and who had the experience to evaluate my performance fully ride herd on me. I'm a valuable resource, but it would be a bit much to expect him to forget my first visit to Yeltsin."

"I see." Honor leaned back, brow furrowed in thought, conscious of Andrew LaFollet's silent presence behind her and tasting Yu's sincerity through Nimitz. She wanted to turn in her chair and look back at Mercedes Brigham, to see what *she* thought of Alfredo Yu, for Mercedes had her own reasons to feel both gratitude and hate for him. She'd been HMS *Madrigal*'s executive officer. It was her ship and her people Yu's ambush had killed, but it was also Yu who'd demanded the Masadans recover *Madrigal*'s survivors. And, Honor thought grimly, it was Yu who'd turned those survivors over to the Masadans.

He couldn't have known what would happen. The man who'd insisted that the rules of war be followed would never have handed helpless prisoners over to people he expected to murder them. But that didn't change the fact that of all *Madrigal*'s captured female personnel, only Mercedes Brigham and Ensign Mai-ling Jackson had lived through the ghastly gang rapes and brutal beatings of their captivity, and Mercedes had been three-quarters dead when Honor's Marines pulled her out of the ruins of Blackbird Base. If it was difficult for Honor to decide how she felt about having Yu under her command, how much harder must it be for Mercedes to serve with him? Especially here, where so many things waited to remind her of the hell she'd endured?

Honor shivered as the thought sent a stab of pain through her. She had trouble enough facing her own wounds; how in the name of God did someone like Mercedes deal with *her* nightmares? And what right did Honor have to put her in the position of serving on a daily basis with the man who'd been responsible, however unknowingly, for the stuff those nightmares were made of?

She closed her eyes, and her hands stroked gently, caressingly, down Nimitz's spine. Every instinct screamed for her to accept Yu's offer and replace him, but her professional judgment insisted just as stubbornly that he was too valuable, too potentially useful to her, to be discarded. She bit the inside of her lip as uncertainty washed about within her like acid—or like proof she'd been right to doubt her own wounded strength.

She closed her eyes tighter and fought to empty her mind of confusion, to summon the detached logic with which Admiral Courvosier had trained her to approach command decisions. And then, almost against her will, Mercedes Brigham's face flashed before her, and she saw once more the small smile Mercedes had given her as she blocked everyone else from the seats behind Honor and Captain Yu. Blocked them, Honor realized, because she'd known what Yu intended to say . . . and given him the space and privacy in which to say it.

The memory of Mercedes' smile stilled the roiling currents of her own emotions. It didn't answer her questions, but somehow it made them *only* questions, not a quagmire of warring instincts that threatened to suck her under, and she opened her eyes to look Yu in the face.

"I appreciate the difficulties of your position, Captain," she said at last, one hand stroking up Nimitz's spine to caress his ears, "and also how difficult it must have been for you to say what you just have. I respect your forthrightness, and I'm grateful for it, but you're right. There have to be some reservations in my mind, and you know it as well as I do. On the other hand," she managed a small smile, "you, Captain Brigham, and I are all newcomers to Grayson, and each of us is here for our own reasons. Maybe it's time we start fresh from that common beginning."

She paused, head cocked, chocolate-dark eyes intent, then shrugged.

"I'll bear your offer in mind, Captain Yu, and I'll think about it. One thing I do know is that you represent far too valuable a resource to be simply thrown away. You deserve equal forthrightness from me, so let me admit that any problems we might have working as a team would arise from personal considerations, not reservations as to your competence. I'd like to think I'm professional enough to put the past behind us and deal solely with the present, but I'm only human. You know as well as I do how important it is for an admiral and her flag captain to have total faith in one another, and, as you say, I didn't even know you'd been given *Terrible*, which means this has all come at me mighty fast. Let me think about it. I'll try not to leave you hanging, but I need to turn it over in my mind. The one thing I promise you is that if I *don't* ask for your replacement, it will be because you have my complete confidence, not simply in your skill, but in your integrity."

"Thank you, My Lady," Yu said quietly. "Both for your honesty, and for your understanding." A tone sounded and a proximity light flashed on the forward bulkhead as the pinnace approached its destination, and he shook himself. "And in the meantime, Lady Harrington," he said, with an almost natural smile of his own, "if you'd care to glance out the view port, I'd be honored to give you your first close look at your new flagship."

• CHAPTER TEN

GNS *Terrible* floated alone in her parking orbit, a double-ended hammerhead of dazzling white, her flanks punctuated with three geometrically precise rows of dots. At first, she looked like some exquisitely detailed model scaled to a child's hand, but the pinnace swept on towards her, closing at an angle to permit Honor a clear view, and her new flagship swelled quickly as the range dropped. *Terrible* seemed to grow rather than come nearer, expanding first from a toy into a ship, and then into the true leviathan she was as the pinnace came close enough to become its own reference point.

From dots, her weapon bays became hatches vast enough to dock the pinnace with ease. Phased radar arrays, point defense laser clusters, and the sharp blades of gravitic sensors swelled into sharp definition, and her drive nodes, four times the pinnace's size, stood out boldly. She was enormous, eight million tons of starship—over four kilometers long and with a maximum beam of six hundred meters, jeweled with the green and white lights of a moored starship—and Honor stared raptly out the view port as the pinnace spiraled along the superdreadnought's length to show her every detail.

Terrible had none of the grace of Honor's last command. HMS *Nike* had been a battlecruiser, sleek and arrogant with carefully blended speed and firepower. *Terrible* wasn't sleek. She was a ponderous mountain of white, built not to raid and run, not to pursue lighter units to destruction or use her own speed to evade more powerful foes, but for the crushing violence of the wall of battle. She was designed to absorb damage that would reduce any less mighty craft to splinters and remain in action, and no mere battlecruiser could live within the reach of her energy batteries.

She wasn't the first SD Honor had served upon, but her power dwarfed any ship she'd ever commanded . . . and there were *six* such vessels in BatRon One. The thought sent a cold shiver down Honor's spine, yet that shiver went almost unnoticed in the intensity of her study. Her trained eye picked out differences between *Terrible* and her Manticoran-built counterparts—the more numerous, closer-spaced tubes of her missile armament, arranged on a single deck rather than intermixed with her energy weapons; the numbers of small craft docking points that supplemented her boat bays; the arrangement of her running lights—and the depths of her mind flickered with first impressions. *Terrible*'s missile armament would give her a heavy throw weight, but she had less magazine space for a sustained engagement than a Manticoran SD. The tubes' tight arrangement made a single hit more likely to take out multiple launchers, as well, Honor mused, then nodded to herself. Peep walls had always seemed overly loose to her, but now she understood. With that missile layout and their poorer point defense, they'd have to maintain separation so ships could roll to interpose their impeller wedges against incoming laser heads or see their own missile batteries blown away from outside energy range, and—

Her thoughts broke off as the pinnace killed its wedge and went to auxiliary thrusters. It swept in below the ship on final approach, and she felt the gentle shudder as the boat bay tractors locked on. The thrusters died, and the pinnace floated up into a vast, brightly lit cavern and settled into the docking buffers. Mechanical mooring arms locked, and Captain Yu stood as the docking tube and umbilicals extended themselves. He stepped back, clearing the way for LaFollet to take his proper position at his Steadholder's shoulder, while the pinnace's flight engineer checked the hatch telltales. A green light announced a good seal and pressure, and the engineer cracked the hatch.

Yu said nothing. He simply stood there, hands clasped behind him, and waited while Honor climbed out of her own seat. She settled Nimitz on her shoulder once more, adjusted her cap, and walked slowly to the hatch while the other passengers got themselves into formation to disembark. Then she drew a deep and (she hoped) unobtrusive breath, reached for the green-hued grab bar, and swung herself into the tube's zero-gee.

A shouted command sounded as Honor swam the last few meters of the tube and caught another grab bar to swing herself over the interface into *Terrible*'s onboard grav field, and she braced herself as the golden notes of a bugle washed over her. Most admirals would have been greeted with the bosun's pipe she was used to; Honor, unfortunately, was a steadholder, which meant she was doomed to hear the fanfare from the Steadholders' March whenever she boarded or left. Under normal circumstances, she rather liked old-fashioned, lung-powered brasses, and she knew the exuberant march was impossible to render on a bosun's pipe, but she made a mental note to have them point the bugle in another direction. The tube made an excellent amplifier.

She stepped forward and reminded herself to salute the Grayson planetary flag on the boat bay's forward bulkhead before facing the side party. That, too, was something new to remember, but at least the GSN had agreed to let its borrowed Manticoran personnel retain the RMN salute they were used to. She snapped her hand down from her cap brim, then turned to the side party and a crowd which seemed too large for any boat bay gallery, even an SD's.

An honor guard of Grayson Marines, their brown-and-green uniforms distinguished from the Army's only by the crossed starships on their collars, stood at attention along the transverse bulkheads. The ship carried a full battalion, plus attached support units, and it seemed all of them must be present, though she knew better. A solid block of ratings and petty officers in blue-and-white undress coveralls stood against the longitudinal bulkhead, and another, smaller block of officers waited beyond the side party, headed by a wiry young man in a commander's uniform who must be Yu's executive officer.

The commander saluted as the bugle died, and Honor returned it.

"Permission to come aboard, Sir?" she asked.

"Permission granted, My Lady." The commander's soft Grayson accent carried clearly through the sudden silence.

"Thank you." Honor stepped across the painted line on the deck, formally boarding her flagship for the first time. Andrew LaFollet followed at her right shoulder with Captain Yu at her left, and then the captain stepped around her to join the commander.

"Welcome aboard *Terrible*, My Lady," he said. "May I present my executive officer, Commander Allenby?"

"Commander." Honor extended her hand, and the right corner of her mouth twitched as she watched the dictates of military courtesy override the older rules Allenby's society had programmed into him. His heels came together with a barely audible click, but he didn't bow over her hand. He simply gripped it firmly, and she approved of the slight twinkle in his brown eyes as he saw her ghost of a smile.

"My Lady," he murmured, and stepped back as Yu beckoned to the officers beyond him.

"Your staff, Admiral. I thought we might wait until you've gotten settled in before introducing you to the remainder of my senior officers, if that's acceptable?"

"Of course, Captain." Honor nodded and turned as the first member of her staff stepped forward.

"Commander Frederick Bagwell, your operations officer, Milady," Mercedes Brigham murmured from beside Yu.

"Commander Bagwell." Honor studied the brown-haired commander as she shook his hand. There wasn't much humor in his lean face, and his precise, very correct air made him seem older than his thirty-odd T-years, but he looked confident enough.

"My Lady," he replied, then stepped aside.

"Commander Allen Sewell, Milady. Your astrogator," Brigham said, and Honor smiled involuntarily as Sewell took her hand and grinned at her. The commander was black-haired and very dark. He was also a veritable giant for a Grayson, barely five centimeters shorter than Honor, and his dark eyes were as mischievous as Bagwell's were serious as he gripped her hand *and* bowed, managing to combine both military and traditional courtesy with total aplomb.

"Welcome aboard, Lady Harrington," he rumbled in a deep, musical bass, and stepped back beside the shorter ops officer.

"Lieutenant Commander Howard Brannigan, your communications officer," Mercedes announced. Brannigan was a hazel-eyed, sandy-haired man, and one of the very few Graysons Honor had seen with facial hair. He sported a magnificent handlebar mustache and a neatly trimmed beard, and though the rings on his uniform cuffs were edged in the white the Grayson Navy used to denote reservists, he had an air of tough competence.

"My Lady," he said gruffly, squeezing her hand hard, and stepped aside for another lieutenant commander.

"Lieutenant Commander Gregory Paxton, Milady. Your intelligence officer," Mercedes said, and Honor nodded.

"Commander Paxton. I've heard High Admiral Matthews speak of you. He seems to think highly of your work."

"Thank you, My Lady." Paxton was older than her other officers, and, like Brannigan, he was a reservist. Unlike the com officer, however, he didn't look a great deal like an officer, despite his uniform. His dark hair was thinning, his sideburns were a startling white, he was more than a bit portly, and he wore a permanent expression of bemusement, but his brown eyes were bright and sharp. He also wore a small pin on his left lapel—a rolled scroll—and Honor reached out to touch it with the forefinger of her free hand.

"You're still a member of the Society, Commander?"

"Yes, My Lady. On extended leave, I'm afraid, but still a member." He seemed pleased by her recognition, and she smiled. Gregory Paxton held a triple doctorate in history, religion, and economics. He'd resigned the Austin Grayson Chair of History at Mayhew University *and* the chairmanship of the Grayson Society to accept his commission, and Honor was both amazed and delighted that Matthews had been willing to spare him from the General Staff.

He gave her hand another squeeze, then stepped back to be replaced by yet another lieutenant commander, this one a flaming redhead with the insignia of the Office of Shipbuilding.

"Lieutenant Commander Stephen Matthews, Milady. Our logistics officer."

"Commander Matthews." Honor felt her head cock despite herself as she took his hand, and Matthews smiled crookedly.

"Yes, My Lady. I'm one of *those* Matthews. The nose always seems to give us away."

"I see." Honor returned his smile and wondered just what his relationship to the high admiral was. The conditions of Grayson's settlement had resulted in enormous, intricately linked clan structures, and she knew the Matthews family was one of the larger ones, but aside from his coloring, the lieutenant commander looked enough like High Admiral Matthews to be his son. He was too old for that—she thought—but the resemblance was almost uncanny.

He seemed to be waiting for her to say something more, which probably wasn't too surprising. He must get a lot of reactions, positive and negative alike, simply because of his family connections.

"Well, I'll try not to hold your nose against you,

Commander," she murmured, and his smile turned into a grin as he stepped back.

"Lieutenant Commander Abraham Jackson, Milady. Your staff chaplain," Mercedes said quietly.

Honor tensed slightly, and Nimitz's ears pricked as Jackson stepped forward. For the first time, she felt more than a bit uncomfortable, for the RMN had no Chaplains Corps, and she was uncertain how to react. Worse, she had no idea how Jackson might feel about serving on an infidel's staff—particularly when that infidel had just been involved in the politically charged defrocking of another priest.

"Lady Harrington." Jackson's pleasant voice was deeper than Matthews' but much lighter than Sewell's. His green eyes met hers frankly as he took her hand, and she felt an inner quiver of released tension at what she saw in them—then scolded herself for feeling it. She should have known High Admiral Matthews and Reverend Hanks would see to it that the man assigned as her staff chaplain was no bigot. Jackson smiled slightly—a curiously gentle smile, uncannily like Reverend Hanks'—and squeezed her hand firmly. "It's a great pleasure to meet you at last, My Lady."

"Thank you, Commander. I hope you feel that way after you've had to put up with me for a while," she said with an answering smile, and he chuckled as he stepped back beside Matthews.

"And last but not least, Milady," Mercedes said, "your flag lieutenant, Lieutenant Jared Sutton."

"Lieutenant." Honor extended her hand once more, and this time she had to bite back a laugh. Sutton was short even by Grayson standards, a wiry young man with intensely black hair and anxious brown eyes that reminded her irresistibly of a puppy's. He was still young enough he'd probably received the original first-generation prolong treatments, and his feet and hands looked too big for the rest of him.

"M-M-My Lady," he got out as he took her hand, then blushed bright red as his stutter betrayed his nervousness.

She felt a wash of compassion for him, but she looked him straight in the eye and made her mouth firm.

"Lieutenant. I hope you're ready to be worked hard." Dismay flickered in his eyes, and she lowered her eyebrows. "An admiral's flag lieutenant is the most overworked officer on her staff," she went on grimly. "He has to know everything she *and* her chief of staff know, and God help him if he screws anything up!" Sutton stared at her and squared his shoulders, snapping to a sort of parade rest without ever releasing her hand, and his expression was too much for her. She felt the grim line of her mouth begin to collapse, and reached out to pat him on the shoulder.

"And he's also the most under-appreciated officer on her staff—by everyone except her," she said, and his dismay vanished into a huge smile.

"Yes, Ma'am!" he said. "I'll try not to let you down, My Lady."

"I'm sure you will, Lieutenant, and I expect you'll succeed." She gave his shoulder another pat, then folded her hands behind her. She didn't know any of them, aside from Mercedes, but they looked good. Solid. And she could tell a lot about Mercedes' estimate of them from the way she'd introduced them. All in all, she thought High Admiral Matthews had done well by her.

"I'm sure we'll all get to know one another quickly," she said after a moment. "We're certainly going to have enough on our plates to see that we do, at any rate!" Several of them smiled back at her, and she nodded. "I'd like to meet with all of you—and especially you, Commander Paxton—for an initial brief as soon as I've had a chance to get settled in." She glanced at the time and date display on the bulkhead. "If you'd be kind enough to assemble in the flag briefing room at ten-hundred, I'll see you all then."

Nods and murmurs of agreement answered, and she turned back to Yu. "I'd appreciate your joining us, as well, Captain," she said more formally.

"Of course, My Lady."

"Thank you. And now, I think it's time I went and got started on that settling in."

"Yes, My Lady," Yu replied. "May I escort you to your quarters?" There was a slight pause between the two sentences, and Honor shook her head.

"No, thank you, Captain. I've taken up enough of your time. Captain Brigham can show me the way; she and I need to discuss a few things, anyway."

"Of course, My Lady," Yu murmured once more, his dark eyes still and just a bit opaque.

"Thank you. I'll see you all at ten-hundred, then." Honor glanced over her shoulder at Mercedes. "Captain Brigham?"

"Yes, Ma'am. If you'll follow me, please?"

The Marines snapped to present arms as Honor followed her chief of staff past them, trailed by her armsmen and James MacGuiness, and she nodded in acknowledgment of the courtesy. Then Mercedes led her into the lift and punched a destination into the panel, and Honor leaned back against the wall and let her breath whoosh out in relief as the doors closed.

"And thank the *Lord* that's done!" she said. Mercedes chuckled, and Honor sniffed. "All very well for *you*. You already knew all those people!"

"Yes, Ma'am, I did. But I'm only a captain—you're an admiral. That gives you a certain advantage when it comes to introductions."

"Ha!" Honor removed her cap to run a hand over her braided hair, and Nimitz bleeked a laugh and made a grab for her hand. She evaded him with practiced ease and gave him a gentle thump on the nose, then waved her cap at the other people in the lift.

"You already know Mac, Mercedes, but let me introduce you to my *other* keepers. This is Major Andrew LaFollet, my personal armsman and the head of my security detachment." Brigham smiled and nodded, and Honor gestured at the others. "And this is Armsman Candless and Armsman Howard. They go everywhere with me, the poor fellows. Gentlemen, in case you missed it, this is Captain Brigham, my chief of staff. Keep an eye on her and don't let that calm demeanor fool you. She has a low and evil sense of humor."

"A base libel, Milady. My sense of humor isn't low."

The armsmen grinned just as a soft chime announced the lift's arrival. Mercedes waited for Honor to lead the way out, then escorted her down a passage. The Marine sentry who would have guarded Honor's quarters aboard a Manticoran warship was nowhere in evidence; instead, Simon Mattingly stood outside the hatch and came to attention at his Steadholder's appearance.

"My Lady. Captain Brigham."

"I see I don't have to make any introductions here," Honor observed.

"No, My Lady. Captain Brigham was very helpful in making the security arrangements."

"As a good chief of staff should be," Honor approved. Mattingly smiled and pressed the admittance key, and Honor turned to LaFollet. "Andrew, take Jamie and Eddy and go get yourselves settled in. Captain Brigham and I have a lot to discuss."

"Of course, My Lady. I'll be back by oh-nine-thirty to escort you to your meeting."

"I don't think that will be nec—" Honor began, then sighed at the familiar mulish look in his eyes. "All right, Andrew. All right! I'll be good."

"Thank you, My Lady," the major said without a flicker of triumph, and Honor shook her head as the hatch slid shut behind her.

"Those people," she said feelingly, "are—"

"—extremely attached to you, Milady," Mercedes interposed. Honor paused, then shut her mouth and nodded.

"Exactly what I was about to say," she agreed, and turned to examine her new quarters. "Heavens, I could play soccer in here!"

"Not quite, Milady, but close," Mercedes agreed. "Peep admirals travel first class, and the GSN didn't see any reason to reduce your cubage."

Honor shook her head and turned in place in the center of her day cabin. She'd always thought Manticoran flag officers were magnificently housed, but this surpassed anything she'd ever imagined. The day cabin was at least ten meters on a side—stupendous for any warship—and the sleeping cabin, just visible through an open hatch, was on the same lavish scale. She waded across the thick, rich carpet of GSN-blue to open a closed hatch and shook her head again as she found a dining cabin large enough to host a state dinner. The original Havenite fittings had been stripped during refit, but the Grayson Navy had refurnished in palatial style, and she pursed her lips as she examined her enormous desk and discovered it was made of natural wood.

"I could get to like this," she announced finally, "but we need to have Nimitz's module gold-plated, Mac. It looks positively plebeian against all this magnificence."

The 'cat made a soft, scolding sound on her shoulder and leapt to the top of his bulkhead-mounted life support module. He sat up and wrapped his tail around his true-feet, craning his head about while he, too, inspected their new quarters, and Honor grinned as he radiated smug satisfaction over their link.

"I believe Nimitz is satisfied the way things are, Ma'am," MacGuiness remarked in a tone which indicated his own agreement with the 'cat.

"Nimitz," Honor said severely, "is a shameless hedonist." She sank onto a comfortable couch and stretched her long legs luxuriously. "Of course, he's not the only shameless hedonist in this cabin."

"Indeed, Ma'am?" MacGuiness said blandly.

"Indeed." Honor closed her eyes, then sat up. "Why don't you go see what your own quarters are like, Mac? Captain Brigham and I have some catching up to do. No doubt she can show me where the buzzer is if I need you."

"Of course, Ma'am." The steward nodded respectfully to the chief of staff and excused himself, and Honor pointed to a chair that faced her couch.

"Sit down, Mercedes," she invited. The older woman accepted with a small smile, crossing her legs and placing her cap in her lap, and Honor studied her from under slightly lowered lids.

Mercedes Brigham was a native of Gryphon. She was also a second-generation prolong recipient and old enough to be Honor's mother, which meant her black hair was stranded with white, and, despite over half a century in space, her dark skin still wore the weathered look of her birth world's climate. She'd never been beautiful, but her comfortable, lived-in face was attractive. They'd first met six T-years ago, when Mercedes had been Honor's sailing master in the light cruiser *Fearless*. Despite her long career, she'd been only a lieutenant at the time, and, after so many years in grade, she'd accepted that she would never attain command rank. Now she sat facing Honor in her captain's uniform, and she was still the same quietly competent, confident officer she'd always been.

And that, Honor thought silently, was truly remarkable, given what had happened to *Madrigal*'s crew on Blackbird.

"Well," she said at last, "I'm delighted to see you again, Mercedes. And, needless to say, I'm also delighted you've finally gotten the rank you always deserved."

"Thank you, Ma'am. I'm still getting used to it myself." Mercedes looked down at the narrower four gold rings on her sleeve. "The Graysons bumped me when the Fleet made me a 'loaner,' but the Admiralty made me a full commander when they let me out of Bassingford. I'm not sure they expected me to keep it, though." She grimaced. "I think BuPers expected it to be my separation rank."

"Oh?" Honor asked in a carefully neutral voice.

"Yes, Ma'am. My counselor advised me to consider retirement—with full pension, of course. I'm afraid I, ah, told her where to stick her advice."

Honor's mouth twitched. "I doubt she took that very well."

"I see you've had your own run-ins with the shrinks,

Ma'am," Mercedes observed, then waved one hand. "Oh, she meant well, and I really am grateful for the way they put me back together, but I don't think they realize how good a job they did. Their own tests passed me fit for duty, and they still figured I should 'take it easy' getting back into harness!"

"I imagine part of it's the nature of what happened to you," Honor said quietly.

"I'm not the first person who was ever raped, Ma'am."

Honor was silent for a moment. What had happened to Mercedes Brigham was far too brutal to dismiss with a single word, even one as ugly as "rape," and still worse had happened to other members of *Madrigal*'s crew. Mercedes' crew. People she was responsible for. Honor knew from bitter experience the terrible guilt an officer felt when she lost her people in combat. How much more terrible must it be to lose them to sadistic, systematic torture?

Yet she detected no evasion or denial in Mercedes' tone. The older woman wasn't trying to pretend what she'd endured had been less hideous than it had. Her voice was simply that of someone who'd come to terms with it more completely than Honor suspected *she* could have, and she shook her head and made herself speak with a matching calm.

"I know you aren't, but I think the Navy feels a sort of institutional guilt. No one expected any of what happened, but the Admiralty knew when they sent us out that neither Masada nor Grayson had ever signed the Deneb Accords—and that they were both . . . a bit backward, shall we say? We all know how POWs can be abused, but it'd been a long time since anything like Blackbird happened to RMN personnel, and we let ourselves forget it might happen to *us*. It's going to be a while before the Fleet forgives itself for that."

"I understand that, but having people who should know better try to wrap you up in cotton isn't exactly the best way to put you back on your feet, Ma'am. And there's a point where having someone explain over and over that it wasn't your fault makes you start wondering if they're telling you that so firmly because they think maybe it *was*. I *know* whose fault it was, and all of 'em are dead now, thanks to you, the Marines, and Grayson. I just wish everyone *else* would figure out I know and let it drop." The captain shook her head. "I know they mean well, but it can get mighty wearing. Still," her eyes darkened, "I suppose sometimes they *have* to tell you an awful lot of times before you start believing it."

"Like Mai-ling," Honor sighed, and Mercedes' face tightened.

"Like Mai-ling," she agreed. She stared down at her cap for a long, silent moment, then inhaled. "I'll be honest, Ma'am—I do have nightmares, but they're not really about me. They're about Mai-ling. About knowing what was happening to *her* at the same time when I couldn't do a damned thing to stop it." She raised her eyes once more. "Accepting that I *couldn't* have kept them off her was harder than accepting what happened to me. She was only a kid, and she couldn't believe *anyone* would do what those animals did to her. That's what I can't forgive, Ma'am—and the reason I'm out here."

"Oh?" Honor said neutrally, and Mercedes smiled grimly.

"I believe in the hair of the dog, Ma'am. That's why I volunteered for the Endicott occupation force. I wanted to watch the bastards who'd sent Captain Williams and his pigs to Blackbird squirm."

"I see." Honor leaned back, and the harshness of Mercedes' voice told her the real reason the psychs had worried about her. "And did you?"

"Yes." The captain looked back down at her cap, and the single word came out leached of all feeling. Then she sighed. "Yes, I saw them squirm. And before you ask, Ma'am, I've already figured out why the shrinks didn't want me out here. They figured their tests might not have caught something and I'd lose it." She looked back up at Honor, and there was a sort of strange whimsy in her grim smile.

"They might even have been right. There was one time—" She broke off and shrugged. "Have you been to Masada since the occupation, Ma'am?"

"No." Honor shook her head. "I've considered it, but never very seriously. If there's one person in the galaxy those lunatics really hate, I'm her, and Andrew would shoot me himself—somewhere harmless, like an arm or a leg—to keep me out of their range."

"That would be wise of him, Ma'am. You know, before I saw the place myself, I wondered why the Kingdom should have to shoulder the full burden of occupying it. I mean, we're stretched way too thin as it is, and Endicott's just a hop and a skip from Yeltsin, so why not let the Graysons supply the troops? But those people—" The chief of staff shook her head and rubbed her upper arms as if against a chill.

"Is it really that bad?" Honor asked quietly.

"Worse," Mercedes said bleakly. "Remember when we first came out here? How hard we found it to understand how Grayson women could accept their status?" Honor nodded, and Mercedes shrugged. "Compared to Graysons, Masadan women are downright scary. They're not even people. They're *property* . . . and ninety percent of them seem to accept that that's the way it's *supposed* to be." She shook her head. "Of the few who don't, half aren't sure the occupation's going to last. They're too terrified to do anything about the way they've been treated, but the ones who aren't afraid are almost worse. The homicide rate on Masada doubled in the first six months of the occupation, and something like two-thirds of the extra bodies were 'husbands'—if you can call the pigs that—who'd been murdered by their 'wives.' Some of them were rather artistic, too, like Elder Simonds' wives. The cops never did find all of *his* body parts."

"Good Lord," Honor murmured, and Mercedes nodded.

"It hasn't just been limited to women getting even with 'husbands,' either. The overwhelming majority of Masadans still believe in their so-called religion, but a lot of those who don't have some pretty nasty personal scores to pay off. A quarter of the church elders were murdered by their parishioners before General Marcel put the others into protective custody . . . and *that* only started the survivors howling about the 'oppression of the Faith'! The whole place is still under martial law, General Marcel's had a hell of a time finding anything resembling a body of responsible moderates to act as the local government, and no one on the planet has any idea how to run a nontheocratic state. Under the circumstances, the mere thought of putting in *Grayson* occupation troops would touch off an explosion, and there's no way Marcel's MPs have managed to confiscate all the weapons on the planet."

Honor leaned further back and steepled her fingers under her chin as she frowned at her chief of staff. The Grayson 'faxes reported on Masada regularly, but they'd taken a distinctly hands-off approach. That had surprised her, given the centuries of hatred between the two planets, and her frown deepened as she wondered for the first time if perhaps the Council hadn't "convinced" the reporters to don kid gloves in hopes of sedating public opinion. Of course, the Star Kingdom, not Grayson, had officially claimed the Endicott System as a protectorate by right of conquest. That gave the Graysons a certain insulation from the Masadan occupation . . . and from what Mercedes was saying, that might be the smartest thing anyone had done yet. It was a pity *anyone* had to occupy the place, but the Alliance couldn't afford to leave a strategically located planet full of implacably hostile fanatics *un*occupied.

"How would you rate the potential for real trouble?" she asked finally, and Mercedes shrugged.

"If you mean a general insurrection, not very great as long as we control the high orbitals. There are still lots of small arms floating around, but Marcel's managed to confiscate all their heavy weapons—we hope!— and they understand what a kinetic interdiction strike would do to anyone stupid enough to come out in the open. Couple that with ground-based Marine combat teams to support the MPs and rapid response forces deployed from orbit, all with modern weapons and battle armor, and any sort of mass resistance would be a quick form of suicide. But that hasn't prevented a lot of sabotage and more or less spontaneous acts of guerrilla warfare. Maybe worse, some of them have figured out we don't like killing people in job lots. We're seeing some really ugly 'peaceful demonstrations,' and their organizers keep pushing. I think they're trying to see how far they can go before someone on our side pulls the trigger and creates a brand new crop of martyrs."

"Wonderful." Honor pinched the bridge of her nose and grimaced. "If they *do* push that far, it'll give the Liberals and Progressives back home another reason to moan about our 'brutal, imperialist' policy in the system!"

"Just thank God the *Masadans* haven't figured that out, Milady," Mercedes said darkly. "Their traditions are so different from ours that they don't seem to realize our government actually has to listen to people who disagree with it. If they ever *do* realize, and start playing to the newsies . . ."

She shrugged once more, and Honor nodded.

"At any rate," Mercedes went on after a moment, "that's the real reason I transferred to Grayson service, Ma'am. They needed officers, and I needed to get away from Masada before I did something I'd regret. I mean, I know the Graysons hanged the bastards who actually raped and murdered my people, but a part of me blames *all* Masadans for it, and with so many of them actively pushing to see how far they can go, it'd be too easy to—"

She broke off and closed her eyes for a moment, and her nostrils flared. Then her eyes reopened. They met her admiral's levelly, and what Honor saw in them reassured her. Mercedes had her own devils, but she recognized them and had them under control. And that, Honor told herself with a familiar tinge of bitterness, was the most anyone could ask of herself. Yet there was still one thing she had to know, and there was only one way to find out.

"And Captain Yu?" She asked the question quietly, and Mercedes smiled faintly.

"You mean do I blame him for what happened to *Madrigal*, Ma'am?" Honor nodded, and she shook her head. "He was doing his job. There was nothing personal in it, and he didn't have a thing to do with what happened on Blackbird. In fact, he protested the way our people were turned over to Williams after he had us picked up."

"He did?" Honor asked sharply. "That never came out at Williams' trial."

"The Grayson prosecutors didn't know about it at the time, Milady, and Yu was never charged. Unlike Theisman, he didn't have any personal knowledge of events on Blackbird, so he wasn't even called to testify, and Williams was the only man on Blackbird who knew about it. Do you think *he* was going to say anything that might make 'that traitor Yu' look better to us?" Mercedes snorted bitterly.

"So how did *you* find out? Did *he* tell you?" Despite herself, Honor couldn't quite keep an uncharacteristic edge out of her tone, and Mercedes looked at her in surprise.

"No, Ma'am. The first things we seized after our initial landings were the Masadan archives and the Havenite embassy records. We were too late to get any of the Peeps' secure files, but we made a pretty clean sweep of the Masadans', and Sword Simonds had filed copies of Captain Yu's 'insubordinate' protests."

"I see." Honor looked away, and her cheekbones heated as she realized she'd *wanted* Yu to be the one who'd told Mercedes about his protests. That she'd wanted to believe they were a self-serving invention. Her flush grew hotter as she faced her own petty desire to cling to something for which she could blame her new flag captain, and Nimitz looked up from his perch on the module. She felt him chiding her for her self-condemning thoughts, but this time she knew he was wrong.

"I see," she repeated more naturally, and returned her gaze to the older woman. "So I take it you don't have any problems serving with him?"

"None," Mercedes said firmly. "He's in a hell of a spot, Ma'am, and I'm damned if *I* would've put myself in one like it. He could've gone back to Manticore after the Office of Shipbuilding finished with him, you know. It was his own decision to stay out here. I don't doubt High Admiral Matthews is glad to have him—he really is as good as his reputation—but whatever he may say, he has to know there are still a lot of Grayson officers who're just waiting for him to make a mistake so they can pounce."

"I know," Honor murmured softly, and felt another stab of shame at her own readiness to do just that. She drummed the fingers of one hand lightly on a couch arm for a moment, then shrugged. "Well, if you're happy with him, Ms. Chief of Staff, then I suppose the least *I* can do is keep an open mind."

Mercedes nodded a wordless acceptance of the admission implicit in those words, and Honor smiled wryly. Mercedes always had been a calm, tactful sort.

"All right, then. Enough about Captain Yu. Let me get Mac in here with some cocoa for me and a cup of coffee for you, and you can give me a thumbnail brief on the rest of the staff, as well."

• CHAPTER ELEVEN

". . . so Earl White Haven is still pressing the Peeps around Nightingale and Trevor's Star, My Lady, but it doesn't look as if they're going to crumble anytime soon."

Lieutenant Commander Paxton paused, touched a key to freeze his memo pad's display, and looked down the conference table as if to invite questions, but Honor only nodded. Paxton's brief on the front had been as comprehensive as she would have expected from someone with his credentials.

"Thank you, Commander," she said now. "To be honest, however, I'm more concerned with our local situation. What can you tell us about Home Fleet?" It felt odd to apply that label to any non-Manticoran formation, but with eleven GSN SDs added to it, it certainly merited the title.

"From all indications, My Lady, I expect to see some major changes shortly. I'm sure Commander Bagwell—" Paxton nodded to the operations officer "—has been better briefed on the details than I have, but my understanding is that the Manties—"

He broke off, and his face darkened with what Honor guessed was a most unusual blush. She raised a hand to hide her smile, but Nimitz was less restrained. His soft bleek of amusement sounded clearly in the silence, and Paxton turned even darker.

"Sorry, My Lady. I meant to say 'the Manticorans.'"

"No, Commander, you meant to say the Manties." Honor lowered her hand and let him see her smile. "I have heard the term before, you know, and as long as

143

you don't add any, ah, pejorative adjectives, I won't hold it against you."

"I—" Paxton paused, then grinned suddenly and raised both hands in surrender. "Mercy, My Lady. I yield." Honor grinned back, and the lieutenant commander shook himself. "At any rate, my understanding is that the *Manticorans* will be pulling their remaining ships of the wall out of Yeltsin sometime in the next few weeks. Fred?"

He glanced at Bagwell for confirmation, and the ops officer nodded.

"It's not official yet, My Lady," he said, "but we've received an informational warning from Command Central. Admiral Suarez has officially informed High Admiral Matthews that the Manticoran Admiralty is reconsidering its deployments. Given conditions at the front, Central expects them to radically reduce the RMN presence in Yeltsin now that we can more or less look after ourselves. Since over half of 'our' Home Fleet's wall of battle still consists of Manticoran units, the impact will be pretty severe."

Honor raised an eyebrow, but Bagwell shook his head quickly.

"Command Central isn't complaining, My Lady. If the Alliance wants to maintain any momentum, the RMN has no choice but to draw reinforcements from *some-where*, and we've become a logical place. Under the circumstances, they've given us a generous lead time on any changes, and BatRon Two's ready to take up the immediate slack. All the same, our defenses *will* become much more dependent on our own resources, and Central wants our squadron ready for operations no later than—" he consulted his own memo pad "—March sixth, as well."

"Um." Honor rubbed her temple while her mind juggled the date. Like every other extra-solar planet, Grayson had a local calendar, but *unlike* most such planets, its people used it only to keep track of the seasons. Nor did they date things from their first colonists' landing as most other systems did. Instead, with a degree of stubbornness unusual even for Graysons, they clung to the ancient Gregorian calendar of Old Earth, which was totally unsuited to the length of their planet's *day*, much less its year, for official dating. Worse, they retained the old Christian Era date . . . and just to make things *really* confusing, they followed it with "A.D.," for "*Anno Domini*," while everyone *else* used that to indicate "Ante Diaspora"! It was enough to thoroughly bewilder any hapless newcomer, and, for some reason, Honor always had trouble remembering whether this was the year 4019 or 4020, despite all the official documents she had to sign. But at least they also used Old Earth's twenty-four-hour day aboard their warships, as well, so she didn't have to convert different day lengths. She only had to remember how many days each month had.

She ran through the silly jingle Howard Clinkscales had taught her to keep track of the days per month, then frowned. February was the short one, which meant March sixth was only forty days away, and her frown deepened as she redid the calculations, hoping she was in error. She wasn't, and she looked at Bagwell and Mercedes Brigham.

"That doesn't give us much time, people." Their expressions told her that was one of the more unnecessary remarks she'd ever made, and the right corner of her mouth quirked. "Can we do it?"

Bagwell looked at Captain Brigham, deferring to the chief of staff and clearly just as happy that he could, and Mercedes frowned.

"We can make a good try, My Lady," she said. "Admiral Brentworth's drilled *Magnificent*, *Courageous*, and *Manticore's Gift* as a single, oversized division for over two months. *Furious* and *Glorious* have only been operational for a couple of weeks, but they're shaping up. Of course, none of them have ever exercised as a complete squadron, and *Terrible* only left the yard Friday. I suppose the real question's how quickly we can get her fully on-line."

"Do you agree, Captain Yu?" Honor heard her voice go just a bit cooler, but Yu seemed not to notice. He simply leaned back in his chair and rubbed his chin, eyes half-closed for a moment, then nodded.

"I think so, My Lady. It'll be close, though. Admiral Brentworth's done well with his exercises, so we've got a solid core to build around, but Admiral Trailman and Admiral Yanakov have only been with the squadron a few days, and so far we haven't even run any sims, much less actual exercises, at the squadron level. I think our COs will pick it up quickly once we get started, but at the same time," his eyes went slightly opaque once more, "*Terrible* still has yard reps on board for final adjustments, and I haven't even completed my full power trials or gunnery checks. We're officially operational, but—" He shrugged and turned those opaque eyes to Honor. "It might be worthwhile to consider transferring your flag to one of the other ships for a few days, My Lady. That would give you a chance to start squaring the squadron away while I complete acceptance trials and deal with any last-minute glitches."

Honor studied him thoughtfully. No captain liked to admit his ship might be less than fully ready for duty, and Yu had more reason than most not to do it. He had to know that if she *did* want to get rid of him as her flag captain, he was offering her the perfect pretext. If *Terrible*'s working up was delayed, she'd have no choice but to use one of the other COs as her acting flag captain. Afterwards, she could always retain that other captain rather than Yu on the basis that she had a proven command team already in place.

Yet there was no evasiveness in his voice. He was giving her his considered judgment of what was best for the squadron, and she knew he was right. Which only woke an oddly perverse disinclination in her to accept his offer. She didn't fully understand her own motives, but she found herself shaking her head.

"Not yet, Captain. Let's see how your trials look, first." She smiled suddenly. "I've commanded a lame duck flagship, myself. The least I can do is be as patient with you as my admiral was with me."

Some of the opacity faded from Yu's eyes. He said nothing, but he ducked his head in a small bob that might have been agreement or thanks, and Honor turned back to Paxton.

"All right, Commander. We'll get to operational matters in a moment. In the meantime, we've wandered a bit afield from your background brief."

"Yes, My Lady." Paxton consulted his memo pad again. "Leaving aside whatever deployment changes we may have here in Yeltsin, High Admiral Matthews has decided to reinforce the Endicott Picket with half the Second Battlecruiser Squadron. This reflects his concern that—"

His clear, precise voice went on painting the details of local deployments and concerns, and Honor tipped back in her chair as she listened.

Citizen Vice Admiral Alexander Thurston read the brief, terse dispatch with a careful lack of expression. It wasn't easy to hide his contempt for the stupidity behind it, but he'd had a lot of practice in the last year or so. He laid the message board on his blotter and took another moment to be sure his mask was properly adjusted before he looked up from it.

Thurston might be the official commander of Operation Dagger, but the man across his desk from him knew better. Citizen Michael Preznikov's simple undress coverall lacked all insignia, yet that very absence of any rank badges was its own brand of arrogance. The fact that Preznikov alone, of every man and woman aboard PNS *Conquistador*, bore no insignia identified him as the battleship's resident people's commissioner and the direct representative of the Committee of Public Safety itself.

And, Thurston reminded himself, as the man who could make anyone *else* aboard *Conquistador*, including any vice admiral foolish enough to criticize those same civilian authorities—or his orders—vanish forever.

It was a point Thurston intended to bear carefully in
mind until the time came to change it.

"A problem, Citizen Admiral?" Preznikov asked now,
and Thurston schooled his tone into one of purely professional concern.

"Another delay," he said as mildly as he could. He
handed over the dispatch, for Preznikov had the right
to see any communication, personal or official, and gritted his teeth as the commissioner read this one.

Alexander Thurston had been one of the very few
officers with no links to any Legislaturalist family to reach
captain's rank in the People's Navy under the old regime.
That gave him certain advantages under the Committee of Public Safety, since the lack of patronage which
would have denied him any chance of flag rank under
the old regime had become a guarantee of it under the
new one. He was well aware of the factors which made
that true . . . and that the Committee wouldn't last forever. Pierre was too much the mob's prisoner; when he
couldn't keep his promises, it would turn on him, and
the resulting chaos would offer a military commander
with a record of success his chance. Thurston was willing
to put up with the inconveniences of the moment to
position himself properly for that chance—but that didn't
mean he liked being second-guessed by a political hack
with absolutely no naval training.

Still, Preznikov was scarcely unique in that respect. The
Committee could hardly select its watchdogs from the
same officer corps it wanted them to watch, and Thurston
supposed he should be grateful he'd at least been spared
one of the commissioners who were ex-enlisted. He'd
seen one or two of them in action; they were even more
insufferable than hacks like Preznikov, and having some
ex-missile tech overruling him on the basis of his "previous naval experience" would have been more than
Thurston could stomach. And dangerous. A fool who
knew a little was far more dangerous than someone who
at least had the wit to admit he knew nothing.

Preznikov finished reading, then laid the board on the

desk and frowned.

"Just how serious is this, Citizen Admiral?"

"That's hard to say, Citizen Commissioner." Even the best of them loved to hear that title, Thurston thought sourly. "We're already two weeks behind schedule. If this—" he tapped the dispatch with a fingertip "—holds and we only lose another week or so, it shouldn't matter too much. But if the delay runs longer than that, it could have serious repercussions."

"Why?" Preznikov asked, and Thurston's other hand fisted under the desktop. Damn it, the man had read the entire operations plan! Surely even an idiot commissioner should know *that* question's answer!

But the citizen vice admiral made his hand relax and nodded as if Preznikov's question were perfectly reasonable. And, he reminded himself, at least he'd asked. That indicated an awareness of his own limitations . . . or Thurston hoped it did, at any rate.

"There are two main reasons, Citizen Commissioner," he said. "First, Dagger depends on the proper execution of Stalking Horse to draw the enemy into positions of our choice, and Stalking Horse's maneuvers have to be carefully coordinated in time and space to have the effect we desire. Even if they succeed entirely, we must be able to strike our actual objective within a very narrow window of time, and anything which makes that window narrower—like a delay in the ops schedule—decreases the odds of our final success."

He paused, and Preznikov nodded for him to continue.

"Secondly, the original ops plan required the assembly of all of Task Force Fourteen here so that we could proceed as a single, unified force. This—" he tapped the message again "—doesn't say anything specifically about the other units of the task force, but if HQ believes the situation around Nightingale is still so dangerous that it's delaying the release of Stalking Horse's superdreadnoughts, it may decide not to reduce the battleship covering forces in other systems around Trevor's Star, either. And since over half our total units are supposed to be drawn from that sector—"

He broke off with a shrug, and Preznikov's frown deepened.

"Why wasn't this possibility allowed for in the preliminary planning?" he asked in a colder voice, and Thurston controlled his own tone very carefully when he replied.

"When my staff and I prepared the original plan for this operation, Citizen Commissioner, we specifically requested that the forces for it be drawn from deeper inside the Republic to avoid this sort of problem. In fact, we originally asked for the Fifteenth and Forty-First Battle Squadrons, and our request was approved. Unfortunately, we were subsequently informed that both those squadrons—which as you know, are currently in Malagasy—had become . . . unavailable. That meant we had to find the ships somewhere else at a very late date, and if we were to avoid unacceptable delays in transit times to assemble the task force, that somewhere else had to be closer to hand. Unhappily, any system close enough for our purposes is also so close to Trevor's Star as to be susceptible to last-minute diversions in response to enemy pressure."

Preznikov's eyes flashed at the mention of the Malagasy System, but Thurston knew he'd scored a point. The squadrons he'd originally been promised were "unavailable" because Malagasy had exploded in the Committee of Public Safety's face. He didn't know precisely what had provoked it, though it seemed likely the officer corps purges had backed someone into too tight a corner. Shortly after Secretary Ransom had started whipping up the Proles, some of the SS "reeducation teams" had taken to shooting suspect officers' families, as well as the officers themselves. It had been among the stupider of many stupid things State Security had done, and he knew the maniacs responsible had exceeded their own authority when they did it, but moderation wasn't in great demand in the People's Republic just now, and he doubted they'd be punished for it. Not, he thought bitterly, until someone realized that little things like wrecking ops plans by diverting desperately needed warships to suppress local revolts were likely to have an adverse effect on the war effort, at least.

"I see," Preznikov said after a moment, sitting back in his chair with an unwilling nod. "But is it really that important to concentrate the entire force in one place before launching the operation?"

"It's extremely important, Citizen Commissioner." Thurston tried not to sound as if he were lecturing a slow student, but it was hard. "If we can't assemble the entire task force *here*, then we'll have to do it somewhere else, possibly in the very face of the enemy. Converging thrusts by widely dispersed forces look good in war games, Citizen Commissioner, but they don't work out well in practice, especially over interstellar distances. In theory, they offer the advantage of surprise by making it harder for the enemy to deduce the target from your beginning deployments, but they only work if every one of those separated forces moves *precisely* on schedule. If your timing is even slightly off, coordination falls apart and whatever part of your force reaches the objective first ends up facing everything the enemy has, which exposes you to the risk of defeat in detail. That," he finished as pointedly as he dared, "is largely what happened when Admiral Rollins moved early and attacked Hancock with only a portion of the strength originally allocated to the operation."

"I see," Preznikov repeated in a much more reasonable tone.

"But that's only part of the problem, Citizen Commissioner," Thurston went on. "If we can't concentrate the task force before we launch Dagger, then I can't brief my officers. This is a very complex operation. A lot of things can go wrong, and let's be honest—our command teams are hardly what I can call experienced." Preznikov frowned but said nothing. Thurston found his lack of response encouraging and went on in a voice of calm dispassion. "That makes human error much more likely, however well motivated our people are, and our operational security instructions mean none of our captains know the details. If I don't even have time to discuss my plans with them before they have to go into action, the chance of fatal misunderstandings increases astronomically."

"Should we consider delaying Dagger, then—even rescheduling it completely?" The question was so sensible it surprised Thurston, but it was also dangerous, and he considered carefully before he replied.

"That's impossible to say for certain, Citizen Commissioner. Dagger is predicated on the strategic situation which exists *now*. If the enemy has time to adjust his position—if, for example, he brings up a substantial portion of the Manty Home Fleet—he'll have a different set of choices when we spring Stalking Horse on him. As things stand, he'll almost have to withdraw forces from our target to respond to our attacks on Candor and Minette without uncovering Grendelsbane. There's no place else he *can* withdraw them from, but if we give him the time to reinforce the front from Manticore, he may choose to divert some of those reinforcements, instead. And if that happens, Citizen Commissioner, our entire task force will be too weak to take our objective or even carry out a worthwhile hit-and-run raid."

"So what you're saying, Citizen Admiral, is that we have to get Dagger in before the balance of forces shifts or else scrub it completely?"

"I'm saying that, depending on what the Manties do, cancellation *may* become our only option," Thurston said even more carefully, for the PN's officers had learned the hard way that disappointing their political masters carried a stiff penalty.

"I understand," Preznikov said with a thin smile. "What can I do to help, Citizen Admiral?"

The offer was almost as surprising as the question which had preceded it. Preznikov would never be anything but a political hack in Thurston's eyes, but at least he seemed to be a hack who was actually willing to *do* something. That was more than many of Thurston's fellow flag officers could count on.

"If you could stress in your own reports that it is imperative to hold any additional delays to the absolute minimum, I would be most grateful, Citizen Commissioner," he said.

"That much I can do," Preznikov agreed with a nod, and his thin smile turned almost warm. "In fact, I'll inform the Committee that I fully share your concerns, Citizen Admiral, and suggest that if they want this operation to succeed, they'd better make sure someone at Fleet HQ gets his thumb out."

"Thank you, Citizen Commissioner. I appreciate that," Thurston told his political master, and the most galling thing about it was that he truly did.

• CHAPTER TWELVE

"Status change! Two unidentified bogies just lit off their drives at zero-eight-niner one-five-three, range five-point-six million klicks! Course two-three-four zero-niner-five relative, base velocity . . . eight-one thousand KPS, accelerating at three-point-niner-four KPS squared."

"I see them, Fred." Honor rose and moved closer to the flag deck's huge holo display. It wasn't as good as a Manticoran plot—though the sensors which fed it had been upgraded, the imagers which drove it were the original Havenite ones—but it was better than the smaller one at her command console, and she smiled. Rear Admiral Yanakov, she thought, was a sneaky devil.

The light codes of Battle Division Thirteen continued to flee with BatDivs Eleven and Twelve in hot pursuit, but she already knew what was about to happen. Walter Brentworth had let Admiral Trailman's BatDiv Twelve get too far ahead of BatDiv Eleven in its efforts to chase down Yanakov's "Aggressor Force," and he was about to pay for it.

"Identification," a voice announced. "The bogies are *Courageous* and *Furious*, Commander."

"What?" Commander Bagwell jerked around, then muttered something venomous under his breath. "It can't be! They're—"

"Howard, inform Admiral Brentworth that he's just suffered a com failure," Honor said, and Bagwell looked at her, then winced as Lieutenant Commander Brannigan passed the message. Honor met her ops officer's gaze with a slightly malicious twinkle and walked back to her command chair.

Her display changed as the computers updated it, and Bagwell crossed to stand at her shoulder.

"Would you mind telling me what Admiral Yanakov thinks he's doing, My Lady?" he asked in a low voice.

"He got sneaky," she replied. "This—" she tapped the light codes BatDiv Twelve was slowly overhauling "—is his screen and a pair of EW drones programmed to mimic SDs. He *wanted* his attempt to 'sneak around us' to be spotted so we'd go in pursuit while *Courageous* and *Furious* hid under their stealth systems. Now that he's sucked us out of position and separated the other two divisions, he plans to cross our sterns and pound BatDiv Eleven one-on-one before Admiral Trailman can decelerate to help out." She shook her head with a small, admiring smile. "It's a gutsy move . . . if he can pull it off."

"But it's not part of the mission brief, My Lady," Bagwell protested. "He was tasked to hit the convoy *without* engaging our wall."

"I know—but he counted on Admiral Brentworth to think that and rewrote his orders to go for the convoy *and* take out a couple of SDs if he can. That's what they call initiative, Fred."

Bagwell's soft sound might charitably have indicated agreement, and though none of it would splash on him, she hoped he'd take the lesson to heart. The whole point of the exercise was for her to observe how her other divisional COs and *their* staffs performed, but it could just as easily have been him and not Brentworth's ops officer who'd walked into BatDiv Thirteen's deep-space ambush.

She watched Yanakov's two isolated superdreadnoughts accelerate at over four hundred gravities on a heading to intersect BatDiv Eleven's base course. New projections appeared in the plot, and she nodded to herself again. Yanakov had guessed well when he pre-positioned his ships and went to silent running, and whoever he'd left to command his screen—Commodore Justman, perhaps?—had led Brentworth to him on the right course.

BatDiv Thirteen would cross astern of BatDiv Eleven, with Brentworth's ships squarely between it and Trailman's division. That would give Trailman's missile crews a litter of kittens if they tried to engage without hitting BatDiv Eleven, and Honor's decision to take Brentworth out of the command loop dropped the entire problem squarely on Trailman's shoulders. Depriving Walter of a chance to retrieve his mistake wasn't very nice of her, but Yanakov had already blown his original plans out the lock, and she wanted to see how the squadron reacted to complete confusion.

She sat back and listened to the com net. With Brentworth out of the loop, Alfredo Yu had become BatDiv Eleven's SO, and she heard him acknowledging Trailman's orders. The admiral sounded both flustered and angry, and she frowned as the plot projected what would happen when BatDiv Eleven executed his commands. He was trying to reunite his separated divisions to engage Yanakov, just as The Book required.

Unfortunately, this time The Book was wrong, and his inexperience showed. BatDiv Twelve was decelerating and diving below the plane of its original advance in a bid to clear the range, and that much, at least, Honor approved. If Trailman could generate enough vertical separation, he could fire "up" past BatDiv Eleven as Yanakov's ships crossed astern of it; it wouldn't be a very good shot—the range would be long, and BatDiv Eleven's emissions would interfere with his fire control—but at least he'd *have* a shot. And if BatDiv Eleven turned to bring its energy batteries to bear as Yanakov passed, the combination of missiles and beams might just do the trick.

But Trailman didn't seem to realize he needed Yu's energy weapons. Or, rather, he'd let Yanakov push him into forgetting that the defense of the convoy was his primary mission. He was intent on protecting his *warships* by getting both divisions out of Yanakov's energy envelope and then using his missile power advantage to nail BatDiv Thirteen if it pressed the attack on BatDiv

Eleven. But if the other two divisions rendezvoused, Yanakov would simply let the maneuver take even BatDiv Eleven out of effective energy range, nip across its rear, and go straight for the convoy. His base velocity was low, but his vector was almost exactly perpendicular to Trailman's. He'd streak across the rest of the squadron's base course like a wet treecat, and Trailman could never generate enough delta vee to stay with him. Worse, the point at which BatDiv Thirteen's course would cross the other divisions' track was far enough astern of BatDiv Twelve to give Yanakov's point defense crews ample tracking time on Trailman's missiles . . . which would have too little time left on their drives for terminal attack maneuvers anyway. Yu's ships would be closer, of course; he'd undoubtedly score at least some hits, but he wouldn't get enough of them to do more than inconvenience Yanakov.

In fact, the convoy's only real chance—and that not much of one—was for Trailman to accept Yanakov's attack on BatDiv Eleven. The odds would be slightly in Yu's favor, since he had screening units in company while Yanakov's were off playing decoy, but the engagement window would be brief and the choice to engage would be Yanakov's. He could accept Yu's fire in order to return it, or he could roll up on his side to block it with the impenetrable tops or bellies of his impeller wedges and hare off after the convoy with impunity.

Only he wouldn't have to do even that. If BatDiv Eleven tried to close with BatDiv Twelve, its own maneuvers would take it beyond the range at which its energy weapons could burn through Yanakov's sidewalls. They'd be harmless to him, and while he might not get any of Trailman's SDs, he'd still sweep through the convoy and annihilate it in passing.

She listened to Yu's calm, unhurried voice accepting Trailman's orders and felt a stab of disappointment. She remained uncomfortable with the former Peep, but she'd expected better than this of him. The consequences of Trailman's maneuver were painfully obvious—to Yanakov, as well as Honor, it appeared. His course was already breaking further to port as he gave up on BatDiv Eleven to turn straight for the convoy, ignoring both of the other divisions in order to head off the scattering freighters.

Minutes ticked past, the projections tracked across the display, sporadic missile fire streaked back and forth, and Honor's disappointment with her flag captain grew. Yu had more experience than any of her Grayson admirals, but Trailman's maneuvers had already taken the ex-Peep's ships well beyond range of the point-blank passing energy engagement that was the convoy's only hope, and he wasn't even arguing about it.

But neither, she realized abruptly, was he obeying Trailman's orders! The plot seemed to swoop sideways as BatDiv Eleven went to full military power and snapped through a howling course change with absolutely no warning. The division and its entire screen swerved like a single ship, in a flawlessly coordinated maneuver, and her eyes widened with astonished respect as she realized Yu must have been busy passing directions of his own even as he acknowledged Trailman's totally different orders.

The abrupt course change completely surprised Trailman. She heard him yelp in dismay, but she herself chuckled in sudden delight. Yu had acknowledged Trailman's orders, all right, yet he'd done it less to deceive Trailman than to deceive *Yanakov!* The aggressor force commander had already demonstrated his cunning with his EW drones, but he'd gone one better even than that. He'd used his com section to tap Trailman's command net, as well!

It wasn't something he could expect to do against real Peeps, but that wasn't the point. A good officer took every advantage he could find, then manufactured more of them any way he could, and it was as audacious as the rest of his plan. But it had just backfired, because Alfredo Yu was even more cunning than he was. Yu couldn't have *known* what Yanakov was doing, yet he'd allowed for the possibility. Trailman had used omnidirectional transmissions to keep all units simultaneously updated on his plans, and Yanakov's com section would have found it fairly easy to tap those. But Yu must have been using tight, directional whisker lasers to coordinate his own units, and Yanakov's people had never noticed. Why should they, when they already knew what his orders from Trailman were? The flag captain's maneuver might have worked even without the added element of deception; with it, his sudden move changed from possibly effective to certainly devastating.

BatDiv Thirteen's heading changed again, shifting crazily as Yanakov realized he'd been out-sneaked, but it was too late, for Yu had timed his turn perfectly. True, the range was too great for his energy weapons to burn through BatDiv Thirteen's sidewalls, but Yanakov had been too sure of what his opponents intended to consider what *else* they might do. He'd let his ships' sterns point just a bit too close to Yu, secure in the knowledge BatDiv Eleven was heading *away* from him; now his overconfidence betrayed him as BatDiv Eleven cleared its broadsides and, for one fleeting moment, two superdreadnoughts, four heavy cruisers, six light cruisers, and six destroyers had perfect "up the kilt" shots through the wide open after-aspect of his impeller wedges.

Lasers and grasers clawed at their targets in brief, titanic fury, with no sidewalls to stop them, and the superdreadnought *Courageous* blew up in a spectacular boil of light. Admiral Yanakov went with his flagship, and more hits ripped into her consort. A wounded *Furious* rolled frantically, twisting through a radical skew turn that snatched her stern away from Yu and interposed the top of her wedge against the incoming fire. But Honor heard Trailman's suddenly exultant voice snapping fresh orders as BatDiv Twelve laid into her with missiles, and the only course that could protect her from Yu's fire turned the open throat of her wedge barely thirty degrees away from Trailman. She went to full

military power as she fought to crab away from her
enemies, but she was already badly hurt, and without
Courageous's support, her point defense was too weak.
A quarter of Trailman's laser heads detonated squarely
in front of her, and debris and atmosphere vomited into
space. Eight minutes after *Courageous* blew up, *Furious* followed suit, and Honor drew a deep breath of
approval.

"All right, Fred. Kill the sim."

The plots died, and she rose and stretched. The visual
display showed her the other ships of her squadron,
and she grinned at the two SDs which had just been
"destroyed," still riding placidly in Grayson orbit as they
ran through the computer-generated simulation.

Commander Bagwell shook himself, still a bit dazed
by how ruthlessly Yanakov—and Yu, she thought with
a broader grin—had violated the exercise's parameters.
Walter was going to be upset with himself, she thought,
but he wasn't the sort to hold it against Yanakov. Or,
for that matter, to let himself be suckered a second time.
And Yanakov was going to be miffed with himself, too.
He'd pulled off a brilliant ambush, then let his initial
success go to his head, and Yu had exacted a devastating price for his overconfidence. He'd waited a bit too
long to make his move—if Yanakov had changed heading
even a few seconds sooner BatDiv Eleven would have
lost its chance for an up the kilt shot, and the range
had been too long for anything else to work—but she'd
make that point to him in private. It had worked, after
all, and he deserved the respect it was going to earn
him from the rest of the squadron.

As a matter of fact, Yanakov deserved a pat on the
back, too. He might have blown it at the last minute,
yet he'd shown imagination and nerve, as well as skill,
in even attempting the ambush. All in all, she was
pleased. There'd been too many mistakes, but mistakes
were what people learned from. Better they should make
them in sims than against the enemy, and she was
delighted by the independence Yanakov and Yu had

displayed. Too much initiative could be disastrous, but too little was more dangerous . . . and far more common. She vastly preferred officers she might need to rein in occasionally to being stuck with ones too timid to act on their own.

She turned away from the visual display.

"Well, that was certainly exciting," she said to Bagwell, and Nimitz bleeked a quiet laugh from his perch on the back of her command chair.

"Ah, yes, My Lady, it was," the commander replied, and Honor's eyes gleamed. Bagwell was just as correct and precise—and tactically formal—as her initial impression had suggested, and he still sounded bemused by it all.

"Indeed it was . . . and I can hardly wait to hear your analysis at the debrief," she said, and her chuckle echoed Nimitz's fresh laugh at the ops officer's expression.

William Fitzclarence, Steadholder Burdette, glowered as Deacon Allman stepped into his office. Burdette House was even larger than Protector's Palace, and far older, as befitted the capital of one of Grayson's original steadings. It was a massive structure of native stone, built when fortresses were needed against fellow steadholders as well as a hostile environment, and his office mirrored its stark, uncompromising presence. One of his first orders as Steadholder had been to strip away the tapestries and paintings the last two steadholders had allowed to soften the office's spartan simplicity. He'd loved his father and grandfather, but they'd let themselves be seduced away from the iron simplicity God expected of His people, and William Fitzclarence had no intention of repeating their error.

Deacon Allman's heels clicked on bare stone as he crossed to Burdette's desk, and something flickered in his otherwise mild eyes as the Steadholder remained seated. Official protocol didn't require a steadholder to rise to greet even a deacon of the Church, but courtesy was something else. Lord Burdette's refusal to stand was a calculated insult, and Allman's exquisitely correct half-bow returned it with interest.

"My Lord," he murmured, and Burdette's nostrils flared. The Sacristy messenger's bland voice offered no overt cause for complaint, but he heard bared steel within it.

"Deacon," he returned shortly, and Allman straightened. The Steadholder didn't offer him a chair, and the churchman folded his hands behind him as he studied the man he'd come to see.

Burdette had the Fitzclarence look—tall for a Grayson, broad shouldered and square, and he'd succeeded to his dignities at an early age. His strong-jawed, handsome face and hard, ice-blue eyes bore the confident stamp of a man accustomed to command . . . and of one *un*accustomed to being thwarted.

The silence stretched out, and despite the moment's tension, Allman was tempted to smile. His high church office had brought him into contact with too many steadholders to be awed by Burdette's birth, and the man's obvious attempt to disconcert him with that steely blue glare amused him. Or would have, he thought more somberly, had the situation been less serious.

"Well?" Burdette growled finally.

"I regret, My Lord, to inform you that the Sacristy has denied your petition. The decision to bar Brother Marchant from his offices will not be rescinded until such time as he makes public acknowledgment of his errors."

"His *errors*!" Burdette's fists clenched on the desk, and his jaw tightened like a steel trap. "Since when has it been a sin for a man of God to speak God's will?"

"My Lord, it is not my place or wish to debate with you," Allman replied calmly. "I am simply a messenger."

"A messenger?" Burdette barked a laugh. "A lap dog, you mean, yapping the 'message' you were ordered to deliver!"

"A messenger," Allman repeated in a harder voice, "charged to deliver the decision of God's Church, My Lord."

"The *Sacristy*," Burdette said coldly, "is not the whole body of Father Church. It consists of *men*, Deacon—men who can fall into error as easily as anyone else."

"No one claims otherwise, My Lord. But the Tester requires men to do their best to understand His will . . . and to act upon that understanding."

"Oh, indeed He does." Burdette's smile was thin, cold, and ugly. "The pity is that the Sacristy chooses to forget that in Brother Marchant's case!"

"The Sacristy," Allman said sternly, "has *not* forgotten, My Lord. No one has attempted to dictate to Brother Marchant's conscience. The Sacristy has found him in error, but if he cannot in good faith agree with the judgment of the Church, then his refusal to do so does him credit. Matters of personal faith are the most difficult Test any of God's children—even those who serve His Church—must face, and the Sacristy is well aware of that. Yet Father Church also has the duty to expose error when it perceives it."

"The Sacristy has been seduced by political expedience," Burdette said flatly, "and *it*, not Brother Marchant, has set itself in opposition to God's will." The Steadholder's voice went harsher and deeper, and his eyes glared. "This foreign woman—this *harlot* who fornicates outside the bonds of holy marriage and poisons us all with her ungodly ways—is an abomination in the eyes of God! She and those who would turn our world into no more than an echo of her own degenerate kingdom are the servants of evil, and the Sacristy seeks to spread their unclean ways among the true children of God!"

"I will not debate your beliefs with you, My Lord. That is not my function. If you disagree with the Sacristy's ruling, it is your ancient right—both as Steadholder and as a child of Father Church—to argue your case before it. It is also the Sacristy's responsibility, as the elected, ordained stewards of Father Church, to reject your arguments if they conflict with its understanding of God's will." Burdette snarled something under his breath, and Allman continued in the same dispassionate tone. "The

Sacristy regrets its inability to grant your petition, but the Elders cannot turn aside from their joint understanding of God's will for any man. Not even for you, My Lord."

"I see." Burdette's eyes, harder—and more contemptuous—than ever, surveyed Allman from head to toe. "So the Sacristy and Protector command me to strip Brother Marchant of the offices God has called him to?"

"The Sacristy and the Protector have already removed Edmond Marchant from the offices he held in trust from God and Father Church," Allman corrected without flinching. "Until he heals the breach between his own teachings and those of Father Church, someone else must discharge those offices for him."

"So you say," Burdette said coldly. Allman made no reply, and he bared his teeth. "Very well, Deacon, you may now bear *my* message. Inform the Sacristy that it may be able to drive a true man of God from his pulpit and publicly humiliate him for remaining true to his Faith, but that it cannot compel me to join its sin. In my eyes, Brother Marchant retains every office of which he has been wrongfully deprived. I will nominate no replacement."

The cold blue eyes glittered as a flash of anger crossed the deacon's face at last. Allman clenched his hands behind him, reminding himself he was a man of God and that Burdette was a steadholder, and clamped his teeth on a hot retort. He took a moment to be sure he had command of his voice, then spoke in the calmest tone he could manage.

"My Lord, whatever your differences with the Sacristy, you, too, have a responsibility. Whether the Sacristy is in error or not, you have no right as a ruler anointed by God to leave the offices of His Church unfilled and His children unministered to."

"The *Sacristy* has done that by removing the man of my choice—and God's—from those offices, Deacon. For myself, I, as the Sacristy, have a duty to act as I believe God wishes me to act. As you say, I *am* a steadholder, and, as such, as much His steward as the Sacristy. To defy God's manifest will is a sin in any man, but especially in one called to carry the steadholder's key, and I refuse to do so. If the Church wishes those offices filled, the Sacristy has only to return them to the man God wishes to hold them. Until the Sacristy does so, however, I will *never* nominate a man repugnant to God to hold them! Better that my people should have no priest than a false one!"

"If you refuse to nominate anyone to the pulpit of Burdette Cathedral, then Father Church will make its own choice, My Lord," Allman said in a voice of steel, and Burdette lunged to his feet at last.

"Then do it!" he shouted. He planted his fists on the desk and leaned over it towards the deacon. "Tell them to *do* it," he hissed in a voice more deadly still for its sudden icy chill. "But they cannot compel me to attend services there or to accept any man not of *my* choosing as my chaplain, *Deacon!* We'll see how the people of Grayson who remain true to God react when a steadholder spits on whatever gutless weakling the Sacristy chooses to foist upon Father Church's holy offices!"

"Beware, Steadholder." Allman's voice was less passionate but equally cold. "God denies no man who seeks Him with an open heart. The only path to Hell is that of a man who chooses to cut *himself* off from God, but that path exists, and you set your feet upon it at your peril."

"Get out," Burdette said in a flat, frozen voice. "Go back to your boot-licking masters. Tell them they may fawn on this foreign whore and attempt to pervert the order God has ordained if they will, but that I refuse. Let them profane their own souls if they so choose; they will never take mine into damnation with them!"

"Very well, My Lord," Allman said, and bowed with frozen dignity. "I will pray for you," he added, and strode from the office while Burdette glared after him in fury.

• CHAPTER THIRTEEN

It was late, and Honor wore a silk kimono over her pajamas as she finished the final report, closed the file on her terminal, and tipped back in her comfortable chair with a pensive expression. She rubbed the tip of her nose for a moment, then reached for the cup of cocoa MacGuiness had left on her desk. He'd given her a severe look, then glanced pointedly at the chrono before he withdrew, and she smiled in memory as she sipped the thick, sweet beverage, swiveling her chair back and forth, but she was far from ready for sleep.

Battle Squadron One remained far short of anything she could consider battleworthy, but her own staff was becoming a crisp, responsive machine. Mercedes Brigham's calm, quietly competent personality was exactly the right balance wheel between Commander Bagwell's humorless detail consciousness and Commander Sewell's freewheeling irreverence. Coupled with Paxton's sharp, analytical intelligence, Mercedes, Bagwell, and Sewell, as the staff's senior members, were proving a formidable instrument, responsive to Honor's orders and able to carry out the tasks delegated to it with smooth efficiency.

But a squadron depended on more than its commander's staff, and this one's COs were still making mistakes no one of their seniority should. Which was understandable, since every one of them had been forced up under glass and required to assume ranks for which they simply didn't have the experience. They were still feeling their way into the potential and power of their ships—and the time their flagship was spending in the slip wasn't helping. Lieutenant Commander Matthews

166

and *Terrible*'s engineers were working hard, but she'd displayed an alarming number of minor post-refit problems, just as Yu had half-predicted, and her repairs had restricted the squadron to too many sims and too little time on actual exercises. Add a squadron commander who still woke herself with nightmares upon occasion, and one had an excellent prescription for disaster in combat.

And yet . . .

She took another sip of cocoa and made a face. Terrible as things might be, they were infinitely better than they *had* been, and they were getting steadily better. What she needed to do was make certain they kept *on* getting better, and she ticked off considerations in the orderly files of her memory.

Yu, Matthews, and the Office of Shipbuilding were doing wonders with *Terrible*. There was still a major glitch in her graser fire control—probably because she'd retained her original Havenite energy armament but acquired a brand-new, Manticoran-designed, Grayson-built fire control suite to go with it—yet the yard assured Honor they'd find it in the next few days. The entire experience made her even more deeply appreciative of how patient Mark Sarnow had been with *her* in Hancock, and she was determined to pass that same patience along to Alfredo Yu and the yard dogs laboring on *Terrible*.

Once the last problem was finally rectified, however, she could buckle down to a solid exercise schedule, and she needed to do just that—badly. She'd worked her people hard in the sims and formed some fairly definite impressions of them, but even the best simulations fell short of actual exercises because everyone *knew* they were sims. She knew she herself tended to react differently, however convincing the computers were, and she was firmly convinced that the only way to evaluate any officer's performance was to watch her actually perform, live, in space. She wanted to see just that where her junior admirals were concerned. More, she wanted *them* to see *her* under the same circumstances, and not just because they needed to develop the "feel" for her tactical thinking that only hard, concentrated drilling could produce.

She wondered, sometimes, if someone who threw tantrums might have gotten faster results. She'd served under admirals who gave their thespian talents free rein, playing the role of screaming martinet to goad their juniors, and for some of them, at least, it had worked. But Honor believed the RMN adage Raoul Courvosier had taught her so long ago: that people performed on an entirely different plane for officers who *led* them. That was one reason she wanted to pry *Terrible* free of the yard. She couldn't fault how hard her people were working, but they needed that *esprit de corps*, that sense of a corporate identity, which only sweat and the chance to prove their competence to one another could provide . . . and that came only when their admiral had proven *her* competence to them, as well. Most of her officers were too new to have witnessed, much less participated with her in, the Battle of Blackbird or Second Yeltsin, and all of them knew the RMN had beached her. Until she showed them she still knew her stuff, she would remain an untried quantity, whatever her reputation, and she needed to resolve any lingering doubts.

She still had to watch herself in her dealings with her Grayson officers, as well. Rear Admiral Trailman, for example, clearly harbored some religion-based reservations about the whole notion of women in uniform, but there, at least, her reputation as the woman who'd saved Grayson from Masada was an enormous help. Honor felt a nagging guilt at trading on that reputation—it seemed cynical and calculating—yet she recognized an effective tool when she saw one, and she needed all the tools she could get for this assignment. And it worked. Trailman might find it difficult to treat most female officers as "real" ones, but he accorded Honor a degree of respect few people jumped from captain to admiral in a single bound could expect.

Of course, respect and authority weren't quite the same thing. All properly brought up Grayson men *respected* women, but that didn't mean they accepted that a woman knew what she was doing in a "man's" role. She rather thought that was how Trailman had been prepared to see her . . . until Yanakov suckered him in the sim, at least. Trailman had been livid over the way the junior admiral had rewritten the "rules," and he hadn't much liked the fact that Yu—a mere captain, and an ex-Peep—had saved his bacon. But Honor had to give the balding Grayson his due. However furious he might have been, he'd honestly admitted his own mistakes, and the fact that she hadn't jumped down his throat hadn't hurt. She'd made a point of praising both Yanakov and Yu (though her praise for the former had been tempered by a few trenchant observations on what happened to admirals who were *too* clever), but she'd delivered her analysis of Trailman's response as dispassionately as she could. There'd been no way to avoid criticizing his decisions, yet she'd refused to denigrate him, either before his fellows or in private. He'd made mistakes, and it was her job to tell him so, but she'd always loathed officers who rubbed subordinates' noses in their errors, and her own experience as Mark Sarnow's flag captain had strengthened her views in that regard. The object was to learn from mistakes, not look for whipping boys. If an officer proved truly incompetent, then it was up to her to remove him; in the meantime, she would make darn sure she had a good reason before she came down on anyone hard.

Still, Trailman was probably the weakest link, she mused. He had a reputation as a fighter, but he was short on finesse, and she couldn't decide whether that was simply part of his personality or reflected an underlying lack of confidence. An officer who distrusted her own capability was often inclined to bull right in, preferring to get to close grips where tenacity was at a premium and the ability to think and maneuver became proportionately less important. Trailman's tendency to react first according to The Book also concerned her, but that was hardly grounds for relieving him, and he was an excellent administrator. More than that, his staff and his COs liked and respected him. That both made him more effective and meant they'd resent his removal, and despite any reservations he might retain about her, *Honor* liked him, too. He was forthright and honest, and if she couldn't count on him for brilliance, he possessed bulldog determination in plenty.

Walter Brentworth, for his part, had proven just as dependable and reliable as she'd expected, and if he'd screwed up by seeing what he expected to see once, he'd taken the lesson to heart since. Unlike Trailman, he was completely comfortable serving with female officers in general, not simply Honor herself, and he operated with a precise attention to detail. His failure to keep BatDiv Twelve in closer company before Yanakov sprang his surprise in the sim might have indicated a failure to appreciate the need to rein in Trailman's attack mentality, but if that had been the case, he'd rectified it since. In fact, if he had a weakness at all, it was his very attention to detail. She suspected that was part of what had happened in the sim. He'd been too fixated on lesser responsibilities he should have delegated to his ops officer or his flag captain to stand back and wonder why Yanakov had tried such a seemingly clumsy initial approach.

If he learned to delegate a bit better, he'd go from very good to outstanding, she judged. Even now, she was eminently satisfied with him as her senior division CO, and she'd been right about his reaction to her critique of the sim. He'd been fully aware of his own mistakes, and he'd resented neither Yanakov's part in creating his problems nor Honor's decision to cut him out of the circuit to see how Trailman would respond. More than that, he'd applied the lessons in their next simulated exercise with telling effect, and he seemed to grow progressively more confident with every passing day.

Yet satisfied as she was with Brentworth's performance, she'd found she had a distinct tendency to gloat over the possession of Rear Admiral Yanakov. Judah Yanakov could have been specifically designed as Trailman's antithesis, both physically and temperamentally. He was the youngest of her divisional commanders, short and wiry, with thick auburn hair and gray eyes, and he moved with a sort of half-tamed energy that the taller, stockier Trailman lacked. He had plenty of aggressiveness, but it was balanced by the cold calculation of a professional gambler. He was also a nephew of Bernard Yanakov, Wesley Matthews' predecessor as High Admiral, which made him a cousin of Protector Benjamin, and he seemed to have no sex-based reservations about her capabilities.

Honor despised officers who played favorites, so she made a deliberate effort to avoid doing so in Yanakov's case, yet she trusted his instincts more than Trailman's—or, for that matter, Brentworth's. As he'd proven in the sim, he could get just a bit too inventive, but he was settling down, and seemed to be losing none of his sense of initiative in the process. In fact, the only real problem she had with him was that *he* had problems with Alfredo Yu.

Honor sighed and rubbed her nose again as she frowned at her now blank terminal. All her Grayson officers had their own reasons for eying askance the man who'd virtually destroyed their pre-Alliance navy, but Walter and Trailman seemed to have overcome theirs. Yanakov hadn't—yet—though he worked hard to keep it from affecting him professionally, and she was guiltily aware that his reasons were all too much akin to her own. She'd blamed Yu for Admiral Courvosier's death; Yanakov blamed Yu for killing his uncle, which probably wasn't very surprising. Honor regretted more and more deeply with passing time that she and the previous high admiral had never had the chance to get past their cultural differences, for everything she'd learned of him only seemed to emphasize what a remarkable man he'd been.

But however outstanding High Admiral Yanakov had been, both as an officer and a man, Honor regretted the wedge his death might be driving between his nephew and Alfredo Yu. She'd been a bit surprised when she first realized she felt that way, yet she did. *She* still felt a lingering personal ambiguity towards Yu, and part of her despised herself for it. She ought to be able to overcome it, she told herself yet again. She thought she was getting on top of it—gradually—but it was taking too long, and it was entirely her own fault.

Her frown deepened as she admitted that. Alfredo Yu was one of the most competent officers she'd ever met. His reaction to Yanakov's ambush had been no flash in the pan; that combination of calm refusal to panic and quick thinking was *typical* of him, and Honor's professional side recognized what an asset he was. Worse, she had a treecat who let her feel the emotions behind his impassive facade. She *knew* his regret for what his orders had required of him in Operation Jericho was genuine, just as she'd come to *know* Mercedes was right about his part in what happened to *Madrigal's* people. And because she knew those things, she couldn't quite forgive her own inability to forgive him.

She sighed, and her eyes softened as she raised them to Nimitz. The 'cat snored softly on his perch, but she knew how he would have reacted if he'd been awake. Nimitz had no reservations about Alfredo Yu, yet he saw no reason his person should blame herself because she *did*, and no doubt he would have scolded her—again—for her sense of guilt. Which changed nothing. Yu was an outstanding officer, as capable a flag captain as any admiral could want . . . and probably more qualified than *she* for flag rank. More, he was a good and decent man, who deserved better of her, and she couldn't give it to him. Not yet. And she didn't like being that small and petulant a person.

She sighed again, then stood and lifted Nimitz from his perch. She carried him towards her sleeping cabin, and he stirred sleepily in her arms, half-opening his eyes and reaching up to pat her cheek with one true-hand. She felt his half-awake satisfaction that she was finally turning in and smiled and rubbed his ears with her free hand. She was tired enough she expected no dreams, good or bad, to trouble her tonight, and the squadron—

and its admiral—were in for a long day tomorrow. It was past time she was asleep herself, and she yawned as she turned out the lights behind her.

Three men sat in the comfort of a library lined with endless shelves of old-fashioned books, and the wine in their long-stemmed glasses glowed blood red as their host set the decanter on a sideboard. The moonless night beyond the library windows was spangled with stars and the small, bright jewels of Grayson's orbital farms, and the massive bulk of Burdette House was quiet about them. It was a calm, even a tranquil scene, but there was nothing tranquil about Lord Burdette's blue eyes as he turned from the sideboard to face them.

"So their decision is final?" one man asked, and Burdette scowled.

"It is," he grated. "The Sacristy's become totally subservient to that gutless wonder in the Protector's chair, and it's ready to take Father Church—and all of us—to damnation with it."

The man who'd spoken shifted in his armchair. Burdette's cold eyes moved to his face in silent question, and the other man shrugged irritably.

"I agree the Sacristy has hardly shown the wisdom God's children have a right to expect, William, but Benjamin Mayhew *is* the Protector."

"Oh?" Burdette's lip curled as he gazed at John Mackenzie.

"Oh," Mackenzie replied without giving an inch. Mackenzie Steading was almost as old as Burdette Steading, and, unlike Burdette, the original Mackenzie family had held steading there in direct line of descent since its founding. "Whatever you think of Protector Benjamin, his family's served Grayson well. I don't care to hear him called a 'gutless wonder' . . . by anyone."

Mackenzie's brown eyes were as hard as Burdette's blue ones, and tension hovered in the air until Burdette's second guest cleared his throat.

"My Lords, we serve neither Grayson's interests nor

God's by quarreling." Steadholder Mueller's voice was calm but pointed, and both of the others looked at him for a moment. Then Burdette grunted.

"You're right." He took a swallow of wine, then turned back to Mackenzie. "I won't take it back, John, but I won't say it again, either." Mackenzie nodded curtly, well aware he'd just gotten as close to an apology as the other was capable of making, and Burdette went on. "Nonetheless, I take it you share my dismay at the godless course he seems hell-bent on pursuing?"

"I do." Mackenzie didn't sound happy to agree, but he did, and Burdette shrugged.

"Then the question is what we do about it, isn't it?"

"I don't see a great deal more we *can* do," Mackenzie replied. "We've supported you this far, and I'm sure we'll continue to." He glanced at Mueller, who nodded, then returned his attention to Burdette. "We've all contributed to support the witnesses we've sent south to try to bring 'Lady' Harrington's people to their senses, and I've added my protests to your own before the Sacristy. I haven't hidden my feelings from the Protector, either. But outside our own steadings, our legal recourses are limited. If the Protector and the Sacristy are both committed to this course, we can only trust in God to show them the error of their ways before it's too late."

"That's not enough," Burdette protested. "God expects His people to act, not just to sit around and wait for Him to intervene. Or are you suggesting we simply turn our backs on the Test He's sent us?"

"I didn't say that." Mackenzie's effort to control his own temper was apparent, and he leaned forward, bracing his hands on his knees. "I simply said our options are limited, and I think we've exercised all of them. And, unlike you, I *do* think God will refuse to let His people be led into sin by anyone. Or are you suggesting we simply forget the power of prayer?"

Burdette's teeth grated and his nostrils flared at the ironic bite of Mackenzie's question, and Mackenzie settled back in his chair once more.

"I'm not saying I disagree, William," his tone was more conciliatory, "and I'll continue to support you however I can, but there's no point pretending we can do more than we can."

"But it's not enough!" Burdette reiterated hotly. "This world is consecrated to God. Saint Austin led our fathers here to build a *holy* place under God's law! Men have no right to chop and prune at His law just because some fancy off-world university's convinced the Protector it's not 'fashionable' anymore! Damn it to Hell, man, can't you *see* that?"

Mackenzie's face went very still. He sat silent for a long, tense moment, then stood. He glanced at Mueller, but his fellow steadholder remained seated and gazed down into his glass, avoiding his eyes.

"I share your sentiments," Mackenzie's voice was level, though the effort he made to keep it so was obvious, "but I've had my say and you've had yours. I believe we've done all we can, that we can only trust God to do what more is required. You obviously disagree, and I've no desire to quarrel with you. Under the circumstances, I think perhaps I'd better leave before one of us says something we'll both regret."

"I think you're right," Burdette grated.

"Samuel?" Mackenzie looked at Mueller again, but the other man only gave a silent headshake without looking up. Mackenzie gazed at him for a moment, then inhaled and looked back at Burdette. The two of them exchanged small, coldly correct bows, and Mackenzie turned and walked from the library with a long, anger-quickened stride.

Silence hovered in his wake until Burdette's third guest rose and carried Mackenzie's abandoned wineglass to the sideboard. The crystal click was loud in the stillness as he set it down, and Mueller looked back up at last.

"He's right, you know, William. We've done all we can legally."

"Legally?" the man who'd so far kept silence repeated. "By whose law, My Lord? God's or man's?"

"I don't like the sound of that, Brother Marchant," Mueller said, but his tone was less stern than it might have been, and the cleric shrugged. He had few doubts about Samuel Mueller. Mueller might be too much the calculator to voice his feelings openly, but he was a man of the Faith, as opposed to Protector Benjamin's "reforms" as Marchant or Lord Burdette themselves. And if he also had more worldly motives, well, God worked with whatever tool He required, and Mueller's ambition and resentment of his own authority's diminution could prove potent tools indeed.

"Perhaps not, My Lord," the cleric said after a moment, "and I mean no disrespect, either to you or to Lord Mackenzie." His voice suggested that part, at least, of his statement was a lie. "But surely you agree God's law supersedes that of man?"

"Of course."

"Then if men, be it willfully or in simple error, violate God's law, do not *other* men have a responsibility to correct those violations?"

"He's right, Samuel." The rage in Burdette's voice was thicker and deeper than he'd let Mackenzie hear. "You and John can talk about 'legal' considerations all you want, but look what happened when we tried to exercise our legal rights. That whore Harrington's thugs almost beat Brother Marchant to death for simply speaking God's will!"

Mueller frowned. He'd seen the press coverage of the episode, and he suspected only the Harrington Guard's intervention had saved Marchant. Still, they'd had to do that, hadn't they? Harrington's Sky Domes personnel had led the strong-arm groups which had broken up the demonstrations outside Harrington House, after all. Most people might not have noticed that, but Mueller had, and felt a grudging respect for how she'd hidden her own involvement. Yet the strategy was blatantly obvious to anyone who knew where to look, and if she'd let the mob kill a priest before her very eyes, other people besides Samuel Mueller might look much more closely.

Under those circumstances, letting her subjects lynch Marchant would only have made her own culpability clear and branded her before the rest of Grayson's people as the agent of sin she was.

"Perhaps so," he said finally, "but I still fail to see what more we can do, William. I deeply regret what's happened to Brother Marchant," he nodded to the ex-priest, "but it was all done legally, and—"

"*Legally!*" Burdette spat. "Since when does an upstart like Mayhew have the right to dictate to one of the Keys in his own steading?!"

"Now just a minute, William!" Burdette's question had touched a nerve, and anger flickered in Mueller's eyes— not at his host, but real all the same—and disgust sharpened his voice. "It wasn't just the Protector; it was the entire Sacristy *and* the Chamber! For that matter, most of the other Keys supported the decision when Reverend Hanks brought the writ before us. I agree Mayhew pushed for it, but he covered himself too well for us to make an open fight of it over steadholder privilege. You know that."

"And why did the Keys support it?" Burdette shot back. "I'll tell you why—for the same reason we all sat there like so many gutless eunuchs and let Mayhew ram that infidel bitch down our throats last year! My God, Samuel, the woman was whoring with that foreign scum—what's his name, Tankersley!—even then, and Mayhew *knew* it! But did he tell us? Of course he didn't! He knew not even he could've gotten her past the Keys if he had!"

"I'm not so sure of that," Mueller said grudgingly. "I mean, infidel or no, she *did* save us from Masada."

"Only so her own side could devour us! We knew the Masadans were enemies, so Satan threw something more insidious at us, didn't he? He offered us Harrington as a 'heroine' and the bait of 'modern technology,' and that fool Mayhew swallowed the poison whole! What does it matter whether Masada destroys us by force of arms or Manticore corrupts us by trickery and bribery?"

Mueller took another sip of wine, and his eyes were hooded. He agreed that Benjamin Mayhew's "reforms" were poisoning his world, but he found his host's rampant religious fervor wearing. And dangerous. Burdette was too much the fanatic, and fanatics could be . . . precipitous. Any hasty action might be disastrous—Mayhew and Harrington were too popular, and before their opponents could accomplish anything, the groundwork to undermine that popularity had to be in place—so perhaps it was time for a note of caution.

"And what about the Havenites?" he asked. "If we break with Manticore, what's to keep *them* from conquering us outright?"

"My Lord, Haven would have no interest in us if Manticore hadn't sucked us into their Alliance," Marchant replied before Burdette could. "It's not enough for *Queen* Elizabeth to corrupt us, she had to bring her ungodly foreign war to us, as well!"

"And it was Mayhew who made that possible," Burdette added in a softer, more persuasive voice. "*He* was the wedge, and he did it for his own selfish reasons. For over a hundred years, the Protector's *Council* governed Grayson. That bastard used the 'crisis'—the crisis *he* created in the first place by convincing the Council to consider allying with Manticore—to turn the clock back and force us all to accept 'personal rule' again. Personal rule!" Burdette actually spat on the library's expensive carpet. "The man's a damned *dictator*, Samuel, and you and John want to talk to me about 'legal' options?"

Mueller started to speak, then stopped and took yet another swallow of wine. The implications of Burdette's tirade were frightening, and he wasn't at all certain he shared Marchant's dismissal of Haven's ambitions. On the other hand, he thought suddenly, how likely *was* the People's Republic to strike at an *ex*-ally of Manticore? Wouldn't they be more inclined to leave Grayson alone? To adopt a hands-off policy to encourage *other* Manticoran allies to consider the advantages of neutrality? And intemperate as Burdette's description of the domestic situation might be, there was a core of truth to it. A hard and painful core.

The Council had reduced the Protectorship to figurehead status long before Benjamin Mayhew's birth, and the Conclave of Steadholders had liked it that way, for they had controlled the Council. But Benjamin had remembered something the Keys had forgotten, Mueller thought bitterly. He'd remembered that the people of Grayson still revered the Mayhew name, and in the crisis of the Masadan War, while the Council and Keys had dithered—Mueller's face burned with shame as he recalled his own panic, but he was too honest with himself to deny it—Benjamin had acted swiftly and decisively.

That probably would have been enough to shatter the Council's power by itself, but then he'd survived the Maccabeans' attempted assassination, as well, and Manticore had gone on to destroy the Masadan threat forever, a combination of events which had devastated the old system. No Protector in centuries had been as popular as Benjamin now was, despite his unholy social "reforms," and, Mueller thought bitterly, the Conclave of Steaders had embraced the renewed power of the Protector with enthusiasm. The Chamber's lower house had become almost as irrelevant as the Protectorship itself as the Council secured its control. Now, in alliance with the Protector, *it* held the balance of power in the Chamber, and if it had been both respectful and moderate in its demands so far, it had also made it clear that it intended to be treated henceforth as the Conclave of Steadholders' equal.

And the worst of it was that there seemed to be nothing anyone could *do* about it. Lord Prestwick remained Mayhew's Chancellor. Indeed, he'd become one of Mayhew's champions, claiming that a stronger executive was critical in time of war, which was a direct slap at his fellow steadholders' failure to provide a strong foreign policy. But there'd been no *need* for a foreign policy, a corner of Mueller's brain protested angrily. Not until Manticore had brought its damned war to Yeltsin's Star—and that was Mayhew's fault, not the Keys'!

The Steadholder's head ached, and he massaged his closed eyes while his mind raced. He was a man of the Faith, he told himself. A servant of God who'd never asked to be born into a time of such turmoil. He'd always tried to live by God's will, to meet the Tests God sent him, but why had God chosen to send him *this* Test? All he'd ever wanted was to do God's will and, someday, in God's good time, pass his steading and his power on to his son and his son's sons.

But Benjamin Mayhew wouldn't let him do that, and Mueller knew it. The Protector *couldn't*, for the old tradition of steadholder autonomy was anathema to the ugly new world he strove to build in despite of God's will. His reforms were but the tip of an iceberg whose true peril was obvious to any discerning pilot. To make them work, they must be applied across the length and breadth of Grayson, and enforcing them would require an enormous increase in the Sword's authority. The Protector would intrude more and more deeply into each steading—always politely, no doubt; always with a pious appeal to the rectitude of his actions in the name of "equality"—unless the power of the Sword was broken soon, decisively. And the Havenite War. The need of a wartime leader for unquestioning obedience. That would be another potent weapon in Mayhew's arsenal, and the only way to take that weapon from his hands was to force a break with Manticore. But the only way to do that . . .

He lowered his hands at last and looked at Burdette.

"What do you want of me, William?" he asked bluntly. "Even Reverend Hanks supports the Protector, and whether we like it or not, our world's at war with the most powerful empire in this part of the galaxy. Unless we can make that just—go away—" he made a throwing away gesture with one hand, "we don't dare give him an excuse to crush us in the name of the war effort."

"But this world is God's." Burdette's soft voice shivered with passion, and his blue eyes blazed like sun-struck sapphires. "What do we have to fear from *any* empire if God is our Captain?"

Mueller stared at him, mesmerized by the glitter of those eyes, and felt something stir inside him. A part of him remembered where he'd heard those words before, heard the echo of the Maccabean fanatics and their Masadan masters, but somehow that seemed suddenly less important. His own heart cried out for the certainty of his faith, the comfort of the world he'd inherited from his father and wanted to pass to his sons, and bitter resentment of the way Benjamin Mayhew and Honor Harrington were warping and changing that world reinforced the seductive power singing in Burdette's soft, fiery words.

"What do you want of me?" he repeated more quietly, and Burdette smiled. He held out his glass to Marchant, and the defrocked priest filled it once more. Then the Steadholder sank back into his own chair, and his voice was quiet and persuasive.

"Nothing, Samuel. Nothing at all right now. But think. Mayhew spurned a century of legal precedent to seize power. He spat on an entire way of government so that he could overturn the way of *life* God intended—what loyalty do we owe a man like that?" Mueller gazed at him silently, and Burdette flicked a look up at Marchant, then continued in that same quietly seductive voice.

"We owe him *nothing*, Samuel—but we owe God *everything*. Surely He has the right to expect us to at least try to preserve the world our people spent a thousand years building obedient to His law. And however Mayhew may have deceived the people into following him into sin, somewhere deep inside, *they* know that as well as we do. All they need is leadership, Samuel. Only a reminder of what God expects of godly men . . . and of what happens to those who embrace the ways of sin."

"What sort of a reminder?" Mueller half-whispered, and a strange eagerness—a half-fearful sense that the weapon he needed to restore the world he understood might lie just beyond his fingertips—quivered deep inside him as Burdette smiled.

• CHAPTER FOURTEEN

Honor leaned back with a small, pleased smile as her pinnace dropped planetward. She wasn't in uniform tonight, and she was delighted to have escaped that monkey suit. After a T-year of acculturation, she cheerfully admitted that female Grayson formal attire was more comfortable even than RMN uniform, much less *Grayson* uniform. And it didn't even have a necktie!

She chuckled at the thought and ran her fingers down Nimitz's spine. The 'cat arched his back, luxuriating in the caress, and she felt his own pleased anticipation. Nimitz liked Benjamin Mayhew and his family, who frankly doted on him in return. They owed him—and Honor, of course—their lives, but while Honor was uncomfortable with their gratitude, Nimitz was shamelessly prepared to luxuriate in it. They always laid in a supply of celery for his visits, and then there were Rachel, Theresa, and Jeanette, the older three Mayhew children, who regarded him as the finest stuffed toy in the universe.

The Protector's personal armsmen had actually cringed when his daughters first discovered Nimitz's sinuous agility and willingness to play, for all of them had seen Palace Security's tapes of him ripping out assassins' throats with gory efficiency, but Honor hadn't been concerned. Treecats were sturdy enough to survive anything even a human two-year-old could dish out, and they loved the uncomplicated delight of children's emotions. Watching the Mayhew girls romp and squeal with Nimitz was like watching her own childhood discovery of him, though without the adoption bond, and she'd grown resigned to his abandonment anytime the kids were up.

Of course, tonight's backdrop was a bit grimmer than for most of her visits, she thought more soberly. She hadn't left her flagship in over a month, but she'd kept abreast of events planet-side, and Greg Paxton had helped her interpret them. She'd learned a lot from the intelligence officer, for he had the rare ability actually to stand back from his own cultural background and the unconscious acceptance of his birth mores which any member of any society took everywhere with him. He approached his world like the scholar he was, intent not simply upon seeing but on *understanding*, and in a way, his analytical viewpoint made him almost as much of an outside observer as Honor.

And, like her, Paxton was deeply troubled by Steadholder Burdette's stubborn refusal to accept the Sacristy's decision on Edmond Marchant. More, he'd pulled together some other alarming indicators she would otherwise have missed. Like how the number of outside protesters being shipped into Harrington Steading had actually increased despite her absence. She'd known that from Colonel Hill's reports, but what she *hadn't* considered was the cost behind the effort. The "protests" were increasingly well organized, their propaganda steadily more sophisticated, and the numbers suggested the protesters' hidden patrons were pouring even more financial support into the effort.

That last point was, in many ways, the most alarming, for it indicated a powerful support structure that was unpleasantly capable of self-concealment. So far, even Colonel Hill had been able to identify only one or two of its members, and they all seemed little more than middlemen.

But who was behind the demonstrations was an almost minor concern compared to their effect. They weren't making any ground in Harrington itself. In fact, Honor's subjects were growing more exasperated with them, not less, yet, perversely, the Harringtons' anger only enhanced their impact in *other* steadings. The news services were covering them, and the fact that the Harrington Guard and HCP had to provide permanent guards to keep her people from assaulting the demonstrators only gave their protests more weight with those already prepared to have reservations about a female steadholder.

Those protests were a constant, nagging irritant, but by themselves, they seemed unlikely to have any major influence on people who weren't already inclined to accept their viewpoint. Unfortunately, Paxton had picked up on another and far more worrisome factor: a handful of steadholders who were coming out in very guarded support of the demonstrations.

That was a new element. Aside from Burdette, who'd made no secret of his feelings from the moment Marchant was attacked, the Keys had initially maintained a dignified silence. Even those who hadn't cared to have a woman in their midst had apparently felt that agitation aimed at any steadholder was an affront to *all* steadholders. But that was changing. Steadholder Mueller had been the first to suggest publicly that perhaps there were two sides to the dispute. Steadholder Harrington was, after all, foreign born, a stranger to Grayson society, who'd refused to join the Church; under the circumstances, it was only natural for Graysons worried about seeing so much power in the hands of an outworlder to express their perfectly natural fears.

It had been a very mild statement, but it had also been the first breach in the united silence of the Keys, and four more steadholders—Lords Kelly, Michaelson, Surtees, and Watson—had chimed in since. Like Mueller, their comments had been too restrained for anyone to call attacks, yet their very restraint lent them a dangerous aura of reasoned argument. People who *weren't* inclined to react with unthinking hostility to the thought of change were more likely to listen to—and ponder—them, particularly when they came from leaders regarded with the deference Grayson extended to its steadholders.

At least the Church was holding firm, but even there Paxton had found signs of subtle erosion. Reverend Hanks and the Sacristy had made the Church's position clear, and none of the Church's lower clergy had opposed the Elders' disciplinary actions against Marchant. But as Paxton had pointed out, there was a vast difference between simply not opposing the Sacristy and *supporting* it. A significant number of priests had chosen to maintain a dignified silence, and there was an ominous correlation between their churches' locations and the steadholders lending the protests such calm and reasonable support.

Honor felt a bit guilty over the time her intelligence officer was spending on something which had nothing whatsoever to do with the military situation, and she hoped he was being pessimistic, but his conclusions worried her. Polls showed the vast majority of Grayson's people continued to give their Protector overwhelming support, but a growing percentage had begun admitting to at least some reservations where *she* was concerned. After all, where there was so much smoke . . .

The balance was shifting, she thought, gazing out the view port. Not quickly or suddenly, but with slow, insidious gradualism. It was nothing overt, nothing anyone could put a finger on—or fight effectively—but it was there, like a thunderstorm on the horizon, and she hoped fervently that she and Paxton were both more alarmed than they ought to be.

Benjamin Mayhew and his family awaited her in the same private dining room where the Maccabeans had tried to kill them all. It wasn't the first time Honor had dined here since that day, yet she felt a small, familiar chill as she entered the room. The carpet which had been soaked with so much blood had been replaced and the bullet-spalled walls had been repaired, but the furnishings were all the same, and she wondered yet again how the Mayhews dealt with the memories when they ate here every night.

Probably they scarcely even thought about it now. Almost four years had passed, and there was a limit to how long any memory, however traumatic, could last before familiarity wore its jagged edges smooth. That reflection and its implications for her own on-going, if blessedly less frequent, bouts of depression struck a spark deep inside her, but she had no time to consider it before a tiny woman called her name with a smile.

"Honor!" Katherine Mayhew, Benjamin's first wife, hurried forward to greet her with a shocking lack of decorum. Of course, this was scarcely a state occasion, as Benjamin's invitation had made clear, but Honor *was* one of the Protector's vassals and a certain amount of standing on ceremony was indicated when she entered his presence.

No one seemed to care, however. Benjamin himself waved to her from across the room without bothering to stand—another gross violation of etiquette for any Grayson male when a woman entered a room—and Rachel, a sturdy six-year-old and the terror of the Palace nursery, made a beeline for Honor in her mother's wake.

"*Nimitz!*" she demanded, and the 'cat bleeked happily, then launched himself from Honor's shoulder. Rachel landed on her posterior with carpet-thumping energy and a crow of delight as ten kilos of treecat catapulted into her waiting arms, and her sisters came swarming forward.

Elaine Mayhew followed them, and Honor noted that Benjamin's junior wife was pregnant again. She was also much younger than Katherine, and she'd been shy and reserved with Honor at first, but now she simply gave her guest a cheerful wave, then waded into the mad swirl of little girls and treecat which was already building to near riot proportions.

"We'll never get them sorted out before dinner." Katherine chuckled.

"I'm sorry. He really does know how to behave better than this, but—" A squeal of delight drowned Honor's apology as Nimitz scurried up Theresa's back, braced velveted true-hands and hand-feet on the crown of her head, and vaulted over her to vanish under a couch. All three girls raced after him—"Catch-the-'Cat" (especially with things like furniture, parents, guests, and stoic armsmen for an obstacle course) was one of their favorite games—and Honor shrugged helplessly. "He likes children," she finished in a wry voice, and Katherine laughed out loud.

"I know he does, and they love him. Don't worry. They'll wear themselves out in a little bit, and we should have at least a lull for the meal. Come on."

Honor followed her over to Benjamin, who rose and clasped her hand firmly. It was her first visit to the Palace since High Admiral Matthews had offered her a commission, and despite the Protector's cheerful demeanor, she felt an unusually searching weight in his eyes as they examined her. Then he gave a little nod and relaxed.

"I'm glad to see you looking so well," he murmured through the racket of three children and a treecat, and Honor smiled a bit more crookedly than her artificial facial nerves could fully account for. Benjamin Mayhew's role in life had made him more adroit than most at concealing his feelings, but Honor didn't need Nimitz to guess what lay behind his scrutiny. Had her damages been *that* obvious, she wondered? And even as she asked herself, she knew the answer.

"Thank you," was all she said, and he smiled again.

"Have a seat." He waved at a comfortable chair, and looked up as his daughters thundered by in pursuit of a cream-and-gray blur of fur. "We figure it'll take about thirty minutes to burn off their initial energy charge, so I ordered dinner for nine."

"I really am sorry about—" Honor began again, and he shook his head.

"If we weren't happy to see it, Elaine would nip it in the bud," he assured her as Elaine forged past in a gallant effort to keep up with the children. Only Jeanette was "hers" in a biological sense, but it made absolutely no difference to any of them, and Honor had to admit that Grayson children had secure childhoods. Any Grayson child had as many mothers as her father had wives, yet it went further than that. The brutality of the Grayson planetary environment, especially in the first terrible generations, had created an infant mortality rate which still harrowed the Grayson soul. They regarded children as the most precious gift God had ever created, and that produced an awesomely nurturing mode of childrearing. Honor suspected Elaine was better at it than Katherine, for she was far more "traditional" than her tiny fellow wife. Katherine was the activist (inasmuch as Grayson *had* female activists yet) who carried the weight of the social and political duties of Grayson's First Consort, but she, too, found time for the children with an apparent ease that astonished Honor. It *couldn't* be as easy as Katherine made it look—Honor knew how full her own career made *her* day—but somehow she managed it.

"Benjamin's right," Katherine said now. "Nimitz is their favorite guest, and they haven't seen him in weeks. If he can stand it, we can."

"Nimitz," Honor said feelingly, "thinks they're the greatest thing since celery."

By that time, Nimitz, children, and Elaine, trailed by a pair of armsmen, had vanished through another door into the family's private quarters. The noise level dropped dramatically, and Benjamin chuckled.

"They seem to reciprocate his feelings," the Protector observed, and Honor sank into the indicated chair at his repeated wave. It was odd, she thought. This man was the direct ruler of an entire planet whose social mores were utterly alien to those of her home world, yet she felt completely relaxed and comfortable in his presence. Was it because Grayson *wasn't* her world by birth? Because she hadn't been raised to regard Benjamin Mayhew as *her* ruler? Or was it simpler than that? They'd been through a lot with each other in a relatively short time, as the universe measured such things.

They *trusted* one another, and she wondered, suddenly, how many people the Protector of Grayson felt genuinely able to trust. The question took on added point in light of her own discussions with Gregory Paxton.

"Well," Benjamin said, breaking into her thoughts, "how do you like your new job, Admiral Harrington?"

"Better than I was afraid I might," she said honestly. "I wasn't too certain High Admiral Matthews was right to offer it to me at first, but—"

She gave a small shrug, and Benjamin nodded.

"I was a little unhappy about letting him ask you," he confessed, "but I think I'm glad I did. You look better, Honor. Much better." Katherine nodded from her own chair, facing Honor's, and Honor shrugged again.

"I *am* better, I think," she admitted.

"And you're satisfied with your squadron?"

"Not yet—but I will be!" Her smile thanked the Protector for the change of subject. "We just finished our first full-scale exercise against High Admiral Matthews and BatRon Two, and he handed us our heads. I had a surprise planned for him, but our execution fell apart. On the other hand, he's had four times as long to work up, and my people are all looking forward to a rematch."

"So you're satisfied with your officers?" There was a subtle emphasis in Benjamin's question, and Honor answered it with a nod.

"I am. High Admiral Matthews was right when he said they needed experience, but they're all working hard, and I'm completely satisfied with my flag captain." Which, she reflected, was true . . . or would be, if she could just get over her lingering, irrationally equivocal feelings. "Give me another two months, and I'll back them against any Manty"—she grinned as she used the word—"squadron you want to name."

"Good!" Benjamin returned her smile, and a last vestige of doubt disappeared from deep inside him. Despite the reports, he'd continued to worry that he might have let Matthews push him into pressing her into GSN uniform too soon, but her almond eyes reassured him.

Shadows still lurked there, but the ghosts had retreated. This was once more the woman who'd saved his family and his world—a naval officer who'd refound the wellsprings of her capability and in the process, perhaps, found herself again, as well.

"Good," he repeated in a more serious voice, and saw her gaze sharpen. "High Admiral Matthews received formal notification from your—I mean, the Manticoran—Admiralty this afternoon. They'll be sending their last two squadrons of dreadnoughts forward to support Admiral White Haven next week."

"I'm surprised they waited so long," Honor said after a moment. "The Peeps have been shoring up the systems around Trevor's Star ever since they stopped him at Nightingale. The pressure to reinforce him has to be heavy."

"It is. I understand Admiral Caparelli also plans to send up two or three squadrons from Manticore's Home Fleet, as well."

"Ah?" Honor crossed her legs and rubbed her nose pensively. "That sounds like they're planning a fresh offensive," she murmured.

"You think they shouldn't?"

"I beg your pardon?" Honor blinked and looked at the Protector.

"I asked if you thought they shouldn't." She raised an eyebrow, and he shrugged. "You sounded a bit . . . oh, doubtful, I suppose."

"Not doubtful, Sir. Thoughtful. I was just wondering whether or not they plan to hit Nightingale again." It was Benjamin's turn to quirk an eyebrow, and she smiled. "Admiral White Haven has been known, on occasion, to, ah, do the unexpected. The Peep fleet base at Nightingale is certainly an important target, but since he knows they know that as well as he does, he might choose to use it for a little misdirection. After all, his real objective is Trevor's Star, and they have to have reinforced Nightingale pretty heavily after his last attack, so if he can convince them he intends to hit them there again and then launch his actual attack someplace *else*—" She broke off, and Benjamin smiled in understanding.

"Well, I think we can safely leave it in his hands, whatever he plans," he observed, and Honor nodded in agreement. "In the meantime, I understand at least one of the Home Fleet squadrons will pay us a visit in passing. High Admiral Matthews has been asked to set up a few days of war games to help it shake down before it joins Admiral White Haven."

"Good! We've exercised with Admiral Suarez, but we can use a new 'Aggressor Force.' Maybe their admiral will have a fresh trick or two to keep us on our toes."

"I'm sure he'll try," Katherine observed dryly.

"I'm sure you're right," Honor agreed, but her tone had changed. "Speaking of keeping people on their toes," she went on more slowly, "I've been a little worried about some of the things I've been hearing about events dirtside here on Grayson."

"Burdette and his fellow idiots, you mean?" Benjamin snorted. She nodded, her expression serious, and he frowned. "I know he's got pretensions of rabble rousing, but so far all he's done is bluster, Honor."

"Maybe, but he's also getting more strident," she countered. "And I can't help thinking that people who take such strong public stances tend to paint themselves into corners and become prisoners of their own rhetoric."

"You mean that he may go so far he has no choice but to go still further?" Katherine asked.

"Something like that. But—" Honor paused, then frowned. "I'm sure you have better sources than I do, but Gregory Paxton and I have been keeping an eye on things as well as we can from off-planet, and I've been in regular contact with Howard and Colonel Hill. And from our perspective, it looks like Lord Burdette may not be the only problem."

"Oh?" Benjamin crossed his own legs, inviting her to continue with his eyes, and she sighed.

"It seems to us that there's more than one strand working out down here, Sir. Lord Burdette and the demonstrators in Harrington are one thread—the loud, public, one you might say—but there's something else going on, as well. Something a lot, well, quieter."

"You mean Mueller, Michaelson, and company?" Benjamin asked.

"Yes, Sir." Honor couldn't quite hide her relief at the Protector's response. He smiled, but it was more of a grimace, really, and she went on carefully. "I don't want to sound paranoid, but to me, they actually seem more dangerous than someone like Marchant or Burdette. They're so much less strident people may actually listen to them. And once people start listening to 'moderate' condemnations, the door's open for the extremists to begin sounding rational to them, as well."

"I see your point," Katherine said. She looked at her husband and frowned. "Didn't you discuss this with Prestwick last week?"

"I did, indeed," Benjamin confirmed. "And at the moment, neither we nor Planetary Security see any immediate cause for concern."

"*Immediate* cause?" his wife repeated, and he smiled sourly.

"You and Lady Harrington have nasty, suspicious minds, Cat," he said, "and you both pay too much attention to qualifiers. Yes, I said 'immediate,' as in 'things may change.'"

"How big a factor do you think the Sacristy's decision to defrock Marchant may be?" Honor asked. He cocked an eyebrow at her, and she shrugged. "Greg and I have been trying to get a read on that, but we don't have enough input. All the same, I'm uneasy about the ammunition it offers the reactionaries, and the last poll I saw was . . . worrying."

"The decision to discipline Marchant was Reverend Hanks' to make," Benjamin said after a moment. "He discussed it with me, since the Protectorship is technically the executive arm of the Church, but his decision to go forward with it was made only after a formal request from the majority of the Sacristy to do so. I suspect he had something to do with that majority's decision to petition him in the first place, but I make it a rule never to interfere in the Church's internal affairs. Given the amount of fire I've drawn over purely secular matters, the last thing I need is to look as if I'm strong-arming the Church into anything!"

He paused until Honor nodded her understanding, then went on.

"Having said that, I agree with his reasoning. Not only was Marchant's behavior unforgivable in any churchman, but it was also a deliberate act of defiance which the Sacristy simply could not overlook. He *had* to be slapped down—hard—before any core of clerical conservatives congealed behind him. I'm aware—as I'm sure you are, Honor, given that you have Paxton working on this— that there's been a sort of passive resistance from some churchmen, but now they have to restrict themselves to actions which don't openly support the error for which Marchant was disciplined or face the same consequences. I think that had to be established, and now that it has, Reverend Hanks is concentrating on starving the fire of fuel, on the one hand, and encouraging the more progressive clergy to speak out on behalf of reason on the other."

Honor nodded, but she also found her right hand playing with the Harrington Key. She grimaced and made herself let go of it.

"And the opinion polls, Sir? It seems to me—and to Greg—that the Marchant decision's been a factor in the numbers. Most of the people who admit to second thoughts about my, ah, suitability as a steadholder indicate that their doubts hinge on my 'infidel' status."

"No doubt," Benjamin acknowledged. "But your own people aren't worried by it, and, frankly, what citizens of other steadings think about you is largely irrelevant. Reverend Hanks and I both anticipated that there'd be a negative initial effect on public opinion, but we've got time for it to smooth out again, and the fact that you've never hidden your own religious convictions should help.

That's the sort of personal integrity Graysons appreciate, once they fully consider it." He shook his head. "Under the circumstances, I think the Reverend's action was a wise one, and, as I say, at least it's told the reactionaries there's a line the Sacristy won't tolerate their crossing."

"I only wish there hadn't been any need for a line in the first place," Honor worried. "I don't like the thought of serving as the focus for all this craziness." She shook her head, irritated by her own choice of words. "What I mean, Sir, is that I regret *providing* a focus for it."

"Honor," Benjamin said quietly, "what *I* regret is having put you in a position where idiots determined to freeze my planet somewhere in the dark ages can attack you for being better than they are."

"I didn't mean—" Honor began with a blush, but he interrupted her gently.

"I understand exactly what you meant. And you're right; you *have* become the focus of the reactionaries. When I first shanghaied you as a steadholder, I told you we needed you as an example and a challenge, and I was right. But what I didn't warn you about—because I hadn't fully considered it myself—was that as an example of what women can and should aspire to, you'd also become the target of every idiot who insists women *can't* be such things. I regret that. At the same time, honesty compels me to admit that even if I had considered it, I wouldn't have let it stop me from drafting you . . . and knowing, as I now do, that your own sense of duty wouldn't have let you turn me down would only have made me feel guilty. It wouldn't have stopped me, because we *do* need you, and I have a responsibility as Protector of Grayson to see to it that we have you." Honor's blush darkened, and he shook his head at her. "But the fact is that if they didn't have you, the reactionaries would only find some other rallying point. People determined to stand in the path of progress can always find some emotional hook to hang their opposition on. You happen to be the hook for this particular bunch of idiots because they see you as the most dangerous person on Grayson, and, from their perspective, they're absolutely right. You are."

"I am?" Honor asked in surprise.

"You are," Benjamin repeated. "You're a hero to our people, even the ones who have doubts about the social reforms, which gives you a dangerous 'constituency' far beyond the bounds of your own steading. The number who have doubts about you may be growing just now, but the majority still sees you as both a woman and an officer who saved our world from our hereditary enemies, which undercuts our society's notions that women are weaker and must be protected. You've done an outstanding job as a steadholder, which presents an intolerable challenge to conservative steadholders who believe no woman could ever do *their* job. And you're an 'infidel' who not only respects and protects the Church in your steading but who's actually studied our Faith so well you can trade citations with a bigot like Marchant and pin his ears back. When you add all of that together, there's not a reactionary on the planet who doesn't see you— you personally, Honor Harrington—as the direct personification of every challenge to his position and pet bigotries, and it's all my fault for dragging you into it."

Honor sat silent, gazing deep into his eyes, then looked at Katherine, who nodded wryly in agreement.

"Sir—Benjamin—I don't want to provide that kind of focus," she repeated finally. He started to speak, but she raised a hand. "Not because I don't want people to hate me. Because I don't want to be the fulcrum they use to attack your reforms."

"If you weren't here, they'd just find another rallying point," Benjamin said again. "You happen to be the key as things stand, and, as it happens, you're a very *good* key from my perspective. Despite any slippage in the polls, you'd have to screw up in some truly spectacular fashion before you became a negative factor, and you're not the sort of person who screws up." He grinned. "Frankly, having the lunatics trying to use *you* as the 'fulcrum,' as you put it, is a vast relief to me. If you're going to be so damned bighearted that you don't blame me for putting you in the middle of such a mess, then for the Tester's sake, don't blame yourself for *being* there!"

"But—" Honor began, then stopped herself with another crooked smile. "All right, I'll shut up and be good. But you *are* keeping an eye on things?"

"Do you keep an eye on enemy force appreciations, Admiral Harrington?" Benjamin asked. She nodded with a wry grin of understanding, and he nodded back. "So do I. The sneaky bastards may surprise me from time to time, but not because I'm not paying attention, I assure you. Fair?"

"Fair, Sir," Honor said.

"Good! Because—" the Protector grinned and cocked an ear as a sudden ruckus headed their way from the nursery "—I think the holy terrors are returning to base, and if we can catch them, it's just about time for dinner!"

• CHAPTER FIFTEEN

Citizen Vice Admiral Esther McQueen hadn't been told Operation Stalking Horse's full purpose, but she knew how hard-pressed the Navy was before Trevor's Star. That suggested Stalking Horse was *very* important, given the strength of her own task force. Not, she corrected herself sourly without looking up from her display, that Task Force Thirty was truly "hers." She was grateful that the Committee of Public Safety had removed the Legislaturalist officer corps from her path, but that didn't mean she liked having one of its lap dogs sitting on her own flag bridge to "oversee" her operations.

She slid that thought back into a well-hidden mental cupboard before she turned from her plot and looked across at Citizen Commissioner Fontein with a candor that was careful to conceal its resentment. *One of these days*, she promised herself. *One of these days . . .*

Fontein smiled at her with his habitual air of slight befuddlement over all things naval, and the satisfaction it woke in her eyes irritated him. He no more enjoyed being thought a fool—especially by someone who hid it so poorly—than the next man. On the other hand, he'd worked hard to convince McQueen he was only one more ignorant Prole who'd risen to his level of incompetence, and he had no intention of revealing how well he actually understood her command's routine operations . . . or how much more thoroughly than she he understood her mission and its implications.

State Security had selected Erasmus Fontein carefully for McQueen's commissioner, though Secretary

Saint-Just had disliked letting him go. Fontein was a wizened little man who looked like someone's harmless uncle, but appearances were deceiving. Most of the citizen commissioners (and, of course, one had to call them all "Citizen" today, Fontein thought dourly; "Prole" was, after all, a plutocratic, elitist denigration) came from the ranks of those who'd most hated the Legislaturalists before the Harris Assassination. In some cases their hatred had been a reasoned thing stemming from the inequities of the old order, but people were people. Most of the Committee's official spies had hated the old regime not on the basis of reason, but solely because they'd been losers under it. Too many of them took a fierce satisfaction in cracking the whip now that it was in their hands, despite the fact that the officers they were charged with overseeing were no more the old regime's minions than *they* were. An officer was an officer, and if they couldn't avenge themselves on the ones they believed had injured them, then they would assuage their hatred by sneering at the ones they *could*.

To a certain extent, that attitude was fine with StateSec and the Committee, neither of whom trusted the military, anyway. The animosity between the Navy's officers and the citizen commissioners both warned those officers that anything which even *looked* like treason would be fatal and insured that they and the commissioners were unlikely to join forces against the new regime.

Unfortunately, there were officers, like Esther McQueen, whose leashes required particularly deft handlers. Her political masters had no doubt where her loyalty lay; they *knew* it lay solely with herself, but she was also, by almost any measure, the best flag officer they had left. They needed her skills, yet the very intelligence which made her so useful meant a clumsy watchdog would be no match for her . . . and that she would maneuver carefully against any commissioner whose capabilities she had cause to respect.

Which was the reason for Fontein's assignment. His

harmless façade concealed a computer's dispassionately amoral mercilessness, and unlike most of the citizen commissioners, he'd done well under the old regime. Indeed, he'd been a major in Saint-Just's old Office of Internal Security, where he'd specialized in keeping an eye on the military. But he'd hungered to do still better, and Major Fontein, whose familiarity with naval operations had been invaluable when Saint-Just and Pierre structured the Harris Assassination so as to implicate the Navy, had been promoted to brigadier when the SS succeeded InSec.

Saint-Just would much preferred to have used a man of his talents to head one of the planetary SS surveillance forces, but the combination of his competence and finely honed paranoia with an in-depth military background McQueen had no idea he possessed made him uniquely valuable as her watchdog.

"So the operation is on schedule, Citizen Admiral?" he asked now in his most undangerous voice, and McQueen nodded.

"It is, Citizen Commissioner. We'll hit the Minette alpha wall almost exactly on time."

"Excellent, Citizen Admiral. I'm sure the Committee will be pleased."

"I'm glad you think so, Citizen Commissioner," McQueen replied, and returned her attention to her plot as fifty-five ships of the People's Navy, headed by the sixteen superdreadnoughts of Battle Squadrons Seven and Twelve, hurtled through hyper space at an apparent n-space velocity of just over thirteen hundred times light-speed.

Vice Admiral of the Red Ludwig Stanton, Royal Manticoran Navy, suppressed an urge to yawn as he carried his coffee cup over to HMS *Majestic*'s master plot and stood gazing down at the light dots of his command.

Every unit of Task Force Minette-01 rode comfortably in orbit around Everest, the single habitable planet of the Minette System. It looked dreadfully complacent, even to him, but his dreadnought flagship's combat information center was tied into an FTL sensor net which covered the entire system. Nothing larger than a cutter could penetrate that kind of coverage under power without detection, and the outer shell of platforms was more than a light-hour out from the system's G3 primary. Using manned vessels as pickets would only have dispersed his strength while adding nothing to his surveillance capabilities, so his destroyers and heavy cruisers were tucked in close, able to respond to any threat in company with his half squadron of dreadnoughts.

It irked Stanton to be this far from the action while Admiral White Haven's forces skirmished back and forth with the main Peep fleet between Nightingale and the Alliance's advanced base at Thetis. Minette wasn't exactly of vital strategic importance. It served as an advanced picket, helping the enormous Grendelsbane fleet base cover the Alliance's southern flank against the Peep bases in Treadway and Solway, but those systems had been stripped of mobile elements as White Haven's offensive headed for Trevor's Star, and their *im*mobile fixed defenses posed no threat. Stanton agreed that Minette's billion inhabitants had to be protected—the Minetians were charter members of the Alliance, and the Star Kingdom had a responsibility to look out for them—but his four ships of the wall represented a lot of firepower to waste a hundred and fifty light-years from the real action.

He sipped more coffee and watched the light dots of impeller-drive freighters plying back and forth between Minette's two asteroid belts and Everest's orbital smelters. Minette's industry was unsophisticated, but the system was an important source of raw materials and heavy industrial products, and there'd been plans, once, to upgrade its defenses by adding a powerful shell of orbital fortresses around Everest itself. Like much else, however, that project had been overtaken by the war. Although it required massive fixed defenses to cover the repair and maintenance bases that supported the Fleet in wartime, they were only built during peacetime. Once the fighting actually started, they cost too much, for not even the Star Kingdom could afford to build *everything*.

It was remarkable that the prewar arms race hadn't wrecked the Manticoran economy, Stanton mused. Although it had been a boom for the armaments industry and done amazing things for applied research, the monetary cost had been staggering. Only the Star Kingdom's enormously productive industrial base and vast merchant marine, coupled with its control of the Manticore Worm Hole Junction, had given it the wealth to absorb such huge peacetime military budgets without major disruptions.

It was getting worse now that the war had actually begun. Taxes and toll fees on the Junction's merchant shipping had already been raised twice. No doubt they'd be going up yet again soon, and finding the trained manpower to simultaneously crew the Fleet and merchant marine *and* sustain the work force might become a problem, but things might have been far worse. No one else in the Peeps' path had possessed the capability to build a war machine that might stand up to them. Only Manticore had been able to do it . . . and even then only with the Liberal and Progressive Parties screaming like gelded hexapumas at "diverting" so many tax dollars into "alarmist, unproductive military hardware."

Well, Stanton thought grimly, only a thin shell of Peep bases still stood between Admiral White Haven's "unproductive military hardware" and Trevor's Star, the single nexus of the Manticore Junction controlled by the People's Republic, and on his way there, White Haven had decisively blunted the Peeps' overwhelming prewar advantage in ships of the wall. At the same time, Stanton admitted, the Peeps had yet to lose a truly vital system. White Haven's capture of Sun-Yat and its major shipyards had hurt them (and, ultimately, with proper technical upgrades, would no doubt *help* Manticore), but Sun-Yat's loss was only a flea bite against the military infrastructure they'd spent fifty years building. Which explained why the Alliance could no longer divert capacity to fortifying its rear areas. It *had* to concentrate on the ships to take the war to the Peeps. And, as certain elements of BuPlan often pointed out, those same starships would also be the most mobile and flexible means of responding to any counteroffensive the Peeps managed to launch.

Unfortunately, the vice admiral thought sourly, even the most mobile starship could be in only one place at a time, and those tied down on picket duty were effectively withdrawn from offensive ops. Worse, the very fact that White Haven had cut so deep left the Alliance with even more volume to protect, and while Stanton much preferred the strain that imposed to the alternative, they were getting dangerously thin in some areas.

He grimaced at the familiar thought and ambled back to his command chair. He couldn't avoid the conclusion that White Haven was right, that this penny-packet dispersal of ships of the wall hurt the Alliance more than it deterred the Peeps. Manticore was on the offensive— for now, at least—and White Haven *needed* those ships to maintain his momentum. The Admiralty ought to stop frittering away detachments in every hole-in-the-wall system and concentrate larger forces in nodal positions responsible for covering several systems each.

Minette itself was an ideal example of what was wrong with the RMN's current strategy. TF M-01 was strong enough to quash any thoughts of a hit-and-run Peep raid, but if the Republic managed to send in a real offensive, Stanton could never stop it. With fewer but more powerful forces covering larger spheres of space, counterattacks could easily squash any Peep activities in the Alliance's rear and simultaneously free dozens of ships of the wall for White Haven, which would let him keep the Peeps far too busy fighting to protect the heart of their empire to poke any hornets' nests in the Alliance's rear areas, anyway.

Vice Admiral Stanton sighed and shook his head, then

stood and stretched. It was late, he was tired, and he'd drunk entirely too much coffee, and that probably explained his moodiness. It was time to turn in and hope things looked better after a good night's sleep.

"Coming up on translation in forty-five minutes, S—Citizen Admiral."

Citizen Vice Admiral Diego Abbot concealed a grimace as his ops officer corrected herself. The only individuals the People's Navy was allowed to call "Sir" or "Ma'am" these days were its citizen commissioners, and while Abbot was no Legislaturalist, there was such a thing as carrying egalitarianism too damned far. Military discipline *required* a certain degree of autocracy, and he resented the constant reminder that he was effectively junior to someone else even on his own flag deck. Especially when the someone in question had been an environmental tech (and *not*, Abbot thought nastily, a particularly good one) one bare T-year before. Not that he had an intention of letting Citizen Commissioner Sigourney recognize his resentment . . . assuming the woman had the intelligence to do so.

"Thank you, Sarah." Like many PN admirals, Abbot had begun making it a habit to use his officers' first names rather than play the "citizen" game with them. He would have avoided such familiarity under the old regime, but it was far better than the comic-opera formality of "Citizen Commander This" and "Citizen Lieutenant That." Besides, it contributed to an "us against them" mentality that made them less likely to try to curry favor with StateSec by turning informer for Sigourney and her like. Or he hoped it did, anyway.

Citizen Commander Hereux nodded in response to his thanks, and he rechecked Task Force Twenty's alignment one last time in his plot. His command was marginally less powerful than Esther McQueen's, but it ought to face lighter opposition, as well, and he was confident of his ability to complete the first stage of Stalking Horse. It would be nice to know *why* he was completing it—

if nothing else, he could have worked up better contingency plans in case something blew up in his face—but the Committee of Public Safety had decreed that the Navy would operate on a strict need-to-know basis, and State Security, not Fleet HQ, decided just how much any admiral needed to know. *Sigourney* probably knew the real objective, but that was precious little consolation. The commissioner lacked the wit to make alternative plans even if she'd had the initiative to consider the need for them.

Abbot finished checking his formation, then sat back in his command chair, crossed his legs to display somewhat more assurance than he could quite feel operating blind this way, and glanced at Hereux.

"We'll send the task force to general quarters in another thirty minutes, Sarah."

"Aye, Citizen Admiral," she replied, and this time he saw the corner of her mouth quirk in wry, bitter amusement at the title.

Rear Admiral of the Green Eloise Meiner leapt from her shower, snatched a towel about herself, and lunged for the com, for the attention signal was the piercing wail of an emergency message. Water runneled off her to soak the decksole as she dashed into her sleeping cabin, but her curse of irritation died unspoken as the sudden, atonal howl of HMS *Hector*'s GQ alarm drowned even the com's wail.

She punched the audio-only acceptance key. Its activation automatically shut down the GQ alert in her quarters, and the silence was a vast relief, but she knew it was going to be an illusory one as her chief of staff appeared on the screen. Commander Montague's expression was strained, and Meiner deliberately made her voice calm and level.

"Yes, Adam?"

"We've just detected multiple hyper footprints, Ma'am." Montague cleared his throat, and his own voice was a shade calmer when he continued. "So far we make it fifty point sources, Ma'am. Looks like maybe fourteen or fifteen ships of the wall with about the same number of battlecruisers. The rest are small fry—light cruisers and tin cans."

"Locus?" Meiner asked more sharply.

"Thirty light-minutes out, Ma'am—two-zero-point-five from the task force, bearing zero-five-niner zero-zero-eight relative from the primary. We're working their vector now. Looks like they made a nice, gentle transit, but they're heading in at four hundred gees. Assuming they make straight for the planet with turnover at about one-eight-four million klicks, they'll come to rest relative to Candor at effective range zero in five-point-three-niner hours."

"Understood." Meiner ran a hand over her soaking hair and her mind raced. Her task force consisted of only twelve battlecruisers and their screen, which the Admiralty regarded as adequate protection for a system as far behind the line as Candor. Unfortunately, the Admiralty appeared to have been wrong.

Damn it to hell, what did the Peeps think they were *doing?* She had no idea how they'd pried a force this big loose from the fighting around Nightingale and sent it this far to the rear. For that matter, *why* had they done it? Candor was a hundred and fifty light-years behind the front, so they had to know there was no *way* they could hold onto it.

None of which meant they couldn't take it away from *her*.

She gave herself a shake. She had five and a half hours before the enemy could come into range of her own command, and it was time to start using some of those hours.

"Alert the planetary authorities," she told Montague. "Pass along your force appreciation and tell President Janakowski I'll do what I can, but that we probably can't stop them. Then pass the word to prep for Omega-One."

Omega-One was the emergency evacuation plan none

of her staff had ever really expected to need, and Montague's mouth tightened, but he nodded.

"Next, send out dispatch boats to Casca, Minette, Yeltsin, Clearaway, Zuckerman, and Doreas. I'm sure they'll all relay, but be sure the Zuckerman courier carries specific orders to inform Grendelsbane."

"Ma'am, we only have three dispatch boats," Montague reminded her.

"I know. Use them for Minette, Yeltsin, and Zuckerman—that's where we need the shortest transit times. Detach destroyers for the others." She saw the look in Montague's eyes and snorted. "*We're* not going to need them, Adam! The best we can do is picket the outer system and keep an eye on these people; we sure as hell can't *fight* them!"

"Yes, Ma'am." Montague's nod was unhappy, but he knew she was right.

"While you're doing that, have Communications set up an all-ships' captain's conference link. I'll be on Flag Bridge to handle it in ten minutes."

"Aye, aye, Ma'am."

She cut the circuit just as Chief Steward Lewis stepped into her cabin. Lewis already wore her own skinsuit, and Meiner's was draped over her shoulder while the admiral's helmet hung from her left hand. Her face was grim, and Meiner made herself smile as she reached for her suit.

It wasn't easy.

"Task Force Twenty should be hitting Minette just about now, Citizen Commissioner," Citizen Vice Admiral McQueen observed.

"Really?" Fontein let a perplexed look cross his face as he studied the chrono on the flag deck bulkhead, then nodded. It wouldn't do to seem *too* incompetent, and it wasn't all that hard to allow for the dilation effect of their own velocity. "And us, Citizen Admiral?"

"Another fifteen minutes," McQueen replied, and looked around the flag deck. Her staff bent intently over their consoles, completing last-minute checks, and a frosty smile lit her green eyes. The Manties remained better than her people—she didn't like admitting that, but there was no point lying to herself—yet that was beginning to change. Their *technological* superiority might be insurmountable, for now at least, but they weren't five meters tall, and a lot of what had happened to the People's Navy had resulted from more mundane factors. Put simply, the Manticorans not only had better equipment, but they were better trained and much more confident, as well.

Well, they also had a five-T-century tradition of winning every war. And though it would never do to say so where someone like Fontein could hear, their better education system explained why their R&D establishment was so much better than Haven's. But the PN was learning, and McQueen's officers were about to receive another lesson in the only school that really mattered. Assuming Intelligence was right, they had enough firepower to annihilate the Manty picket in Minette whatever the enemy tried, and every battle the PN fought gave it that much more insight into Manty doctrine and capabilities. And more experience and confidence in itself.

"Do you expect much resistance, Citizen Admiral?" Fontein asked.

"That depends on how stupid their CO is, Citizen Commissioner." McQueen was *damned* if she would call this man "Sir." "He'll have the initial advantage, thanks to his sensor net. I understand Intelligence thinks it's figured out how they can real-time tactical data on us, but until we manage to produce matching systems, we can't do the same thing to them."

Fontein frowned, but McQueen wasn't worried. What she'd said was self-evident and not quite a criticism of her own superiors, but if Fontein reported it, it might just goad some of those same superiors into finding a way to match the Manties' technology. Their new com system was technically elegant, if Intelligence was right about how they were doing it, and McQueen had her

own ideas about how to deal with the Republic's own
R&D types' inability to duplicate it. The Solarian League
had embargoed technology and war materials to both
sides in this war, but the human race had sought an
FTL means of communication for almost two thousand
T-years. If the Republic could give the League a hint
about how the Manties were doing it, then some greedy
bastard in one of the League's member navies would
be *delighted* to work a deal that guaranteed the PN
an equal share in the hardware its raw information
allowed the Leaguers to produce.

After all, she thought cynically, the embargo had been
around a long time, and it wouldn't be the first time
the Republic had found someone willing to violate it for
the right price.

"For the moment, however," she went on, "it shouldn't
matter much. I'm not planning on anything fancy, Citizen
Commissioner, and they shouldn't have the firepower
to do anything fancy to *us*, either. If they want to stand
and fight, we'll smash them to wreckage; if they choose
to withdraw, we'll just gather in the system and laugh
at them."

A soft almost-growl rose from her staff, and she bared
her teeth at Fontein. She had plans of her own, but she
wasn't immune to the Navy's collective desire for revenge.
The Manties had made them look bad too often; it was
about time the People's Navy got a little of its own back
. . . and they didn't need any damned "citizen commissioners" to make them want *that*.

"It's confirmed, Sir. Sixteen SDs, seven BCs, and thirty-
two lighter units." Vice Admiral Stanton grimaced as his
ops officer cataloged the enemy's strength. It was very
quiet on *Majestic*'s flag deck, and the red light codes
advancing on Everest seemed to pulse with menace in
the plot. They'd translated into n-space right on the 20.7
light-minute hyper limit of a G3, and they were boring straight in to catch the planet between them and
the primary.

And, he thought, there was nothing he could do to stop them.

"Tracking's latest estimate, Sir."

Captain Truscot, his chief of staff, passed over a message board, and Stanton grimaced again as he scanned its display. Just under three hours on their present course, assuming they maintained their current accel the entire way. Of course, that would also bring them scorching past Everest at well over 44,600 KPS, and the planet had to be their primary objective. It was, at any rate, the one thing in the system they'd *know* he had to fight for—assuming he stood and fought at all—so it was more likely they'd go for turnover at the halfway point.

He drew a deep breath and stood back from the plot. At the moment, the enemy was still close to two hundred and fifty million kilometers from the planet, which meant he couldn't even see Stanton's ships. But that would change as soon as TF M-01 lit off its drives, and gravitic sensors were FTL. Unless he chose to hold his power settings down to something his stealth systems could hide, they'd be able to track him in real time, just as *Majestic* was doing to them now through the FTL net. They wouldn't be able to tell *what* his units were until they got much closer, but they could tell *where* they were.

Not good, he thought. Not good at all. Manticoran missiles were at least thirty percent more effective than Peep missiles, and Stanton's ECM and point defense had similar, if slimmer, margins of superiority. But his biggest ship was a mere dreadnought, and he had only four of them, while there were sixteen Peep *super*dreadnoughts out there. Those odds would make even a missile duel suicidal, and if he tried to defend Everest, they could pin him against it and close to energy range. In *that* sort of engagement, his task force *might* last twenty whole minutes. He'd hurt them before they killed him, but the loss of his own ships would hurt the Alliance worse than whatever he did to them . . . and buy Everest less than half an hour.

"We can't stop them," he said quietly, and Truscot nodded tightly. The chief of staff's eyes were bitter, but there was no point pretending they could do the impossible.

"Helen," Stanton looked at his communication officer, "get me a direct link to Premier Jones." The com officer nodded, and Stanton turned back to Truscot and Commander Ryan, his ops officer. "George, you and Pete set up for a passing engagement on a direct reciprocal. There's no sense thinking we can hold 'em, but I want them hurt as we go by. Plot a course that will bring us past them at a range of five million klicks. If they decide to maneuver against us, it'll buy Jones and the evacuation ships a little more time; if they don't maneuver, I want to burn past them with the max possible velocity. They'll probably decel to increase the engagement window, but they won't be able to stretch it too far, and I want our magazines emptied into them on the way by. Rapid fire with everything we've got till the tubes run dry."

"Sir, if we do that—"

"I know, we won't dare let them back into missile range later, because we won't have anything left to shoot at them with." Stanton shook his head hard, angry not with Truscot for protesting but with the circumstances which drove his own plan. "George, we can't afford any extended engagement against that many launchers whatever we do. This way we can at least slam them with the maximum throw weight in the shortest possible time, and their point defense is more susceptible to overload. If we saturate 'em, we should get at least a few good hits."

Truscot considered for a moment, then nodded.

"Yes, Sir," he said. "Targeting priorities?"

"We'll go for the big boys. We could probably kill more of the battlecruisers, but if we hammer one or two of the SDs hard enough it'll make taking the system back easier when we get around to it."

"Yes, Sir." Truscot sounded more positive this time.

"Admiral, I have the Premier," his com officer said, and Stanton held up a hand at her.

"Just a second, Helen," he said, still looking at Truscot. "Once you and Pete work out the rough plan, let him finish it up while you make sure Tracking Central blows all the inner-system platforms, George. Tell Central I want them to *confirm* their own scuttling charges before they bail out, then detach *Seeress* and *Oracle* to pick them up and get them the hell out of here while the rest of us deal with the Peeps. I do *not* want any of those grav techs winding up as Peep POWs, understood?"

"Aye, aye, Sir." Truscot nodded grimly. Blowing the FTL sensor platforms would cost Stanton a major tactical advantage, but he wasn't planning on standing and fighting, and the grav-pulse transmitters were one of the RMN's most closely held secrets. None of them were to be allowed to fall into Peep hands. In the case of a ship like *Majestic*, that would require massive internal destruction to wreck her own com section beyond reconstruction; in Tracking Central's case, it would require *total* destruction. Even more to the point, perhaps, among them, the techs in Tracking Central had the specs on the system filed in their brains, as well as their computers.

"All right." Stanton drew a deep, bitter breath and straightened his spine as he turned to the com officer. "I'll talk to the Premier now, Helen," he said quietly.

• CHAPTER SIXTEEN

"He's done *what?*"

"He's placed Brother Jouet under house arrest and returned Marchant to Burdette Cathedral's pulpit, Your Grace," Lord Prestwick repeated.

"*House ar—*!" Benjamin Mayhew bit off the words before he could echo his Chancellor yet again like some idiot. For just a moment, all he felt was shock at Burdette's sheer insolence, but then his eyes turned to narrowed slits of stone. "I presume he used his own armsmen to do it?"

"Yes, Your Grace." Prestwick kept his reply level, but it was hard. Benjamin's voice matched his eyes, and its icy timbre reminded the Chancellor that the Mayhew dynasty had reigned for almost a thousand T-years. Not all those years had been kind and gentle . . . and neither had the Protectors who'd weathered them.

"I see." Benjamin's voice was hard enough to cut diamonds. "And just how did he justify his actions?"

"As you know," Prestwick said carefully, "he's always maintained that the Sacristy erred in instigating Marchant's removal. Now he's broadened that position by claiming that, quite aside from the rectitude of the Sacristy's decision, *you* lacked the legal authority to implement it."

"Indeed?" The single word demanded explanation, and Prestwick sighed.

"Essentially, he's called your reassumption of personal rule unconstitutional, Your Grace, and that's scary. I know the High Court disagrees, but though the Keys have never explicitly challenged that opinion, they've never

212

formally accepted it, either. If the reactionaries can use the religious outrage he's generating to push a challenge to it, they can argue that every action you've taken *since* reassuming power was illegal, as well."

Mayhew's jaw tightened, and the cold fire in his eyes turned hot, but Prestwick clearly disliked reporting Burdette's argument, and there was no point venting his temper on the Chancellor. Besides, the tack Burdette had taken must put Prestwick in an unhappy position.

"Please sit down, Henry," he made himself say more calmly, and produced a wintry smile as Prestwick sank into the comfortable chair in front of his desk. The Chancellor was a good man, he thought, but he was also in a difficult position. He'd inherited the steadholdership of Prestwick from his childless nephew just two years ago, and that totally unexpected event had made him a member of the Conclave as well as Chancellor, with what could all too easily become competing loyalties under the new Grayson political equation. He was often uncomfortable treating with other steadholders as their peer, and there were times he seemed to forget he was a reigning head of state's first minister, whose function was to lay down the law to them rather than accept the Keys' direction. He could also be a bit too fussy about details and protocols, but he was solid, dependable, and—more importantly—a man of principle. Many men would have resigned rather than continue to serve the man who'd displaced them from control of the government in the so-called Mayhew Restoration, particularly when continuing as both Chancellor and Steadholder complicated his life so. Prestwick hadn't, and he'd been utterly invaluable over the last four years.

"Tell me, Henry. What do you think of his argument?" Benjamin asked more naturally, and Prestwick shrugged.

"I think it's based on shaky legal ground, Your Grace."

"How shaky?" Mayhew pressed.

"*Very* shaky," Prestwick replied with a small, wry grin. "Your Grace, if my predecessors and I intended to establish permanent ministerial control of the government, we made a serious error—as the Court reminded us—in not amending the Constitution." His smile grew a bit wider, and Benjamin returned it tightly, but then Prestwick leaned forward with a more serious air.

"The problem, Your Grace, is that for over a hundred years, precedent said the Protector was the symbolic guarantor of a stable continuity, but that the actual business of running the government was his Council's affair, while the Constitution still said he was the head of *government*, not just the state." He shrugged. "When you reasserted your authority, you certainly violated that precedent, but the written Constitution—which every Grayson steadholder and military officer is sworn to uphold—gave you every right to do so. We simply never anticipated that you would."

"And do you think it was a good thing?" Benjamin had never asked that question before—not in so many words—and Prestwick paused a moment. Then—

"Yes, Your Grace, I do," he said quietly.

"Why?" Benjamin asked, equally quietly.

"Because you were right: we do need a stronger executive." The Chancellor looked away, gazing out the office windows as he went on. "I supported your position on the treaty with Manticore even before you, ah, reclaimed your authority, because I agreed that we needed the industrial and economic advantages, not to mention the military ones, it would bring. But despite that, I truly hadn't realized—then—how completely the Keys dominated the Council. I should have, since I was part of the system, but I was too busy dealing with day-to-day details to see any larger picture. And because I was, I hadn't realized we were actually in danger of returning to the Five Keys."

Benjamin sighed in relief, and the Chancellor gave him another faint smile. The truth, as the Protector now knew both of them realized, was that Grayson's steadholders had slipped steadily back into a dangerous, autocratic autonomy over the last century and a half. It hadn't been anything clear-cut and overt—the process had been too gradual for that—but the great feudal lords had slowly yet inevitably reasserted their independence of central authority.

It was understandable, if one was a student of Grayson history, for the struggle between the Sword and the Keys had been a long, often bitter one, and the Keys held several advantages. From the colony's earliest days, it had been the steadholders who'd led their people's grim fight for survival. Someone had had to make the hard decisions, to determine who died so that others might live, and that someone had been the steadholder. Even today, a steadholder's decree had the force of law within his steading, so long as it did not conflict with the Constitution, and there'd been a period, known by Grayson historians as the Time of the Five Keys, when there *was* no Constitution. When the great steadholders, dominated by the lords of the five original steadings—Mayhew, Burdette, Mackenzie, Yanakov, and Bancroft—had ruled as independent kings in all but name. When their power had been checked only by the Church, and the Protector had been simply first among equals, without even an army he could call his own. If he happened to be Steadholder Mayhew, as well as Protector (a state of affairs the other Keys saw to it seldom applied), he could utilize the Mayhew Guard, but that was all the military muscle the most powerful Protector could command, and it was scarcely enough to challenge the Keys as a group.

Custom had decreed that the Protector be a Mayhew, for it had been Oliver Mayhew who'd almost single-handedly preserved the original colony from destruction. But for four centuries, the Protector had been elected from all the adult males of the line by the Conclave of Steadholders, and the Keys had chosen weakness, not strength. They'd wanted a Protector unable to challenge their own power, and if they accidentally got one who was too strong for them, there'd been ways to correct the situation. Benjamin II, Oliver IV, and Bernard III had all died by assassination, and Cyrus the Weak had actually been imprisoned by an alliance of steadholders. Every Protector had known he would reign only so long as the Keys permitted it, and it had taken four hundred T-years—and the ghastly carnage of Grayson's Civil War—to change that state of affairs.

The Keys had been virtually annihilated in the first hour of the Civil War. Fifty-three of Grayson's then fifty-six steadholders, all with their heirs in attendance, had assembled for the special Conclave summoned by Protector John II on the petition of Jeremiah Bancroft. There'd been some surprise when Steadholder Bancroft sent word he and two of his fellows had been delayed, yet no one had guessed the true reason for their tardiness. All had known Bancroft for a zealot, but none had known he was also a traitor . . . and because they hadn't known, all of them had died when the Faithful's armsmen stormed the Chamber. Of all Grayson's steadholders, only Bancroft, Oswald, and Simonds, the leaders of the Faithful, had survived, and there'd been no one left to rally their murdered peers' steaders—or armsmen—against them.

No one, that was, except the Protector's son Benjamin.

The Mayhew armsmen had been as surprised as any, but somehow—to this day, no one knew how—a handful of them had cut a way out of the trap for John's son. The opening was brief, however it was created, but John's armsmen had died to a man, with their Protector fighting at their head, to cover Benjamin IV's escape from the murderers of the Fifty-Three and *their* heirs.

But he was the *only* escapee, and Mayhew Steading was the very first one the Faithful occupied. He'd been only seventeen, a mere boy who no longer had a single armsman to call his own, and the Faithful had dismissed him as a threat . . . but that seventeen-year-old boy was to go down in Grayson history as Benjamin the Great. He fled to Mackenzie Steading, and, somehow, he rallied the shattered remnants of the other steadholders' Guards to him. The Faithful controlled two-thirds of the planet before he could do it, but he built an army of those leaderless men. It was *his* army, one which would have followed him into the jaws of Hell itself, and in fourteen savage years of war, he and that army retook their planet one bloody meter at a time, until they drove the Faithful into total rout and exile to Masada.

It was an incredible achievement, and the written Constitution which emerged from the horrors of the war had recognized Grayson's debt to the man who accomplished it. It had merged the confiscated steadings of Bancroft, Oswald, and Simonds into a single demesne held by the Protector (*not* Steadholder Mayhew), made his title hereditary, restricted the size of the Keys' personal guards, and created a standing planetary army under his command.

Benjamin IV had sworn upon his father's grave to defer his official investment as Protector until the Faithful were defeated, and, like every other promise he ever made, he kept that oath. But when at last he was proclaimed Protector, it was not "by acclamation of the Conclave" but "by God's grace," and at his investiture he also passed the Mayhew Key to his eldest son and chose a new symbol for himself. The key had always symbolized a *steadholder's* authority, and the fact that the Protector carried it had only emphasized his coequal status with his peers. But the Protector no longer *had* a legal peer, and no one had misunderstood Benjamin IV's meaning when he exchanged his key for a bared sword.

Yet that had been six hundred T-years ago, and the steadholders had only been humbled, not broken. Nor had all Protectors been Benjamin the Great's equal, and by Benjamin IX's birth, the Keys, through the Council, had once more asserted de facto control of Grayson.

Benjamin had read, during his years at Harvard University's Bogota campus, of the parliament of the ancient Kingdom of Poland in which every baron had a seat and unanimous consent was required for any decision, with the predictable result that nothing ever *was* decided. Grayson's situation hadn't been quite that bad, but it had been bad enough, for the members of the

Protector's Council had to be approved by the Conclave of Steadholders. That ancient right was still reserved to it under the Constitution, and over time, a succession of weak protectors had permitted the Keys to assume outright control of the Council's membership. The great steadholders of their day—men like Burdette, Mueller, Mackenzie, and Garth—had divided the Council among themselves and doled out the ministries like conquered fiefs. Each of them, with a small group of lesser allies, had controlled the appointment of the Councilman who headed "his" ministry, and those ministers, each responsible to his own patron steadholders, had controlled the appointment of the men who staffed their ministries. It had been a simple progression, a matter of who actually commanded the loyalties of each shell of the government and its bureaucracies, which had extended itself insidiously until the Protector had controlled only his own household. As in the Time of the Five Keys, it had been the steadholders who formulated domestic policy, and that policy had been directed towards insuring their own autonomy. As for foreign policy, there simply hadn't been one—aside from the traditional hostility to Masada—for no one had been interested in making one until the confrontation between Manticore and Haven had suddenly given their star system crucial strategic importance.

But, the Keys had failed to amend the Constitution . . . or to recognize the prestige the Mayhew name still commanded among their steaders. When the Council found itself paralyzed by Haven's attempt to seize Yeltsin's Star through its Masadan proxies, it had been a Mayhew who broke the paralysis. And, once again, that act had made a man named Benjamin Protector of Grayson in fact, as well as name.

The Sword had regained its keenness, and there was nothing—legally—the Keys could do about it. At one time, Grayson's Church and civil law had been identical, with the Sacristy as the planetary High Court. But the same carnage which had produced the Constitution had taught the Church a painful lesson in the consequences of religious interference in secular matters. Grayson law still enshrined the theocratic tenets which had always infused it, but for six centuries, sitting judges had been legally barred from Church office. A distinctly secular element had crept into the law as a result, but the Church still trained the planet's jurists. And it also retained the right to approve appointments to the High Court, which, among other things, exercised judicial review of constitutional matters.

That right of approval had been critical to the events of four years past, for Julius Hanks had been the Sacristy's guiding force—first as Second Elder, and then as Reverend and First Elder—for over three decades, and the Keys' increasing arrogance had worried him. His options had been limited, but he'd exercised the ones he had, and the High Court judges approved under his leadership had been strict constructionalists. The Keys hadn't worried about it overmuch. Perhaps they hadn't even considered the implications . . . until the Mayhew Restoration, when the Court ruled that the written Constitution, not the precedent which had violated it for a hundred years, was the law of Grayson.

That had stymied legal steadholder opposition to direct rule, and even if they'd wanted to, no Key had dared resort to *extra*legal means. The Protector enjoyed the full support of the Grayson Navy and Army, and those organizations were more powerful than they'd ever before been, even in Benjamin the Great's day. He enjoyed the support of the common steaders of Grayson, and the Conclave of Steaders—after a century in which its power had waned in lock step with the Sword's—had rediscovered its legal equality with the Keys. And he also enjoyed the support of Reverend Hanks and the Church of Humanity Unchained, which gave him God's own imprimatur. Powerful as any Steadholder might be within his own steading, the central authority on Grayson lay firmly in Benjamin Mayhew's grip, and he had no intention of surrendering it until he'd dragged his planet out of the past and into the present.

Which, unfortunately, Lord Burdette seemed to have recognized. And if this was the opening shot in a formal attempt to derail the Mayhew Restoration, it might be far more dangerous than first impressions suggested. The High Court, after all, had been approved by the Sacristy, not the General Convocation of the Church, and it was the *Sacristy* with whom Burdette had picked his quarrel. If he could convince enough people the Sacristy had erred in Marchant's case, the Court decision in Benjamin's favor might also become suspect by association. And if *that* happened . . .

Despite his confident words to Lady Harrington, Benjamin Mayhew had always recognized the gamble he'd chosen to run. Most Graysons were prepared to follow where he led, but if he stumbled—if the destination to which he led them exploded in their faces, or if a solid block of those who feared the changes it entailed coalesced in opposition—that could change. In the ultimate sense, his authority derived from the fact that those he governed chose that he should do so, and even if he'd believed the attempt could have succeeded, he had no ambition to use the military power he commanded to change that.

And that, for all his fanaticism, made Burdette a threat. The Steadholder spoke for the large minority who feared change, and by couching his opposition in religious terms, he'd appealed to a mighty force. The Grayson belief that each man must face his own Test, holding to his own view of God's will for him, whatever the cost, lent him a dangerous legitimacy, and if he was reaching for yet another weapon, his argument shed a suddenly much more ominous light on the public positions men like Lord Mueller had taken of late. Whether they acted from religious conviction or in a cynical bid to regain the power they'd lost, an organized opposition within the steadholders—especially one with any claim to legitimacy—would be a perilous adversary.

Yet Benjamin held potent cards of his own. The Masadan threat had been ended at last, after half a dozen wars (which had been "minor" only by major star nations' standards) over more than two centuries. Despite the social strains of his reforms and the war against the Peeps, Grayson's economy was stronger than it had ever been and growing stronger by the week. More than that, modern medicine—less outwardly spectacular, perhaps, than the glittering machinery of "hard" technology—had come to Grayson, and people now living, like his own brother Michael and his daughters, would live for two or even three centuries. Benjamin IX was less than forty, yet that was still too old for prolong to be effective, and despite a certain bittersweet regret, he accepted that he would not live to see the end result of his reforms. But his brother and his children would, and the implications were staggering.

All of those things had resulted directly from Benjamin's policies, and the people of Grayson knew it. More, they knew they'd been born into a time of tumult and change, of danger and uncertainty, and, as Graysons always had, they looked to their Church and the Mayhew dynasty for safety. If Lord Burdette allowed himself to forget that, Benjamin thought grimly, the consequences for his own position would be profound.

But for now . . .

"All right, Henry. I take it Burdette's claiming that my 'usurpation' of power justifies him in acting in his own stead against the Sacristy?"

"Yes, Your Grace."

"And on that basis, he's used his own armsmen to 'arrest' Brother Jouet?" Prestwick nodded, and Benjamin snorted. "I don't suppose he mentioned that, usurper or no, I issued the writ to remove Marchant only after the Sacristy had properly petitioned me to do so?"

"As a matter of fact, Your Grace, he did." Mayhew quirked an eyebrow, and Prestwick raised one hand, palm uppermost. "As I say, he's repeated his claim that the Sacristy acted in error. In fact, he's gone further than his earlier statements. He claims 'the present Sacristy's support of the heretical changes poisoning our Faith and society' deprive it of any right to pass judgment 'on a true man of God for denouncing a foreign-born adulteress's perversion of the God-given dignity of the Steadholder's Key.'" The Chancellor grimaced. "I'm sorry, Your Grace, but those are direct quotes."

"I see." Benjamin stared into the distance for several seconds, and his mind raced. Burdette's new, stronger rhetoric tied in ominously well with Benjamin's suspicions of where he was headed, but the very speed with which the Steadholder was moving posed its own danger for his strategy.

"I suppose," the Protector said after a moment, "that he figured since Reverend Hanks supports me anyway, he might as well take us both on at once. But even steadholders who might like to see *me* taken down are going to back away from declaring war on the Sacristy, as well, which means he's divided the potential opposition for us."

"Well, yes, Your Grace, but he may also have divided those who might *support* you. As you yourself demonstrated four years ago, loyalty to the Mayhew name has always been strongest among the most traditional—and conservative—of our people. That means many who might otherwise come out in *your* support may hesitate to support the reforms you've initiated."

"Um." Benjamin tipped his chair back. For someone who'd once been "too busy with details" to see the bigger picture, Prestwick had developed an impressive ability to see it now. "I still think it'll hurt him more than us," he said after a moment. "In order to play the religion card in *his* favor, he has to convince people the Sacristy's 'betrayed' the Faith. He's not going to generate any sort of united opposition to Reverend Hanks overnight, and until they can do that, he and his cronies have to be careful about presenting too united a front. If they come out into the open too soon and give me a target I can attack as a group, with a united Church behind me, I'll cut their legs off before they realize what's happening."

"They've been careful about that so far, Your Grace,"

Prestwick pointed out, "and the way they're using Burdette as their point worries me. The man's too much like one of the old-line Faithful for my taste, but he *does* have an impressive reputation for personal piety. Touch him, and *you* may polarize the religious issues, and Tester only knows where that might end!"

"True." Benjamin drummed on the desk, then looked up sharply. "Has he done anything except replace Brother Jouet with Marchant?"

"Not yet. He clearly stepped over the line in confining a clergyman, but he only ordered Brother Jouet's 'arrest' when he refused to leave the cathedral, and all of my sources say the Burdette armsmen treated him with great respect. So far, Lord Burdette is making this a confrontation purely on the basis of his own personal faith, and despite his charge that you seized power illegally, he's been very careful not to touch a single secular arm of the Sword within Burdette."

"Damn," Benjamin said mildly. That was better tactics than he'd expected. In fact, it was clever enough to make him wonder if someone else might be calling the plays. But whoever had thought it up, Burdette's actions left the next move squarely up to him. He could—and no doubt should—assert the Sword's religious authority as the Church's guardian to reverse Burdette's actions. But if he did, he risked escalating the entire affair, especially if Burdette was prepared to go so far as forcible resistance. The image of a man meeting the hour of his Test by opposing the suppression of his personal faith was a powerful one on Grayson. If Benjamin brought the Sword's full weight to bear on a single steadholder, the sheer imbalance of strength might make Burdette a hero of sorts . . . and if some of the other steadholders *had* gathered quietly in the wings to oppose him, they'd be primed to spring to Burdette's defense by defending a steadholder's traditional authority within his own steading. But if he *didn't* act, then Burdette and his cronies had won the first round, which could only increase their prestige for the next one.

"All right, Henry. I agree we have to move carefully. If he's restricting himself to a purely religious confrontation for the moment, perhaps we should do the same, and if we do that, then Reverend Hanks and the Sacristy become our strongest weapon."

"Agreed, Your Grace."

"All right," Benjamin repeated. "In that case, please ask the Reverend to come to Protector's Palace at his earliest convenience. Then put together a statement deploring Lord Burdette's actions in assailing Father Church. I want something that condemns him without attacking too openly. Something that stresses our own moderation and regrets his wrongheadedness and hastiness without throwing down any gauntlets where he can pick them up. Our position will be that what he's done is wrong, but that the Faith is too important to become a pretext for secular confrontations. If Reverend Hanks agrees, we may want to call a general convocation of the Church to condemn his actions—make it a matter of Burdette against the entire body of the Church, not just the Sacristy."

"That's a bit risky, Your Grace." Prestwick looked worried. "The Sacristy Elders are closely united; I'm not sure a general convocation would be, and if anything like a sizable minority were to back Marchant, it would only strengthen Burdette's hand."

"Reverend Hanks will be the best judge of that," Benjamin replied, "but for the moment, I think the general outrage at the way Marchant—and, for that matter, Burdette himself, now—have attacked Lady Harrington will work in our favor. Burdette's made her the focal point for his opposition to all the other changes, but she remains immensely popular. Under the circumstances, what we may need to do is use some of that popularity."

"Use it, Your Grace?"

"Of course. She's a military hero, and the way her steading's come along—especially the way Sky Domes is impacting the entire planet—is the best testimonial we have for the positive consequences of the Alliance and the reforms. Besides, Marchant and Burdette made a serious mistake by attacking her personally. Not only have they publicly assailed a steadholder—and we'll play up *that* point for Burdette's allies, if any, as well as everyone else—but they've insulted a woman. That'll put the traditionalists most concerned over social changes in a serious quandary, however much they hate those changes." The Protector smiled coldly. "If Burdette wants to attack Lady Harrington to rally support, then let's stick his own tactic right up his ass."

Samuel M. Harding was new at his job, but he was hardly alone in that. In the last three months, as the orders poured in from other steadings, Grayson Sky Domes, Ltd., had quadrupled its workforce. The corporation had been forced to hire at an incredible rate and then to train all of its personnel to operate their off-world equipment, and that left very little time for getting to know its new employees.

Fortunately, Harding's job wasn't all that complicated, for his Manticoran-built power bore was designed to be user-friendly. Its software was carefully crafted to provide quick, positive control, with hardwired safety features to make its operation nearly foolproof, and Harding was a fast learner. He'd needed less than three weeks to master his new duties, and he'd passed the final safety check that cleared him to operate without close supervision just in time for assignment to the lead team for Sky Domes' latest project.

Now he sat in his comfortable control chair, overseeing the operation of his quarter-million-austin machine, and watched the remote view as Power Bore Number Four's refractory alloy cutting heads sliced through bedrock like so much crumbly cheese. The racket was appalling— he knew, for part of his training program had included direct, on-site observation, though his actual operating station was three kilometers from the bore's present activity—and he watched the visual display beside him with something very like awe. The bore was sinking its meter-wide shaft at almost ten centimeters per minute, and, at that, it had slowed by over sixty percent when it got through the last clay and hit solid rock.

It truly was a magnificent tool, he thought, eyes on the cloud of dust and debris fountaining from the discharge hopper as the screaming, bellowing bore chewed rock. Lumps of stone spat from the hopper like bullets; long, agile "fingers" of battle steel moved with darting speed and micrometric precision, picking the spinning cutting heads' teeth on the fly lest their own voracious appetite jam them with pulverized rock; and high-pressure coolant circulated through channels in the heads lest even their alloy overheat and shatter. The cutting teeth whirled faster than the turbine of Harding's new, Manticoran-built air car, and he turned his head slightly to check the bore's actual performance against the profile in his computer.

There was something oddly unreal about his task. He only had to look at the visual display to see the high-speed, shrieking intensity of the bore and recognize the incredible power he controlled. Yet the air-conditioned comfort of the control room about him was almost hushed, isolated from the howling monster he commanded, and he and he alone actually knew—or worried about—what it was doing at any given moment.

Half a dozen other workers sat at matching panels in the same room, but none had any attention to spare for Harding. Each was equally intent on the machine *he* controlled, for the people about him were men with a mission. They were bringing their world yet another new wonder from Manticore's high-tech cornucopia, and in the process, earning the income Harrington Steading needed so badly. It was an exhilarating opportunity, and Sky Domes' workers were vociferously loyal to their Steadholder for making it possible and allowing them to be a part of it.

Samuel Harding understood that, and he, too, was grateful for the chance to be here, for he, too, had a

mission—if not the same one as Sky Domes' other workers. He typed a brief correction into his terminal,
resetting the bore's parameters. It wasn't a large change,
but it was enough. The shaft Harding was sinking would
soon provide the footing for one of the new dome's primary load-bearing supports . . . but that shaft would be
ever so slightly off profile. Not by much. In fact, it would
take careful measurement by someone who *expected* to
find a problem to detect one.

In itself, the discrepancy would hardly matter, but
Samuel Harding would be drilling two more shafts this
afternoon and five more every day after that, until the
project was completed. Each of them would be the least
bit off profile, as well, and Harding knew he wasn't the
only man who knew they would be. When the crew
responsible for setting the supports in place moved on-
site, certain of its members would have a detailed list
of the holes Harding had drilled and precisely how each
of them differed from the original specifications. Those
supports were fabricated from yet another of Manticore's
marvelous alloys, and each was a precision part of the
intricately interlocking structure Adam Gerrick and his
team had designed. Once in place, buttressed by
minutely calculated stress and counter-stress, they would
provide the dome with walls stronger than steel. And
because those walls were elastic, with many separate
supports woven into a single whole, they would have
the flexible redundancy to survive anything short of an
earthquake without so much as cracking a single
crystoplast pane.

Except for the supports in the holes Harding had
drilled, where the ceramacrete footings would be fused
almost correctly in shafts which were *almost* perfectly
aligned. The ones whose load-bearing ability had been
just as precisely calculated as their fellows, but toward
a very different outcome.

Samuel Harding didn't know whether the collapse
would come while the dome was still going up or only
after it had been in place for a period, but he knew what

would happen in God's good time. A part of him hoped that not too many would be killed or maimed when the moment came, but sacrifices sometimes had to be made to do God's will. His deepest regret, and the one for which he beseeched God's understanding each night, was that so many of those who died would die outside a state of grace, seduced into sin by the out-world harlot to whom they'd given their loyalty. The thought of what their error might cost their souls was a heavy weight for him to bear, yet he consoled himself with the thought that God knew how those men had been deceived and lured astray, and God was as merciful as He was terrible in His wrath. Perhaps He would take into consideration how they'd been betrayed by the false shepherds who'd led them away from His law.

But whatever might become of others, Samuel Harding had a responsibility to meet his own Test, and he knew God's hand was about him, protecting him as he bent to the task God had sent him, for no one had the least suspicion of what he was actually doing. His fellow employees accepted him as one of their own, unaware he recognized the true nature of the false mistress they served and the menace she and her Star Kingdom represented for all of God's people. Why, they hadn't even realized the name he'd given them was false, and as a result, none of them even guessed that his mother's maiden name had been "Marchant."

• CHAPTER SEVENTEEN

"There! You see that?"

Honor pointed into the depths of CIC's huge master display and looked at Mercedes Brigham and Fred Bagwell. The three of them stood in *Terrible*'s combat information center to watch the replay of their last exercise, because the flag deck plots were too small for the detail Honor had wanted. Now she watched their faces, tasting their concentration through her link to Nimitz as they pondered the faint light at the heart of the holo sphere. She felt them trying to understand what she'd already deduced had to be there, then heard a muttered expletive from Mercedes, though Bagwell still looked perplexed.

"I see it, My Lady, but I don't know what it is," he admitted, peering at the small, ghostlike trace reading. That was one of the things Honor most liked about him. His determination to make everything go precisely to plan could make him a fussy pain in the posterior, but when he didn't know something he admitted it.

"Mercedes?" she prompted, and the chief of staff sighed.

"Yes, Milady. *I* know what it is," she admitted wryly, and turned to Bagwell. "What that is, Fred, is a powered down, stealthed reconnaissance drone—and it went right through the middle of our formation."

"An RD?" Bagwell blinked, and then the light went on behind his eyes. "Is *that* how Admiral Henries knew what we were up to?"

"It is, indeed," Honor murmured with a rueful smile. She hadn't thought Sir Alfred Henries, CO of the

229

Manticoran battle squadron which had dropped by for maneuvers on its way to Thetis, was quite that devious.

She shook her head and folded her arms. She'd spent hours with Mercedes and Bagwell planning her surprise for Henries, and it should have worked. In fact, but for that RD, it *would* have worked.

Peep EW systems were inferior to those of the RMN. Getting comparable performance out of them required much more massive installations, and the Grayson Navy hadn't been able to resist the temptation of all that available volume when they refitted their prize vessels. They'd gutted their new SDs' original EW sections and then filled the same space with *Manticoran* systems, which meant *Terrible* boasted almost the same electronic warfare capabilities as a sixteen-million-ton orbital fortress, and that was just fine with Honor. If someone was going to be shooting at her flagship, she wanted all the nasty tricks she could get to play on that someone's fire control.

Still, she *had* been a bit surprised to learn that Grayson's new-build warships were also more heavily equipped with EW systems than their Manticoran counterparts. Not by as great a margin as the SDs, perhaps, but they carried considerably more capable suites on a class-for-class basis, though the GSN hadn't yet learned to use the potential of its systems to full effect.

The discovery of all that capability had inspired Honor, and her formation for the exercise had *looked* like a standard deployment, with her SDs in tight and her escorts covering its flanks while a squadron of battlecruisers screened its line of advance. Only the "battlecruisers" had actually been superdreadnoughts, using their EW to mask the true power of their emissions, and the "superdreadnoughts" had actually been battlecruisers using *their* EW to *augment* their emissions. It should have been impossible for Henries to detect at anything over four million klicks, which should have let Honor flush her towed missile pods *and* get in the first, devastating broadsides from her SDs before his own ships of the wall even realized where the fire was coming from.

Unfortunately, Sir Alfred's wiliness had taken most of the punch out of her surprise, and that was her own fault. She'd deliberately come in on a completely predictable course to help him see what she wanted him to. But that had also given him the opportunity to deploy recon drones from beyond the range at which her own sensors could detect their drives. He'd accelerated them up to speed, then shut down their impellers and let them coast straight down her nice, predictable line of approach to such close range that no EW could fool them, and the RDs' lack of power, coupled with their built-in stealth features, had caused her people to miss them even when one physically penetrated her formation.

"That's how he did it," she repeated to Bagwell. "Sneaky devil, isn't he?"

"Well, yes, My Lady, I suppose he is. Which just means *we* have to be even sneakier tomorrow."

"Exactly." Honor smiled at him, and he smiled back. He would never be truly comfortable with unconventional tactics, but he'd come a long way, and so far, BatRon One had held its own against Henries. Despite the way Sir Alfred had trumped her latest ploy with his RDs, the honors had been about evenly split over the past week. In a total of four exercises, BatRon One had won one hands down, two had been draws, and Henries had won the last one by a narrow, if respectable, margin. No doubt he was pleased by yesterday's outcome, but she knew he hadn't expected things to be quite so hard. Oh, he'd been polite, but there'd been a certain confidence, almost an arrogance, about him at the initial conferences.

She snorted in memory, and Nimitz bleeked a laugh on her shoulder. She was becoming more Grayson than Manticoran, she thought wryly, and wondered whether the Graysons had thought *she* was arrogant when they first met? She knew Henries hadn't meant anything by it. He probably hadn't even realized he had what Honor's mother had always called "an attitude." The RMN had a tradition of victory, after all, and it had done very well so far in this war. Its officers *expected* to be better than anyone they met, and it had showed.

Well, Sir Alfred ought to have known better where Grayson was concerned . . . and Honor and her squadron had cleaned his clock in the first exercise, so perhaps she shouldn't begrudge his victory in this one. Not that she intended to give him any more.

"All right," she said more crisply, turning from the display. "We get another chance at him tomorrow. It's our last crack before he moves on to Thetis, and I want to go for match point. Have we received the ops order yet?"

"Yes, My Lady." Bagwell took a message board from under his arm and keyed it alive. "The umpires have decided to upgrade his battlecruisers to dreadnoughts for the exercise. That will give him eight SDs and six DNs, but *we'll* have BatRon Two under command."

Honor hid an internal grimace behind an expression of calm attention. High Admiral Matthews personally commanded Grayson's second battle squadron, and he'd be coming along as an observer. BatRon Two had had time to drill to a much higher level of readiness than her own squadron, and she'd be glad to have his well-trained ships' companies. But she wasn't as familiar with BatRon Two's captains as with her own, and knowing her commander in chief would be looking over her shoulder made their support a mixed blessing.

"We'll only have eleven of the wall to his fourteen," Bagwell went on, "but ours will all be SDs, so—"

"Excuse me, My Lady?"

Honor turned her head. Jared Sutton stood behind her with another message board. Her flag lieutenant had become much more relaxed over the past months. He'd gone from an almost painful deference to actually responding to her teasing in kind. Respectfully, of course—God help any lieutenant who got *too* familiar with his admiral, however much she liked him!—but almost as comfortably as she would have expected from a Manticoran. Which, considering that she was both a steadholder and female, said quite a lot. But his puppy dog eyes were hooded now, and he wore no expression at all.

"Yes, Jared?" she said, and her eyebrows rose as he extended the board wordlessly. A wisp of uneasiness came to her from him over Nimitz's empathic link, and then her own face tensed as she scanned the board. She felt Bagwell and Mercedes reacting to her expression, but that seemed unimportant as the dispatch's contents sank home.

She scrolled ahead to the second page, then the third, and her mouth tightened. It was worse than she'd thought, and she made her lips relax as she finished the message and looked up again.

"Thank you, Jared. Please ask Commander Brannigan to inform the High Admiral that I'll join him on *Vengeance* as soon as possible. And ask Mac to lay out my dress uniform."

"Yes, My Lady." Sutton came briefly to attention, then hurried away, and she looked at the armsman standing unobtrusively against a bulkhead.

"Simon, inform Andrew that I'll be leaving the ship in fifteen minutes. Have him alert my pinnace crew and meet me in Boat Bay One."

"Yes, My Lady." Simon Mattingly reached for his com, and Honor turned back to her staff officers and smiled thinly at their questioning expressions.

"The High Admiral didn't specifically invite chiefs of staff, Mercedes, but maybe you'd better come along. I don't think we'll need you, Fred, and you'll have enough to do here. I want a complete readiness update from every unit on my desk terminal within the hour."

"Of course, My Lady. May I ask what's happening?"

"You may." She handed him the message board. "The Peeps have taken Minette and Candor." Mercedes stiffened in disbelief, and Honor nodded. "High Admiral Matthews has confirmation from both systems. We don't know what they're up to, but it changes the situation rather radically."

"It certainly does, Milady," Mercedes said, then shook herself. "How heavy are their forces?"

"Heavier than I would have thought they could pry loose from Trevor's Star. According to the dispatches, they used over thirty SDs." Mercedes pursed her lips silently, and Honor nodded again. "Of course, that's split between both systems, so they're still pretty thin if they intend to hold them."

"Unless they reinforce, My Lady," Bagwell pointed out.

"Exactly." Honor shook herself and glanced at the chrono. "Well, we don't have time to dwell on it now. I'll meet you in Boat Bay One, Mercedes, and you'd better get started on that readiness report, Fred."

High Admiral Wesley Matthews rose in greeting as Lady Harrington stepped into his flag briefing room. Admiral Henries had had a shorter flight, and he'd arrived several minutes earlier, but he was still reading the original dispatches when Lady Harrington appeared with her chief of staff and trailed by two of her armsmen. Matthews saw Major LaFollet's eyes flick once about the briefing room in the automatic threat-search of his calling, but a small motion from Lady Harrington sent both armsmen back through the hatch. Matthews appreciated the gesture, though he had no security qualms where her bodyguards were concerned and this was hardly something that could be kept quiet for long.

Nor was it something he looked forward to dealing with. Admiral Henries was thirty T-years older than Lady Harrington, which made Matthews the youngest person present. Unfortunately, he was also the senior Allied officer, which made it *his* job to decide what to do about this mess.

"Please, be seated, My Lady," he invited.

Honor took the indicated seat. Mercedes slipped into the chair beside her and keyed a terminal, scanning the dispatches, but Honor kept her eyes on Matthews and raised one eyebrow. The high admiral had time for one frank look, exposing his own uncertainty to her, before

Henries looked up and he banished his worry with a professional expression.

"I will be dipped in shit if I ever expected anything like this," Henries said frankly, and Matthews nodded. Hearing such language in Lady Harrington's presence annoyed him, but no doubt she'd heard worse, and it was typical of Henries. Sir Alfred was a highly competent officer, but he'd started out as a merchant spacer and earned his flag—and knighthood—the hard way. That might be easier in the RMN than in many other navies, but it remained a remarkable achievement, and he cultivated a certain deliberate bluntness as if to remind everyone of it. He was short and stocky for a Manticoran, though still several centimeters taller than Matthews himself, and his brown eyes were worried as he ran a hand through sandy hair he wore as short as most Graysons.

"How in hell did they pry that much tonnage loose?" Henries went on, unconsciously echoing Honor's earlier remark to Mercedes. "And if they had it to use someplace, why not throw it at Thetis? Surely that's more important to them than a raid on somewhere like Minette or Candor!"

"If it *is* a raid, Sir Alfred," Honor said quietly. Henries looked at her, and she shrugged. "You're right. They've sent a good seven percent of their total surviving wall a hundred-plus light-years *behind* the front and used it to take two systems that aren't especially vital to us. That seems like an awfully stupid diversion when they have to be aware of what will happen to them if Admiral White Haven breaks through to Trevor's Star." Henries' grunt of agreement held an interrogative note, as if asking what her point was, and she shrugged again. "I don't object to the enemy doing stupid things, Sir Alfred, but when it's something *this* stupid, I have to wonder if there's something behind it that we just haven't seen yet."

"You don't suppose they're trying to force Earl White Haven to weaken his own forces, do you?" Henries asked. "Figuring he'll detach from his own command to take them back?"

"They could be. Or they could be after something else entirely. The question is what."

Henries nodded again, thoughtfully, Matthews noted. Despite his occasionally rough-edged language in her presence, Sir Alfred had always shown Lady Harrington the respect her Grayson rank demanded, in spite of the fact that her permanent Manticoran rank was only that of captain. It was one of the things Matthews liked about Henries, and probably also a sign of the RMN's professional respect for her, half-pay or no.

"That's the question, My Lady," the high admiral said now, "but since we can't answer it, a more immediate question is deciding how to respond."

He pressed a button, and a holo display of a conical volume of space defined by the Manticore Binary System, Clairmont, and Grendelsbane blinked to life. Most of the stars were the green of the Manticoran Alliance, but Minette and Candor now burned a sullen red.

"They've driven a wedge into our flank," he pointed out. "I suppose they might be planning to stage followup attacks through Solway and Treadway, but Lady Harrington is right; diverting enough ships of the wall to make it effective will weaken them before Trevor's Star. If they maintain their strength at Nightingale, then they'll have to divert from Maastricht or Solon, and weakening either of those systems will let Admiral White Haven hook around Nightingale's flank. Somehow I can't quite see them doing that."

Honor and Henries nodded. The Peeps had to realize Trevor's Star was the true target of Earl White Haven's campaign, for the Republic's possession of the system constituted a direct threat to the Manticore Binary System. Trevor's Star was over two hundred light-years from Manticore. It would take a superdreadnought over a month to make the hyper-space voyage between them, but Trevor's Star also contained one terminus of the Manticore Worm Hole Junction, and a battle fleet could make the same trip effectively instantaneously via the Junction.

Relieving that threat was one of Manticore's primary strategic goals, but the Star Kingdom had more than one motive. If White Haven could take the system, its Junction terminus would become a direct link to Manticore for the *Alliance*. Developed into a forward base inside the Republic, Trevor's Star would represent a secure bridgehead, a springboard for future offensives. Transit times between the Star Kingdom's shipyards and home-system fleet bases would become negligible. There wouldn't even be any need to detach convoy escorts to protect the long, vulnerable logistical chain between Manticore and a base like Thetis; unescorted merchantmen could pop through to Trevor's Star with total impunity, whenever they chose.

All of which meant the Peeps *had* to hold the system, and they'd been scraping the bottom of the barrel for months to do just that, which made this latest escapade still more inexplicable.

And, High Admiral Wesley Matthews reminded himself grimly, it made Lady Harrington's observation even more pertinent. If it looked this stupid, there *had* to be more to it than met the eye.

"Well, High Admiral," Henries said after a moment, eyes on the holo display, "whatever they're up to, I don't see that we've got any choice but to bounce their asses out. They're a direct threat to Doreas and Casca—neither of those systems is much more heavily picketed than Candor was—or they could hook up and try to retake Quest, I suppose." The stocky Manticoran admiral brooded over the green and red stars, then sighed. "Whatever they're after, they've damned well picked a couple of targets we have to take back from them!"

"Which may be all they really want," Matthews pointed out. "As you say, they may hope we'll detach forces from Admiral White Haven to do it."

"It may be what they want," Honor murmured, "but they have to know they're unlikely to get it. They must have a pretty accurate order of battle on the Earl, so simple math should tell them we still have more than enough ships of the wall in other places—like the Manticoran Home Fleet, or right here, for that matter— to throw them back out again. They can make us uncover, or at least weaken, other systems to concentrate a relief force, but we can do it without weakening Admiral White Haven. And once we *do* concentrate it, they won't risk losing that many SDs by trying to hold two relatively unimportant systems so far from Trevor's Star."

"Lady Harrington's right, High Admiral," Henries said. "All they can really make us do is burn the time to assemble our forces. Oh," he waved, "if they go ahead and try for Casca or Quest or Doreas, they can make us burn some *more* time, but they don't have enough ships of the wall to risk any sort of serious defense against the numerical superiority we can throw at them."

"Any word on what the Peeps are doing in the systems, Sir?" Honor asked, and Matthews shook his head. "Not really. All we've got so far are the preliminary dispatches from the station commanders. I assume Admiral Stanton and Admiral Meiner are still managing to picket the outer systems, but we can't even be certain of that. As of the last report we have, the Peeps weren't carrying out any systematic destruction of the system infrastructures, though."

"Then maybe they *are* planning to stay," Henries said. "If they think they can hold them, they wouldn't want to wreck anything they could use."

"I see your logic," Matthews said, "but it only emphasizes that we don't know what they're after. And whatever it is, it seems to me that the immediate problem is to get enough strength into the vicinity to sit on them."

"According to Admiral Stanton's dispatch, he took his lumps, but he hurt them pretty badly in his single pass, Sir," Mercedes Brigham put in. She looked at Honor and tapped the terminal in front of her. "He lost four heavy cruisers and took heavy damage to *Majestic* and

Orion, but he nailed one of their SDs, hit a second one hard, and took out a battlecruiser for good measure. They know they've been nudged, Milady."

"True, but he expended virtually his full missile load to do it," Henries pointed out. "He can picket the outer system, but until we get some missile resupply to him, he can't do anything more, and he's got cripples to worry about. Admiral Meiner's got full magazines and no crips, but battlecruisers can't go toe-to-toe with SDs."

"But *we* can," Matthews said. Honor and Henries looked at him, and he used the holo controls to throw a cursor into the display. He moved it to touch Grendelsbane, and neat letters displayed the Alliance strength in the system.

"As you can see, Admiral Hemphill has half-again the strength of either of these forces sitting down here on their southern flank." He touched the tracker ball, and the cursor whipped across to Clairmont. "At the same time, Admiral Koga has two divisions of dreadnoughts up here, and—" the cursor dashed up off the upper edge of the display and another star appeared in previously empty space "—Admiral Truman has a division of SDs up here at Klien Station. That gives us six ships of the wall north of Candor, though it'll take some time to concentrate them."

"Six against fifteen, Sir?" Henries couldn't quite keep the doubt out of his voice, and Matthews shook his head once more.

"No, *nineteen* against fifteen, Sir Alfred," he said quietly. "It's time Grayson made a little payback for all Manticore's done for us."

"Sir?" Henries sat straighter, and Matthews gave him a thin smile.

"I realize your orders are to report to Admiral White Haven, Sir Alfred, but I'm countermanding them. Battle Squadron Two will combine with your command and depart within three hours for Casca. At the same time, I'll send dispatches to Admiral Koga and Admiral Truman, instructing them to join us there at their best speed. If the Peeps haven't already pinched the system out from Candor, you and I should have enough strength to discourage them from making the attempt. Once the other divisions join us, we'll move in and throw them out of Candor, then advance on Minette. With any luck, we can coordinate with Admiral Hemphill to take that system back, as well, and do it without diverting a single ship from Thetis."

"Have you discussed this with Protector Benjamin, Sir?" Henries asked, regarding the high admiral with pronounced respect. "That's half your battle fleet, High Admiral, and, with all due respect, you haven't had a hell of a lot of time to drill your people."

"We've had long enough for Lady Harrington to hold her own against you, Sir Alfred," Matthews pointed out with a smile. "BatRon Two's had considerably longer to drill than her squadron has—that's why I'm tapping it for this operation instead of BatRon One," he added almost apologetically to Honor, though his eyes never left Henries'. "If we can do that well against you Manticorans, I think we can manage against Peeps."

"Yes, Sir, I imagine you damned well can," Henries agreed with a slow grin. "But it's still a lot of exposure for your Navy."

"It is, but I have, indeed, received the Protector's approval."

"In that case, High Admiral, all I can say on behalf of my Queen is thank you. Thank you very much."

"It's no more than you've done for us already, Sir Alfred," Matthews said. Their eyes held a moment longer, and then the high admiral looked squarely at Honor. "I wish we could take you along as well, My Lady," he said, "but someone has to stay home to mind the store, and—"

He shrugged, and Honor nodded silently. A part of her demanded to go with Matthews and Henries, yet she knew he was right. He was already reducing Grayson's security by almost half, and well as her people were now doing in the sims and exercises, they still had a dangerous number of rough edges. If anyone was going to be left to, as he put it, "mind the store," then it made sense to leave the units whose combat effectiveness was most doubtful.

And, she realized with a trace of surprise, however inexperienced her ships might still be at working together, he was also leaving the more seasoned command team. He himself would have three veteran Manticoran admirals—Koga, Truman, and Henries—upon whom to lean, but he was leaving his most experienced admiral—her—behind, with an equally experienced flag captain, to cover Yeltsin's Star. The realization sent a shiver through her, but then she took herself to task. She'd held the system once with only a heavy cruiser and a destroyer; she could darned well do the same thing with an almost full-strength squadron of superdreadnoughts! Especially, she thought wryly, with Alfredo Yu on *her* side for a change.

She knew she was whistling in the dark, that any threat she might have to counter today would be vastly stronger than the Masadan threat of four years past, but she ordered herself to forget that part. Nimitz stirred uneasily on her shoulder, and she reached up to rub his ears, but she kept her eyes on High Admiral Matthews.

"I'll leave covering orders for you, My Lady, but mostly they'll just be to use your discretion. I'll also leave the picket in Endicott alone. If you feel the need, you can draw on them, but I'd prefer you didn't expose Masada any more than you can help."

Honor nodded. The Endicott picket had nothing heavier than a battlecruiser, and, if Endicott was less strategically important than Yeltsin's Star, Masada also lacked Grayson's heavy orbital fortifications. More to the point, perhaps, even the briefest of raids could have catastrophic consequences if the Peeps only realized it. If they managed just to drive out the pickets and pick off the relatively weak orbital bases the Star Kingdom had placed in Masada orbit, General Marcel's ground forces would be hopelessly inadequate to police the planet. The Peeps wouldn't have to get involved in ground combat at all; all they'd have to do would be isolate the planet from outside relief, then sit back and watch the fanatics dirt-side swamp Marcel's people. The resultant massacre of the "infidel occupiers" and the government of moderates Marcel had managed to put in place would force Manticore to mount a punitive expedition and, all too probably, produce a long, bloody, ugly guerrilla war before control could be reasserted.

The effect of that on the Star Kingdom's domestic opinion could be catastrophic to public support for the war and the Cromarty Government, and that didn't even count the price in blood and suffering, Masadan as well as Manticoran, it would entail.

"I understand, Sir," she said, and Matthews nodded. "I thought you would." He looked back and forth between the two older—and junior—admirals for a moment, then drew a deep breath and shoved himself to his feet. "Very well, then. Let's—" he smiled at Honor as he used one of her favorite phrases "—be about it."

• CHAPTER EIGHTEEN

"Ahhhhhhh! Here we go, S—Citizen Commander. We've got customers."

Citizen Commander Caslet grimaced and crossed quickly to the tactical section, hoping—without much hope—that Citizen Commissioner Jourdain hadn't heard Shannon's slip. PNS *Vaubon*, unlike most of the PN's ships, had survived the last year of purges with her crew essentially intact, and that had tended to shield the light cruiser's company from some of the Republic's harsher realities. Caslet had reminded his people again and again that the Committee of Public Safety and its minions were *serious* about their egalitarianism, yet some of them, and especially Citizen Lieutenant Shannon Foraker, had a hard time remembering it. Shannon did fine when she took time to think before speaking, but she was a quint-essential example of what was still called "a techno nerd." She was brilliant in her area of specialization, but her social skills were an afterthought. When the tactical situation hit the fan—or when she simply got particularly intent on a task—she dropped back into old habits of speech without even realizing she'd done it.

But at least Jourdain was a pretty decent sort for a citizen commissioner, and Caslet had explained to him (at length) why Foraker was especially valuable to him. Shannon's talent for extrapolating data amounted to witchcraft, and she was one of the few Havenite tac officers immune to the PN's collective sense of techno-inferiority. She knew her instrumentation wasn't as good as the Manties', but she took it as a challenge, not a cause for despair. Caslet only hoped Jourdain grasped how important that was and would remain willing to put up with a few lapses in Shannon's revolutionary vocabulary.

He shook the thought aside and leaned over her shoulder to peer at her displays. Shannon was already bringing her computers fully on-line to enhance her passive sensors' data, and *Vaubon*'s captain frowned as the distant light codes crept slowly across the plot.

"What do you make of it, Shannon?"

"Well, now, Skipper, that's hard to say just yet." She tapped in a fresh enhancement command. "Sure wish we were a little closer," she grumbled. "This passive shit's for the birds at this range, Sir."

"*Citizen Commander*, Shannon!" Caslet whispered, and hid a sigh as the tac officer blinked, then shrugged the reminder aside. She had more important things on her mind, and Caslet darted an apologetic look at Jourdain. The commissioner didn't look happy, but he only strolled across the bridge to examine the environmental readouts. That put him far enough away to pretend he wasn't hearing anything, and Caslet thought a very loud mental thank-you in his direction, then turned back to Foraker.

The tac officer was muttering to herself while her fingers caressed her keypad with surgical skill, and Caslet waited as patiently as he could for her to remember to report to the rest of the universe. Unfortunately, she seemed too intent on the marvelous toys the People's Navy had obviously provided for her sole entertainment, and he cleared his throat.

"Talk to me, Shannon!" he said sternly, and she straightened with a start. She looked at him blankly for a moment, then grinned.

"Sorry, Skip. What did you say?"

"I said tell me what we've got." Caslet spoke with the patience one normally reserved for a small child, and Foraker had the grace to blush.

"Uh, yes, S—Citizen Commander. The problem is, I'm not entirely *sure* what we've got. Is there any way we could maybe sneak in a little closer?" she asked in a wheedling tone.

"No, there isn't," Caslet replied repressively. Shannon was familiar with their orders and knew better than to ask—which was the main reason he didn't add that *he* wished they could close on the contacts, too. Unfortunately, his instructions were clear: he was to keep *Vaubon's* presence completely covert, which meant no live impellers where the Manties might see them.

In Citizen Commander Warner Caslet's considered opinion, that was a pretty damned silly restriction. *Vaubon* was a hundred thousand klicks outside the Casca hyper limit; he could dart in for a closer look, make *positive* identification on his targets, then vanish into hyper before anyone could do anything about it, and he couldn't quite see why he shouldn't do so. It wasn't as if finding a Republican picket watching the system should surprise the Manties. They wouldn't be reinforcing unless they believed Haven might be interested in Casca, and confirmation that the People's Navy was keeping an eye on it should only encourage that belief. Which, as he understood it, had been the whole purpose of Operation Stalking Horse in the first place.

Orders, he thought. *Something unfortunate must happen to a person's brain when he turns into a flag officer.*

"Well, anything I tell you from this far out's gonna be a guess, Skipper," Shannon warned.

"So guess."

"Yes, Sir." The tac officer tapped a function key, and two of the thirteen capital ship codes on her display were suddenly ringed in white. "It looks like they must've refitted even more heavily than we figured they would," she said, "'cause I'm getting Manty emissions off all of them. Looks like they've done the next best thing to a complete replacement on their active sensors, but I'm picking up emissions from an Alpha-Romeo-Seven-Baker off these two puppies here, Skip."

"Are you, indeed?" Caslet murmured, and Foraker

nodded happily. The AR-7(b) was the standard search radar mounted in PN dreadnoughts and superdreadnoughts. It wasn't as good as the Manty equivalent—after all, he thought sourly, what Republican equipment *was?*—but that was mostly because the Manties' enhancement let them do more with the data they picked up. The AR-7 was about as powerful as its Manticoran equivalent and, all in all, a damned good installation, so it made sense that the Grayson Navy would have retained it if it had survived the ships' capture.

"Yep," Foraker replied cheerfully, but then her smile faded. "Problem is, Skip, that these're the *only* two I'm sure about. I've got the computers trying to run a correlation between impeller strength and acceleration, but we know the Manties are refitting across the board with the new inertial compensator. We're still guessing how much that improves their efficiency, and these birds are taking it mighty easy, so I don't have max power signatures to work with, but it may give us something on their masses." She shrugged. "Our SDs are smaller than theirs are. If I can get an idea—"

She broke off as an alarm chimed softly. Her fingers flickered across her panel again, and her face lit with a devilish smile.

"Well, now! I may just owe my 'puters an apology." She touched another function key, and three more light codes suddenly grew white rims. "Okay, what we've got here is speculative as hell, Skipper, but stay with me for a minute." Caslet nodded, and the tac officer tapped one of the light codes which *wasn't* ringed in white. "What I've done, Sir—oh, damn. I mean Citizen Commander." She sighed, looking past Caslet at Jourdain with an expression that mingled repentance and impatience, then shrugged. "At any rate, what I've done is make the best read I can from this range on their impeller strengths and correlate it with their observed acceleration rate. It's not going to tell us much about absolute masses, but it *can* indicate which ships are bigger than others, right?"

"Right." Caslet tried very hard not to sigh. Shannon really didn't understand how irritating it was to have things you already knew explained to you. On the other hand, her lecture mode normally insured that she caught anything you might *not* know . . . or that you'd simply forgotten to consider.

"All right," the tac officer said. "What I can tell you for certain, Skip, is that *this*—" she tapped the display again "—is the biggest single ship I've got good reads on, and that makes her an SD." Caslet nodded again. That was an unprovable assumption, but it was also a virtual certainty, and his eyes narrowed as Foraker flicked a finger at the trio of lights she'd just painted with white borders. "Well, these three here are in the same mass neighborhood, but they're pulling the same accel with only point-niner-five the impeller strength. Assuming that all of 'em have the new compensators, then that means they're *smaller* than our big boy, but not a lot. If the big guy *is* an SD, that means they're a hell of a lot bigger than any DN I've ever seen. Matter of fact, they match pretty damned well with the impeller strengths on the two we know have our radars aboard."

"The Manties have some smaller superdreadnoughts," Caslet pointed out, and Foraker nodded.

"Yep, but we know how *many* of 'em they've got, and that's the other thing my 'puters've been up to. See, Intelligence says they've got thirty-two of those smaller SDs at Thetis and Lowell, and the spooks put another five of 'em down south at Grendelsbane. That only leaves sixteen more in the whole Manty navy, and ten of *them're* supposed to be in their Home Fleet. There's no way anything could've gotten here from Manticore this fast, so we can ignore those ten—assuming Intelligence isn't talking out its ass again—and that gets us down to six unaccounted for. So since all five of these are smaller than Mister Big Fella, they're either five of the *DuQuesne*-class SDs the Manties gave Grayson or else they just happen to've sent out eighty-odd percent of all the Manty-built ships they *could* be in one fell swoop.

I don't know what the odds against that are, Skip, but they've gotta be pretty high."

"Very *good*, Shannon," Caslet said with a smile, and patted her on the shoulder. She was right—it was speculative. But it was good, intelligent speculation, and if their orders wouldn't let them go in for a decent look that was about the best he could hope for. "Anything else?"

"You want pretzels with your beer, Skipper? There's no way I can say anything more certain from this far out." Foraker frowned and tapped in yet another command, then grimaced. "Nope. All those other drive sources are kicking up too much interference. I can tell you there are at least five more of the wall on the far side of their main body, but I can't tell you anything about them. And on this heading, they're not gonna give me a good look before they go completely out of range into the inner system."

"All right, Shannon." He gazed at her display for another moment, then shrugged. "You did good to get this much."

"Any chance anyone else's gonna get a look at the other side of their formation?" Foraker asked hopefully.

"I'm afraid not," Caslet sighed. "*De Conde* is over there, but we're spread too far, and—" he grinned suddenly "—Citizen Commander Hewlett's tac witch isn't as good as mine." Foraker grinned back, and he patted her shoulder again before he turned and crossed the bridge to Jourdain.

"Well, Citizen Commander?" the commissioner asked.

"As I warned you, Citizen Commissioner," Caslet said formally, "we're too far out to be certain." Jourdain nodded with a trace of impatience, and Caslet shrugged. "With that proviso, I have to say it *looks* like the operation is succeeding. If you'd come with me?"

Jourdain followed him over to the astrogator's station, and he waved at the display. "As you can see, they came in on the right heading for a least-time passage from Yeltsin's Star. Moreover, Citizen Lieutenant Foraker has positively confirmed emissions from our own radar systems aboard two ships of the wall, which would seem to prove that they're two of the prize ships the Manties handed over to the Graysons.

"We also have evidence that at least three more of their ships are smaller than most Manticoran SDs. Again, that probably indicates that they're ex-PN prizes, but that conclusion is based solely on inferential evidence. There's no way we can confirm it without closing with the enemy, and our orders preclude that."

Jourdain nodded, and Caslet sighed.

"The main thing that worries me, Citizen Commissioner, is that there seem to be too many of them."

"Too many?" Jourdain repeated.

"Yes, Sir. We count thirteen of the wall."

"Ah." Jourdain gazed down at the astro display and plucked at his lip, and Caslet was grateful for the obvious intensity of the other man's thoughts. Jourdain had an undeniable edge of priggish revolutionary ardor, but he was also an intelligent man who paid as much attention to mission briefs as to the political reliability of *Vaubon's* crew.

"Exactly," the citizen commander said, after letting the commissioner ponder for a moment. "If these *are* the Grayson SDs, then they've picked up a pair of hitch-hikers somewhere."

"There could be any number of explanations for that," Jourdain countered. "The Manties are probably pulling in everything they can to respond to our attacks on Minette and Candor. This could be no more than a pair of dreadnoughts detached from convoy escort."

"No, Sir. At least one of them is an SD."

"They could still be convoy escorts."

"They could be, Citizen Commissioner, but it's not like the Manties to have single divisions of superdreadnoughts wandering around."

"Agreed," Jourdain sighed. He stood pondering the astro display a moment longer, then shrugged. "Well, whatever they are, they came in on a heading from Yeltsin, as you say. For that matter, Intelligence only gives

250 David M. Weber

about a sixty percent chance that even the Manticorans
could have gotten all eleven prizes back into service this
quickly. The Graysons are probably a bit slower than that,
so it's possible we're looking at two divisions of Manty
SDs, not one, and they're more likely to have been
moving a half-squadron independently than they are to
move a single division."

Caslet nodded thoughtfully. That was a possibility he
hadn't considered, and it made sense.

"At any rate," Jourdain went on, "if at least five of
them *are* Grayson ships, it seems likely they brought
everything Yeltsin could spare." The citizen commissioner
sounded a bit as if he were trying to convince himself
of that, Caslet noted, and said nothing. A brief silence
stretched out between them once more, and then
Jourdain nodded sharply to himself.

"All right," said. "If we've gotten all the information
we can from this range, then I suppose that's the best
we can do, Citizen Commander. Let's pull out for the
rendezvous."

• CHAPTER NINETEEN

Armsman Yard clicked to attention outside Honor's quarters at her approach, and she wondered if the procession looked as silly as it felt. Andrew LaFollet led the way, Jared Sutton and Abraham Jackson, the latter still in surplice and cassock, followed her, and Jamie Candless brought up the rear like an escorting destroyer. It still seemed awfully complicated to her, and she remembered the first time she'd dined with Benjamin Mayhew and his family. Her mouth quirked at the memory of how grateful she'd been that *she* didn't have to put up with twenty-four-hour security oversight. God, she'd decided long ago, had a strange sense of humor.

Candless and LaFollet peeled off as she and her two staff officers continued into the cabin. The dining cabin hatch was open, and MacGuiness had just finished setting the table.

"Ready for us, Mac?" she asked while Sutton and Jackson followed her across the carpet.

"Whenever you are, Milady," MacGuiness assured her, and pulled Nimitz's highchair back from the table. The 'cat leapt from her shoulder to the chair, and Honor grinned at her steward.

"I'm sure Commander Jackson needs to, ah, slip into something a bit more comfortable, first," she said. The chaplain chuckled, then peeled off his surplice, and MacGuiness shook his head reprovingly at Honor as he draped the spotless white garment carefully over his forearm.

"That's all, Mac," Jackson said with a smile of his own,

and ran a hand down his black cassock to smooth away a wrinkle. "I'm quite comfortable now, My Lady," he told Honor cheerfully. "After all, I wore *this* uniform for over five T-years before I ever tried on the Navy's."

"In that case, let's be seated, gentlemen," she invited. She took her own place, with Nimitz to her right and Sutton to her left while Jackson faced her from the table's far end, and watched MacGuiness pour the wine. The Gryphon vintage, a blush chablis from Wishbone, Gryphon's small, southern continent, was a bit sweet for Honor. She preferred a good, tart rosé or rich burgundy, but the Star Kingdom's softer wines had proven popular with Grayson palates, and it made an acceptable apéritif.

The steward finished pouring and withdrew, and Honor watched her guests sample their wine. She'd made a point of inviting Jackson to lunch after each Sunday's services, and Sutton joined her for virtually every meal as part of his ongoing professional education. He was far more confident and comfortable with his duties than he had been, but the social skills which went with a flag lieutenant's role still needed a little polishing. Besides, he was a member of her official "family," and she liked him.

She took a sip from her own glass, then looked at Jackson.

"If you don't mind an infidel's opinion, I particularly liked today's hymns, Abraham. Especially the one after the second lesson."

"I never mind compliments, My Lady," the chaplain replied, "and I'm rather fond of that one myself."

"It didn't sound much like the other Grayson hymns I've heard, though," Honor observed.

"That's because it's much older than most of our sacred music, My Lady. I believe the original version was written back in the nineteenth century—ah, the third century Ante Diaspora, that is—on Old Earth by a man named Whiting. Of course, that predated space travel. In fact, it predated manned aircraft, and it's been revised and updated several times since. Still, I think the original feeling comes through, and you're right: it is beautiful. And appropriate to naval service, I think."

"I agree. But, then, I usually like your taste in music. I only wish *I* had a singing voice that didn't sound like a GQ alarm." Jackson's raised glass acknowledged both the compliment and her wry commentary on her own voice, and she smiled back, but then her expression turned thoughtful.

"You know," she said slowly, "it still feels . . . odd to me to hold official church services on a warship." Jackson quirked an eyebrow, and she shook her head quickly. "Not *wrong*, Abraham, just odd. Manticoran warships do have services, and any captain always tries to adjust her duty schedules around them, but they're purely voluntary, and the people who conduct them usually have other duties, as well. The RMN doesn't have a Chaplain's Corps, you know."

"Well, fair's fair, My Lady," Jackson said after a moment. "A Grayson would find the notion that any Navy could survive without chaplains equally odd. Of course, we've made some concessions—and rightfully so, I think—since we started 'borrowing' so many Manticoran personnel. Attendance at service used to be compulsory, not optional, which would hardly be suitable now. Besides, even when everyone in uniform belonged to the Church, I always felt conscripting worshipers probably wasn't exactly what God had in mind."

Sutton started to speak, then closed his mouth and shifted in his chair, and Honor glanced at him.

"Yes, Jared?" she invited. The flag lieutenant hesitated a moment longer—he was still uncomfortable about injecting himself into a conversation between his seniors—then made a small grimace.

"I was just thinking, My Lady, that it's a pity certain other people don't feel the way Brother Jackson does about 'conscripting worshipers.' " He looked down the table at the chaplain. There was a hint of apology in his eyes, but also a lot of anger. Jared Sutton had developed a strong, personal loyalty to his admiral, and he didn't like Edmond Marchant a bit.

"If you're referring to Lord Burdette, you don't have to worry about *my* feelings, Jared." Jackson shook his head wryly, but the bitterness poisoning his usually cheerful expression belied his light tone. "I don't have a clue where that situation's going to end, but I know Reverend Hanks well enough to suspect he's not taking Burdette's activities very kindly. Bad enough for the man to remove the Sacristy's choice from the pulpit by force without *ordering* his steaders to attend services conducted by that sorry bas—" The chaplain broke off and flushed. The noun anger had almost betrayed him into using was hardly suitable for a clergyman, and especially not in Honor's presence. "I mean, by Marchant," he finished instead.

"Yes, well, that's getting a bit afield from my observation." Honor moved the subject firmly away from Burdette and Grayson's religious . . . well, crisis probably wasn't the right word yet, but it was moving in the right direction, and Jackson accepted the shift.

"You were saying something about official and unofficial worship services, My Lady?" he asked politely.

"I was saying Manticoran ships don't have official chaplains. Of course, we've got so many religions and denominations that providing a chaplain for each of them would be the next best thing to impossible even if we tried." She smiled suddenly. "On the first SD I ever served in, the captain was a Roman Catholic—Second Reformation, I think; not the Old Earth denomination—the exec was an Orthodox Jew, the astrogator was a Buddhist, and the com officer was a Scientologist Agnostic. If I remember correctly, the tac officer—my direct superior—was a Mithran, and Chief O'Brien, my tracking yeoman, was a Shinto priest. All of that, mind you, just on the command deck! We had another six thousand odd people in the ship's company, and God only knows how many different religions *they* represented."

"Merciful Tester!" Jackson murmured in a voice that

was only half humorous. "How do any of you manage to keep things straight?"

"Well, Manticore was settled by a bunch of secularists," Honor pointed out. "I hope you won't take this wrongly, but I sometimes think that what Grayson actually has is a church which spawned a state as a sort of accidental appendage. I realize things have changed, especially since the Civil War, but the very notion of a church-dominated state would have been anathema to the Manticoran colonists. They'd had too much historical experience with state churches back home."

Jackson cocked his head as he listened to her, then nodded with an air of thoughtful comprehension, but Sutton looked puzzled.

"Excuse me, My Lady, but I don't quite understand," he said.

"What the Steadholder means, Jared, is—" Jackson began, then broke off with a grimace. "Excuse me, My Lady. I believe *you* were making a point." His grimace became a grin. "Sometimes I tend to backslide into confirmation class mode."

"No, really?" Honor teased gently. The chaplain bent his head in a gesture of surrender, and she turned to Sutton. "Both the people who settled Grayson and the people who settled Manticore came mainly from Old Earth's western hemisphere, Jared, but they had very different reasons for leaving the Sol System.

"The Manticoran colonists primarily wanted to get away from a grossly overcrowded planet. They felt crowded and hemmed in and they were looking for both living space and economic opportunity elsewhere, but very few of them signed on because they felt like a persecuted minority.

"Grayson's colonists, on the other hand, were classic religious emigrés who *did* regard themselves as a persecuted minority. So whereas the Manticorans came from the entire spectrum of Old Earth's religious backgrounds, *your* ancestors came from a single one. That was, in fact, what set them apart from the entire civilization they were fleeing, which made it inevitable that they should develop a single state church and a theocratic state here."

"I see that, My Lady, but what did you mean about the Manties' 'historical experience with state churches'?"

"Two-thirds of Manticore's colonists were from Europe, and Europe had a history of sectarian violence and religious conflict that went back to, oh, the sixth century Ante Diaspora, at least. Whole nations had spent centuries trying to kill each other over religious differences—like your own Civil War. The colonists didn't want anything like that happening to them, so they adopted the traditions of those of their numbers who came from North America, where separation between church and state had been part of the fundamental law. In the Star Kingdom, the state is legally *prohibited* from interfering in religious matters, and vice versa."

Sutton blinked. The notion of an explicit split between church and state seemed so alien that he looked at Jackson as if seeking confirmation that such a thing was even possible.

"Lady Harrington's quite correct," the chaplain told him gently. "And given the wide religious diversity in the Star Kingdom, its founders were very wise to set things up that way." He smiled sadly. "Anyone who studies history eventually comes up against the same cruel irony, Jared. Man has probably spent more time killing his fellows 'in God's name' than for any other single reason. Look at our own Civil War, or those lunatics on Masada." He sighed. "I know He loves us, but we must be a terrible disappointment to Him from time to time."

The primary supports were all in, and Adam Gerrick stood on the scaffolding which crowned what would become the dome's number one access annex and watched huge, glittering panes of crystoplast rising delicately into place. Although the crystoplast was barely three millimeters thick and far lighter than an equal volume of glass, the smallest panel was over six meters on a side, and while Grayson's gravity was less than that of Lady

Harrington's home world, it was seventeen percent higher than Old Earth's. Only four years before, the men maneuvering them into place would have relied upon grunting, snorting cranes and brute force; now they used counter-grav to nudge the shimmering, near-invisible panes into position with cautious ease, and Gerrick felt a thrill of pride he hadn't yet learned to take for granted.

He turned in place to survey the entire site. This was one of the smaller jobs, for Lord Mueller had decided he needed a demonstration project before he committed to something the size of a farm or city dome, but he'd certainly picked a gorgeous spot to put it. When the project was finished, it would protect the brand new Winston Mueller Middle School, set atop a bluff overlooking God's Tears, the most beautiful chain of lakes on the continent of Idaho. The school's buildings were in, and once the bluff wore its dome like a gleaming, high-tech crown, work crews would plant Old Terran grass and lay out playing fields, and—Gerrick chuckled—Lady Harrington was donating one of her "swimming pools." The school administrator had expressed his thanks, but the poor man still seemed dreadfully confused by the whole idea.

Small as it was, the project was certainly one of the most satisfying Sky Domes had underway. Especially for him. The entire dome concept had been his, but in the beginning, he'd thought of it primarily as a fascinating challenge to adapt Manticoran technology to Grayson needs, without really considering all its implications. Now that those implications had become a reality, he felt a deep, complex joy, a happiness that mingled the satisfaction of a challenge met with that sense of accomplishment—of knowing he would leave his world a better place than he had found it—which only the most fortunate of engineers got to savor.

And, he admitted with a broad smile, the fact that he was also in the process of becoming one of the wealthiest men in Grayson's history was pretty nice icing for his cake.

He turned back to the east and watched as the first section went into the uppermost tier. The dome looked lopsided and dangerously unbalanced with that single pane leaning so far out over the center of the school, but Gerrick saw with an engineer's eye. He'd personally checked every decimal place of the stress calculations, and he'd designed a safety margin of well over five hundred percent into the support structure.

The paneling teams sealed the pane with an instantly-setting caulking compound and moved quickly to the west side of the dome. Despite the safety factor, they wanted to complete the first full cross section of roof quickly to balance the stress, and Gerrick approved. Engineers believed as firmly in their calculations as they did in God, but they also believed in minimizing exposure to the Demon Murphy.

Gerrick smiled at the familiar thought and looked down as the high, clear sound of a child's voice cut through the work site's noise. A group of kids—students-to-be in the middle school—had asked permission to watch the completion of the main dome, and their teachers, after checking with the site supervisors, had organized a field trip. Needless to say, the Sky Domes staff had impressed them with the dangers the construction equipment represented, and Grayson children learned early to take adults' warnings to heart. They were well back under the completed eastern wall, and they were staying there, but that didn't mute their avid interest. He could see their excitement even from here as they watched the panels drifting upward on their countergrav like some sort of impossibly beautiful seed pods and chattered to one another, and he smiled. He'd talked to some of those youngsters himself this morning, and two or three had looked like they had the making of good engineers.

He let his eyes sweep proudly back up the glittering wall above the kids . . . and that meant he saw it all happen.

It started almost gently, as the most terrible accidents

so often do. The first movement was tiny, so slight he thought he'd imagined it, but he hadn't. One of the primary load-bearing supports—a solid shaft of alloy orders of magnitude stronger than titanium set in a hole bored fourteen meters into solid bedrock and sealed with over a hundred tons of ceramacrete—swayed like a young tree in a breeze. But that support was no sapling. It was a vital component of the dome's integrity, and even as Gerrick stared at it in disbelief it was turning, *twisting* in its socket as if it had been tamped into place with so much sand and not sealed into the densest, hardest mineral building material known to man. It couldn't happen. It wasn't just unlikely, it was *impossible*, and Gerrick knew it, for he was the man who'd designed it . . . but it was also happening.

His eyes whipped unerringly to the supports which shared that shaft's component of the dome's weight. An untrained eye wouldn't even have known which ones to look at; to Gerrick, it was as obvious as if he'd spent hours pouring over the schematics that very morning, and his heart leapt into his throat with horror as he saw one of *them* shifting as well!

He stared at it for one terrible, endless instant, his engineer's mind leaping ahead to the disaster to come. It was only a moment, no more than four seconds—possibly five; certainly not more than six—yet that moment of stunned inactivity would haunt Adam Gerrick. It didn't make any difference. He knew that—didn't *think* it, but *knew* it. Too much mass was in motion. The inevitable chain of events was beyond the control of any man, and nothing he did or didn't do could make the slightest difference, yet Gerrick would never forgive himself for that moment of stasis.

A soft, almost inaudible groan came from the moving supports, and a pane of crystoplast popped free. The glittering panel dropped, no longer drifting and lovely in its counter-grav supports but slashing downward like a gleaming guillotine, and Adam Gerrick began to run.

He flung himself down the scaffolding, screaming a

warning, running straight towards the collapsing horror of his dream. It was madness—a race which could end only in his own death if he won it—but he didn't think about that. He thought only of the children, standing in what was supposed to be the safest part of the entire site . . . directly under those creaking, groaning, treacherously shifting supports.

Perhaps, he told himself later, if he'd reacted faster, if he'd started running sooner, if he'd screamed a louder warning, perhaps it would have made a difference. The engineer in him, the part of his brain and soul which manipulated numbers and load factors and vectors of force knew better, but Gerrick had two children of his own, and the father in him would never, ever, forgive himself for not having *made* it make a difference.

He saw one of the kids turn and look at him. It was a girl, no more than eleven, and Adam Gerrick saw her smile, unaware of what was happening. He saw her wave at him, happy and excited by all the activity . . . and then he saw eighty thousand metric tons of alloy and crystoplast and plunging horror come crashing down and blot that smile away forever.

• CHAPTER TWENTY

Honor Harrington sat in her quarters and stared numbly at nothing while Nimitz curled in her arms and buried his muzzle against her. For once, even he was quenched, too crushed to comfort her, for he, too, loved children.

Thirty of them, she thought emptily. Thirty *children*, the oldest of them thirteen, wiped away in a moment of transcendent horror. Crushed to death, ground to mangled ruin under eighty thousand tons of wreckage, and it was her fault. Whatever had happened, whatever had led to the disaster, *she* was the one who'd originally bankrolled Sky Domes. It was her money which had made the company a success, and her eagerness to win jobs and income for her steaders which had spread it across the entire planet.

A tear flowed down her face, prickling and alien feeling to the artificial nerves of her left cheek, and she made no move to dry it. Children, she thought despairingly. Intentionally or not, she'd killed *children*.

And fifty-two other people had died with them, a cruel corner of her brain reminded her. Three had been teachers supervising their students—teachers who'd undoubtedly had a moment of horror to realize what was happening to their charges—but the others had been Sky Domes employees. *Honor's* employees, most of them her own steaders.

She drew a deep, shuddering breath and hugged Nimitz's warm, living weight while the tears flowed faster and her memory replayed Adam Gerrick's com message with merciless clarity. She saw his tattered clothing, the

ripped and torn hands which had fought madly to heave
wreckage off small, crushed bodies . . . the bloodstains
and his haggard, tear-stained face. He was a man who'd
looked upon Hell. A man who wished he'd died with
the victims of his dream, and she understood perfectly.

"*No*, damn it!" Adam Gerrick shouted, and his torn
hands quivered with the desire to strangle the officious
bastard in front of him. "My people *have* to be part of
the investigation!"

"I'm afraid that will be impossible," the building
inspector replied with cold, bitter venom. They faced
each another in the tangled wreckage of Winston Mueller
Middle School, and their crews stood behind them like
two hostile armies. The surviving Sky Domes people had
worked like demons, risking life and limb side by side
with the Mueller rescue personnel in a frantic effort to
save as many lives as possible. But the last survivor had
been removed hours ago. It would be days, even with
Manticoran equipment, before the last body was recovered, and now that the desperation which had prevented
them from considering *how* it had happened had eased,
the shock which had made them allies had turned into
searing anger.

"Then *make* it possible!" Gerrick raged. "Damn it,
man, I've got twenty-three *other* projects! I've *got* to
know what happened here!"

"What happened, Mr. Gerrick," the inspector said in
that same cold, vicious voice, "is that your workers just
killed eighty-two people—including thirty *children* who
were citizens of this steading." Gerrick flinched as if he'd
been struck, and the inspector's eyes glowed with savage satisfaction. "As for why it happened, I have no doubt
we'll discover substandard construction materials and
practices brought it about."

"No," Gerrick half-whispered. He shook his head vio-
lently. "Sky Domes would never do something like that!
My God, fifty of *our* people died here. Do you think
we'd . . . we'd—"

"I don't have to *think*, Mr. Gerrick!" The inspector nodded to one of his assistants, and the man held out a lump of what should have been heat-fused ceramacrete. The assistant looked straight into Adam Gerrick's eyes and closed his fist, and the "ceramacrete" crumbled like a clod of sun-dried mud. Dust drifted from his fingers on the evening breeze, and there was naked hate in the eyes staring into Gerrick's.

"If you think for one minute that I'm going to give you *bastards* a chance to cover this up, then I'm here to tell you you're wrong, *Mr.* Gerrick." The inspector's voice was far more terrible for its total, icy control. "I am going to personally validate every single example of substandard workmanship on this project," he said. "And after I've done that, I'm going to personally see that you and every officer of your goddamned company are prosecuted for *murder*, and if one of you—even *one* of you— is still on this site in ten minutes, then my men will by God shoot the bastard!"

"My God," Benjamin Mayhew whispered. His eyes were locked to the live reports from Mueller Steading, and his face was white. Chancellor Prestwick stood beside his desk, staring at the same reportage, and his face was even whiter and more drawn than the Protector's.

"My God in Heaven," Mayhew repeated in a harrowed voice. "*How*, Henry? How did something like this *happen?*"

"I don't know, Your Grace," Prestwick murmured ashenly. He watched a massive beam being moved aside, and his eyes were sick as another small, broken body was lifted tenderly from under it. Work lights poured pitiless brilliance over the night-struck scene, and Mueller Guard armsmen formed a cordon around the site. The parents of the dead children stood just beyond that cordon, fathers with their arms about their wives, faces twisted with terrible grief, and the Chancellor's hands shook as he lowered himself into a chair at last.

"The Mueller inspectors claim it's the result of substandard materials, Your Grace," he said finally, and winced at the look the Protector threw him.

"Lady Harrington would never condone that!" Benjamin snapped. "And our own people saw every facet of that design. It *exceeded* code standards in every parameter, and Sky Domes was still going to show a twenty-five percent profit margin! My God, Henry, what possible motive could she have had?"

"I didn't say she did, Your Grace," the Chancellor replied, but he shook his head as he spoke. "Nor did I say *she* knew anything about it. But look at the scale of the projects. Think about all the opportunities for someone *else* to skim off the top by substituting sub-code materials."

"Never." Benjamin's voice was ice.

"Your Grace," Prestwick said heavily, "the Mueller inspectors have sent ceramacrete samples to the Sword laboratories here in Austin. I've seen the preliminary reports. The final product did *not* meet code standards."

Benjamin stared at him, trying to understand, but the scale of such a crime was too vast to comprehend. To use substandard materials for a school's dome was unthinkable. No Grayson would put *children* at risk! Their entire society—their whole way of life—was built on *protecting* their children!

"I'm sorry, Your Grace," Prestwick said more gently. "Sorrier than I can say, but I've *seen* the reports."

"Lady Harrington couldn't have known," the Protector whispered. "Whatever your reports say, she *couldn't have known*, Henry. She would *never* have permitted something like this, and neither would Adam Gerrick."

"I agree with you, Your Grace, but—forgive me if I seem cold—but what does that matter? Lady Harrington is Sky Domes' majority stockholder, Gerrick is their chief engineer—even Howard Clinkscales is their CEO. However it happened, the legal responsibility falls squarely on them. It was their *job* to see to it that a disaster like this never, ever, happened . . . and they didn't do it."

The Protector scrubbed his face with his hands, and

a cold chill went through him, one that was totally independent of the death and destruction on his HD. He loathed himself for feeling it, but he had no choice; he was the Protector of Grayson. He *had* to be a political animal as well as a father with children of his own.

Henry had seen the reports. Within days—hours—the news people would have them, as well, and what the Chancellor had just said would be being said over every news channel on the planet. Nothing—*nothing*—could have been better calculated to infuriate Graysons, and every person who'd ever denounced Honor Harrington, every person who'd ever even entertained private *doubts* about her, would hear those reports and awaken to a deep, implacable hatred for the woman who'd let this happen. And hard on the heels of that hate would come the denunciations, no longer whispers but shouts of fury. "Look!" they would cry. "Look what happens when you let a *woman* exercise a man's authority! Look at our murdered children and tell me *this* was God's will!"

Benjamin Mayhew could already hear those anguished, heartfelt cries, and in them he heard the utter destruction of his reforms.

"Dear Tester, what have we *done?*" William Fitzclarence whispered. He, too, sat staring at an HD, and Samuel Mueller and Edmond Marchant sat on either side of him. "Children," Lord Burdette groaned. "We've killed *children!*"

"No, My Lord," Marchant said. Burdette looked at him, blue eyes dark with horror, and the defrocked priest shook his head, his own eyes dark with purpose, not shock. "*We* killed no one, My Lord," he said in a soft, persuasive voice. "It was God's will that the innocent perish, not ours."

"*God's* will?" Burdette repeated numbly, and Marchant nodded.

"You know how little choice we have in doing His work, My Lord. We *must* bring the people to their senses, show them the danger of allowing themselves to be poisoned by this harlot and her corrupt society."

"But this—!" Burdette's voice was a bit stronger, and a hint of color flowed back into his ashen face, and Marchant sighed sadly.

"I know, My Lord, yet it *was* God's will. We had no way to know children would be present, but He did. Would He have allowed the dome to collapse when it did if it wasn't part of His plan? Terrible as their deaths were, their souls are with Him now—innocent of sin, untouched by the world's temptations—and their deaths have multiplied the effect of our plan a thousand fold. Our entire *world* now sees the consequences of embracing Manticore and the Protector's 'reforms,' and nothing, My Lord, *nothing*, could have driven that lesson home as this has. Those children are the Lord's martyrs, fallen in His service as surely as any martyr ever perished for his Faith."

"He's right, William," Mueller said quietly. Burdette turned to his fellow Steadholder, and Mueller raised one hand. "My inspectors have already found the substandard ceramacrete. I'll wait a day or so before announcing it—long enough for us to check and recheck the analyses, so that no one can possibly question our conclusions—but the proof is there. The *proof*, William. There's no way that harlot or the Protector can weasel their way around it. We didn't pick the moment it would collapse; God did that, and in doing so he made our original plan enormously more successful than we'd ever dared hope."

"Maybe . . . maybe you're right," Burdette said slowly. The horror had faded in his eyes, replaced by the supporting self-righteousness of his faith . . . and a cold light of calculation. "It's *her* fault," he murmured, "not ours. *She's* the one who drove us to this."

"Of course she is, My Lord," Marchant agreed. "It takes a sharp sword to cut away Satan's mask, and we who wield the Lord's blade can only accept whatever price He thinks mete to ask of us."

"You're right, Edmond," Burdette said in a stronger

voice. He nodded and looked back at the HD, and this time there as a slight, sneering curl to his lip as he listened to the reporter's grief-fogged voice.

"You're right," Steadholder Burdette repeated. "We've set our hands to God's work. If He demands we bear the blood price, then His will be done, and may that harlot burn in Hell for all eternity for driving us to this."

Adam Gerrick walked into the conference room, and his face was terrible. The young man who'd left for Mueller Steading that morning had died with the collapse of his shining dream. The Adam Gerrick who'd returned to Harrington was a haunted man, with the joy of accomplishment quenched to bitter ashes in his eyes.

But he was also an angry man, filled with rage and determined to find out what had happened. He'd find the man whose greed was responsible for this carnage—this murder—he promised himself, and when he did, he'd kill the cold, calculating bastard with his two bare hands.

"All right," he said harshly to his senior engineers, "the Mueller inspectors have barred us from the site, but we still have our own records. We know what was *supposed* to go into that project, and we are going to find out what *actually* went into it . . . and how."

"But—" The man who'd started to speak closed his mouth as cold, burning eyes swiveled to his face. He licked his lips and looked appealingly at his colleagues, then turned unwillingly back to his superior.

"What?" Gerrick asked in a liquid helium voice.

"I've already *pulled* the records, Adam," Frederick Bennington said. "I've checked everything that went to the site and compared expenditures in every category against what we still have in invoice."

"And?"

"And it all checks!" Bennington said forcefully. "We didn't skimp anywhere, Adam, I swear it." He laid a minicomp on the table. "There are the records, and they're not just mine. I'm in charge of procurement, and that makes me the logical suspect. I know that. So when I pulled the records, I took Jake Howell from Accounting with me, and I brought in three inspectors from the Harrington Bureau of Records. These figures are *solid*, Adam. We checked them five times. Every single item we bought and shipped to that site met or surpassed Sword code standards."

"Then someone swapped them on-site," Gerrick rasped. "Some bastard skimmed the code materials and replaced them with crap."

"No way, Adam." Despite his own shock, Bennington's voice was flat with assurance. "Not possible. We're working round-the-clock shifts, and we've maintained continuous on-site visual records. You know that." Gerrick nodded slowly, his expression suddenly intent, for Sky Domes was in the midst of a motion efficiency study, and that required detailed visual records of all their procedures.

"All right," Bennington went on, "if anyone *had* stolen materials from the site, we'd have at least some evidence of it on record. But every air lorry that entered or left that site is on chip, Adam, and aside from the disposal lorries headed for reclamation or the landfill, none of them—I repeat, *none* of them—left loaded. All materials movement was *into* the site."

"But I *saw* the ceramacrete," Gerrick said. "One of the inspectors crushed it, Fred. Just crushed it in his hand, like . . . like so much packing material!"

"I can't help that," Bennington replied. "All I can tell you is that we have certified records that it *couldn't* have been substandard materials."

"Records no one will believe." Howard Clinkscales' voice was harsh as he spoke at last, and every eye turned to him. "*We* may know they're accurate, but who's going to take our word? If Adam saw substandard materials, then there are substandard materials on the site. We don't know how they got there, but we can't dispute their existence, and our *Steadholder* is Sky Domes' majority stockholder. If we make our records public, all we'll do is destroy any last vestige of trust in her. Burdette and his supporters will scream that we doctored them—that *her* inspectors signed off on their falsification because she told them to—and we can't prove that didn't happen. Not with physical proof of wrongdoing sitting right there in Mueller."

He looked around the table, and his heart felt old and frozen as he saw the understanding on the engineers' faces. But Adam Gerrick shook his head, and there was no surrender in his eyes.

"You're wrong, Lord Clinkscales," he said flatly. The regent blinked at him, unaccustomed to being contradicted in such a hard, certain voice. "You're not an engineer, Sir. No doubt you're right about what will happen if we turn Fred's records over to the press, but we *can* prove what happened."

"How?" Clinkscales's desire to believe showed in his voice, but there was little hope behind it.

"Because *we*—" Gerrick waved at the men around the table "—*are* engineers. The *best* damned engineers on this damned planet, and we *know* our records are accurate. More than that, we have a complete visual record of everything that happened at that site, including the collapse itself. And on top of that, we've got not just the plans and the final specs that went into them, we've got all the original calculations, from the first rough site survey through every step of the process."

"And?"

"And that means we have all the pieces, My Lord. If Fred's right about the quality of the materials we shipped to that site, then someone, somewhere, *made* that dome collapse, and we've got the data we need to figure out how the bastard did it."

"*Made* it collapse?" Clinkscales stared at the younger man. "Adam, I know you don't want to believe it was our fault—dear God, *I* don't want to believe it!—but if it wasn't a simple case of materials theft, what else *could* it be? Surely you're not suggesting someone *wanted* it to collapse!"

"When you eliminate all the impossible factors, whatever's left must be the truth. And I am telling you, My Lord, that *if* that dome was built with the materials we specified and *if* the plans we provided were followed, then the collapse I saw this morning *could not happen*."

"But—" Clinkscales paused, and something happened in his eyes. The man who'd once been Planetary Security's commanding general looked suddenly out of them, and his voice changed. "Why would anyone deliberately sabotage the project?" he asked, and he was no longer rejecting the notion; he was looking for answers. "What sort of evil monster would murder *children*, Adam?"

"I don't know the answer to that yet, Sir—but I intend to find out," Gerrick said grimly.

"How can you?"

"The first thing we'll do," Gerrick said, turning to his staff, "is put the visual records through the computers. I want an exact analysis of what happened. The collapse started in the alpha ring of the east quadrant—I saw it go myself—but I want a detailed breakdown of every step of the process."

"I can handle that," one of the others said in the voice of a man thankful for a task he could perform. "It'll take ten or twelve hours to break down all the visual records, but I'll guarantee what we get will be solid."

"All right. Once we have *that*, we model every possible combination of factors that could have caused it. Somebody get us the Mueller met records for the last three months. I don't see how it could have happened, but it's just possible some sort of freak weather effect could have contributed."

"Not likely, Adam," someone else objected.

"Of course it isn't, but we need to consider *every* possibility, and not just for our own analysis. I want the sick son-of-a-bitch who did this. I want him in front of a court of law, and I want a front row seat for his hanging. I *saw* those kids die." Gerrick shivered, and his face was drawn and even older for just a moment. Then he shook himself. "I saw them die," he repeated, "and when we find the man who murdered them, I don't want there to be one scrap of doubt about it."

A low, harsh growl of agreement answered him, and then Clinkscales frowned thoughtfully.

"You're right, Adam. If—and at this point it's *only* an 'if'—but *if* someone deliberately caused this, then our data has to be absolutely solid. No loose ends anyone can question." Gerrick nodded sharply, and the regent went on in that same, thoughtful tone which did nothing to hide his own anger. "And there's something else you need to consider. You and your staff may be able to tell us *what* happened, and *how*, but there's still the question of who and why, and we have to nail that down just as tight."

"That may be harder, Sir—especially the 'why,'" Gerrick cautioned.

"Adam," Clinkscales said with a cold, frightening smile, "you're an engineer. I used to be a policeman, and, I like to think, a pretty good one. If there's a who and a why, I'll find them." He turned his gaze on another man, at the far end of the table. "Chet, I want the personnel records on that work crew. While you start your analysis of what happened, I'm going to be looking at every single human being who had a hand in the construction. If this was deliberate, then somewhere, somebody left a fingerprint. When you people can tell me what they did and how they did it, I'll know where to look for the person or persons behind it. And when I find them, Adam," he said with an even more terrifying smile, "I promise you'll have that front row seat you wanted."

• CHAPTER TWENTY-ONE

Citizen Rear Admiral Thomas Theisman stepped into PNS *Conquistador*'s flag briefing room with Citizen Commissioner Dennis LePic at his heels. Theisman didn't much care for LePic, but he knew most of that stemmed from his dislike for carrying a constant political anchor around with him. He'd seen the consequences of political interference in military operations often enough without ferrying politicians to the very site of the action so they could screw things up even faster.

On the other hand, he also knew how fortunate he was to be here himself. He'd survived Haven's original fiasco in Yeltsin only because he'd been lucky enough (and luck, he knew, was precisely the right word for it) to damage several of Honor Harrington's ships before his destroyer was forced to surrender to her. Only that achievement, coupled with the distraction of Captain Yu's defection to Manticore, had saved him from the Legislaturalist admirals seeking a scapegoat for that particular screw-up. And, he admitted, only the destruction of the old regime had saved him from the consequences of what had happened to the Ninth Cruiser Squadron in the opening moves of the current war. He'd made his Legislaturalist commodore look like an idiot, and her patrons would have squashed him like a bug for daring to be right when she was wrong. But the *new* regime had been looking for *Legislaturalist* scapegoats, so Commodore Reichman had been shot and Captain Theisman had been promoted.

The universe, he reflected, was not precisely overrunning with fairness, but it did seem that what went around came around. A point the Committee of Public Safety might want to bear in mind.

He shook off his thoughts as he took his seat at the conference table and LePic slid into the chair beside him. Citizen Vice Admiral Thurston and Citizen Commissioner Preznikov were already ensconced at the head of the table, and Meredith Chavez, Task Group 14.1's CO, nodded to Theisman from across the table. Theisman didn't know George DuPres, Chavez's commissioner, but he was rumored to be more willing than most to let the professionals get on with their profession, which probably helped explain Meredith's cheerful demeanor.

Citizen Rear Admiral Chernov and Citizen Commissioner Johnson of TG 14.3 arrived less than three minutes after Theisman, and Task Force Fourteen's command team was complete. Except, of course, for their chiefs of staff, whom what passed for Fleet HQ these days had decreed could not be informed of the details until Operation Dagger was actually launched. *Not* the most promising of preparations for an op this complex, although, to give the staff pukes their due, Dagger should be a piece of cake if Stalking Horse had succeeded.

Of course, "if" wasn't a word Thomas Theisman had ever been particularly happy about including in operational planning.

"I see we're all here," Thurston remarked. "And since we are, I can tell you that Stalking Horse seems to have worked out quite nicely."

Chavez and Chernov grinned, but Theisman contented himself with a nod. "Seems." Another of those words with unfortunate connotations.

Thurston activated the holo display, and a star map appeared above the table. He manipulated controls briefly, and Minette and Candor blinked red. A moment later, Casca, Doreas, and Grendelsbane also began flashing, but their lights were amber, not red.

"All right," he said. "You all know Citizen Admiral McQueen and Citizen Admiral Abbot have secured control of Minette and Candor. McQueen took a heavier hit from the Manty pickets than we anticipated, but they burned off all their missiles to do it. All they can do now is stooge around the outer system and watch her, and they took losses of their own. What they've got left couldn't take her on even with full magazines.

"Citizen Admiral Abbot's in even better shape. He got in without a shot, and the Manties don't have anything heavier than a battlecruiser to picket him."

Thurston paused and looked around the table to make sure everyone was with him, then used a cursor to indicate Grendelsbane.

"As you also know, we've had light, covert pickets in place around Grendelsbane and Casca for over a month, and Admiral Hemphill seems to be playing it very cautiously in Grendelsbane. She's retained her ships of the wall there—probably to be sure we don't make another flank pounce if she uncovers it—but she's dispatched a heavy battlecruiser force to support the Doreas pickets. In addition, some of her light units have joined the Manty picket still in Minette. That suggests her attention's focused there while she waits for reinforcements before going in to take it back . . . just as we want her to do.

"More to the point," the cursor swooped up to Casca, "our scouts up here report the arrival of a pretty damned powerful task force. I wonder where *they* came from?"

Thurston bared his teeth, and this time even Theisman smiled back. *Damn*, he thought. *The man's a calculating son-of-a-bitch, but he* does *know how to work a crowd!*

"We didn't get as good a read on them as I'd like," Thurston admitted, "but what we did get seems to indicate they've done what we wanted. We have positive confirmation of at least five ex-PN prize ships there, and their arrival time works out right for an immediate response from Yeltsin to Stalking Horse. In addition, the entire force arrived as a single unit, which indicates it was pulled *out* as a unit. This isn't something they put together by scraping up ships from other locations, people."

Theisman nodded, but something about Thurston's confident explanation nagged at him, and he raised a hand.

"Citizen Admiral Theisman?"

"You say we have confirmation on *five* ex-PN prizes, Citizen Admiral?"

"That's correct."

"But *only* five?" Theisman pressed respectfully, and Thurston exchanged glances with Preznikov before he nodded.

"That's correct, Citizen Admiral," he repeated. "The range was quite long, and you know how hard it can be to interpret passive data. In addition, the Manties and Graysons seem to have refitted them even more heavily than we'd anticipated, which makes emission analysis proportionately more difficult. Given the timing, however, and the size of the force, my staff and I are confident several of the capital ships our scouts were unable to positively identify were actually prizes which had simply been refitted too extensively for us to ID with certainty."

"How many other ships are we talking about, Citizen Admiral?"

"Eight of the wall—*probably* eight, that is." Theisman frowned thoughtfully, and Thurston shrugged. "No doubt they picked up a couple of Manty extras that happened to be in-system. We know they've pulled all of the Manty ships of the wall which were stationed in Yeltsin out of the area—they've been positively IDed at Thetis—but it's a logical place to stage through. A good area for final exercises before they commit new units to the front."

Theisman sat back with a nod, for Thurston was certainly right about that. And the fact that the *Graysons* doubtlessly needed all the training they could get would only make the practice even more attractive to the Manties. Still . . .

He ran his mind back over his own intelligence package. Assuming Intelligence had it right, even Manticoran yards couldn't have more than eight or *possibly* nine of

Grayson's eleven prizes back into service yet. If the original damage estimates were correct, he thought sardonically, the *Republic* couldn't have gotten more than six of them back on-line this soon, and it was unlikely Grayson could be as efficient as Manties were. Not yet, anyway. And if Intelligence's estimate was accurate, and if five of the prize ships had been positively located at Casca, Thurston was probably right: the Alliance *had* stripped the system to cover against the threat from Candor.

"On the basis of that intelligence," Thurston went on, "Citizen Commissioner Preznikov and I have decided to activate Operation Dagger in seventy-two hours. We'd like to start immediately, but we've agreed that it would be wise to spend two or three days rehearsing the operation now that we're cleared to brief your staffs and unit commanders."

Well, thank God for that, Theisman thought. Task Force Fourteen had over a hundred and sixty ships on its order of battle, including thirty-six battleships and twenty-four battlecruisers. That sounded impressive as hell, but operational security had been so tight that virtually none of their ships' companies had the least idea what Operation Dagger was about. Theisman himself, with LePic's clandestine approval, had "accidentally" leaked the ops plan to his own staff, so he'd managed to put together a series of contingency plans he could live with, but none of his captains knew what was supposed to happen. The Committee of Public Safety had seen to it that they'd learned not to ask questions, too. The chance to brief and rehearse them, even if only for a couple of days, would be invaluable, and Theisman wondered how Thurston had gotten Preznikov to agree to it. It was possible the commissioner had succumbed to the force of logic, but Theisman warned himself not to indulge his optimism too wildly on that point.

"All right," Thurston went on. "Here's what I have in mind. First, I'll give you three hours to brief in your staffs and unit COs. At thirteen hundred, Commissioner

Preznikov and I will set up a task force conference net to handle any questions you or any of your people may have. After that—at, say, sixteen hundred—we'll start with a sim of the primary plan of attack, with Citizen Admiral Chavez coordinating. Citizen Commissioner Preznikov and I will observe and run the Graysons for the first sim. After that—"

The news, as the Protector had known it must, had leaked, and the media was playing the story for all it was worth.

No, he told himself sternly, that wasn't fair. The Grayson press corps was more responsible than most. In fact, it was possibly a bit too much on the "tame" side—as a reflection of its society's deference-based mores and traditional respect for authority, no doubt—and the newsies had checked their facts carefully before going public. Unfortunately, they had those facts straight, and one thing Benjamin Mayhew had learned from others' mistakes was to never, ever lie to reporters. Refusing to comment and keeping a lid on stories was one thing; destroying his credibility forever was something else entirely, and it was a deadly simple thing to do.

So he'd confirmed the lab reports in as noninflammatory a fashion as possible and preserved his credibility . . . for whatever that was worth.

Shock and grief had swept the planet even before the reports made the news. Despite its ancient tradition of steading autonomy, Grayson was a world whose people rallied almost instinctively to their neighbors' support in time of trouble. But Mueller's internal resources had sufficed to do what pitifully little could be done for the victims and their families, which meant there'd been no place for outsiders to help, and that had only strengthened the rest of Grayson's grief and sympathy. The combination of their religion and planetary environment meant Graysons were programmed on an almost genetic level to *help*, which was one of the things Benjamin most liked about his people. But when they *couldn't* help they felt as if they'd somehow failed, and in this instance, that was the worst thing they could have felt. People who already felt vaguely guilty themselves had a natural tendency to be even angrier with someone whose guilt was real and unquestionable.

And, as the reports from the laboratories and inspections had made clear, someone *was* guilty. Most of the Mueller Middle School dome's supports appeared to have been properly set in high-standard ceramacrete, but some had not, and what made it even more heartbreaking was that the problems with the ceramacrete seemed to be entirely the fault of poor quality control. The material had all the proper ingredients, in precisely the right proportions. As far as Benjamin's own experts could determine, the entire disaster had stemmed solely from a simple failure to *fuse* it properly. A stupid, unforgivable, easily preventable mistake which—as the reporters had figured out—pointed at either poor equipment maintenance or grossly inadequate training. Either the fusers themselves had been defective, or else the people operating them hadn't known what they were doing, and in either case, the blame rested squarely on the management of Grayson Sky Domes, Ltd.

Greed. That was the damning verdict of the media. Sky Domes had been too greedy to invest in proper maintenance of its equipment, or else it had expanded its work force so rapidly—again, out of greed to cash in on the contracts available to it—that it had put half-trained, or possibly even totally *un*trained, workers into the field. And the hell of it, Benjamin thought, was that there was no way to disprove that verdict. The evidence was there, in the improperly prepared ceramacrete, and the discovery had caused a panic. Of the twenty-three other projects Sky Domes had had simultaneously under construction, eight had been suspended by the buyers. The other fifteen had been canceled outright, and no one had even commented on the fact that Sky Domes itself had put an immediate hold on all of them even before the customers reacted. Benjamin knew that order had come from Honor Harrington herself. She'd refused to allow *any* project to proceed until she knew what had happened in Mueller and was positive it wouldn't happen anywhere else, and no one even seemed to care . . . despite the fact that if Sky Domes failed to meet those projects' completion deadlines, the penalty clauses in the contracts would wipe out even Lady Harrington's off-world fortune. She'd put every penny she had on the line by ordering the hold, and all public opinion could do was scream about the "greed" with which she'd risked the lives of their children!

It was a disaster in every sense of the word. The earlier attacks upon her had suddenly acquired a damning currency, and her role as the heroine of Grayson was no protection against the charge of child-murder. Even some of her own steaders recoiled from supporting anyone responsible for the deaths of children, and her enemies were fanning the fire with savage enthusiasm.

Steadholder Mueller's first grief-wracked news conference after the collapse had done incredible damage. Rescue operations had still been underway when he first faced the reporters. The safety inspectors hadn't even begun their initial examinations at that point, and he'd been careful not to point any fingers. But the very way he hadn't pointed them, the way he'd bent over backward to avoid accusing Lady Harrington of any wrongdoing, had only made people more certain of her guilt. And since the inspectors' reports had been made public, Mueller's grief had turned into rage at the parties responsible for the deaths.

Nor was he the only one crying out for punishment of the guilty. Lord Burdette had launched a brutal attack on Sky Domes, Lady Harrington, and the consequences of allowing women to exercise a man's authority within an hour of the dome's collapse. And while most of Grayson's clergy were still conducting services to pray for God's mercy on the disaster's victims and their families, Edmond Burdette was preaching fire and damnation from the stolen pulpit of Burdette Cathedral—which was now packed for every fiery sermon.

For the moment, Benjamin thought grimly, he could still keep a lid on things . . . but *only* for the moment. The fury against Honor Harrington was gathering like a tidal wave, and when that wave crashed ashore, everything Benjamin Mayhew had fought to bring to his planet was all too likely to be smashed away in the general destruction.

"That's odd."

The soft murmur drew Adam Gerrick's attention from his own terminal. Stuart Matthews, the leader of the pattern analysis team, stood gazing down at a detailed holographic model of the collapsed dome. The ghastly tangle of wreckage was brutally clear, but at least the bodies had been omitted. Gerrick was grateful for that, but even now his mind insisted on supplying the crushed victims, and a fresh shudder of anguish ran through him as he remembered a smiling little girl's final seconds of life.

He closed his eyes, fighting off the pain that threatened his ability to think, then stood and walked over to the holo.

"What?" His voice was a croak, and his eyes were red-rimmed and swollen in a sunken face. He'd had less than ten hours' sleep in the ninety-odd hours since the dome's collapse, and he'd gotten those only because the medics had flatly refused to prescribe any more stimulants unless he did. Matthews was in little better shape. Like all of Sky Domes' senior engineers, he'd been skipping sleep, meals, and baths, and his own exhaustion showed as he blinked owlishly, then ran one hand through the oily tangle of his thinning black hair.

"I've been running the actual event against our models of what *could* have happened."

"And?"

"And they won't match, Adam. Not even if we allow for defective ceramacrete in every footing pour."

"What?" Gerrick propped his buttocks on a work table to take the weight off his shaky legs, but though his shoulders slumped with grinding fatigue, his stim-fired brain worked with a sort of detached smoothness.

"I said what happened doesn't match any of them."

"It has to," Gerrick said reasonably. "Are you sure we've allowed for all the factors?"

"Damn straight I am." Matthews' temper was on as frayed a leash as anyone else's, and his voice was sharp with exhausted belligerence, but he clamped his teeth and fought it down, then took a deep breath and held up a thick folio of data chips. "We've got *everything* in here, Adam. I guarantee it. Hell, I even went back and applied all the met data from the period between our original survey and the start of construction just to see if it could have had some unanticipated effect on the soil strata. And I'm telling you that nothing in our models can account for what happened here."

"Why not?"

"Watch." Matthews tapped instructions into the computers driving the holo display. The tangled wreckage reassembled itself into an intact, half-completed dome, and Gerrick shoved himself up off the worktable and stepped closer for a better view. "I'm running this at a one-to-sixty retardation rate for better detail," Matthews said without turning his head. "Keep your eyes on the alpha ring down here in the eastern quadrant."

Gerrick grunted agreement, then folded his arms and waited. Nothing happened for a moment, and then he detected the same, tiny movement he'd seen the first time. It brought back all his nightmare memories, but this time his angle of view was different . . . and this time he wasn't actually standing there watching children die. He could *think* about what he was seeing, not simply know he was trapped in an obscene tragedy.

The first support member began its fall, and despite his detachment, Gerrick's heart spasmed as he saw another begin to move. Then another. But then his eyes narrowed, for there was a pattern here. One he hadn't

seen at the time, and one he still couldn't quite isolate.
His trained instincts *saw* it, but it eluded his reason, and
he leaned still closer to the holo, fighting to isolate the
element that was indefinably yet utterly *wrong*.

"There!" Matthews froze the holo. Plunging crystoplast
and alloy were abruptly suspended in mid-fall, and he
pointed. "Look here, down in the alpha ring. See this?"
He frowned and tapped more keys, and a clutch of struc-
tural members abruptly shifted color, blazing bright
crimson in the display.

"Yessssss," Gerrick said slowly, brow furrowed in
thought, and the other engineer shook his head.

"Couldn't happen that way, Adam. Look." He input
still more commands, and glowing vector analyses
appeared beside the crimson supports. "See, those suck-
ers are *turning*. They're not just falling, they're *rotat-
ing* in the holes."

"But—" Gerrick began, then stopped, and his frown
mirrored Matthews'. He remembered his original impression on the site, the way the collapsing shafts had twisted
sickeningly as they fell, and his frown deepened.

"But that *is* what happened," he said after a moment,
very slowly. "I was there, Stu. I saw it."

"I know it is," Matthews said tiredly. "This isn't a
model; it's a recreation from the visual records of the
real event. The only problem is, what you're seeing is
impossible. The crosscuts in the holes would have prevented that twisting motion."

"Come on, Stu. There's a hell of a lot of mass coming down out there, and the footings don't have to
actually turn to impart that kind of motion. Even the
six-nineteen alloys would warp under that much stress."

"Sure they would, but not this soon. We're barely three
seconds into the event, Adam. They would've held longer
than that. And when they *did* start warping, they'd do
it as individuals, in a cascade effect. Not only that, but
if you look closely, you'll see there's very little deformation of the supports. In fact, if you check the post-
collapse reports, the ones I've highlighted actually show

less deformation than any other beams in the entire structure—and *none* of them actually sheared." Matthews shook his head. "No, Adam. These bastards started turning *before* they started *falling*."

Gerrick grunted as if he'd been punched in the belly, for Matthews was right. What had happened in Mueller *couldn't* have happened. The support bores narrowed once they reached bedrock, and each of them incorporated a squared-off crosscut a half-meter wider than the diameter of the lower bore. The rectangular support shafts socketed into those crosscuts, for their cross-section was also greater than the diameter of the lower bores. The last ten meters of every shaft was, in effect, locked into a supporting matrix of bedrock even before the ceramacrete footing was poured. Without proper ceramacrete, the native rock couldn't have held a support once the collapse began—but it *should* have kept the supports from turning until far more shearing force was exerted on the stone. The supports should have fallen straight *inward* for the first dozen meters and only started to twist in the last two-thirds or so of their collapse.

And, he thought, his eyes suddenly even more intent, *only* the supports Stu had tagged in crimson showed that motion pattern. The ones between them were falling exactly the way the models said they should, and he was right about the final degree of deformation, too. It was as if something had actually relieved the stress on the marked support members . . . and that, he realized suddenly, was exactly what *would* have happened if they'd been free to turn in the holes. More than that, there was another pattern that—

"We've input the data on the bad ceramacrete?"

"Of course we have," Matthews said a bit snappishly, touched on his exhausted professional pride, and Gerrick raised a placating hand.

"Highlight the supports with the bad footings in amber," he said intently. Matthews looked at him a moment, then shrugged and typed more instructions into the computer. Nothing happened for an instant while the molycirc genius considered its orders, and then most of the crimson-coded support members began to flash alternating crimson and amber. But not *all* of them, Gerrick noted, and leaned closer to look at the two which didn't.

His eyes darted over the displayed vector analyses beside the two steadily crimson supports, and then he grunted again. The numbers didn't match those of their red-and-yellow fellows, but allowing for the fact that they'd had good ceramacrete and the others hadn't . . .

And then the rest of the pattern hit him.

"Son-of-a-bitch," he whispered. "*Son*-of-a-*bitch!*"

"What?" Matthews said sharply.

"Look! Look at the spacing of the bad holes!"

"What about it?" Matthews asked blankly, and Gerrick shoved him aside to get at the controls. He frowned for a moment, making his brain give up the information he needed, then started inputting commands, and the display began to flash with additional light codes.

"We had a total of seven power bores working this project," he reminded his colleague without ever looking away from his keyboard and the holo. "Each of them put in five holes a day, right?"

"Right." Matthews' reply came out slowly, as if his thoughts were almost catching up with Gerrick's. More lights flashed in the holo, picking out support members in seven different colors, and then Gerrick stood back.

"You see?" He reached out and caught Matthews' shoulder as if to drag him physically inside the holo with him, and his voice was a whisper. "Do you *see* it, Stu? Every goddamned one of those 'turning' supports was set in a hole drilled by the *same* bore-operator! And look at this!" He tapped more keys, and a final indicator of lurid, poison-green light flickered and danced in the display. "You see it?" he said again. "Two of the holes the son-of-a-bitch drilled got good ceramacrete, *but every single instance of* bad *ceramacrete is in one of the holes he drilled!*"

"But that means—" Matthews began, and Gerrick nodded savagely, then whirled from the display.

"Chet! Get me a priority line to the Regent!"

"What?" Sky Domes' personnel manager sounded confused, and Gerrick actually stamped a foot in fury.

"Get me Lord Clinkscales *now*, damn it!" he barked. "And then get me the name of the motherless bastard responsible for—" he bent to peer at his own inputs for a moment "—Power Bore Number Four!"

• CHAPTER TWENTY-TWO

Andrew LaFollet watched through the boat bay gallery's armorplast as the civilian shuttle docked, and his mind was sick and weary behind the mask of his steady gray eyes. He'd come down personally to escort the shuttle's passenger to the Steadholder because he hoped that this time there might be some good news buried in all the horror, yet another part of him knew there *was* no good news, and the weight of his personal despair was like some agonizing yet pale shadow of Lady Harrington's.

LaFollet was a Grayson. He was unmarried and had no children, yet he understood his people's fury deep in his bones. He didn't—couldn't—blame them for feeling it, but he also knew how skillfully Lady Harrington's enemies were using that fury against her. The callous manipulation of such heart-deep anguish sickened him, yet there was nothing he could do about it. And because there wasn't, he couldn't protect his Steadholder from others' anger. . . or from her own cruel, self-inflicted wounds.

He remembered his sense of futility when Lady Harrington had learned of Paul Tankersley's death. She'd been shattered by her loss, white-faced and stricken, and she'd shut out the entire universe, even Nimitz, for three terrible days. LaFollet had been terrified that they were going to lose her, that she was simply going to go out like a light, but somehow she'd survived. Avenging Tankersley's bought and paid for murder had helped, he thought. It hadn't been enough to prevent the deep wounds not even a full T-year had yet completely healed, for no amount of vengeance could ever restore the man she'd loved to her, but it had helped.

Only this time, there was no one to seek vengeance from, and the only person she could punish for what her company had done was herself.

LaFollet's mind shied away from what this was doing to her. She hadn't withdrawn this time, but the person who looked out through her eyes was no longer his Steadholder. She was a stranger, fulfilling her duties as a naval officer only because some remnant of her deep, personal sense of honor required that she do so. Yet she fulfilled them like a robot, locked in her own private hell and hating herself even more than the people on the planet her ships orbited hated her. There was no cruel, vicious charge anyone could hurl at her which she hadn't already hurled at herself, and the fresh damage had ripped her old wounds wide.

He watched the green pressure signal light over the docking tube and remembered the first night after the dome's collapse. He'd been off duty when MacGuiness commed him frantically, and he'd rushed to her quarters to find her writhing in the sweat-soaked grip of a nightmare. He had no idea what agonies she'd been inflicting upon herself, but one look at Nimitz had told him they were terrible.

Even when she'd withdrawn into her numb, frozen cocoon after Tankersley's death, she'd never truly been alone, for Nimitz had been with her. He'd shared her pain, but he'd *fought* for her, pouring his love and support into her while he handled the anguish beating at him through their empathic link and refused to let it suck him under with her or make him let her go.

Not this time. This time her agony had claimed him, as well, and a hissing, red-eyed, bare-fanged demon had crouched on the carpet just inside her sleeping cabin when MacGuiness keyed the hatch. Andrew LaFollet was no coward, but he'd seen the videotapes of the Maccabeus coup attempt, seen Nimitz kill and maim men who threatened Honor Harrington, and it would

have been more than his life was worth to dare that
door guard's fury. He and MacGuiness had talked to
the 'cat, gently, soothingly, almost begging him to let
them pass, and there'd been no response. None at all.
Nimitz had been lost in his person's agony, hammered
back to the bloody-fanged violence of his evolutionary
past.

And then, thankfully, the nightmare had released her,
and the 'cat had dropped to the carpet, shaking his head
and whimpering in reaction. LaFollet had never seen
Nimitz frightened. The 'cat's supreme confidence in his
person and himself was a fundamental bulwark of his
personality. Yet this time he'd huddled in a lump, trembling, his belly pressed to the carpet in a futile defensive posture against the threat he couldn't fight, and his
fear had wrung LaFollet's heart.

The major had stood motionless, frozen by the implications, but MacGuiness had crossed to the treecat. He'd
scooped Nimitz up in his arms like a beaten child, and
the 'cat had buried his face against the steward and
moaned. It was the only word for the sound he'd made,
and Andrew LaFollet had watched in despair as Mac-
Guiness carried his frightened, shivering friend from the
sleeping cabin while he murmured useless, soothing
words to him.

That had been the worst night, the major thought
. . . but for how long? How long before the hatred
building on the surface of Grayson fused with the
Steadholder's own self-hatred and destroyed her outright?

The docking tube hatch slid open, and Andrew
LaFollet braced himself to meet Adam Gerrick while
he prayed that it wasn't still more bad news which
brought him here.

Honor Harrington sat before her blank terminal. She
should be working, a dreary corner of her brain told her,
but she couldn't. She knew Walter Brentworth and
Alfredo Yu were carrying the full weight of her

responsibilities to the squadron, and the knowledge was one more weight in the scales of her self-hatred. She couldn't even do her *job* anymore, she thought with bitter self-loathing. She could only sit here, knowing she was beaten, knowing that the part of her life she'd turned to to rebuild her universe after Paul's death had been as brutally destroyed as Paul had been. She went through the rote motions, pretended there was something left inside her, and every evening she felt the terror of sleep looming before her with its promise of fresh and hideous nightmares.

She'd failed. Worse than failed. She was responsible for the deaths of children and men who'd worked in her employ. It was *her* dome which had killed them, and even through her own black despair, she recognized that her guilt was the flail with which Benjamin Mayhew's enemies would pound his reforms to dust. It was her fault, a cruel inner voice whispered. In her pride and arrogance, she'd accepted responsibilities she was unfit to discharge, and the consequences of her failure stood stark and plain in her mind. She'd actually thought *she* could be a steadholder, make a difference, play a part on a stage too great for her pitiful capabilities, and this was the result. Death and destruction, the collapse of an effort to bring an entire world into the present out of the past. And now she couldn't even do the one job she'd always believed she could and had to rely on people who had the right to expect—demand—leadership from her to hide the utter totality of her failure from anyone outside the squadron.

She raised her dull, almond eyes to Nimitz. The 'cat was huddled on his perch above her desk, watching over her, and his own eyes were dark. He was afraid, she thought. *Afraid.* She'd failed even Nimitz, for he could no more hide his emotions from her than she could hide hers from him, and for the first time in all their years together, he feared his link to her.

He made a soft sound, trying to disagree with her, his unflawed love battling against his fear, but she knew, just as he did, and the two of them mourned the ruin of all they'd been to one another as they mourned those crushed child bodies in Mueller Steading.

He made another soft sound and dropped from his perch. He crossed her desk and stretched out from its edge, putting his true-hands on her shoulders and rubbing his muzzle against her cheek, and tears burned behind her eyes as he begged her to relinquish the self-hate which was destroying them both. But she couldn't. She *deserved* her destruction, and knowing how terribly it hurt *him* only made her hate herself still more.

She took him in her arms, burying her face in his fur, and tried to use physical caresses as a substitute for the emotional ones she could no longer give him. He purred to her, pressing back against her, promising her his love . . . and under the love the bitter taste of fear still burned. The courage with which he exposed himself to her pain was a dagger, twisting within her, and she felt her tears soak into his fur like the acid of self-loathing.

She didn't know how long they huddled together, each trying uselessly to comfort the other, but finally the soft chime of the admittance signal broke in upon them. She tensed, muscles tightening to reject the summons, but she couldn't do that, either. She still had to pretend, she thought wearily. She was trapped, compelled to assume the mask of someone who could do the jobs she'd failed at, and she drew a deep, ragged breath, then pressed a kiss between Nimitz's ears and stood. She set him gently back on his perch and scrubbed away her tears, and his soft, loving croon as she turned away from the desk tore at her heart.

She pressed the admittance stud without even checking to see who it was. It didn't matter, anyway.

The hatch opened, and Andrew LaFollet stepped through it. She saw his face, the concern and trust—and fear—that echoed Nimitz's, however hard he tried to hide them, and her mouth moved in a parody of a smile. But then she saw Adam Gerrick behind her armsman, and her stomach knotted. *Please*, she thought.

Oh, please, God! Not more disaster. I can't survive any more guilt.

"Andrew." Her own voice startled her, for she hadn't ordered it to speak, but it carried on without her, another rote automaton pretending the person it belonged to still functioned.

"My Lady," LaFollet said quietly, and stepped out of Gerrick's way.

"Adam," her voice said.

"My Lady." The engineer looked dreadful, she thought distantly, as if he hadn't slept since it happened. Yet even as she thought that, another equally distant part of her realized something had changed. The last time they'd spoken over the com, Adam Gerrick's self-hatred had been the mirror of her own, but there was something different now. The hate was still there, but it was hotter. It no longer burned like slow acid, and its fiery heat reached out to her as if from the door of an opened furnace.

"What can I do for you, Adam?" she asked listlessly, and his answer stunned her.

"You can listen to me, My Lady," he said grimly, "and then you can help me find the murdering bastards who sabotaged the Mueller dome."

It was the first time he'd ever used even the mildest profanity in her presence. That was her first thought, but it barely had time to register before she jerked as if she'd been slapped.

"Sabotaged?" she repeated, and her suddenly taut soprano voice was hoarse, no longer numb.

"Sabotaged." The engineer's reply was a thing of cold iron, as quenched in certainty as in outrage, and Honor swayed. LaFollet stepped quickly forward as she put out a hand, gripping her desk for support, but she didn't even notice. Her eyes were locked on Gerrick's face, begging him to be right, to know what he was talking about, and his short, savage nod answered her plea.

She dropped into her chair, distantly ashamed of her weakness, but things were shifting and roaring in her head. Vast, terrible weights plunged through the dark spaces of her mind, crashing into one another in showers of white-hot splinters, and she drew a deep, strangled breath.

"Are . . . are you sure, Adam?" she whispered. "It was *deliberate?*"

"It was, My Lady. Stu Matthews spotted it four hours ago."

"Four hours?" she repeated. "You. . . you've known for *four hours?*" Her voice broke, and shame flashed across Gerrick's expression.

"Yes, My Lady. Forgive me. I should have commed you and told you then, but I wanted to be sure—to be *positive*—before I brought it to you." His nostrils flared and he tossed his head. "Now I am . . . and so are Lord Clinkscales, Planetary Security, and Protector Benjamin."

"My God," Honor whispered. She heard the soft thud of Nimitz's weight on the desk behind her, felt his arms go about her neck from behind, and her eyes clung to Gerrick like her last, faint hope of salvation.

"*Oh, my God!*" she whispered again, and this time it was a cry from the heart, ragged with the agony she'd tried to hide for so long. She buried her face in her hands, rocking in her chair, and her entire body jerked with the force of her sobs.

"My Lady!" LaFollet cried. She felt him there, on his knees beside her, his hands on her forearms. He pulled with gentle strength, forcing her hands down, making her stare at him through her tears, and his voice was deep and soft. "It wasn't us, My Lady," he told her. "It wasn't an accident, wasn't carelessness. My Lady, *it wasn't your fault.*"

She stared at him—ashamed of her weakness, grateful for his comfort—and he smiled at her. He *smiled*, without a trace of contempt for her broken reaction, and she twisted her forearms in his grip, sliding them down to clasp his hands and squeeze them tightly before she looked back at Gerrick.

"How, Adam?" she asked, and her voice was almost

her own again. "How did they do it? And how did you find out?"

"How we found out is a long story, My Lady. The short version of it is that we've been modeling and analyzing the collapse ever since it happened, and we finally realized there was a pattern. We—"

He paused suddenly, then shook his head like an annoyed horse and gave her a weary, lopsided smile.

"My Lady, would you mind if I sit? I'm afraid I'm a little tired."

"Of course," she said quickly, and he sank into a facing chair. "I'll buzz Mac," she went on, knowing she sounded inane but unable to think of anything else to say. "We need—"

"My Lady," LaFollet's gentle voice summoned her eyes back to him, and he smiled again. "I already told him, My Lady, and he asked me to tell you he'd be here as soon as he found the . . . Delacourt, I think he said."

"The—?" Honor blinked at her armsman, for the first time truly realizing how exhausted and drained she was, and then she laughed softly. "The Delacourt," she repeated with a crooked smile of her own. "Mac always has had a nice sense of the appropriate."

"Indeed he has, and—"

LaFollet broke off as the dining cabin hatch opened and MacGuiness stepped through it. The steward carried a silver tray with three tall-stemmed glasses and a bottle from her father's personal cellars on Manticore, and the smile he gave wrenched at her heart. He carried the tray to her desk and set it down, and she blinked misty eyes as she saw the small bowl of celery he'd taken time to prepare for Nimitz.

"I thought you might want this, Ma'am," he said quietly as he poured ruby wine into a glass. He handed it to her, then filled two more glasses and handed them to LaFollet and Gerrick before he stood back, still holding the bottle, and she reached out and touched his hand.

"Thank you, Mac," she said softly. "You always seem to know, don't you?"

"A minor talent, Ma'am," he said equally softly, and freed his other hand from the bottle to cover hers. Then he stepped back and set the bottle on the tray. "Buzz if you need anything else, Milady," he said with a small, formal bow, and withdrew from the cabin.

Honor watched him go, then turned back to Gerrick and LaFollet. The armsman stood formally beside her chair, but she shook her head and pointed to the couch. He hesitated a moment, then drew a deep breath, nodded, and obeyed her gesture, and she waited for him to settle before she looked back at Gerrick.

"Tell me," she commanded, and her voice was *hers* again. Still strained with grief and pain, but hers.

"In a sense, My Lady, it *was* our fault," Gerrick said quietly, "but only because we let the bas—" He paused, as if his anger had finally cooled enough for him to remember his language, then went on. "Only because we let whoever planned this slip their own people into our workforce, My Lady." He shrugged. "It never occurred to us that anyone might deliberately cause a disaster like this. We were only concerned with getting people who could do the job and then training them to do it right; security measures against sabotage never even crossed our minds."

"There was no reason they should have, My Lady," LaFollet said, and she glanced at him. "Oh, in hindsight, yes, it's something you ought to have considered. But hindsight is always perfect, and going in, there was no more reason for you to think any of your employees were mass murderers than for any other company to worry about it."

Honor nodded, grateful for his reassurance but not really needing it—not now—and looked back at Gerrick.

"Major LaFollet's right, My Lady, and this was no case of an individual maniac, either. It took at least eighteen or twenty people, acting in concert, to pull this off. That makes it a conspiracy, as well as murder."

"How did they do it?" she asked.

"They had two strings to their bow," Gerrick replied.

"Either of them *might* have done it alone; with both of them in place, I'm amazed we got as far as we did before the dome collapsed." The engineer made a little face, and if his voice was no less angry, it was also dry and factual when he continued.

"One of their people got himself hired as a power bore operator, My Lady, and he altered the profile on the holes he drilled to hold the main support units. You're familiar with the original design?"

"Only in general terms," Honor said. She'd examined the plans, but they hadn't been her area of expertise.

"Do you remember how we'd designed the holes to give the maximum volume for the ceramacrete footings while simultaneously locking the base of each support into a natural load-bearing matrix?" Gerrick asked, and she nodded. "Well, with the supports socketed into the crosscuts and a hundred-plus tons of ceramacrete poured into each footing on top of that, each support in the alpha ring should have been the next best thing to inde-structible."

Honor nodded. Had the ceramacrete been properly fused, it would have formed the equivalent of a plug of solid igneous rock stronger and harder than obsid-ian. Coupled with the socketing effect of the crosscuts, the support members should have been like extrusions of the planet's very bones.

"All right, My Lady, what actually happened is this. When the man on the power bore drilled his holes, they *looked* close to specs, but the portion that was supposed to 'neck down' actually had a diameter equal to the support's width, which meant the beams didn't engage in the crosscuts and knocked out that part of the design's stress redundancy. We've only managed to check two of the holes, since the Mueller inspectors won't let us on-site, but we had good visual records on those two. The people who shot the chips were holo-vid techs, not engineers, so they never noticed the proportions were off, and none of our technical people viewed the chips prior to the accident. But we've viewed them now, and we've been able to scale the holes from the HD chips. It's a computer reconstruction, but it'll stand up in any court, and the holes themselves are still there and available for physical examination to confirm it."

Honor nodded once more, and Gerrick rubbed his eyebrow in a gesture of tired triumph before he continued.

"In addition to the diameter shift, the bottoms of each of the holes we've checked were also off profile, My Lady. They were cut on a slight angle, so that only the edge of each support actually had any bearing surface. Again, with good ceramacrete, that wouldn't have mattered, since the pour would have come in under the unsupported portion of each upright before it was fused. With *bad* ceramacrete, it became an important factor in what happened."

"Didn't we check the profiles?"

"Yes and no, My Lady," Gerrick said with a grimace. "The specs were locked into the bores' software. For them to be off required the bore operator to deliberately alter them, and we run diagnostics and self-check programs on all our equipment between shifts to catch any accidental modifications. That meant whoever altered them also had to *reset* them before he went off shift, which he did. That deprived us of any warning from that end . . . and, just incidentally, proves that what happened *wasn't* an accident.

"But we had a second built-in check, My Lady. The crews who set the supports also had the proper profiles in *their* software. If the holes were off, they should have caught them—*would* have caught them, if they hadn't been deliberately covering for whoever drilled them in the first place. That's how we know there were at least two teams involved in this. And, finally, we had on-site supervisors who were responsible for spot-checking the footings after they were in. But the point is that we were checking for *accidents*, not deliberate sabotage, and whoever planned this knew it.

"As nearly as we can piece it together at this point,

the crews who put the supports into the bad holes knew which ones were off. They put in their beams, then poured the ceramacrete, but they only fused the top half meter or so of it. Two of the bad holes had good ceramacrete, so we're assuming one of our supervisors happened by during those pours and that the saboteurs were afraid to hold back on the fusing process in his presence because they figured he'd spot it. As far as the others are concerned, though, our inspectors—and the Mueller Steading inspectors, for that matter—only drill twenty-centimeter cores for our quality control samples. That's the standard for Sword and steading inspectors, My Lady, partly because it's so hard to drill through ceramacrete in the first place. Given what's happened here, however, I've already recommended to the Protector that the requirement be changed to a full-depth sampling technique.

"What it meant, though, was that a half-meter of good ceramacrete gave a valid quality control check for the entire footing—a footing which, in fact, came nowhere close to meeting the stress loading we'd designed into it. In fact, it wouldn't have been enough to handle the loads in a *good* hole, but they weren't taking any chances."

The engineer paused with a bitter smile, then took another sip of his wine and leaned back in his chair.

"So what happened, My Lady, is that approximately fourteen percent of the main load-bearing elements of the dome had been designed to fail, and the angle cut into the bottom of each hole actually threw the mass of those supports *against* the other elements of the dome. There was no way, My Lady, no way at all, that dome was going to stand with that kind of bugger factor built into it, and whoever did it knew exactly what was going to happen."

"Who, Adam?" Honor's eyes were hard, and the engineer shrugged.

"At this point, My Lady, we're still figuring out exactly how they did it. We can't identify the crews who set the supports and poured the ceramacrete from our own work orders, but Security is working with the site visual records, and Lord Clinkscales fully expects to find their faces in our employee database. But we can positively identify the bore operator right now, because we know which bore drilled which holes and who was the assigned operator on each bore."

"And?"

"According to our records, it was a Lawrence Maguire, My Lady," Gerrick said flatly. "He's one of the workers who 'resigned in protest' when the first reports of substandard materials came out, and we don't know where he went after that. We've already checked the address he listed as his residence and discovered that it was a boardinghouse. He rented rooms there only a week before he applied to us for a job, however, and none of the other personal background he gave on his application form checks out."

"Then we don't know who he really was?" Honor tried to keep the disappointment from her voice and knew she'd failed. It was vital that they find the man. If they couldn't identify him, establish a motive for his murderous actions, then her enemies would insist he was a figment of her company's imagination—that there'd been no deliberate saboteurs and that the faulty execution which had caused the disaster were only the "mistakes by poorly trained personnel" they were already being called.

"I didn't say that, My Lady," Gerrick said with a thin smile. "I said *our records* don't tell us where to look for him, and they don't. But while he falsified his application information, he had to give us his real fingerprints. I guess he figured we'd never put it together and even realize we should be looking for him, but we've got them, and we handed them over to Lord Clinkscales. He ran them against the Harrington database without finding anything, which confirmed our suspicion 'Maguire' was an outsider, but he also transmitted them under a deep security cover to a contact of his in Planetary Security, who ran them through the *Sword* database. And it just happens, My Lady, that as a teenager, Mr. 'Maguire' was once picked up for participating in a civil disturbance. It was a 'demonstration' against the Jerimites—they're a small, independent-minded group some members of the Church consider heretics—that turned violent, but because of his youth, he got off with a reprimand. He may not even have realized that the steading records on all criminal arrests, even the most petty ones, go into the Sword database and stay there.

"At any rate, My Lady, Protector Benjamin's people have IDed him. His real name is Samuel *Marchant* Harding." Honor's eyes flared, and the engineer nodded slowly. "That's right, My Lady. He's a first cousin of *Edmond* Marchant's . . . and his official place of residence is Burdette City, Steading of Burdette."

• CHAPTER TWENTY-THREE

"So it's confirmed, Your Grace?"

"As positively as it can be without tipping our hand, Reverend," Benjamin IX replied. "We can't use it in court until our own forensic people have duplicated Sky Domes' models, and we probably need to actually excavate the foundations, but no one who's seen the analysis doubts it. At this point, all contacts with Planetary Security have been restricted to a group Regent Clinkscales personally trusts to keep them quiet, but a senior engineer in Security's Building Safety Directorate has checked the Sky Domes material and completely endorses its conclusions, and we have positive confirmation of Harding's identity." The Protector shook his head. "It hasn't been 'proven' in the sense in which the courts use that verb, Reverend. But it will be when the time comes."

"I see." Reverend Hanks leaned back in his armchair, and distress and anger warred with relief in his eyes. Chancellor Prestwick sat beside the Reverend, and Benjamin wondered which of the three of them looked most exhausted. It would, he was sure, have been a very close call.

"I do not want to believe anyone who calls himself a man of God could conspire in the murder of children." Hanks' deep, resonant voice was dark and heavy with sorrow. "But given the speed with which Lord Burdette and Marchant reacted to the initial reports—"

The Reverend shook his head sadly, yet the anger in his eyes only grew. The spiritual head of the Church of Humanity Unchained was a gentle and compassionate man, but the Church, too, had borne a sword in its time.

"I agree, Reverend," Prestwick said soberly, "but, if you'll forgive me, the secular side is even more complicated. We have proof a Burdette steader was involved, but so far any evidence of collusion—even with Marchant—is entirely speculative. At the moment, Harding could have acted alone."

Benjamin looked at the Chancellor in disbelief, and Prestwick shrugged.

"If Lord Clinkscales and Security can identify the workmen who sabotaged the ceramacrete and we can link them to Harding, we'll have convincing proof of a conspiracy, Your Grace. But unless we can demonstrate a link between the conspirators and Lord Burdette, we won't have enough evidence to impeach him before the Keys. At this stage no one can predict whether or not we can ever make that linkage at all, but we *do* know we can't assemble the evidence which might demonstrate it without a formal investigation."

"And if I authorize a formal investigation," Benjamin sighed, "we'll have to bring in so many people Burdette is bound to get wind of it."

"I'm very much afraid so, Your Grace. Especially with his . . . historical links to Justice."

"And if he *is* guilty, he'll take steps to destroy the evidence we need before we get our hands on it," Benjamin said sourly. "And steadholder autonomy means he can probably stall the admission of any Sword investigation team to Burdette long enough to get away with it."

"Perhaps more to the point, Your Grace," Hanks pointed out, "the verdict of the court of public opinion may be delivered before the Ministry of Justice can set the official wheels in motion. The Sacristy has been firm in its instructions, but many of our priests—even those who neither distrusted nor feared Lady Harrington before the dome collapse—are ignoring those instructions. The nature of the disaster, the deaths of so many children—" He sighed and shook his head once more. "This sort of catastrophe produces the strongest reaction in the best of men. Their very goodness drives them to cry out against perceived injustice, and the evidence has been so outwardly damning that none of them question it. The situation is already badly inflamed, and it will only get worse until we can *prove* Lady Harrington is the blameless victim of someone else's conspiracy. Indeed, some of the damage may already be beyond repair, even if a court of law clears her. She is, after all, a Steadholder. Her enemies will be quick to circulate the rumor that she used her rank to engineer a coverup, that the court's verdict was a whitewash which you and Father Church supported out of political expediency, and some will believe it. Once people become sufficiently convinced of her guilt, a taint will always cling to her in some minds, and the longer we delay public revelation of the new evidence, the more convinced people will become."

"He's right, Your Grace." Prestwick rubbed his hands together in his lap, and his eyes were troubled. "We're already hearing charges that you're delaying the investigation to protect Lady Harrington, and we're also seeing incidents of organized vandalism against Sky Domes. Eight million austins worth of their equipment was firebombed in Surtees Steading the day after the collapse. Worse, three Sky Domes workers were attacked by a mob in Watson Steading last night. One of the victims may not live—he's in a coma, and the doctors aren't optimistic—and I have reports that almost equally ugly incidents are being directed against people just because they're from Harrington, whether they have any links to Sky Domes or not."

The Chancellor rubbed his aching eyes, then met his Protector's gaze squarely.

"Bad as all that is, Your Grace, it's only a symptom. The real outrage is aimed directly—and personally—at Lady Harrington, and it's assuming frightening proportions. I've received petitions from thirty-eight steadholders and over ninety members of the Conclave of Steaders for her immediate recall as an admiral and impeachment and formal trial for murder. If only six more steadholders endorse the impeachment petition, we'll have no choice but to implement it. And if that happens—"

He shrugged unhappily, and Benjamin nodded. The evidence Adam Gerrick had put together—and what a brilliant piece of reconstruction that had been, the Protector thought admiringly—was almost certain to defeat any impeachment. Unfortunately, the very process of clearing Honor before the Keys would expose their evidence to the man behind the entire plot. More than that, impeachment proceedings would be broadcast throughout the star system, which was only too likely to taint that evidence for later legal prosecutions. If Harding and his fellow murderers were ever brought to trial, their attorneys would undoubtedly argue that the evidence presented at the impeachment had prejudiced anyone who might be selected as a juror, and they might very well be right.

But how did he head that off? Reverend Hanks was right; this was precisely the sort of crime which evoked the most anger in the best of men, and aside from the people behind it, all of the Keys genuinely believed Honor was guilty of it. Their fury was completely understandable, yet it was virtually certain to generate the six additional signatures a writ of impeachment required. If that happened, not even he could quash the proceedings—and the true guilty parties might well escape as a consequence.

He tipped his chair back and frowned as he thought. He was the Protector of Grayson. It was his job to insure that anyone who committed a crime such as this did *not* escape, and he was coldly determined to do just that. But it was also his job to protect the innocent, and that meant he had to get a handle on the groundswell of violence building against Sky Domes and the steaders of Harrington, as well as Honor, and how in God's name did he do *that* without handing Gerrick's analysis to the Keys and the press?

"All right," he sighed finally. "This nest of snakes has too many heads; however we reach into it, we're going to get bitten somewhere, so the best we can do, I think, is try to minimize the consequences." Prestwick nodded unhappily, and Reverend Hanks looked grave.

"Henry," the Protector turned his gaze on the Chancellor, "I want you to sit down with Security. Take Councilman Sidemore with you." Prestwick nodded again; Aaron Sidemore was the Minister of Justice, and they had to bring him into this quickly. Fortunately, he was a new appointee, with none of the ties to the old patronage system which might have led to leaks to the Keys, and a man who took his responsibilities seriously.

"This has to be handled very carefully," Benjamin went on. "As of this moment, the Sword has made an official finding of the possibility of treason on the part of a steadholder. I'll give you written confirmation of that for Sidemore."

Prestwick nodded again, but his face was more tense than it had been, and Benjamin smiled grimly. No Protector had exerted his constitutional authority to police the Keys for over a T-century, and dusting off the old laws which governed that process was almost certain to provoke a constitutional crisis if any member of the Keys challenged them. But by invoking a Sword finding of possible treason, Benjamin could also empower Justice to investigate in absolute secrecy. By law, he could keep the investigation "black" for no more than three weeks; after that, he had to file formal charges against a specific steadholder, convince a majority of the Joint Steadholder-Steader Judiciary Committee that a continuation of the finding was justified, or else withdraw it, but at least they could get a running start on the case and *probably* not alert Burdette.

"In the meantime," the Protector mused, "we have to head off this impeachment talk or risk blowing the entire case against the real criminals." He gnawed his lower lip for a moment, then sighed. "I don't see any way to do that without giving Burdette at least a little warning. To stop the impeachment, I'll have to give the Keys at least some of what we suspect."

"Risky, Your Grace," Prestwick pointed out. "Giving them enough to convince them this isn't just a political ploy—that you have substantive reason to believe the collapse was deliberately engineered by someone besides Lady Harrington—is going to require you to expose at least some of the critical evidence."

"I realize that, but we're damned if we do and damned if we don't, Henry. A formal impeachment will put *all* the evidence on the table. What I'm hoping is to play it by ear, reveal only a little of Gerrick's analysis and suggest that there's reason to reexamine the original findings of the site inspectors in light of it."

"They'll never accept that as sufficient, Your Grace," the Chancellor said flatly.

"You're probably right, and if I have to go further, I will. But I can at least *try* to limit the damage first."

"Well, yes, Your Grace. I suppose we can try," Prestwick agreed doubtfully.

"Your Grace," Reverend Hanks' tone was unusually formal, "the Church does not normally take a hand in the affairs of the Keys. In this instance, however, you have the support of my office, and, I believe, of the Sacristy at large. If you wish, I will appear before the Keys and appeal to them to accept your plea for a delay without divulgence of the evidence. If I inform them that *I* have seen the full body of evidence and endorse your conclusions, perhaps we can convince them not to push."

"Thank you, Reverend." Benjamin's voice and expression showed his profound gratitude for Hanks' offer. While the Reverend was correct about the Church's normal impartiality, it was also true that his position *as* Reverend gave him the legal standing of a steadholder. In fact, it made him a member both of the Protector's Council and of the Keys, and if he was willing to throw the Church's weight behind a plea to delay any formal impeachment proceedings, it might—*might*—turn the trick without revealing their evidence to Burdette.

"Your Grace, if there is the slightest possibility that even an ex-priest has involved himself in the murder of children, Father Church has no choice but to exert his full influence to see justice done," the gentle Reverend said sternly, and Benjamin nodded soberly.

"In that case, Henry, as soon as you and Sidemore have finished your preliminary discussions, I want you to transmit writs of summons for a special—and closed—session of the Keys. We'll try to keep this quiet enough the media doesn't get involved."

"Yes, Your Grace."

"Where's Gerrick now?" the Protector asked, and Prestwick frowned for a moment, then nodded to himself.

"I believe he's still aboard *Terrible*, Your Grace. Lord Clinkscales tells me he went up to explain his findings to Lady Harrington and *Terrible*'s surgeon ordered him straight to bed after he'd done so."

"Wise of him, no doubt," Benjamin murmured, remembering the gray-faced, exhausted young man he'd seen on his own com screen—was it really only three hours ago? He shook his head, then brought his chair back upright.

"I think we should leave him there for now," he said slowly, then nodded. "In fact, let's *announce* where he is, Henry. Put together a press release to the effect that he's there to confer with Lady Harrington but without including any hint of what they're conferring about. Don't tell any lies; just stick to the bare facts of his presence and I feel sure the newsies will draw the conclusion we want."

"The conclusion we want, Your Grace?" Hanks repeated, and Benjamin smiled.

"Reverend, unless they already know about the Sky Domes analysis, the people really responsible for this must feel pretty confident just now, and I'm sure they figure Lady Harrington must be growing desperate. Well,

I'd like to use that against them, and if we can convince
them that she's summoned her chief engineer to a 'spin
control' conference in an attempt to salvage *something*
from the wreck, it should make them even more confident . . . and less wary. Besides, I'd just as soon have
Gerrick out of reach of the media at least until after
the special session's behind us."

"I think that's wise, Your Grace," Prestwick put in. "In
fact, if you approve, I'll also contact Howard Clinkscales.
Between the two of us, I'm sure we can concoct an
absolutely truthful—and highly misleading—release to
reinforce that image, and I'll also ask him to warn the
rest of Sky Domes' engineers to keep a low profile."

"Good idea, Henry. Good idea." Benjamin pinched his
nose and tried to think of what else they could do, but
nothing occurred to his weary brain.

"With your permission, Your Grace, I think I'll go up
to *Terrible*, as well," Reverend Hanks said. Benjamin
quirked an eyebrow, and Hanks shrugged. "I know Lady
Harrington well enough to realize this must have been
a terrible ordeal for her, Your Grace. I'd like the opportunity to speak with her, and I could also take her the
writ of summons for the Conclave without putting it
through official Navy channels or sending a Sword courier." The Reverend frowned thoughtfully, then nodded.
"In fact, I'm sure Chancellor Prestwick will have the writs
prepared by the time I've been able to speak with the
Sacristy and explain what's happening to the Elders I
can trust not to accidentally let something slip. In that
case, she could return for the special session with me
the following day. That would probably be the quick-
est—and most confidential—way to complete the
arrangements."

"It would, indeed, Reverend, though I feel a bit
uncomfortable using the head of Father Church as a
mere courier!"

"There's nothing 'mere' about it, under the circumstances, Your Grace," Hanks replied, "and Father
Church—and the people of Grayson—owe Lady

Harrington any service we can legitimately perform for her."

"You're right, of course," Benjamin agreed, then looked back and forth between the two older men on the far side of his desk. "In that case, gentlemen, I think we should get things organized."

"Well, *that* was an . . . interesting disaster," Citizen Rear Admiral Theisman observed. His tone was so dry that even Citizen Commissioner LePic grinned, but there was point to the comment. Task Group 14.2, Theisman's own command of twelve battleships and screening elements, had performed flawlessly in the latest sim. Unfortunately, Citizen Admiral Chernov's TG 14.3 had completely misunderstood its orders. He'd strayed badly out of position on the approach to Masada, and the computers ruled that the Grayson battlecruisers protecting Endicott had managed a successful interception. They'd taken heavy losses from Chernov's escorts, but not heavy enough to keep them from killing both his troop transports and four of his five freighters full of weapons.

Theisman sighed. He wasn't at all happy about arming a planet full of religious fanatics—especially when he knew from personal experience what they were capable of—but if he had to do it, he preferred to do it right. No doubt his fellow task group commander was getting an earful from Thurston and Preznikov at this very moment, but it really hadn't been Chernov's fault. This was a more complex op than even Theisman had fully suspected. Neither he nor Chernov had known, for example, that the entire task force was going to arrive in Yeltsin in a single body before detaching the Endicott attack force . . . for the very simple reason that it hadn't been part of the original plan. Theisman thought it an eminently sensible alteration—he'd never been happy about splitting the task force into two forces and having them go in completely independent of one another—but it would have been nice if he and the other task group COs had been informed of it a bit sooner. As it was, the entire maneuver had come at them almost cold, and it was hardly surprising that Chernov's astrogation had been off.

Still, he reflected, the whole purpose of a sim was to figure out what could go wrong and fix it. You never found all the problems, of course. The best you could do was disaster-proof your ops plan against the screwups you knew about and hope the others didn't bite you on the ass too hard.

"All right," he told his staff, "we had a little accident. These things happen. The idea is to keep them from happening the same way twice, so let's look over all our movement orders. Tomorrow's the last day of simulations we get, people. Five days from now, we have to get it right the first time, or we're going to be looking at something a damn sight more serious than data bits in a computer, right?"

"Right, Citizen Admiral," LePic said firmly, and the rest of the staff nodded.

"In that case," Theisman said, turning to his ops officer, "let's pull up the general operational schematic first, Megan. I want to see if we can't integrate Citizen Admiral Chernov's task group a bit more intimately with ours from the outset. If we'd had him inside our own com net, we'd have realized he was drifting off course *before* we went into hyper leaving Yeltsin."

"Yes, Citizen Admiral," the ops officer said, tapping commands into her terminal to summon the proper files. "In fact, Citizen Admiral, I was thinking that what we might want to do is—"

Thomas Theisman leaned back in his chair, listening to his staff tear into the problem, and hoped like hell that Yeltsin really was as bare as Thurston's intelligence appreciations suggested. Because if it wasn't, and if they didn't get a much larger percentage of the bugs exterminated before they got there, God alone knew how Operation Dagger was *really* going to end up.

• CHAPTER TWENTY-FOUR

Samuel Mueller frowned down at the archaic sheet of parchment on his blotter. The writ of summons' stilted, old-fashioned legalese was familiar enough—except for the last sentence, which no living steadholder had ever seen. Mayhew had the right to append it under the old Constitution, but that made Mueller no happier to be ordered to keep the session secret "upon peril of the Sword's displeasure." It was like a throwback to the bad old days when the Protector had been able to threaten his steadholders, and the fact that Mayhew truly *could* threaten them only made it more disagreeable.

For now, at least, Mueller thought as he reviewed recent events.

His colleagues had been bloodthirsty enough *devising* their plan, but deciding where to execute it had been a problem. For them, at least. Samuel Mueller had seen the ideal spot immediately, and the others were enormously grateful to him—once he'd maneuvered them into suggesting it.

Burdette's repugnance at the thought of killing his own steaders had been plain from the outset; all Mueller had needed to do was look grave and encourage his fellow steadholder to gird his loins to the task God had sent them. His own stern acceptance of the distasteful necessity of Marchant's plan, coupled with the thoughtful observation that it wouldn't do to choose a Sky Domes project in the steading of Harrington's most bitter critic, had prompted Burdette to suggest that perhaps, in that case, Mueller Steading might be a better location. Mueller had allowed himself to appear horrified . . .

which had brought Marchant neatly into the argument at Burdette's side. The defrocked priest and his Steadholder had made their case with passion, and when he'd finally, grudgingly, allowed himself to be talked into it, they'd expressed their admiration for his willingness to pay the price of God's work most becomingly. They'd been too busy finding reasons to arrange the accident somewhere—anywhere—other than in Burdette to even consider the benefits Mueller's "sacrifice" would buy him.

Well, perhaps the purity of their motives blinded them to the more worldly possibilities so evident to Mueller. He was as committed to God's work as anyone, but he saw no reason to ignore the opportunities God chose to offer him in its doing. Not that it had been an easy decision. He had no more wish to kill his own steaders than the next man—he had, after all, assumed an obligation to them when he swore fealty to Benjamin IX's grandfather—but as Burdette and Marchant had said themselves, sacrifices had to be made. And while he was truly shocked by the deaths of children, which had never been part of the original plan, Marchant had been right again. They *were* about God's work, it *had* made their strategy far more effective . . . and the added tragedy had only enhanced the advantages Mueller's fellow conspirators failed to perceive.

Neither Burdette nor Marchant had yet realized how deep in his debt they now stood. Nor had it occurred to Burdette that what he might not choose to give Mueller out of gratitude could be secured hereafter by other means. Burdette hadn't even noticed that while there was no evidence linking Mueller to the plot, he had complete details on every phase of *their* operations. With that in hand, his steading's investigative agencies could always "discover" evidence of the others' involvement later, and any allegations Marchant and Burdette might make about his own complicity would be futile. And *that*, he thought with another smile, would give him an iron hold on Lord Burdette for the rest of his life.

Nor was that the only, or even the greatest, advantage

he'd secured, for he and his steaders were the victims of this atrocity. That not only made him the last person anyone would suspect of involvement, but also positioned him nicely to lead the attack on Harrington—and, indirectly, on Mayhew—as a matter of principle. He could wax as bitter in his rhetoric as he pleased, and it would be put down to perfectly natural outrage rather than to ambition. And if worst came to worst and somehow their plan to brand Harrington with responsibility miscarried, he was also positioned to recoil in shock and adopt the voice of sweet reason in order to "heal the wounds" left by this tragedy. Best of all, any concessions he made to that end would gain him enormous sympathy as a wise and judicious statesman and put that upstart Mayhew publicly in his debt.

Not, of course, that he intended to fail. But it never hurt to cover all possibilities, and one thing he was determined upon. He had no intention of passing his son a hollow authority in his own, God-given steading, and he was only fifty-two. With the new medical advances, he could expect to last well into his nineties, even without prolong, and, he thought with grim humor, that would give him plenty of time to, as the verse from his childhood had put it, "try, try again."

He paused and frowned as a new thought occurred to him. If he was going to think about covering possibilities, he ought to be certain his flanks were covered, as well. The only six people with direct knowledge of his involvement in any plans against Harrington and Mayhew were Burdette, Marchant, and Samuel Harding, on the one hand, and Surtees, Michaelson, and Watson on the other. The latter three were no threat, since he'd kept both sets of plans separate and they had no knowledge of any illegal acts. But the others might become a problem—and so, for that matter, might the other workmen who'd sabotaged the site. Mueller had taken pains to insure his own security, and, aside from Harding, he'd never met any of the saboteurs. But he wasn't at all certain the need for internal security would occur to fanatics of Marchant's stripe . . . or how much he might confide in his tools. After all, he and Burdette had told *Mueller* the names of the others involved in the plot, hadn't they?

His frown deepened, and he nodded to himself. Burdette and Marchant were obvious threats; the others were more problematical, but he couldn't rule out the possibility that they'd heard his name mentioned. A third-party investigation he couldn't control might just be able to tie him to it with enough corroborating testimony, and it wouldn't pay to take chances. Not with dead children to tighten the nooses about the necks of anyone who got caught.

No, it was time to take out a little insurance, and he knew just the man to whom he could safely entrust the task.

"A secret session, My Lord?" Edmond Marchant frowned at his patron. Neither man was bothered by the fact that Burdette had just broken the law to inform Marchant of the session. After all, it was only Man's law, not God's. But the timing was disturbing, and Marchant's frown deepened.

Things were going well, but Satan was a cunning foe, and while it was true they were God's warriors and God was master of the Devil, that didn't mean Satan would take this lying down. He'd spent years grooming Mayhew and his harlot for their tasks, and scorpions must be gnawing his vitals over what God's servants had wrought to thwart him. Surely he was working all his infernal wiles to salvage his plans, so where were the signs of his handiwork? That there were such signs was a given, but Edmond Marchant, strive as he might, had yet to perceive them, and that worried him.

He leaned back in his chair and rubbed his upper lip in thought. If Mayhew had summoned the Keys, then he had something he thought could be effective, and the fact that it was a *secret* session suggested he wanted to conceal whatever it was to the last possible moment.

Which, in turn, suggested Marchant and his Steadholder should be wary and, if possible, discover just what that something was.

But what could it be? The people were arising to smite the whore Harrington. If Mayhew and the corrupt Sacristy tried to preserve her, they would only draw the people's wrath down on themselves. Unless they thought there was some way they could *turn* that wrath . . . ?

"My Lord, have you heard anything about the reasons for this session?" he asked finally.

"No," Burdette snorted. "No doubt he plans on whining and pleading for 'restraint' in the matter of the bitch's impeachment."

"But why do that in *secret*, My Lord?" Marchant probed, trying as much to get his own thoughts in order as stir the Steadholder to consider it.

"Because he's afraid of the people," Burdette returned shortly.

"Possibly, My Lord. Possibly. But what if he has some other reason? One he feels can succeed only if he produces it as a surprise?" Marchant's eyes sharpened as he heard his own words, and Burdette cocked his head.

"What is it, Brother Marchant?" he asked in a less abrupt tone. "You suspect something specific?"

"I don't know, My Lord. . . ." Marchant's voice trailed off, and his brain worked even more furiously. Satan was cunning, and, like God, though surely to a lesser extent, he knew far more than any mortal. Was it possible that—? The cleric's heart raced with sudden, fearful suspicion, but he made his expression remain calm and considering.

"My Lord, do you still have contacts in the Ministry of Justice?" he asked in a merely thoughtful tone.

"A few," Burdette said with a fresh edge of anger. Prior to the accursed "Mayhew Restoration," Burdette had controlled Justice, and he bitterly resented the way Councilman Sidemore had moved steadily to "retire" the appointees who might still be loyal to their one-time patron.

"In that case, My Lord, it might be wise to see what you can discover about Security's investigation into the dome collapse. It would be well to know exactly what evidence they may have amassed against the harlot. That information would be of help in planning your own remarks before the Conclave."

Burdette considered for a moment, then nodded. His expression showed no shadow of the doubt which had sprung to sudden life in Marchant's own heart, but he saw the logic of the argument the priest had chosen to advance.

It was a pity, Marchant thought sadly, that men who sought only to do God's will must be so circumspect about their actions, even with one another. But his Steadholder was a man of passions, and if Marchant's suspicion had no foundation, it would be wise never to suggest it to him. The worst thing Marchant could do was set the same worry in the Steadholder's mind when there was no way to prove or disprove it. That sort of concern would only prey upon him, and might well weaken his will when they stood upon the very threshold of success.

"Councilman Sidemore has set things in motion, Your Grace," Prestwick said. "He's assembled a team to sift the evidence, but he and Security say they need a rather larger effort than we'd originally hoped."

"I see." Benjamin frowned at the screen. He and Prestwick had hoped to get things moving with only a handful of senior, completely trustworthy men, but the Chancellor's tone told him they'd been overly optimistic. Well, he thought, a justice ministry responsible for an entire planet was, by its very nature, a huge, complex organism. Like any respectable dinosaur, it needed secondary brains scattered throughout its body to make things work.

"I understand, Henry," he said after a moment. "Please thank the Councilman . . . and stress once more the importance of confidentiality." He smiled wryly. "Feel free to seek his commiseration for my harping on the matter, but get the message across."

"Of course, Your Grace," Prestwick replied, and Benjamin nodded and cut the circuit. For the first time since this disaster had begun, he realized with some surprise, he actually felt a bit cheerful over his prospects.

A dangerous sign, he told himself immediately. Any conspirators who could bring their plot this far were dangerous, and his own options had too many built-in risks. He couldn't afford complacency-born mistakes.

"Welcome aboard *Terrible*, Reverend Hanks."

"Thank you, My Lady. As always, it's a pleasure to see you." Hanks deliberately projected his voice to the ears of all the officers and ratings gathered in the boat bay gallery. He had no doubt the Navy's personnel had been as horrified by the dome collapse as anyone on the planet. Military discipline might hide it, but they were Graysons, and many of them must entertain doubts about their admiral. The Reverend was too astute a student of human nature to blame them for that, but he wanted the cordiality of his greeting to Lady Harrington to sink into any minds where those doubts had found a home.

"Will you accompany me to my quarters, Sir?" Honor asked.

"Thank you, My Lady. I'd be honored," Hanks replied, and glanced sideways at her profile as she escorted him towards the boat bay lift. She looked better than he'd feared, but the marks of grief remained plain on her face, and his heart went out to her. She was no member of his Church, but she was—as, indeed, he'd told the Keys at her investment—a good and a godly woman who deserved so much better than vile and ambitious men had done to her.

"Protector Benjamin and his family charged me to remind you of their debt to you—and of their love," he said, and she smiled gratefully at him as they stepped into the lift. He let the doors close, and then went on. "In addition, My Lady, the Protector sends you this."

He handed her the writ of summons, and her eyebrows rose as she examined the heavy, official envelope. He simply waited, and she broke the seal and scanned its contents, then she looked back at him in silent question.

"The Chamber is growing restless, My Lady," he explained quietly, "and there's been . . . well, some talk of impeaching you." A spark of anger flared in her eyes—a healthful sign, he thought—and he shook his head. "To date, those who want you formally charged before the Keys lack the numbers to demand it, My Lady, but that could change. The Protector hopes to head that off by a personal appeal—and, if that fails, by revealing at least a little of Mr. Gerrick's findings. The hard part," his sudden, wry smile made him look almost boyish, "will be to do it without revealing precisely who else he suspects may be behind it."

"If you'll pardon my saying so, Reverend, that will be an impressive trick," Honor observed, and Hanks nodded.

"No doubt. However, the Protector wishes you to bring Mr. Gerrick along as an expert witness. And, of course, I've also been summoned to the session, where I will be only too happy to offer you my own modest support."

"'Modest support'!" Honor snorted, and smiled warmly at the kindly old man who'd done so much to help her on Grayson despite the turmoil her mere presence had spawned. "Your Grace," she said, reaching out to lay her hand on his shoulder, "your 'modest support' is more firepower than any reasonable person could expect to call on. Thank you. Thank you very much."

"There's no need to thank me, My Lady," the Reverend said simply, reaching up to cover the hand on his shoulder with his own. "I will consider it both my privilege and my honor to serve you in any way I can, at any time."

• CHAPTER TWENTY-FIVE

Thomas Theisman relaxed at last as TF Fourteen made its alpha translation. Operation Dagger was finally underway, and, as always, it was a vast relief now that the op had actually begun, yet his relief was not unalloyed.

So far, things had gone well, he told his nagging edge of worry. Although the entire force had lain less than nine hours' hyper flight from Casca while it rehearsed, interstellar space was one vast hiding hole. And even more gratifying than knowing operational security had been maintained, the last sims had gone much better than any of their predecessors. The computers estimated that TF Fourteen had taken only trifling losses and attained all of Dagger's objectives well within the specified timetable.

Was his problem the old superstition that a bad dress rehearsal was the best harbinger of a successful performance? Or was it the fact that, despite their proximity to Casca, they'd failed to confirm the presence of more Grayson superdreadnoughts in that system? He tried to calm his qualms by repeating Intelligence's estimates of Grayson refit times to himself once more, but somehow it wasn't quite enough.

He drew a deep breath and looked around almost surreptitiously as he finally admitted the truth in the privacy of his own thoughts. The last update from Intelligence had included a reference which Thomas Theisman found most unsettling. StateSec had clamped down on the distribution of intelligence since the coup. *All* of it was now handled solely on a "need to know" basis, and StateSec apparently assumed naval officers had no particular need to know anything. Nonetheless, what had once been NavInt before StateSec ingested it had finally confirmed reports that Honor Harrington had retired to Yeltsin in disgrace after that disastrous duel on Manticore.

Theisman shook his head. How could anyone be stupid enough to beach *Harrington* over something like that? The most cursory glance at the raw newsfax stories showed Pavel Young had deserved everything he'd gotten, and Thomas Theisman was pleased, in an oddly proprietary way, that Harrington had given it to him. The thought amused him, yet it was true. He regarded Honor Harrington as an enemy, but she was an honorable one, who'd treated him and his people with respect and dignity after their surrender to her in Yeltsin—and that despite the fact that, whatever the official cover story, she'd *known* the PRH had deliberately attacked and killed Manticoran personnel.

She was also, he thought, one of the best in the business. Even the PN officers who hated her, and they were many, admitted that. She was the sort of officer any navy would kill to enlist, and the RMN had *beached* her? For shooting a piece of aristocratic scum in a fair—and legal—fight? Incredible.

But however stupid the Manties might've been, Theisman doubted the Graysons shared their opinion. No, if Harrington was in Yeltsin, the GSN had offered her a commission. And given Grayson's need for experienced officers, she'd probably been bumped even higher in rank than *he* had, as well.

Of course, if Stalking Horse had succeeded, she was also sitting there in Casca along with all of Grayson's ships of the wall. But if it *hadn't* succeeded, there was a chance he might find himself facing her once more, this time with an SD or two in her kit bag, and wouldn't *that* be fun? For all his ambition and planning ability, Alexander Thurston was no match for Honor Harrington once the shit began to fly. And while Theisman himself had scored off her once, he was only too well aware of the fluke circumstances which had let him. If she happened to be in command in Grayson and had any capital ships at all to work with, TF Fourteen was going to get hurt.

But even if they did, they could still pull it off, he told himself. However good she was, thirty-six battleships would be ample to handle the two or three SDs Grayson might have retained for local defense.

He nodded to himself, amused, in a grim sort of way, by his own near-superstitious respect for her, and settled himself in his command chair. One way or the other, it would all be over within the next four days.

"That *bitch!*" Lord Burdette slammed his fists on his desk, then flung himself up out of his chair. "That cunning *whore* of Satan! How? How did she *do* this?"

Edmond Marchant made himself as small and inoffensive-looking as possible while his Steadholder stormed about his office like a caged beast. Burdette's normally handsome face was ugly with fury—and fear—and the cleric felt an icy fist about his own heart as he contemplated the news from his Steadholder's Justice Ministry contacts.

The most infuriating, and frightening, thing about that news was that it was fragmentary. Aaron Sidemore had done his job of replacing Burdette loyalists well, and none of the handful of remaining bureaucrats still mindful of past obligations to the Steadholder were members of the small, tight task force the Councilman had established. All they had was bits and pieces, but what they did know was bad enough, and Marchant's brain echoed his Steadholder's impassioned question.

How had they done it? How had Sky Domes reconstructed events when they'd been completely barred from the site? Marchant had personally recruited the engineers who'd planned the operation. Those men had been given exact copies of the original plans, and they'd sworn to him—sworn on their own souls—that their sabotage would be almost impossible to detect even from direct, on-site examination. So how had Sky Domes even realized it had been deliberate, far less how it had been done, all the way from Harrington?

Satan. It had to be direct, demonic intervention. The icy fist squeezed tighter about his heart at the thought. He'd known the Devil would fight to preserve his tools, but how had even *he* managed this? Were not his Steadholder and he God's champions? Would God permit Satan to defeat them?

No! The Lord would *never* let that happen! There was—must be!—a way yet, if only he could meet the Test of finding it. But what *was* it?

He closed his eyes in prayer, begging God to show him the answer even as his mind churned back over the maddening bits and pieces they knew.

Gerrick, he thought. Adam Gerrick, Sky Domes' chief engineer. Lord Burdette's Justice sources all agreed that whatever was happening had started with him, and Harrington had him safely tucked away aboard her flagship, so—

Wait! *Why* was he in hiding on Harrington's ship? If his was the guiding hand behind the investigation, why did she have him hidden rather than down on Grayson leading Justice's hounds along Marchant's trail? There had to be a reason, the cleric told himself fiercely. There *had* to be! But what was it? What, what, *what?*

And then he realized. Justice was *beginning* an investigation. That meant they didn't *know* anything yet, didn't it? If they'd really known what had happened, that heretic Mayhew would already have taken formal steps against Lord Burdette, and he hadn't. Instead, he'd summoned a closed session of the Keys. That must mean he intended to lay the story before the steadholders *before* Justice had investigated, and that made sense, didn't it? The public's hatred for Harrington was rising to levels higher than Marchant had dared let himself hope for, so it followed that the Protector was desperate to quell the mounting fury before it reached a stage at which not even proof the Mueller dome had been sabotaged could repair public confidence in her.

Of course it did! Marchant nodded to himself, and his eyes screwed even more tightly shut as his brain raced through the possibilities.

If Justice hadn't yet amassed any hard evidence—and they couldn't have without Lord Mueller's warning them Justice inspectors were examining the site—then Mayhew's only "proof" was Sky Domes' unsupported *allegations*. Even if Gerrick had figured out everything, only he and his staff knew the truth. *That* was why Harrington had him aboard her ship. She was protecting him against any possible danger from the godly until she trotted him out for the Keys.

And if that was so, if he was Mayhew's star witness, she was wise to do just that. Much as Marchant hated her, his humiliation in their public confrontation had cured him of any tendency to underestimate her, and he nodded in sour acknowledgement of her cunning. If the godly could only get to Gerrick, silence him, buy even a few more days for the public's hatred to build, not even a full dress Justice investigation could—

His eyes popped open. Of course! That was it—the answer he'd begged God to show him! How could he have missed seeing it from the outset?

"—that *whore!* That scheming, fornicating, rutting *bitch!* I'll kill her—kill her with my own two hands! I'll—"

"My Lord!" Marchant spoke loudly to break into his Steadholder's furious monologue, and Burdette whirled. His blue eyes were furnaces, so hot the cleric quailed inwardly, but he dared not falter. He was God's servant, and he knew the answer now.

"What?" Burdette snapped in a hard, savage voice he'd never before used to his chaplain, and Marchant forced his own words to come out calmly and reasonably.

"My Lord, I know what we must do," he said quietly.

"*Do?* What *can* we do?"

"We can still assure God's triumph, My Lord."

"How?" Rage still choked William Fitzclarence, but the cleric's calm tone was having its effect. He shook himself, and his voice was almost normal when he repeated the question. "How, Edmond? If they know what happened—"

"But they don't, My Lord. Not yet. So far all they can possibly have is conjecture—*Sky Domes'* conjecture."

"What?" Burdette looked puzzled, and Marchant leaned forward.

"My Lord, if they had real evidence, would Mayhew and his sycophants hesitate one moment before making public charges against you?"

"But what if that's precisely what he *does* intend to do at this cursed secret session of his?!"

"If he meant to do that, he wouldn't have asked for a *secret* session, My Lord. Don't you see? That *proves* he has only a theory. The hatred against Harrington is so intense now that he would never delay any public statement which could defuse it, so he must intend to lay Sky Domes' theories—*theories*, My Lord—before the Keys."

"He—" Burdette paused with an arrested expression. "Yes," he murmured. "Yes, that *would* make sense, wouldn't it? He has no proof, but he hopes to buy time, postpone the harlot's impeachment."

"Precisely, My Lord. Until she's stripped of her steadholder's immunity, no civil charges can be brought against her. All he needs to do to preserve her, for the moment, at least, is head off the writ of impeachment. And, My Lord, that's all he can *hope* to do at this point. I'm certain of it."

Burdette stood for a moment, jaw locked in concentration, then sank back into his chair. He frowned at his blotter for several seconds, then shook his head.

"I'm afraid that doesn't matter in the long run, Edmond. If he manages to delay her impeachment— and if this Gerrick and his staff have, indeed, deduced what happened—they'll find proof eventually. They may not be able to prove who did it, but if they know exactly what to look for—"

"But, My Lord, all *we* need to do is prevent Mayhew

from winning the time for his investigation," Marchant said quietly. Burdette's head popped up, and the cleric nodded. "My Lord, in a very few more days it will no longer matter what actually happened. All that will matter is that we've awakened all of Grayson to the consequences of putting a steadholder's key in the hands of a woman. In fact, we don't even need to impeach Harrington."

"But the plan—" Burdette began, only to have Marchant interrupt him yet again.

"I know the plan, My Lord, but think. If there *is* any physical evidence, the plan to convict her of murder will fail. But if she's never brought to trial, if neither she nor Gerrick, the man responsible for the dome's original design, are allowed to present their stories, her innocence will never be fully proven in the people's minds. If Harrington *herself*, personally, is never exonerated in a court of law, many—possibly most—of Grayson's people will never truly be convinced the collapse was contrived. A kernel of doubt will remain, like God's mustard seed. Even if we don't fully succeed at this time, all we truly need is to assure that we do not fully *fail*. In His Own good time, God will bring that seed to fruition."

Burdette leaned back, gazing at Marchant with intent, narrow eyes, and the cleric smiled thinly.

"At this moment the only two people who present a genuine threat to God's will are Gerrick and Harrington. They, and they alone, are the focus around which Satan may rally his minions in time to undo God's work. And we, My Lord, know where they are . . . and where they will be in twelve hours' time."

• CHAPTER TWENTY-SIX

"Ready, Jared?"

"Just a second, My Lady. I— Ah!" Jared Sutton finally got the carryall sealed and slung its strap over his shoulder. "*Now* I'm ready, My Lady. One flag lieutenant, reporting for escort duty."

He grinned, and Honor shook her head. Jared had no official business coming along tonight, but she was grateful he'd volunteered. Adam was loaded to near-capacity with his own mini-comp, data chips, and miniature HD unit, but he'd also brought along complete hardcopy documentation of every stage of the Mueller project and his study teams' conclusions. That ran to over thirty kilos of paper, which Jared had offered to carry for her.

"I appreciate this, Jared," she said gravely as she scooped Nimitz from his perch and set him on her shoulder. The 'cat had snapped back more quickly from their shared, killing depression than she had, and he bleeked a cheerful endorsement of her thanks to the flag lieutenant.

"My Lady, you once told me a flag lieutenant was the most overworked and underappreciated member of an admiral's staff. Well, you've been mighty generous about not overworking me, and you don't kick me *too* often. The least I can do is play porter for you on a night this important."

Honor smiled and started to say something more, then settled for patting his shoulder and turned to survey the rest of her party.

MacGuiness had Adam looking almost human again.

He'd had the Harrington House staff collect several changes of clothing from the engineer's senior wife and fly them up to *Terrible*, and he'd almost sat on the younger man to make him eat properly. Honor knew from experience what too many stims did to a person, and she was grateful for the way Mac had fussed over Adam. Of course, he'd had plenty of practice fussing over *her*, hadn't he?

Eddy Howard, the third man of her usual "travel" detachment, was down with a virus, but Arthur Yard was substituting for him, and he, Andrew LaFollet, and Jamie Candless had taken special pains with their always perfect appearance. Her armsmen had shared the communal sense of guilt which had enveloped Harrington Steading after the Mueller disaster, and the knowledge that it *hadn't* been Sky Domes' fault had done wonders for them. More, they saw the special session of the Keys as the first step in vindicating their Steadholder and punishing the men who'd deliberately planned that atrocity to destroy her, and there was a grim, hard light in their eyes at the prospect.

Reverend Hanks wore his customary clerical black with the round, white collar, and Honor cocked her head.

"Reverend, I've always meant to ask—what *is* that collar made of?"

"An ancient and well-kept secret, My Lady," Hanks said gravely, then chuckled. "As a matter of fact, it's celluloid. Old-fashioned, stiff, *sweaty* celluloid. Ever since I became Reverend, I've toyed with the notion of changing it, but I suppose I'm more a creature of tradition than my critics think. Besides, a little mortification is good for the flesh, as long as you don't get carried away."

Honor laughed, then squared her shoulders. She wasn't wearing uniform tonight, for she was in her persona as Steadholder, not Admiral, and she was just as glad. She had no special desire to mortify *her* flesh— though, now that she considered it, that was a remarkably apt description of the GSN's uniform. Besides, it was important that she not seem to be hiding behind her naval rank . . . and it wouldn't hurt to soothe the traditionalists' sensibilities by refraining from appearing in Steadholders' Hall in trousers.

"All right, gentlemen. Let's be about it," she said, and LaFollet nodded to Candless to open the hatch.

Edward Martin tried to grind his tension into submission as the air car sped south, but they were over ocean now, approaching the southernmost continent of Goshen, and the retired Burdette armsman felt the shuddery wings of fear beating in his belly.

Yet it was only natural to feel fear, he told himself, for the time had come for him to meet the Test of his life and return that life to Him Who had created it. He accepted that, but the body's physical fear was something not even faith could completely overcome and no cause for shame. God had given Man fear to warn him of danger, and so long as a man didn't let that natural fear deter him from doing God's will, God asked no more of him, and his welcome in the arms of the Lord was certain.

He glanced at the man in the seat beside him. Austin Taylor was nineteen years younger than he, and his own anxiety was obvious, but Austin had already proven his faith, working as one of the men who'd brought about the collapse of the harlot's project in Mueller. Martin had reached the rank of sergeant in the Burdette Steadholder's Guard before a broken leg that never quite healed properly retired him, and that had barred him from the Sky Domes infiltration teams. Brother Marchant had explained why they could risk no connection between any man who might be caught and the Steadholder, and, in truth, Martin was glad of it. He was willing to lay down his own life for the Faith, yet he thanked his God for sparing him the more terrible task He had demanded of Austin and his fellows. One could harden one's soul to slay men in the service of Satan's handmaiden, but children, little children—

Martin bit his lip and blinked on angry tears. God had willed it. It was He Who'd chosen the time for the collapse, knowing—as He knew all things—that those children would be present, and their innocent souls had been gathered to His bosom, the agony and terror of their last moments of life soothed away by the merciful touch of the Almighty. In their innocence, they'd been spared the harsher task God demanded of Edward Martin: the taking of a human life, be it ever so lost to sin, and the knowing sacrifice of his own.

He glanced down at his sleeve and grimaced. He'd always been proud of his Burdette uniform, but tonight he wore another, one whose very sight he loathed. He knew why he had to wear it, yet simply donning the green-on-green of the harlot's own Guard defiled him, for it represented all the evils Satan had brought to pass on Grayson.

His nostrils flared with contempt for the so-called Churchmen who'd let themselves be seduced into abandoning God's way like so many whores, but then he shook his head, instantly contrite for his own lack of charity. Most of the Elders were good and godly men, he knew. He'd once met Reverend Hanks when the Reverend had celebrated services in Burdette Cathedral, and he understood why the Reverend was so beloved. The depth of his personal faith had cried out to Martin, and he'd felt an instant—a fleeting instant, but real—when the Reverend's faith had linked with his, making his own belief an even brighter and more glorious thing. But neither of them had known then the snare that Satan would lay before the Reverend's feet, he thought grimly. Indeed, Edward Martin's greatest anger was reserved for whatever wile of Satan had led a decent, God-fearing man like Julius Hanks into such error. How could a man like that not see that inciting wives and daughters to turn upon husbands and fathers, rejecting the Faith under which Grayson had endured for almost a thousand years as God's Own planet, was the Devil's work? What sorcery had that foreign harlot worked upon him to make him overlook even the mortal sin of her fornication outside marriage's sanctified bounds? A fornication she'd publicly admitted—*boasted* of!—when another man of God charged her to repent her sins? How had she blinded the Reverend to the effect *that* example would have on other women? The mortal peril to their very souls into which it must tempt them?

Martin knew some men treated their wives and daughters badly, yet that was because Man was fallible, and it was the duty of other men and the Church to censure and punish such behavior, just as they would punish any who victimized the weak. He was even willing to admit Protector Benjamin might have *some* good ideas. Perhaps it *was* time to relax the outdated laws an older, harsher time had required, to permit women to seek genteel employment, even to vote. But to *force* them to shoulder burdens God had never meant them to bear, even to serve in the *military*? Edward Martin knew what military life was like, for he'd lived it for eighteen proud, grueling years, and no woman could live like that and remain what God had intended her to be. Look at Harrington herself—the best possible example of how it coarsened and defiled them!

No, he told himself, Reverend Hanks had been deceived, tricked into approving the changes the Protector demanded. The Reverend's admiration for Harrington's courage—and, Martin admitted, there was no gainsaying the woman's bravery—blinded him to her sins and the corrupt message they proclaimed to Grayson. But even the best men made mistakes, and God never held it against them if they acknowledged their errors and turned once more to Him. That was the entire purpose of the sacrifice Martin was about to make this night, and he prayed—prayed with all his heart—that Reverend Hanks and the other Elders would embrace their God once more when the corruption poisoning their souls had been cleansed at last.

* * *

All navies seem convinced of the need to make an astounding amount of fuss whenever an admiral leaves her flagship in order to sufficiently emphasize the importance of such an august personage. When the admiral in question is also a great feudal lady, things can get *truly* involved.

Honor had allowed for it in the schedule, and she maintained a properly grave expression as she walked through the inspection the honor guard expected of her, then took her farewell of Captain Yu. It was all as gravely formal as if she meant never to return rather than be back aboard in barely six hours, but she knew better than to complain.

The bugle fanfare announced her official departure as she swung into the boarding tube, but at least she'd gotten them to aim it in a different direction, though the bugler had looked a bit hurt by her tactful request. She smiled at the thought, now that no one could see her face, and swam down the tube, trailed at an unusually discreet distance by her armsman, given what zero-gee did to her ridiculous gown.

Her smile became an urchin's grin at *that* thought, and then she swung into the pinnace's gravity and adjusted her skirts before she moved forward. The pinnace had started life as a standard RMN Mark Thirty, designed to land a half-company of Marines on a hostile surface and/ or give them fire support once they were down. It still retained the capability for the latter mission, but a superdreadnought's small craft capacity was great enough that the GSN had decided to gut the troop compartment of one of each SD's pinnaces and refit it as a VIP transport. The results were downright opulent, with double-wide aisles—something Honor appreciated at the moment. Her key of office's chain had gotten tangled with the ribbon of the Star of Grayson while she swam the tube, and it was a relief to have an aisle wide enough to let her look down while she disentangled them without tripping over things. She completed the task, then slipped into her seat and looked up at the flight engineer.

"How's the schedule?"

"We're looking good, My Lady. In fact, we're running a bit ahead. I'm afraid there's going to be a five-minute delay before we undock."

"Why am I not surprised?" she murmured, and glanced across the aisle to watch Adam Gerrick settle into his seat. Nimitz curled comfortably down in her lap, and she looked over her shoulder at Sutton.

The flag lieutenant was struggling to get the carryall into the overhead luggage compartment, and her eyes twinkled as he muttered something she wasn't supposed to hear. She considered teasing him about it, but the side of his face she could see was already red with embarrassment, and she decided to show clemency. Lieutenants would feel neglected if their admirals *never* gave them problems, but there was a time and a place for everything.

Reverend Hanks settled into the seat beside her as his rank demanded, and she shook her head.

"It would be a lot simpler to just go straight to Austin City," she observed quietly, and he snorted.

"And violate a thousand years of tradition, My Lady? Never! A steadholder flies to the capital in his—or her—official vehicle from his—or her—official residence. Tester only knows what would happen if we suggested that the practice can be a bit, um, inefficient!"

"Even if it means spending two extra hours each way in an air car?"

"I will agree your steading's distance from Austin makes it a bit more difficult, My Lady, but that's *all* I'm prepared to agree to. Someone might report me if I admitted anything more."

Honor laughed and then leaned back in her seat as the pinnace abruptly shivered. The mechanical docking arms unlatched, and the pilot drifted the small craft free on a gentle puff of belly thrusters, then backed out of the bay stern-first. Undocking was a routine maneuver, but he accomplished it with an effortless grace, and

Honor nodded in approval as he turned the pinnace's nose planetward.

"We're late," Taylor said, and Martin nodded tensely. Brother Marchant's followers had done unbelievably well to assemble all they needed for the mission as quickly as they had, but they'd had to duplicate Harrington uniforms, paint an air car in official Harrington colors, and cobble up IDs that could pass muster. Without the practice they'd had preparing covers for the people they'd inserted into the Sky Domes crews they could never have gotten it done in time.

Only, Martin thought, glaring at the dash chrono, they *hadn't* done it in time—not quite. The blur of surf that marked the rocky northern headlands of Goshen was still invisible in the darkness ahead of them, and the flight plan one of the Burdette Space Facility controllers had pulled from Orbital Control gave them less than eighty more minutes to get into position. They'd need seventy of those minutes just to reach Harrington Space Facility, and if they hit even the slightest delay getting onto the grounds—

"We'll never get the car through the traffic control points in time. We'll have to go to the backup plan and ditch it at the west gate," he said, thinking aloud for Austin's benefit. Taylor nodded tautly. HSF was Grayson's newest space facility. It was over ten kilometers from Harrington City, and the usual clutter of service establishments only just now growing up around it was concentrated to the east, between it and the steading's capital.

"I don't like leaving the car," the younger man said after a pause. "The launcher's going to be pretty obvious, Ed."

"Then we'll just have to be sure no one sees us," Martin replied, trying to coax a little more speed from his turbines as the coastline finally appeared before them

The ride down was taking longer than usual because

of who the pinnace's passengers were. Orbital Control had cleared a special security corridor for it, and its flight path had been planned for a gentle atmospheric insertion, but Honor rather wished they'd opted for a shorter flight, even at the expense of a little roughness. She needed to meet with Sky Domes' other engineers before she left for Steadholders' Hall, and time was short, but there was no point fretting over what couldn't be changed, she reminded herself.

Martin and Taylor parked their air car in a bay just out of sight of the west personnel gate and took the time to lock it. Its interior didn't match a real HSG car's, and they couldn't risk someone noticing that and sounding an alarm.

The ex-sergeant glanced at his chrono and swore softly as he pocketed the keys. He'd gotten a little more speed out of the car than he'd hoped, but they had less than twelve minutes to get into position, and that was cutting things too tight. He felt a moment of panic, but then he forced it down. They were about God's work. He would see to it that they met His schedule.

"Give me your ID," he said. Taylor handed the folio over, and Martin drew his own from his breast pocket. "Stay behind me and try to keep your body between the guard and the launcher."

"I'll try, Ed, but—"

Martin nodded. The weapon was one of the accursed Manticorans' latest designs—there was a certain sweetness in that thought—for a portable, shoulder-fired, surface-to-air missile, and like all such weapons, it used its own impeller wedge rather than a warhead to destroy its target. Of course, the drive which could be crammed into a portable weapon produced a wedge smaller than those of larger vehicle- or aircraft-mounted missiles, which reduced its lethal zone and put a correspondingly greater premium on accuracy. But it also meant the weapon was small enough that its carrying case could—barely—be forced into an outsized civilian carryall. That, unfortunately, was a mixed blessing, since armsmen had no business carrying civilian luggage on duty. Well, if the gate guard pressed the point they could always claim Austin was delivering it for a friend before he checked in.

He drew a deep breath and headed for the person-nel gate at the best pace he could manage without look-ing too obviously hurried. *If I find myself too busy to remember You properly, Lord,* he prayed silently, *do not forget me. I am about Your work. Guide me, that my actions may save Your people from sin and damnation.*

Honor glanced back out the view port. Even in the darkness, she saw water gleaming below and recognized the Goshen Sea. Good! The diamond-shaped sea cut deep into the continent of the same name from the northwest, and Harrington City lay at its eastern end. If the sea was below her, she'd be home in another ten minutes, so perhaps she'd have time for that meeting after all.

The single guard was even younger than Austin—an armsman first class, but so new he squeaked—and that was good, for Martin wore a captain's insignia. It was a higher rank than he'd ever expected to hold, but coupled with his age, it should make him a reassuringly senior presence and help defuse any doubts the young-ster might have.

"Good evening, Armsman," he said briskly as he stepped fully into the illumination cast by the gate lights.

"Good evening, Sir!" The Afc snapped to attention and saluted, and Martin returned it.

"Lonely out here," he remarked as he handed over the two ID folios.

"Yes, Sir, it is," the Harrington replied. He opened the first ID and glanced at it, then looked up to match Martin's face to it. "Lonely, I mean," he went on as he closed Martin's ID and opened Taylor's, "but my re—"

He paused suddenly, and Martin's belly tensed as he

looked up. Austin had stepped into the light—he'd had no choice but to come forward so the Harrington could check his face against his ID—and the carryall was damnably evident. The sentry gazed at it for a moment, then shrugged and looked back down at the ID, and Martin relaxed . . . only to tense anew as the Harrington stiffened. The youngster was looking at *him* now, and then his eyes flipped back to Austin. Not at the carryall this time, but at something else.

At, Martin suddenly realized, Austin's *gun belt*. His own eyes dropped to the Harrington's sidearm, and his jaw tightened as he saw the sleek, lethal pulser. It was a modern weapon, too expensive for most steadholders to have reequipped their armsmen with . . . and totally unlike the old-fashioned machine pistols he and Austin carried.

This possibility had occurred to none of their planners—it was always the simple damned things that tripped people up—but he didn't take time to think about it. The Harrington had just started to step back, his own mind still grappling with the implications of what his eye had seen but his brain had not yet fully assimilated, when Martin struck.

There was no time to be gentle, and his eyes were hard as his knuckles smashed into the young armsman's throat. The Harrington's head flew back with a horrible, choking gurgle. His hands went to his throat in an involuntary reflex of agony, and Martin carried through with the attack. The young man was probably already dying of a crushed larynx, a corner of his mind told him, but his right leg swept the Harrington's feet from under him and his hands darted out. They caught the sentry's head and twisted explosively against the angle of his fall, and the sharp, crunching snap of a broken neck was shockingly loud in the silent night.

"*Shit!*" Taylor whispered, and Martin shot him a glare. This was no time for obscenity, he thought, and knew even as he did what a stupid thing it was to think.

He lowered the twitching body gently, smelling the

sewer smell of a death-relaxed sphincter, and grimaced as he dragged the corpse out of the light. It was cruel how death robbed even the best men of dignity, and a heartfelt stab of remorse went through him. This young man had served a sinful mistress, but that was hardly his fault, and he'd done his duty well.

"May God forgive me—and you," he whispered to the corpse, then beckoned sharply to Taylor and led the way through the gate.

"Five minutes, My Lady," the flight engineer announced, and Honor nodded.

"It'll be nice to get down, My Lady." Hanks sighed beside her. "I mean no disrespect, but I've lived on a planet all my life, and while your flagship is a splendid vessel, I prefer solid ground under my feet."

The position wasn't perfect, but it was the best Martin could expect to find, and it wasn't as if they had to worry about target identification. The harlot was Harrington's Steadholder; all other traffic in and out of HSF had been shut down for fifteen minutes on either side of her arrival as a security measure, and they knew the bearing from which her pinnace would approach.

The ex-sergeant went down on one knee in the dense, black shadow of the parked air lorry, pistol in hand, and scanned the field nervously while Taylor unpacked the missile and attached the sighting unit to the launcher.

Senior Corporal Anthony Whitehead, HSG, was in a hurry. All the scurrying about to prepare for the Steadholder's arrival had delayed him, and he was over fifteen minutes late for the gate change. He had no doubt Armsman Sully wondered where the hell he was, and he couldn't blame the kid.

He half-jogged around the last bend, the better to show Sully that even NCOs were aware of their obligations, then slowed to a halt, and his sympathy disappeared into instant anger. Damn it to hell, where *was* he? Just because a man's relief was a little late was no reason to go dashing off and leave his post unguarded! When he got his hands on that young twerp, he'd—

His mental tirade broke off as his cognitive processes caught up with his instant anger. Frederick Sully was no "twerp." Young, yes, but well trained and sharp. He'd made Afc in record time, and Whitehead and his platoon sergeant had their eyes on him for further promotion. There was no *way* Sully would just wander off with the entire facility on a heightened alert level. Feelings were running high, and the Steadholder's armsmen had no intention of taking chances with her life.

But if he hadn't wandered, then—

The corporal snatched out his com.

"Security alert! This is Corporal Whitehead at Gate Five! I've just arrived on-site, and there's no sign of the sentry!" Something poked at his mind, and he scowled, then swore as something he'd seen without seeing it flashed through his brain. "Central, Whitehead. There's an HSG air car parked out here on the hangar apron, Bay Seven-Niner-Three. Was that cleared?"

His answer was the sudden, strident howl of security alarms throughout the facility.

"Sweet Tester!" Taylor gasped as sirens began to scream, and Martin bit back a matching expletive as he remembered what the dead guard had said. It was lonely, "but my re—" His *relief*, of course!

"W-What do we d-do, Ed?" Taylor stuttered, and the ex-sergeant gave him a steady look.

"We do God's work," he said quietly through the alarms' howl, "and if it's His will that we escape alive, we do that, too. Arm your launcher."

Master Chief Coxswain Gilbert Troubridge was Navy, not a member of the Harrington Guard, but the GSN did not encourage its pilots to take chances with the safety of flag officers. More to the point, Troubridge was as aware as anyone of the high state of tension on the planet, and his com was tied into both the HSF and HSG nets.

"Security alert?" He turned in his seat to glare at the com tech. "What *kind* of security alert, damn it?"

"I don't know, Gil," the rating replied tautly. "Some HSG corporal just came up on the air. Something about an unguarded gate."

"Shit!" The pinnace was already on final. If he had to abort, his counter-grav could take him up like a homesick meteor, but with no more information than he had, he couldn't know if that was necessary. Or, for that matter, a good idea.

Master Chief Troubridge made a decision. A Fleet pinnace's active tactical sensors would play hell with HSF's navigation and control systems, but he had an admiral who also happened to be a steadholder onboard.

His finger stabbed a button on his flight console.

"Seeking . . . seeking . . . seeking . . ." Taylor's singsong chant sawed at Martin's nerves, but he forced himself not to shout at the younger man to be silent. Neither of them was likely to live another ten minutes, and he would not go to God having cursed a man seeking to do His will.

"*Acquisition!*" Taylor cried suddenly, and squeezed the stud.

"Missile launch—zero-zero-ten!" Troubridge's copilot shouted, and the master chief's belly turned to frozen lead. Impeller drive. Had to be from the accel. Coming up at over forty degrees.

The data snapped into his brain, and he knew there was no way he could climb out of its path. In fact, there was only one thing he could do.

He killed the counter-grav and dove straight for the ground.

"Sweet Tester!" the senior controller in HSF Flight

Ops gasped. There was no exhaust flare from an impeller-drive missile, and his instrumentation was too badly hashed by the pinnace's sensor emissions for him to tell precisely where it had come from, but he knew what it was, and he stabbed a button that dropped his mike into the HSF security net as well as its link to Lady Harrington's pinnace.

"SAM launch, somewhere on the west approach apron!"

"My God—at the *Steadholder*?" someone else shouted from behind him, but the controller didn't even look up. His horrified eyes were locked to the pinnace's plunging radar return.

Honor's head flew up as the pinnace suddenly lurched, then fell heavily off to port and dove vertically. For a moment she thought the pilot had lost it, but then she heard the scream of air-breathing turbines rammed to full power and realized the pinnace was still veering sharply left. It was an *intentional* maneuver, but why—?

Nimitz reared up in her lap, and she locked her arms about him, then bent her body across his in instant, protective reaction. She freed one arm from the 'cat to reach out and jerk Reverend Hanks' head down, and that was absolutely all she could do.

Operation. There was too much power from an engine close to redline, and his master's union was too tightly locked by the ultimate control systems for him to risk prematurely what it had come from, but he knew what it was, and...

He let go a picture.

"SAM launch!" snapped from the very approach

• CHAPTER TWENTY-SEVEN

In technical terms, what Master Chief Troubridge was trying to do was generate a miss. In layman's terms, he was deliberately crashing his own pinnace in a desperation bid to drop out of the SAM's acquisition envelope . . . and praying he could recover in the instant before he hit the ground and killed everyone on board himself. It was a virtually impossible maneuver, but Gil Troubridge was very, very good, and he almost managed it.

Almost.

He *had* to pull up, and he hauled the nose desperately back, riding his abused, howling turbines and air foils and simultaneously throwing in the counter-grav, but he was perhaps one meter low, and the pinnace's tail slammed into the ground. The impact snapped the sleek craft almost straight upright, but it didn't *quite* go over. For an instant it hung there, and Troubridge felt a moment of terrible relief. His copilot had gotten the emergency landing skids deployed. When the bird came down on them, it would be all—

That was when the SAM executed its terminal attack run.

The small, high-tech kamikaze had lost its target when Troubridge dove for the deck, but its seekers had reacquired lock, and it came slashing in at over ten kilometers per second. Even so, the pilot had *almost* denied it a hit, and its impeller wedge's leading edge caught the pinnace's rearing nose one bare meter aft of the radome.

A guillotine of gravitic energy slammed through the fuselage like an axe through butter, and the raw kinetic energy of the impact tore the first ten meters of the pinnace apart. Troubridge, his copilot, and his com tech died instantly, and the impact energy completed what the tail strike had begun. The dying pinnace twisted impossibly, snapping all the way up and over, then slammed into the ground like a dolphin arcing backwards into the water. But it was no dolphin, and the spaceport approaches were paved with forty centimeters of ceramacrete that was much, much harder than water.

"Oh, dear God, she's down," the controller whispered. "My God, my God, *she's down!*"

Emergency vehicles were screaming into the night, and he stared through the tower's windows in horror as his Steadholder's disintegrating pinnace porpoised across the parking apron on its back.

Had it been a civilian shuttle, everyone aboard would have died with the flight deck crew, but the pinnace was a naval craft, intended for high-threat environments. Its armored hull was built of battle steel, and the people who'd designed it had produced the most crash-survivable vehicle their technology could build.

Number two turbine ripped free, rocketed across the field, and slammed into a fuel tanker, and a huge, blue fireball spalled the night. The tanker's driver never even knew he was dead, and his ground-effect vehicle blew sideways into Service Bay Twelve. Two atmospheric passenger buses and eighteen technicians were torn apart in the resultant explosion, and the pinnace slithered onward in a screaming shower of sparks and shredded alloy.

The hydrogen reservoirs went next, but they, too, were designed to be crash-survivable, and jettisoning charges hurled them away from the splintering fuselage before they could explode. They fell like bombs, and, mercifully, three of them landed in empty, open space. The fourth slammed into the main terminal, and the staggering concussion when it blew turned a thousand square

meters of exterior wall to shrapnel and sent it shrieking through the civilians in Concourse B. Two crash
vehicles narrowly survived the explosion of another of
the tanks square in their path, but their crews had no
time to waste on their miraculous survival, and they
reefed around in hairpin turns to charge after the disintegrating pinnace.

Honor grunted in anguish as something smashed into
her right side. She sensed more than felt something else
coming and instinctively angled her own body to the left
to protect Reverend Hanks' frail, ancient bones just as
a hammer-like impact slammed into her. She heard the
Reverend cry out in pain as her shoulder was driven into
him, and someone screamed from the rear of the cabin.
The terrible sound of agony cut off with even more
terrible suddenness, and the world cartwheeled and spun
and shook about her in a lightning nightmare that somehow seemed to last forever.

But then, miraculously, the pinnace slammed back over
onto its belly and was still. She heard groans and strange,
thick-voiced shouts around her and thrust herself upright.
The overhead luggage rack had come down—that must
have been what knocked her into Hanks—but it had
broken completely loose from its brackets, and her
Sphinx-bred muscles heaved it aside. Her hands were
already feeling for Nimitz, assuring herself she hadn't
lost her grip and that he was uninjured, even as she
turned her head to look for the Reverend.

He was alive, and relief flooded her as he shook his
head dazedly. He'd cut his forehead and bloodied his
mouth, but there was intelligence in his eyes—and concern for her, she noticed—as she fought her way clear
of the air bag which had automatically deployed from
the bulkhead in front of her.

"My Lady! *Lady Harrington!*" She didn't know how
LaFollet had gotten there so soon, but his arm darted
out as she came unsteadily upright. The pain in her right
side told her she had at least one broken rib, and more
pain said her left shoulder was damaged, as well, but

those were minor, distant thoughts, for she smelled the actinic stink of an electrical fire.

"Off! Get everybody off—*now!*" she shouted. The hydrogen reservoirs must have separated properly, or they'd all have been dead, but the emergency thrusters were another matter. Designed for a last-ditch effort to land a battle-damaged pinnace in one piece, *their* tankage was buried deep inside the hull. The fuel lines were filled with inert gas under normal flight conditions, and the tanks themselves were heavily armored in near-indestructible alloy, but *nothing* was truly indestructible.

Hands grabbed her, and she turned her head as LaFollet literally yanked her off her feet and threw her at Jamie Candless. The younger armsman's face was cut and bloody, but he caught her and turned instantly for the nearest rent in the hull.

"Don't worry about me! Help Adam!"

The fuselage's starboard side had been ripped wide open, and Gerrick twisted weakly, moaning with pain. One leg was snapped back at an unnatural angle, trapped under the mangled base of his seat. Splintered bone thrust from a bloodsoaked thigh, and more blood pulsed from a deep wound in his shoulder.

"Let me go—*help Adam!*" she shouted again, but Jamie Candless was a Grayson armsman whose Steadholder was in danger. She twisted in his grip, but he hauled her grimly towards the hole in the hull, despite her greater height and strength, and someone else appeared on her other side.

Arthur Yard gripped her other arm, tearing it free of Nimitz, but the 'cat's arms were about her neck, and he clung to her like a limpet. Between them, Yard and Candless dragged her bodily from the pinnace while Andrew LaFollet bent over Reverend Hanks behind her. His life was even more important to Grayson than the Steadholder's, and there was no time to worry about any injuries the old man might have. The major yanked him to his feet, flung him over his shoulders in a fireman's carry, and charged after his Steadholder.

Honor heaved madly, but her armsmen refused to let her go and ran desperately towards the shelter of a nearby drainage culvert.

She twisted her head and saw LaFollet right behind her with Hanks while Jared Sutton brought up the rear. Her flag lieutenant seemed intact, though he was obviously dazed, but there was no sign of the pinnace's crew. The cockpit crew couldn't possibly have survived, but where was the engineer? Then she remembered the chopped off terrible scream, and she knew.

Candless and Yard reached the culvert and flung her flat in the deep ditch it served, and Candless threw his body over hers. His weight crushed her down on Nimitz, and she writhed out from under him. He tried to drag her back, but an elbow slammed into his belly with the precision of thirty-six years of unarmed combat training. It didn't even occur to Honor that he was trying to save her life. All she could think of was Adam. She started back, only to go down as Yard tackled her bodily from behind, and LaFollet dropped Reverend Hanks less gently than the old man's years deserved and flung himself into the struggle to restrain his Steadholder's insane charge back into the wreckage.

"*No*, My Lady! We can't risk you!"

"I'll go, My Lady!" Sutton had gotten his mind working again, and he dashed back towards the pinnace, his soul writhing in shame as he realized he'd left an injured man trapped while he ran. Candless was still clutching his belly and whooping in agony from Honor's elbow strike, and the other armsmen had all they could do to keep her from following her lieutenant without injuring her themselves.

"*No, goddamn it!*" LaFollet screamed in her face, and the sheer shock of hearing him swear did what all his physical efforts could not. She froze, staring into his wild gray eyes and panting, and only then noticed the tears flowing down his face. "We can't *risk* you!" he half-sobbed, shaking her in his fear for her. "Don't you *understand* that?"

"He's right, My Lady." Reverend Hanks hobbled over to her. He favored his left leg and his face was blood-streaked, but his voice was unnaturally calm, almost gentle, and that gave it even more weight than LaFollet's passionate plea. "He's right," the Reverend said again, even more quietly, and she slumped in her armsmen's grip.

"All right," she whispered.

"Give me your word, My Lady," LaFollet demanded. She looked at him, and he managed a strained carica-ture of a smile. "Give me your word you'll stay here—stay *here!*—and we'll go back after Mr. Gerrick."

"I give you my word," she said dully. He stared into her eyes for one more moment, then released her and jerked his head at Yard, and the two of them started climbing back up out of the ditch.

"Did we get them? *Did we get them?*" Taylor demanded, and Martin shook his head irritably.

"I don't know."

He stood upright, staring out across the field. He'd been certain, at first, that all the explosions and fire meant they'd succeeded, but now he saw the battered, buckled pinnace, not fifty meters away, looming against a backdrop of flame as the first rescue vehicle slammed to a halt beside it. The damage was terrible yet not total, and it was just possible some of the passengers had survived.

He looked around and, despite his faith, swallowed a thick, choking bolus of fear. There were other ground cars out there now, not rescue vehicles, but HSG patrol cars, sweeping directly towards Austin and him. He looked the other way and saw still more of them, clos-ing in along the sides of an isosceles triangle with the wreckage at its base.

"We're not going to get out, Austin," he said, and the calmness of his own voice surprised him. Taylor stared at him for a moment, his mouth working, then dropped the empty launcher with a sigh.

"I guess not," he said with a matching calm, and Martin nodded.

"In that case, I think we should make certain we accomplished what we came for."

LaFollet and Yard heaved themselves out of the ditch, whose side seemed far steeper than it had when they'd dragged their Steadholder down it, and Honor stood beside Reverend Hanks. Enough sanity had returned for her to realize Andrew and the Reverend were right. She was who she was, and she could no longer rush into avoidable danger. Too many people depended upon her for too much, but the acceptance was bitter, bitter poison on her tongue while she watched her armsmen start back towards the pinnace. Nimitz crooned to her, sharing her wretched sense of shame as she let duty hold her back, and Reverend Hanks rested one hand on her shoulder in silent understanding.

Jamie Candless coughed and shoved himself to his knees, and Honor shook her head and knelt beside him.

"Sorry, Jamie," she said with true contrition, and he shook his head.

"Not . . . not a bad hit, My Lady," he gasped with something like a smile, and she set Nimitz down to help him to his feet. The 'cat scampered up to the lip of the ditch and perched there, watching the wreckage and the rescue workers he was far too small to help, and Honor slid an arm around Candless' shoulders. He muttered something and leaned against her—something he would never have done if he hadn't been all but out on his feet—and the two of them turned to look at the wreckage.

Emergency personnel moved with trained, desperate haste. Half a dozen charged straight into the wreckage, looking for survivors, while others pumped thick, white foam over the wreckage, and she recognized the green-on-green uniforms of two more guardsmen running towards her. They must be from the HSF detachment, she thought as they circled wide of the pinnace and dashed in her direction, and wondered how they'd gotten here so quickly.

"There! By the culvert!" Martin hissed, and heard Taylor growl something foul as they saw the tall, slim figure in the deep ditch. The roaring flames struck glittering splinters from the golden key and star about her throat, and the two of them ran even faster, desperate to reach her before a real armsman challenged them.

LaFollet and Yard had gotten no more than twenty meters from the ditch when it happened, and only the fact that they were both looking at the wreck saved their lives.

The hole in the propellant tank wasn't large . . . but enough fumes had finally gathered inside the hull, where the fire-suppressing foam hadn't quite reached in time. The first, brief warning was a lurid sheet of flame, shooting up out of the wreckage like some obscenely beautiful fan of scarlet and gold and blue, and both armsmen flung themselves flat a fraction of a second before the world blew apart.

The concussion threw Honor, Candless, and Hanks from their feet, and Honor's face went whiter than bone as Adam Gerrick, Jared Sutton, and forty-two HSF rescue personnel were turned from living human beings to so much seared and shredded flesh. She felt the thermal bloom reaching out over the ditch, heard the shriek of flying metal, and loss and guilt worse than any agony of the flesh smashed through her as the explosion hurled her to the ground.

Edward Martin, like Andrew LaFollet and Arthur Yard, had seen and recognized the first dreadful flare. He was older than his companion, and his reflexes weren't what they once had been, but Taylor cried out in confusion as the ex-sergeant tackled him. Then the paving came up and smashed them both in the face as the concussion hit, and Martin felt Taylor's shocked understanding through the arms still pinning the younger man down.

The explosion went on and on, like the Wrath of God Himself. A heavy weight slammed down less than five meters away, then bounced over them and went crashing into the darkness, and he raised his head cautiously.

What had been a pinnace was a flaming crater crowned with tattered scraps of wreckage and the blazing hulks of rescue vehicles, and he wondered numbly how many more men he'd just killed. Then he shoved upright and reached down to drag Taylor up beside him.

"Come on, Austin," he said, and his voice held an eerie calm. The blood guilt for so many innocent lives crushed down on him, but he was about God's work, and he clung to that assurance desperately. It was his talisman, the only thing that kept him sane in this nightmare of fiery mass death. "We have work to do."

Andrew LaFollet and Arthur Yard were alive, but Yard was unconscious, and the major was little better. He heaved up on his knees and looked for the pinnace. One glance was all he needed to know he could do nothing for anyone who'd been close to it, and he bent over Yard to check his injuries.

Thank God I talked her into staying in the ditch, he thought, and then sighed in relief as his fingers found the throb of Yard's pulse.

Honor crawled up the side of the ditch, looking for Nimitz. She could feel him through their link and knew he was both frightened and appalled by the destruction. A bright, sharp jitter of anger in his emotions suggested he hadn't gotten off totally unscathed—and resented the fact—but at least she knew he was in one piece and not badly damaged, which was more than she was certain she could say for herself at the moment.

She'd already known she had at least one broken rib; now her entire side was afire with pain and blood stung her eyes with its thick salt. She couldn't tell if her forehead was cut or just badly scraped, but she knew she'd split her lower lip when her face hit the ground, and she was still more than half-dazed when her head rose over the edge of the ditch.

There! Nimitz had found the ceramacrete lip of the culvert. Now he crouched behind it, peering over it at the flames, and she sighed in relief. His pelt was singed in more than one place, but she should have known he had the sense—and reflexes—to get under cover.

She looked back over her shoulder and grimaced in sympathy as she watched Candless struggling stubbornly to pick himself up once more. *Poor Jamie's having a bad day,* she thought with a something that would have been hysterical amusement if she hadn't been so detached. *First a pinnace wreck, then his own Steadholder tries to put him down for the count, and now the entire world blows up in his face. It's a wonder he can even move.*

A hand touched her shoulder, and she looked up. Reverend Hanks stood beside her, his face a mask of blood and grief as he stared at the carnage, and he shook his head sadly.

"Here, My Lady," he said, "let me help you."

He reached down and pulled her to her feet—just as Nimitz suddenly whipped around to his left with the tearing-canvas snarl of his war cry.

"Pretend it's a target range, Austin," Martin said softly as they jogged towards the ditch as fast as their rubbery legs would let them. Taylor nodded convulsively, but the ex-sergeant didn't really expect much from him. Austin was as brave and willing a companion as a man could ask to die with, yet he lacked the training for this. Martin knew he'd do his best, but he also knew the job was really up to him.

Forgive me, God—for what I've already done, and for what I am about to do, he prayed. *I know she is Your enemy, an infidel and a harlot, yet she's also a woman. Give me the strength to do what I know I must in Your Name.*

*   *   *

Honor's head snapped around as a streak of singed gray-and-cream fur rocketed across the flame-struck ground. Her eyes were already tracking him, but her brain had been through too much. Even with her link to the 'cat, it took her precious seconds to realize what was happening, and they were seconds she didn't have.

"Sweet Tes—!"

Austin Taylor's shout became a gurgling shriek as ten kilos of Sphinx treecat exploded from the ground and went for his throat. He managed to get an arm up to guard his jugular, but all the instant, instinctive reaction bought him was a few more endless seconds of agony as a six-limbed buzz saw exploded in his face. Nimitz's first strike took out his eyes, and the blind, screaming assassin tottered wildly, staggering about in the steps of some hellish dance while claws and fangs ripped his life out one bloody centimeter at a time.

Edward Martin flinched as Austin screamed, then gagged in horror as he realized what had happened. The snarling, hissing fury slashing and tearing at Austin could only be the harlot's demon familiar, and he cringed as Austin's shrieks tore at his ears, but even in that he recognized God's providence. The treecat had attacked the wrong man, leaving the more dangerous killer free to act, and he charged forward with his pistol ready.

There! His entire universe narrowed to that single tall figure. He saw the blood coating her alien, sharply beautiful face, noted the way she leaned to the right, favoring the ribs on that side, saw the dirt and blood on her once-elegant gown. His mind noted every detail as she turned towards him. He saw her puzzlement, recognized her dawning comprehension, and none of it mattered. He was too far away for her off-world combat techniques to be a threat, yet far too close to miss his shot, and he skidded to a stop and brought his pistol up in both hands. Someone moved at the corner of his vision, but nothing mattered. Nothing but the woman he'd come to kill.

Forgive me, God, a corner of his brain whispered yet again, and he squeezed the trigger.

Honor heard the screams as Nimitz hit his target, but there was other movement out there, as well. She fought her confusion, trying to make her battered mind work, but too much horror had come at her too fast this night, and she couldn't quite grasp what was happening.

Then she saw the gun, and in one, searing instant, she understood. It hadn't been a terrible accident. Someone had killed all those other people as a mere byproduct of an effort to kill *her* . . . and now they *were* going to kill her, and there was nothing at all she could do about it.

"My L—!"

The shout died in a staccato chatter as the Reverend Julius Hanks, First Elder of the Church of Humanity Unchained, flung himself between her and her assassin. Bullets ripped through a frail old body in a spray of blood, and Honor cried out—in horrified grief and useless denial as much as pain—as those same bullets smashed into her chest. She went down, fighting for the breath the impact had hammered out of her, but she wore her formal gown and vest, not her uniform, and it was the vest Andrew LaFollet liked so much—the one designed with Nimitz's claws in mind. The one that could stop even light pulser fire. It wouldn't normally have stopped the machine-pistol's heavy slugs, not from this close, but their passage through Reverend Hanks' body had slowed them, absorbed just enough kinetic energy to keep them from penetrating.

She lay at the bottom of the ditch, drenched in Hanks' blood and pinned by his weight, stunned by the brutal impact of bullets and gasping for breath, and her killer came to the lip of the ditch. He knelt there and extended the pistol at arms' length for the final, careful head shot to end it.

*   *   *

Martin went to his knees, clinging to his sanity by his fingernails. Alive. She was still *alive!* How many times must he muster all the courage in him to *kill* this woman? And how many more innocents must perish before she died?!

The thought of all the blood he'd taken upon his soul, even in the name of God's work, tore at him, and his eyes dropped compassionately to the armsman who'd given his life to save his Steadholder's. *A good man,* he thought. *Another good man, just like that kid at—*

Edward Martin's universe came apart in one terrible, incandescent burst of recognition. The light of the fires spilled over the face of the man lying across Harrington's body, and he heard the hideous triumph of Satan's laughter in the roar of the flames, for he knew that face. He *knew* it, and it was no armsman's.

The pistol fell from his hand, and he stared in utter horror at the man he'd killed. The man whose murder would damn his own soul to Hell for all eternity.

"My God!" he cried in agony. "My God, my God— *what have You let me do?"*

Honor jerked in astonishment as the assassin dropped his weapon, and then, through the howl of sirens and the bellow of flames, she heard his anguished cry. She saw the horror on his face—the total disbelief that turned instantly into a hopeless agony so deep, so terrible, that she felt a wrenching stab of pity for the man who'd tried to kill her. Who *had* killed the gentle, compassionate Reverend . . . and who, in that horrible moment of recognition, *knew* he had.

Someone else moved, and she rolled her head as Jamie Candless lurched to his feet. She felt the terrible effort with which the swaying armsman fought off the collapse of his abused body, and his face was a mask of blood and hate as he stared at Reverend Hanks' murderer. He drew his pulser with the slow, dreadful precision of an executioner while the killer sobbed and rocked on his knees. The weapon rose and steadied, aimed at a head less than three meters from it, and Candless's trigger finger began to tighten.

"Alive!" It took all Honor's strength to get the word out, but somehow she did. "We need him *alive!*"

She was still breathless, her voice hoarse, and, for an instant she thought Candless hadn't heard her. For another, even more terrible moment she thought he would refuse to obey, but he was an armsman. His lips drew back in a snarl of baffled, murderous hate, and then he staggered the two steps it took to reach Martin, and the pulser in his hand rose and came crashing down.

Candless went back to his own knees with the force of his blow. He lacked the strength to rise off them a third time, but there was no need. The pulser butt struck the back of Edward Martin's head like a hammer, and merciful unconsciousness dragged him away from the horror of his own deed.

• CHAPTER TWENTY-EIGHT

William Fitzclarence glared at his HD's nonstop news bulletins in bloodshot exhaustion, and hopeless, unanswerable questions stuttered through his brain.

By now, all Grayson knew something terrible had happened at Harrington Space Facility, but no one knew *what*. The Harrington Guard had clamped a steel cordon *no one* was getting through about the facility. The first—and only—news crew to try entering HSF airspace had come within millimeters of being shot out of the sky, and freedom of the press or no, none of their colleagues had felt the slightest temptation to try their own luck.

But Lord Burdette, unlike the newsies, knew what was *supposed* to have happened, and that made him far more desperate for information. Because what he *didn't* know was whether or not Taylor and Martin had succeeded. Grim-faced steading spokesmen had already confirmed over eighty dead, but they refused to release any names, and the shouted questions about Steadholder Harrington had been answered with stony silence. Did that mean the bitch *was* dead? Or, far more frightening, did it mean she *wasn't?* And what about Martin and Taylor? He knew they would never let themselves be taken alive, but if they'd somehow escaped, he would have heard from them by now. Had they been engulfed in the holocaust their attack had ignited, burned beyond recognition? Or had their bodies been identified?

The Steadholder scrubbed his face with trembling hands and longed for Brother Marchant's comforting presence. But the cleric was out pumping his own information sources, and he was alone with the terror of what he'd unleashed.

Damn it, the harlot had *deserved* to die! Her very existence was an offense against God, and Burdette did not—would not—feel remorse for her. But he'd never counted on all those other deaths, and somehow it had never occurred to him that he wouldn't know whether his men had even been found, much less identified. He'd been so sure, so confident, God would insure their success, as He'd insured their success against the Mueller dome. Now he didn't know, but if the bitch *had* lived—if Satan had somehow preserved her yet again—or if Martin or Taylor *had* been identified—

He swore again, then snapped his mouth shut and begged God to forgive his doubts, the unseemly panic he couldn't shake.

But God said nothing, and Burdette groaned deep in his throat at His silence.

Edward Martin sat in the small, bare cell and stared numbly at nothing. He'd been stripped to his underwear, his hands were cuffed behind him, and his head was a pounding drum filled with dull pain, but his captors had treated him far more gently than he'd expected. Than he'd *wanted* them to. The horror of what he'd done was a bleeding wound, oozing black despair and self-hate that cried out for punishment, and punishment had been denied him.

He sat in the hard, metal chair bolted to the floor, and the eternity he'd laid up for himself in Hell sat with him. He'd killed the *Reverend*. He hadn't meant to, hadn't planned to—hadn't even known Reverend Hanks would *be* there! But none of that mattered. He'd laid his hands on the weapons of violence in God's name, and Satan had taken him in the cruelest snare of all, used him to destroy God's chosen steward.

He'd been so sure—so certain—he'd heard God's voice. Had it truly been Satan's all along? And if it had, what did that say about Lady Harrington? *Was* she the

Devil's tool? She still could be, he thought desperately. She *could*! Satan's laughter would rock Hell at the thought of using his tool to trick Martin into destroying the head of God's Church. But . . . what if she *wasn't*? What if Reverend Hanks had been right all along, that *God's* will, not Satan's, had sent her to Grayson? Had he allowed his own fear to blind him and listened to Satan's lies as God's Own truth?

Had he killed Reverend Hanks—and all those other men—and helped others kill *children* for *nothing*?

He moaned and writhed in the chair, longing for death and terrified it might find him before he had a chance to beg the forgiveness of God and Man, and only the echo of his own anguished sound came back from the barren cell walls in answer.

Damn it to hell, what had the man been *thinking* about? Or *had* he thought at all?

Samuel Mueller had no doubt who was responsible for the events in Harrington. He could even reconstruct the logic behind them, but what the *hell* had possessed Burdette to try something as blatant—and chancy—as this?

He grabbed the remote and killed his HD with a vicious snap. One thing was plain: whether Harrington had lived or died, whoever was in charge was stonewalling all questions. Was it Mayhew? Mueller frowned, then nodded. It could be. More, it *should* be. The Protector would want a total lock on the facts until he'd decided how to handle them, whatever they were.

Mueller leaned back in his chair, rubbing his upper lip, and his mind raced. Aside from Maccabeus, no one had tried to assassinate a steadholder in over four centuries. He had no idea how the shock of that would impact on the anti-Harrington hatred he'd worked so hard to help Burdette and Marchant create, but if she'd survived, it was at least possible the attack would swing opinion in her favor. That was bad enough, but if whoever Burdette had used for it could be identified, traced back to him, then the fool had put Mueller at risk along with himself.

Well, he'd made his own plans for that eventuality. It wouldn't do to execute them prematurely. If Burdette survived this undetected, he would remain too valuable an ally—assuming he could be prevented from doing something else equally stupid—to turn into an enemy with attacks on his fellow fanatics. But if this disaster was as complete as it could be . . .

Lord Mueller walked to his desk and activated his com. The face of a man in the yellow and red of the Mueller Steadholder's Guard appeared, and Mueller spoke before the armsman could open his mouth.

"Get your teams into Burdette and position them now," he said coldly.

The cell door opened.

Martin's head jerked up, and his eyes widened—dark with terror and the burden of agonizing doubt—as he recognized the men in the opening. Benjamin IX, Protector of Grayson, and Jeremiah Sullivan, Second Elder of the Sacristy, stood looking at him, and somehow he found the strength to rise. He couldn't raise his gaze to theirs, but at least he could meet them on his feet.

"Edward Julian Martin," Elder Sullivan's voice was cold with doom, "do you know what you've done this night?"

He tried to answer. He truly tried, but the words choked him, and he felt the tears sliding down his face, and all he could do was nod.

"Then you know what you have laid up for yourself in the eyes of God and under the law of Man," Sullivan told him. Martin nodded once more, and the Second Elder stepped closer to him. "Look at me, Edward Martin," he commanded, and, against his will, Martin obeyed. He stared into the dark, bushy-browed eyes set on either side of Sullivan's strong, hooked nose, and what he saw there shriveled his soul within him.

"To my shame," the Second Elder said in that same slow, cold voice, "I cannot forgive you. What you have done tonight—what you *tried* to do—" The bald head shook slowly, but then the Second Elder inhaled. "Yet it isn't *my* forgiveness you need, and whatever we who serve Father Church think or feel, we are Father Church's servants, and God's, and God can forgive what Man cannot. Would you make confession of your sins, Edward Martin, to the lords temporal and secular of Grayson, and seek God's mercy upon yourself?"

The prisoner's white, tear-streaked face twisted, and a last, desperate need to believe he'd been right, that it *had* been God's voice he'd heard, warred with the terrible suspicion that it hadn't. And then he sank slowly to his knees at Sullivan's feet and bent his head.

"Yes." His voice was a tattered, broken thing, but it came out with all the tormented guilt which filled him. "Hear my confession, Second Elder." He whispered the words he'd said to priests so often during his life with a desperate need he'd never before dreamed was possible. "Help . . . help me find God's forgiveness, for I have failed in the Test He sent me, and I am afraid."

"Do you voluntarily make confession to the secular powers of Grayson, releasing me from the seal of your contrition?" Sullivan asked.

"I—" Martin swallowed and reached deep for the strength to repair his sin in whatever pitiful way he could. "I do," he whispered, and the Second Elder reached into the pocket of his cassock. He withdrew the scarlet stole of Father Church and draped it about his neck, and when he spoke again, his voice was no less implacable, yet touched somehow with the compassion of his calling.

"Then begin, Edward Martin, and as you value your immortal soul and your chance of Heaven, may your confession be true and complete so that you may find the omnipotent mercy of the Lord our God."

• CHAPTER TWENTY-NINE

The whisper of conversation seemed small and lost as the steadholders waited. No one dared raise his voice, and the tension in their ancient, horseshoe-shaped Conclave Chamber could have been chipped with a knife. No one knew what was to happen here this day, yet all feared it.

The events in Harrington Steading hung heavy in their minds. Fifty hours had passed since the first stunning reports, and still all they knew were rumors. But what had been ordered as a closed session of the Keys had become something else, and holo-vid cameras rimmed the Spectators' Gallery above them, waiting to carry whatever was to transpire here to every HD in the star system.

Yet they had no idea, no hint, of what that was to be. It was unheard of for them to be so ignorant, for there to be no Council leaks—not even a single media snippet—to provide *some* clue, yet it had happened. And so they sat, awaiting the Protector's arrival in confusion as great as any of their steaders', and like the cameras, their eyes clung to the vacant desk directly below the Protector's throne. The one blazoned with the Harrington arms and the seal of the Protector's Champion, whose velvet-padded brackets bore the naked blade of the Grayson Sword of State.

The one whose owner, if the rumors were true, lay dead or dying even as they sat and wondered.

Something happened. A stir ran through the Gallery, and the cameras swung towards the Chamber doors. The steadholders' eyes followed the lenses, their murmured conversations died, and when the massive wooden panels swung open, the whispering creak of their hinges was ear-shattering in the sudden silence.

Benjamin IX walked through those doors and into that silence with a face of stone. For the first time in living memory, the Door Warden neither challenged nor announced the Protector's entrance, and more than one steadholder's mouth went dry as the significance sank home.

There was one time, and only one, when the Protector might ignore the Keys' corporate equality with him in this, their Chamber . . . and that time was when he came to pass judgment upon one of them.

Burdette fought to control his expression, but his face tightened as the Protector walked to his throne in the horseshoe's bend with a slow, deliberate stride. Benjamin mounted to the dais and turned, seating himself, and only then did the Keys realize someone else was missing. Reverend Hanks, as the temporal head of Grayson, should have accompanied the Protector, and a hushed almost-sound of fresh confusion ran through the stillness as his absence registered.

"My Lords," Benjamin's voice was harsh as cold iron, "I come here tonight with the gravest news a Protector has brought this Conclave in six hundred years. I come with news of a treason which surpasses even that of Jared Mayhew, who called himself Maccabeus. A treason, My Lords, I did not believe any Grayson capable of committing . . . until Tuesday night."

Sweat dotted Burdette's brow, and he dared not blot it lest he betray himself to his peers. His heart hammered, and he stared out across the floor of the horseshoe at Samuel Mueller, but his ally looked as confused as any other man there, with no slightest hint that he suspected what Mayhew was talking about. Nor did he spare Burdette so much as a glance . . . and then the Protector spoke again, and all eyes, even Burdette's, snapped back to him as filings to a magnet.

"Tuesday night, My Lords, I had summoned you to a closed session. Each of you knew it. Each of you was pledged, and charged by law, to keep that summons secret. The purpose of that session was to acquaint you with new information concerning the collapse of the Mueller Middle School dome. I had informed none of you of that purpose, but someone among you guessed, and that someone did not wish you to learn of what I had discovered."

Benjamin paused, and the silence was absolute. Not even a reporter whispered into his hush phone.

"My Lords," the Protector said, "the collapse of that dome was not an accident." Someone gasped, but Benjamin continued in that same iron voice. "Nor was it the result of bad design, nor even, as you have been told, of faulty construction materials. That dome, My Lords, was *made* to collapse by men whose sole purpose was to discredit Steadholder Harrington."

A vast, deep susurration ran around the chamber, but the Protector continued speaking, and the sound died instantly.

"Tuesday night, I could only have told you my investigators *believed* that to be the case, and we knew even that much only because Adam Gerrick, Sky Domes' chief engineer, had performed a brilliant piece of reconstruction. For that reason, I wished Mr. Gerrick to be present, so that he could, if you so desired, explain his conclusions. I regret to inform you that it will not now be possible for him to do so, however, for Adam Gerrick is dead—dead with ninety-five other men and women in the crash of Lady Harrington's pinnace in Harrington Steading. And like the Mueller dome collapse, that crash was no accident. Adam Gerrick and the others who died with him were *murdered*. Murdered by the men who used a surface-to-air missile to shoot down that pinnace because Lady Harrington was aboard it. The same men, Steadholders of Grayson, who also murdered Reverend Julius Hanks."

For perhaps as much as ten seconds it totally failed to register. Benjamin hadn't even raised his voice, and the enormity of what he'd said was too vast for comprehension. The words meant nothing, for their meaning was impossible. They simply *could not* be true.

But then, suddenly, it *did* register, and a strangled shout sprang as a single, anguished cry of disbelief from seventy-nine throats, then died in an instant of fresh, stunned silence—of shock too profound for any words. But this silence lasted only a moment, and the sound which broke it was indescribable. Not yet words, for, once more, there *were* no words to hold the first, formless stirring of its fury.

William Fitzclarence staggered, clutching at his desk for support. No! *It couldn't be!*

His eyes darted to Mueller, but this time Mueller was as genuinely stunned as anyone—as stunned as Burdette himself—and when his shock faded, it was replaced by fury as dark as that of any other man in the Chamber. Nor was that fury feigned. It was all he could do not to glare accusingly at Burdette, but he stopped himself just in time, for to do so would be to reveal his own knowledge and brand himself as the man's accomplice.

The fool! Oh, the damned, bungling, incompetent *fool*! He couldn't have known Hanks would be there—not even *he* was stupid enough to do something like this knowingly! But neither had he checked, and if Mayhew truly knew who'd been responsible, if even the thinnest thread of evidence linking Mueller to Burdette were found—

Benjamin Mayhew sat on his throne and watched shock smash through the Conclave. He watched the first total disbelief change, saw its numb anesthesia vanish into the awareness of loss, into pain and a soul-deep rage he knew was mirrored in the face of every person watching the HD broadcast of this Conclave session, and then he stood.

That silent movement did what no shouted plea for order could have. It jerked every eye back to him, stilled every tongue, and his gaze swept from one end of the horseshoe of steadholders to the other.

"My Lords," his voice was harsh, still cold but wrapped

now around a core of white-hot anger, "Tuesday night was the most shameful night in Grayson's history since the Fifty-Three were murdered in this very Chamber. For the first time in my memory, I am *ashamed* to own myself a Grayson and confess that I spring from the same planet as the men who could plan such acts out of bigotry, intolerance, fear, and ambition!"

His fury lashed them like a whip, and more than one steadholder physically recoiled from its ferocity.

"Yes, Reverend Hanks was murdered. The leader of our Church and Faith, the man chosen by Father Church as God's steward on this planet, was *murdered*, yet the motives for that crime are almost worse than the crime itself, for he wasn't even its true target. Oh, no, My Lords! The true target of this vicious, cowardly attack was a woman, a steadholder, a naval officer whose courage saved our world from conquest. The *true* purpose was to murder a woman whose sole offense was to be incomparably better than this planet has just proven it deserves!"

Benjamin Mayhew's wrath was a living presence, stalking through the Chamber with claws and fangs of fire, but then he closed his eyes and drew a deep breath, and when he spoke again, his voice was very, very quiet.

"What have we become, My Lords? What has happened to our world and our Faith that Grayson men can convince themselves God Himself calls them to destroy a blameless woman simply because she is different? Simply because she challenges us to grow beyond ourselves, to become more and better than we are, just as the Tester Himself demands of us? What possible explanation—what conceivable *reason*—can men who claim to love God give for using the murder of children—our *children*, My Lords!—to destroy a woman who has done only good for our world and offered her very life to protect *all* its children? Tell me that, My Lords. For the love of the God we say we serve, how did we let this *happen*? How *could* we let it happen?"

No voice answered. No word was spoken, for the shame cut too deep. For all their fear, all their resentment of the changes in their world and the erosion of their power, most of the men in that Chamber were decent ones whose limitations were those of their rearing. In the final analysis, their anger at Honor Harrington and Benjamin Mayhew sprang from the way in which she and the Protector's reforms offended their concept of proper social behavior, and that concept rested upon rules they'd been taught as children. But they were no longer children, and in that moment, they saw themselves through the pitiless lens of their Protector's anguished words and shrank from what they saw.

"My Lords, Tuesday night Reverend Hanks faced that question, and he answered it," Benjamin said softly, and saw his own pain etched in the steadholders' faces as he spoke Hanks' name. "Reverend Hanks knew how poisoned with hate Lady Harrington's enemies had become, and he took our duty to prevent such crimes upon his own shoulders and, as the Tester's own Son calls upon each of us to do at need, he chose to die so that someone else might live. When the murderers who shot down Lady Harrington's pinnace realized she'd survived its crash—" a fresh stir ran through the Chamber at the news that she *had* survived, but his words gave them no chance to consider it yet "—they attacked her more directly, determined to complete the foulness to which they had set their hands, and they found her alone and defenseless, for she had sent her armsmen back to attempt the rescue of those still trapped in the wreckage of her pinnace.

"But she was not *quite* alone," Benjamin said more softly yet, "for when a man who'd donned the uniform of her own Guard came upon her with a gun, Reverend Hanks was with her. And when the Reverend realized the purpose of that man, he put his own body between her and her killer, and that—*that*, My Lords— is how our Reverend died. Giving his life to protect the blameless, as all who call themselves godly have been charged to do by the Tester, the Intercessor, and the Comforter."

He stopped speaking and raised his hand as if in signal. The silence in the Chamber was once more a living thing as the whipsawed steadholders wondered what that signal foretold, and then, unexpectedly, the massive doors opened once more, and Honor Harrington stepped through them.

The click of her heels echoed and reechoed in the stillness as she moved down the stone-floored Chamber's length like a tall, slender flame of white and green. The Harrington Key glittered on her breast below the Star of Grayson, and the Star's scarlet ribbon was stained with darker spots whose origin every man in that chamber guessed. The dark line of a deep cut, already responding to quick heal, seamed her forehead, and her right cheek was brutally bruised and discolored. The fluffy pelt of the treecat on her shoulder was singed and scorched, yet he held his head as high as she held her own, gazing, as she, straight at the Protector. It was as if they and Benjamin were alone in the Chamber, and the pain in her eyes—the sorrow for the deaths of her own people, and always and above all for the gentle and compassionate man who had died for her—was a weight no man there could face. They stared at her, frozen in shame, grief, and fear, and she ignored them all as she walked to the foot of Benjamin IX's throne.

"Your Grace, I come before you for justice." Her soprano voice was a thing of cold steel, the pain in it deeper even than the pain in her eyes. "By my oath to you, I call upon yours to me. As I swore to protect and guard my people, so I now require your aid to that end, for he who has killed and maimed my steaders carries the key of a steadholder, and I may not touch him while he shelters behind its protection."

The entire Chamber held its breath as it recognized the formal appeal to the Protector's Justice, unheard in this Chamber in generations, and then Benjamin spoke.

"By my oath to you, I honor your demand for justice,

My Lady. If any man in this Chamber has offended against you or yours, name him, and if you bear proof of his crimes, then steadholder or no, he shall answer for them as the laws of God and Man decree."

William Fitzclarence stared in horror at the woman before the throne, for he knew, now. Even through his own shock at the news of Reverend Hanks' death, he knew. Mayhew would never have allowed it to go this far unless the harlot *did* have proof, and his promise of justice was a sentence of death.

"Your Grace, I have proof," Honor said, and her anguish at the deaths of Julius Hanks, Adam Gerrick, Jared Sutton, Frederick Sully, Gilbert Troubridge, and ninety-one other men and women fused with a rage as deep and bitter as that of any man in that Chamber as she turned from the throne at last and looked straight at Burdette.

"I name my enemy William Allen Hillman Fitzclarence, Steadholder Burdette," she said in a voice colder than the heart of space. Her treecat hissed, baring his fangs, and Burdette's knees sagged as every eye in the Chamber turned upon him like the closing jaws of a trap. "I accuse him of murder, of treason, of my own attempted assassination, and of the deaths of children and of Reverend Julius Hanks. I bring before you the witnessed and sealed confession of Edward Julius Martin of Burdette Steading, freely offered under the law of Church and Sword, that William Fitzclarence personally ordered my death; that William Fitzclarence, Edmond Augustus Marchant, his steader, Samuel Marchant Harding, also his steader, Austin Vincent Taylor, also his steader, and twenty-seven other men in his service, contrived the collapse of the Mueller Middle School dome and the deaths of fifty-two men and thirty children; and that as a direct consequence of William Fitzclarence's orders, the Reverend Julius Hanks, First Elder of the Church of Humanity Unchained, died giving his own life that I might live."

She paused, and Burdette's ragged breathing was the

only sound in the vast, hushed Chamber. She let the silence linger while a small cruel part of her—one whose vicious strength shocked her—savored what must be running through his mind, and then she raised her right hand and pointed at him.

"Your Grace, by your oath to me and the proofs I have offered, I claim the life of William Allen Hillman Fitzclarence as forfeit for his crimes, for his cruelty, and for his violation of his sacred oaths to you, to this Conclave, to the People of Grayson, and to God Himself."

"My Lady," Benjamin Mayhew said softly, "by my oath to you, you shall have it."

William Fitzclarence stared at Honor Harrington as his fellow steadholders recoiled from him, and terror filled him. No. No, it couldn't happen! Mayhew and the bitch had twisted and perverted all he'd tried to accomplish, made God's Own work into something ugly and vile, and now his very *life* had been cast into the hands of an infidel whore unworthy to breathe the air of God's world? God would not permit this. *He wouldn't!*

Yet even as he thought that, the stone-faced Protector gestured, and four armsmen of the Steadholders' Guard, each in the colors of a different steading, crossed the Chamber floor and started up the shallow steps towards him. Their faces were as hard as the Protector's own, their eyes as filled with hate for him—for *God's warrior!*—as those of the bitch who'd brought Satan's poison into his world, and he knew it *was* happening. That his life would end, and that he would be remembered not as the man who'd fought with every weapon at his command against sin and damnation, but as a murderer of children. As the man who'd ordered the murder of God's Steward when he hadn't even known Hanks was *there!* The ruin of his world, the destruction of all he believed in, of God's Own law was upon him, and there was nothing he could d—

"Wait!"

He lunged to his feet, and his bellow shook the

Chamber. He saw Mayhew twitch at his sudden shout, but the bitch didn't even blink, and somehow that gave him fresh strength. There was a way, he told himself. There was still a way to destroy her and, in her destruction, *prove* he was God's champion.

For a moment he thought the oncoming armsmen would ignore his cry, but then the officer at their head looked at the Protector, and Mayhew raised a hand. He said nothing, simply stood waiting with contempt plain on his face, and Burdette descended to the Conclave floor. He brushed through the armsmen with cold disdain and threw the bitch a single hate-filled glare, then turned to face the Keys of Grayson.

"My Lords," he cried, "I do not dispute the facts this harlot claims, nor do I regret any of my acts! I say only that I neither desired nor ordered Reverend Hanks' death, and that no man can prove against me, for I never even knew he would be present. But yes—*yes*, My Lords!—I did each and every other thing this foreign-born whore claims, and I would do them again—do them a thousand times again!—before I let an infidel fornicator and this traitor who calls himself Protector pollute and poison a world sacred to God!"

He saw the other steadholders' shock as he admitted his guilt. No, as he *proclaimed* it and flung it in the bitch's face! And he understood their confusion, for they didn't know what he intended. A rush of power, the assurance that God was with him yet, filled him, and he wheeled to glare at Benjamin Mayhew.

"I reject your right to condemn me to death in order to silence God's voice of opposition to your corrupt abuse of power! As is my ancient right before God, the law, and this Conclave, I challenge your decree! Let your Champion stand forth and prove the true will of God sword-to-sword, in the ancient way of our fathers, and may God preserve the righteous!"

Exultation filled him as he saw Mayhew's astonishment, and he snarled in triumph, for he'd trapped the bastard in his own snare. If he would assume the ancient powers of the Protector, turn back the clock and exert his despotism, then he must accept the Protector's ancient *limitations*, as well, and his so-called "Champion" was the bitch on the Conclave floor. The harlot God had brought openly within reach of Burdette's own sword at last.

Echoes of consternation ran around the Chamber, and centuries of decorum were forgotten as a dozen steadholders shouted in protest. But Burdette ignored them and locked his triumphant eyes with Mayhew's. He knew the harlot had toyed with the sword since her own people had driven her to Grayson in disgrace, but she'd been here little more than a year and spent the last three months in space. No doubt what little she'd learned had slipped away through lack of practice, while *he* held the rank of Master Second. Like any other Grayson, he'd thought the sword's serious use a thing of the past, but now he understood at last the true reason God had inspired him to become its master.

It was for this moment. This single day, when he would master *another* Sword by striking down the Harlot of Satan before the eyes of every Grayson in the star system. And when she fell, when God's will was made evident to every eye, her death would also nullify Mayhew's sentence of death, for under the Protector's own precious Constitution, a steadholder's victory protected him forever from any aspect of the decree for which he'd cried challenge!

Benjamin Mayhew gazed down at Burdette's triumphant face, and his heart was cold within him while he cursed his own stupidity. He should have considered this possibility, should have allowed for it, but no one had claimed challenge right in over three hundred years! It was a throwback to barbarism, but he should have expected it, for this man *was* a barbarian.

His right hand fisted at his side, and his eyes went bleak and cold. In that moment, he wanted nothing in the universe as much as he wanted William Fitzclarence dead on the Chamber floor. Yet whatever he wanted, he also knew Honor had slept for less than three hours in the fifty since her pinnace went down, that she had four broken ribs quick heal had only begun to repair, and that under her clothing she was covered with brutal bruises. She was running on adrenaline and stim tabs, and he had no idea how she could show so little sign of fatigue or physical pain as she stood proudly erect before the Keys, but he knew she was in no fit state to meet a man with Burdette's sword skill. Even if she'd been fresh and unhurt, she'd first touched even a practice blade barely a year before, while Burdette had advanced to the planetary quarterfinals no less than three times, and the rogue steadholder would never settle for first blood. He meant to kill her, and the odds were overwhelming that he could.

He could renounce his own decree, Benjamin thought, and in the renunciation accept his Champion's defeat without exposing Honor to Burdette's blade, but the entire population of Yeltsin's Star was watching. The blow to the Protectorship's power and prestige would be severe, and if the people of Grayson thought he'd surrendered because Honor was afraid to face Burdette—

But then he looked down at Honor, at her waiting eyes—calm and still, despite Burdette's challenge and her own pain—and knew he had no choice. Legally, it made no difference if the Protector accepted defeat or his Champion was slain. In either case, his decree was nullified, and Benjamin Mayhew had no right to ask this woman he owed so much to throw away her life on the threadbare chance that she might, somehow, defeat an opponent with thirty times her experience.

"My Lady, I know of your injuries," he said, and pitched his voice so that it carried to every ear and microphone. He was determined that everyone watching should know he'd surrendered only because of her injuries, and not because he'd ever doubted her courage. "I do not believe you are physically fit to accept this man's challenge in my defense, and so—"

Honor raised a hand, and shock stopped him in midsentence. No one *ever* interrupted the Protector of

Grayson when he spoke from the throne! It was unheard of, but she seemed unaware of that. She simply gazed up at him, never even turning to glance at Burdette, and her cold, dispassionate soprano was as clear and carrying as his own voice had been.

"Your Grace," she said, "I have only one question. Do you wish this man crippled, or dead?"

Benjamin twitched in surprise too great to conceal and a gasp of disbelief went up from the steadholders, but her question had snatched any chance to avoid the challenge from his hands. It was *her* choice now, not his, and as he gazed down into her dark, almond eyes, he saw again the woman who'd saved his own family from assassination against impossible odds. For just one moment he prayed desperately that she could somehow work one more miracle for herself, for him, and for his world, and then he drew a deep breath.

"My Lady," the Protector of Grayson told his Champion, "I do not wish him to leave this Chamber alive."

"As you will it, Your Grace." Honor bowed in formal salute and stepped up to her own desk. She lifted Nimitz from her shoulder, and he sat tall and still, ears flat but quiet, as she took the Grayson Sword of State from its padded brackets. That jeweled yet deadly weapon had been forged six hundred years before for the hand of Benjamin the Great, but it remained as lethal as of old, and its polished blade—marked with the ripple pattern of what Old Terra had called Damascus steel—flashed in her own hand as she stepped back down to face her enemy.

"My Lord," Lady Honor Harrington said coldly, "send for your sword—and may God preserve the righteous."

William Fitzclarence stood with his eyes on Harrington, and sneered inwardly at her stupidity. Did she actually believe even her demonic master could protect her *now?* Was she *that* stupid?

He glanced at his chrono again, taking care to look almost bored. By law, he could not leave the Chamber without forfeiting the legal protection of his challenge, so he'd been forced to send one of his armsmen to fetch his sword. How fortunate that he'd brought it to the capital with him. He always did, of course, when he was unsure how long he would be here, for he made it a point to work out with it regularly. But, no, it wasn't fortune at all, was it? It was part of God's plan to make him the Sword of the Lord.

There was a stir among the steadholders seated above him, hovering like so many frightened birds, as the Chamber doors opened once more. His armsman entered, carrying the sheathed Burdette blade that forty generations of steadholders had called their own, and he held out his hand. The well-worn hilt slid into his palm like an old and trusted friend, and he turned to the harlot.

She stood as she'd stood since he'd sent for his sword, waiting, the Sword of State braced upright on the polished stone floor before her, hands folded on its pommel, and there was no expression on her face. Not fear, not hate, not concern, not even anger. Nothing at all, only those cold, still eyes.

He felt a sudden, unexpected shiver as his own gaze met those eyes directly, for their very emptiness held something frightening. *I am Death*, they seemed to say, but only for a moment. Only until he reminded himself of his own skill, and he snorted in contempt. *This* fornicating trollop thought she was Death? His lip curled, and he spat on the polished floor. She was only the Devil's whore, and her eyes were only eyes, whatever lies they tried to tell. The time had come to close them forever, and steel whispered as he drew his blade.

Honor watched Burdette draw his sword and saw the glitter of its edge. Like the ancient Japanese blades they so resembled, the swords of Grayson were the work of craftsmen who knew perfection was an impossible goal yet forever sought to attain it. For a millennium they'd polished and perfected their art, and even today, the handful who remained forged the glowing steel blow by blow upon the anvil. They folded each blade again and again to give it its magnificent temper, then honed it to an edge any razor might envy and few could match, and the very perfection of its function defined the form which gave it such lethal beauty.

No doubt modern technology could have duplicated those swords, but they weren't the proper product of modern technology. And preposterous though it was for a modern naval officer to meet a murderous religious fanatic with a weapon which had been five hundred years out of date before ever Man left Old Terra for the stars, there was an indefinable rightness to this moment. She knew Burdette was far more experienced than she, that he'd spent years proving his ability in the fencing salles of Grayson, and she felt the aches and stabbing pain flashes of a body too battered for something like this. But that didn't change her strange, perfect sense of rightness.

She toed off her shoes and stepped forward, gown swirling about her legs, her stockinged feet silent on the stone floor, and despite her fatigue, her mind was as still as her face. She took her position directly before Benjamin's throne, and knew every man in that enormous room expected to see her die.

Yet for all his confidence, Burdette had forgotten—or perhaps never learned—something Honor knew only too well. He thought it would be like the fencing salle. But they weren't in a salle, and unlike him, she knew where they truly were, for it was a place she'd been before . . . and he hadn't. He'd ordered murder done, but he himself had never killed—just as he'd never before come in reach of an intended victim with a weapon in her hand.

Burdette advanced to face her with the arrogant, confident stride of a conqueror. He paused to execute a brief limbering up exercise, and she watched impassively, wondering if he even began to appreciate the difference between competition fencing and this. Fencing was like a training *kata* in *coup de vitesse*. It was designed to perfect the moves, to practice them, not to *use* them. And in the salle, a touch was only a touch.

*   *   *

Burdette finished loosening his muscles, and that confident corner of his mind sneered afresh as the harlot took her stance. She'd adopted a low-guard position, with the blade extended at a slight diagonal, the hilt just above her waist and the tip angled down. She tried to hide it, but she was favoring her right side—perhaps that was the "injury" Mayhew had mentioned? If so, it might well explain her stance, for the low-guard put less strain on the muscles there.

But the low-guard, as his very first swordmaster had taught him, was a position of weakness. It invited attack rather than positioning *to* attack, and his sword rose into the high-guard as he took his own stance, weight spread evenly, right foot cocked and slightly back, and his hilt just above eye-level so that he could see her clearly while his blade hovered to strike.

Honor watched him with the eyes of a woman who'd trained in the martial arts for almost forty years, and the hard-learned, poised relaxation of all those years hummed softly within her. She felt her weariness, the pain of broken ribs, the ache in bruised muscles, the stiffness of her left shoulder, but then she commanded her body to ignore those things, and her body obeyed.

There were two terms Master Thomas had taught her in her first week of training. "The dominance" and "the crease," he'd called them. The "dominance" was the clash of wills, the war of personal confidence fought before the first blow was struck to establish who held psychological domination over the other. But the "crease" was something else, a reference to the tiny wrinkling of the forehead when the moment of decision came. Of course, "crease" was only a convenient label for an infinite set of permutations, he'd stressed, for every swordsman announced the commitment to attack in a different way. All fencers were taught to look for the crease, and competition fencers researched opponents exhaustively before a match, for though the signal might be subtle, it was also constant. *Every* swordsman had one; it was something he simply could not train completely out of himself. But because there were so very many possible creases, Master Thomas had explained while they sat cross-legged in sunlight on the salle floor, most sword-masters emphasized the dominance over the crease, for it was a simpler and a surer thing to defeat your opponent's will than to look for something one might or might not recognize even if one saw it.

But the true *master* of the sword, he'd said that quiet day, was she who had learned to rely not on her enemy's weakness, but upon her own strength. She who understood that the difference between the salle and what Honor faced today—between fencing, the art, and life or death by the sword—was always in the crease, not the dominance.

Honor knew she'd taken longer to grasp his meaning than someone with her background should have. But once she had, and after she'd studied the library information on Japan, she'd also realized why—on Grayson, as in the ancient islands of the samurai—a formal duel almost always both began and ended with a single stroke.

An edge of puzzlement flickered in Burdette's mind as she simply stood there. He, too, had been taught about the dominance and the crease, and he'd used both to his advantage in many competitions. But he was certain she had no more idea of what his crease was than he did of *hers*; surely she didn't think she could somehow deduce it at this late date!

Or perhaps she did. Perhaps she was too new to the sword to have sorted out all the metaphysical claptrap from the practical reality, but William Fitzclarence was too experienced to allow himself to be distracted from the real and practical when he held a live blade.

He held his position, and his upper lip curled as he reached out for the dominance. That was the part of every match he'd always enjoyed most. The invisible thrust and parry, that tension as the stronger will drove the weaker to open itself to attack, and he licked mental chops at the thought of driving the harlot.

But then the curl smoothed from his lip and his eyes widened, for there *was* no clash. His intense concentration simply disappeared against her, like a sword thrust into bottomless black water which enveloped it without resistance, and a bead of sweat trickled down his cheek. What was *wrong* with her? He was the master here, she the tyro. She *had* to feel the pressure, the gnawing tension . . . the fear. Why wasn't she attacking to *end* it?

Honor waited, poised and still, centered physically and mentally, her eyes watching every part of his body without focusing on any. She felt his frustration, but it was as distant and unimportant as the ache of her broken ribs. She simply waited—and then, suddenly, she moved.

She never knew, then or later, what William Fitzclarence's "crease" was. She simply knew she'd recognized it. That something deep inside her saw the moment he committed himself, the instant his arms tightened to bring his blade slashing down.

The instant in which he was entirely focused on the attack, and not on defense.

Her body responded to that recognition with the trained reaction speed of someone born and bred at the bottom of a gravity well fifteen percent more powerful than her opponent's. Her blade flashed up in a blinding, backhand arc, and the Sword of State's razor-sharp spine opened Burdette's torso from right hip to left shoulder. Clothing and flesh parted like cobwebs, and she heard the start of his explosive cry as shock and pain froze his blade. But he never completed that scream, for even as it rose in his throat and he began to fold forward over his opened belly, her wrists turned easily, and she slashed back to her left in a flashing continuation of her original movement, backed by all the whip-crack power of her body, and William Fitzclarence's head leapt from his shoulders in a geyser of blood.

• CHAPTER THIRTY

Honor sat in another pinnace and watched indigo
atmosphere gave way to space-black ebony beyond the
view port. The survivors of the party which had accompanied her down to the planet fifty-three hours before
sat quietly behind her, and she felt them through her
link to Nimitz. Felt their grief like a shadow of her own
. . . and their savage satisfaction at Fitzclarence's death.

She turned her eyes to the seat beside hers, twin to
the one in which Reverend Hanks had ridden to his
death. A sword sat upright in that seat. Once it had been
the Burdette Sword; now it was the Harrington Sword,
and she tried to analyze her feelings as she gazed at it.

Exhaustion, she thought with a small, bleak smile. That
was what she felt most strongly just now, through the
shimmery false energy of too many stims. But under that
there were other emotions.

It wasn't like her duel with Pavel Young. Then she'd
felt nothing but . . . relief. A grim sense of completion,
yes, but nothing more than that, for she'd known it would
never bring Paul back to her. It had been something
she'd *had* to do, something she couldn't *not* have done,
yet in its own way it had been as empty as Young himself, for it had healed nothing. Prevented nothing.

But this time was different. Burdette's death could
no more atone for his crimes than Young's had, but he'd
been a danger to others, as well. He'd been a danger
to Benjamin Mayhew and his reforms and to all the other
people he would have destroyed in the service of his
fanaticism, and now he would destroy no more. She'd
managed that much, she thought. She'd stopped him

from killing again, and this time no voice had condemned her actions. She'd killed him, yes, but she'd done so as Steadholder and Champion, executing the power of high justice that was hers as Steadholder Harrington in full accord with the law even as she discharged her sworn duty to her Protector.

She sighed and leaned back, hugging Nimitz against her, and felt his fierce approval. There were no qualifications in *his* feelings, for treecats were less complicated than humans, and for all their intelligence, they held to a simple code. For them, those who threatened them or their adopted humans came in only two categories: those who had been suitably dealt with, and those who were still alive. Nimitz accepted that it would sometimes be impossible to deal with Honor's enemies properly, for humans embraced a variety of often silly philosophical conventions, but that didn't dampen his satisfaction when it was possible. More to the point, perhaps, a dead enemy was no longer a matter of much concern to him.

Not for the first time, Honor wished her own feelings could be as straightforward, but they weren't. She felt no regret for killing Burdette, yet his hatred of *her* had been the catalyst for all his murderous actions, and she hadn't stopped him in time. Intellectually, she knew it was stupid to blame herself for his fanaticism; emotionally, it was hard—so hard—not to feel somehow responsible. And whoever had been to blame, killing him had undone nothing he'd already done, just as the sword in the seat beside her could never fill the emptiness left by Julius Hanks in her own life and the life of Grayson. And because of that, she thought wearily, this time Nimitz was wrong. There were debts no death could pay, and she was so tired of death.

They'd reach *Terrible* soon, and all those men and women in uniform would remind her painfully of how Jared Sutton had died. Yet even so she longed to get back aboard. She had too many dead to mourn; no place could be free of reminders of them all, and at least her flagship was also a refuge. It was a world she understood, one in which she could shelter while her body recovered and her soul healed, and she knew how badly she needed that refuge now.

Alfredo Yu and Mercedes Brigham stood in the boat bay gallery. Just this once, as Lady Harrington had requested, there was no side party, no honor guard of Marines. Only her flag captain and her chief of staff waited to greet her, and if that was a gross violation of naval etiquette, neither of them very much cared.

The docking tube hatch opened, and the two captains turned to face it, waiting side by side until Honor Harrington caught the grab bar and swung herself into *Terrible's* onboard gravity. Mercedes hid an inner wince as she saw the bruised face and cut forehead, the still haunted eyes . . . and the dark, dried spatters on her vest and skirt where her enemy's blood had splashed. She'd never seen Honor look so exhausted, and she hesitated, uncertain of what to do or say, but even as she searched for words, Yu stepped forward without them. He extended his hand, and this time Honor took it without hesitation, for his eyes were no longer opaque. She looked into them and saw his relief—*felt* his relief, through Nimitz—at her safety, and knew that whatever they might once have been, they were enemies no longer. A moment passed in silence, and then he smiled.

"Welcome home, My Lady," he said softly, and she returned his smile.

"Thank you, Alfredo." She saw a flash of pleasure as she used his first name at last and squeezed his hand, then looked past him as her chief of staff followed him over.

"Mercedes." She gripped Brigham's hand in turn while her armsmen followed her from the tube. They looked as battered as she did, and Andrew LaFollet and Arthur Yard moved even more stiffly than she, but the major also carried a sheathed sword. His bandaged hands were almost reverent on the gemmed scabbard, and his gray eyes were grimly satisfied.

Honor felt herself drooping and squared her shoulders, then started for the lift, accompanied by her officers and her armsmen.

"I spoke to Jared's parents," she said quietly to Mercedes. "They deserved to know how he died, but——" She closed her eyes for just a moment. "I hadn't realized he was an only son, Mercedes. He never told me."

"I know, Milady," Mercedes said equally quietly. "I commed them as soon as you notified us."

"It's never easy, My Lady," Yu said. Honor looked at him, and he shook his head. "I'm twenty T-years older than you, and it's never easy, and it never gets any easier. Or I never want to serve under an officer for whom it does."

The lift doors sighed open, and Yu stepped aside. He and Mercedes stood and watched Honor step into the lift, and she felt a weary glow of gratitude. They'd come down to greet her not simply because regs required it, but because they truly cared, yet they also knew she needed to be alone, to recuperate before she turned her mind once more to the squadron.

She waited while her armsmen joined her in the lift, then sighed.

"I'm going to my quarters," she said. "Mercedes, would you buzz Mac and tell him I'm on the way?"

"Of course, Milady."

"Alfredo, please set up a conference link with all our divisional and unit COs for tomorrow morning. Make it eleven hundred, if you would." She smiled wanly. "I don't think I'm going to be good for much before then."

"I'll see to it, My Lady," her flag captain assured her, and she gave him a grateful nod and glanced back at Brigham.

"Mercedes, I'll sit down with the staff forty-five minutes before the conference. Ask Fred and Greg to have a quick, thumbnail brief ready to bring me back up to speed."

"It'll be ready when you are, Milady."

"Thank you. Thank you both," she said, and let the lift doors close.

"ETA now one hour fifteen minutes, Citizen Vice Admiral."

Citizen Vice Admiral Thurston blinked and looked up from his tactical plot. He'd expressly requested the reminder, yet he'd been so deep in his review of the final task force exercises that he'd actually managed to forget, temporarily, at least, and put aside the tingling mixture of anticipation and tension.

But it was back now . . . and its elements seemed to have grown stronger while they'd been away. He smiled wryly at the thought and nodded to the petty officer who'd spoken.

"Thank you, Citizen Chief," he said, and glanced at Preznikov. "Well, Citizen Commissioner, it's about time. I'll be sending the task force to battle stations in thirty minutes. Do you have any final suggestions?"

Preznikov returned his gaze for several seconds, and Thurston saw a shadow of his own tautness in the other's eyes and wondered how much the commissioner truly understood about what they were about to do. Preznikov had attended all the briefings, studied the plans, even offered a few worthwhile suggestions, but he was a civilian, a politician, and he'd never seen a naval battle. Thurston had. Operation Dagger was only the first step in his own personal campaign—one whose full extent he devoutly hoped neither Preznikov nor his superiors had figured out—and the outcome he anticipated would be the Republic's first offensive victory of the war. The prestige of that should position him nicely to begin the other campaign, but first he had to win the battle. And while the citizen vice admiral was confident his firepower could crush the Grayson Navy, he also knew that navy was going to fight. It had to, for this was its home star system, and he refused to make the mistake of underestimating the Graysons' courage or skill.

And that meant that, preponderance of firepower or no, Task Force Fourteen would take losses, possibly even among the battleships. Possibly even aboard a battleship named *Conquistador*.

It was odd how difficult it was actually to believe that. Oh, he accepted it intellectually—but to actually *believe* he himself might be among the thousands of dead his battle plan was about to create? No, that was more than he could truthfully do. Dying, he thought with a wry mental smile, would be so inconvenient, after all. But if it was hard for him to accept the possibility when he *knew* what could happen, then how much harder must it be for civilians like Preznikov or LePic or DuPres?

The seconds ticked past while Preznikov gazed at him, and it suddenly occurred to Thurston that perhaps the citizen commissioner was looking for something in *his* eyes even as he looked for the same thing in Preznikov's. Now there was an amusing thought, but if his civilian watchdog searched for signs of weakness, he failed to find them, and he shook his head.

"No, Citizen Vice Admiral. I'm satisfied."

"Thank you, Sir," Thurston said, and looked at his ops officer. "Citizen Captain Jordan," he said formally, "have Communications pass the word to bring all units to battle stations at nineteen hundred hours."

An alert bell rang, and the rear admiral who had the duty in Command Central looked up. His eyes found the blinking yellow light of a hyper footprint on the master plot, then moved automatically to the scheduled arrivals on System Control's status boards, and he grimaced as he found none listed. Great. Just great. Like himself, every other man in the vast command center had been glued to his HD before coming on duty. They'd all seen the traumatic events in the Conclave Chamber, and they'd been half-distracted by them, and now he had a whole damned unscheduled convoy to—

The yellow light code turned abruptly blood red as

the FTL sensor net began to report, and the admiral's irritation was suddenly a thing of the past.

The two-toned priority buzz of Honor's bedside com yanked her awake with all the gentleness of a garrote. She hissed in pain as broken ribs and bruised muscles protested their abuse, but the spinal-reflex reactions of thirty years of naval service were ruthless, and she shoved the pain aside and swung her feet to the deck even as she rubbed at sleep-gummy eyes. She didn't need the querulous sound Nimitz made from his nest in the blankets to tell her they'd gotten barely an hour's sack time. Her thoughts felt slow and logy, floating on a drift of fatigue, and she made herself take another few seconds to fight herself awake before she pressed the audio-only acceptance key.

"Yes?" She heard the husky weariness of her voice and cleared her throat.

"Sorry to disturb you, Milady," Mercedes Brigham said tensely, "but Command Central just sent out a Flash One."

Honor's nostrils flared as a jolt of adrenaline punched at her foggy brain. She touched the vision key, and the terminal flashed alight in the darkened sleeping cabin. Mercedes looked out of it at her, and she saw the flag bridge, already coming fully on-line, behind her chief of staff.

"Numbers and locus?"

"Numbers are still rough, Milady. It looks like—" Mercedes paused and looked up as Fred Bagwell appeared at her shoulder. The ops officer handed her a message board, and she glanced at it, then looked back at Honor with a grim expression. "Update from Central, Milady. They make it one-sixty-plus point sources approximately two-four-point-four-seven light-minutes from the primary at zero-eight-five, right on the ecliptic. The sensor net's still reporting in, but it looks like a standard Peep task force formation."

Honor tried to keep her face from reacting, but her

mind raced, despite the streamers of fatigue which clogged it. Although the sensor platform's grav-pulse transmitters were FTL capable, each pulse took time to generate, which meant their data transmission *rate* was slow. At the moment, all Mercedes' information was based on the intruders' hyper footprint and impeller signatures, both of which were also FTL and could be directly observed from Grayson, but which told very little—other than raw numbers—about the ships who'd made them. It would be several minutes yet before the closest sensor platforms could send Central anything definite on the Peeps' light-speed emissions, but if it *was* a standard Peep formation, that high a unit count argued for at least twenty-five ships of the wall . . . and she had six.

"All right, Mercedes," she heard her own voice say calmly. "Send the squadron to quarters, then tell Central I'm activating Sierra-Delta-One." Brigham nodded. System Defense One was the emergency contingency plan which put every unit in Yeltsin under Honor's direct command in support of BatRon One . . . for whatever good it was going to do. "After you've done that, set up the Sierra-One net; I want every squadron and division commander tied into our command net—and be sure we include every SD's skipper, as well as the flag officers."

"Aye, aye, Milady."

"After that—" Honor looked up as MacGuiness appeared in her quarters, carrying her skinsuit "—get with Fred and CIC. I need strength estimates and course projections soonest."

"You'll have them, Milady."

"Good. I'll see you on the flag bridge in ten minutes."

"Well, Citizen Commissioner," Thomas Theisman murmured to Dennis LePic, "they know we're here."

"How soon do you expect a response?" LePic asked a bit nervously, and Theisman looked up from his plot with a wry smile.

"Soon enough, Citizen Commissioner. Soon enough. It's not like they can just ignore us and we'll go away, now is it?"

"Message from *Conquistador*, Citizen Admiral," Theisman turned his head and cocked an eyebrow, and his com officer cleared his throat. "'From CO TF Fourteen to all units. Stand by to execute Bravo-One on my signal.'"

"Very well." Theisman looked at his ops officer. "Bravo-One, Megan. Execute on the Flag's signal—but be sure our own net is tied in with Citizen Admiral Chernov's, and have Astro run a continuous course update in case we get an alpha revision."

"Aye, Citizen Admiral."

Terrible's flag bridge was a scene of orderly fury when Honor stepped onto it with Simon Mattingly at her heels. Mercedes Brigham and Fred Bagwell had their heads together and looked up simultaneously at her entry, but she held up her right hand to fend them off long enough to cross to the master plot and take a quick glance. For the first time in all their years together, she'd brought Nimitz to action stations rather than closing him in the life support module in her cabin. She cradled the 'cat against her side with a crooked left arm, the helmet of the skinsuit Paul Tankersley had designed for him hanging down his back, and rubbed his ears while she gazed down into the holo tank.

It did look like a standard Peep task force, but there was something . . . odd, about it. She tried to put her finger on that oddness, but it eluded her, and she gave herself an angry mental shake at her inability to pin it down. She knew she was exhausted. She couldn't have been anything else, under the circumstances, and *Terrible*'s doctor had flatly refused to allow her more stims. She knew he was right, but she also knew the energy lift of adrenaline rushing through her system was a false friend. There was a limit to how long it could sustain her, and when it ran out . . .

She closed her eyes and braced her right hand on the frame of the tank as traitor knees tried to betray her. Her ribs spasmed as her arm took her weight, and she felt a matching spasm of terrible, futile rage at the universe. *Why*, she thought bitterly. *Why now? Why does it have to be right this minute?*

The universe returned no answer, and she felt a deep, cowardly temptation to pass responsibility to Command Central. She'd been through too much, lost too much, built up too vast a debt of physical and emotional exhaustion. Barely an hour before, she'd looked desperately forward to a period of rest and recovery; now she had *this* to deal with, and it was too much to expect of her. Let Command Central handle it. They were fresh. *They* hadn't been shot out of the sky, seen people they cared about blown into bloody meat, fought a duel on the floor of the Conclave Chamber, so let *them* make the decisions. That was what they were *there* for, wasn't it?

Shame twisted her, and she gritted her teeth, forced her eyes back open, and commanded her knees to support her as she glared down into the tank and cursed her own self-pitying cowardice. So she was tired, was she? Well, no rule required the enemy to wait till they were sure she was fresh as a daisy, did it? And while she was whimpering about how unfair it was to *her*, what about the Graysons? It was their star system which was about to be blown apart, and High Admiral Matthews had offered her this job because she had more experience than any of them did. How would he feel if she told him he'd been wrong after all? That she needed a little rest—that she'd get back to him after the battle, if there was still a star system to defend?

Humiliation straightened her spine, and she turned from the master plot. She crossed to her command chair and set Nimitz on its back, and the 'cat's nimble truehands snapped the specially installed safety harness to its attachment points on his skinsuit while she racked her helmet. Then she seated herself and tapped the activation code into the keypad on the chair's right arm. Displays flickered to life before her, and she gazed at them for one more moment through almond eyes hard with contempt for her own cowardice. Then she drew a deep breath, leaned back in her chair, and turned it to face her chief of staff and her ops officer.

"All right, people." Admiral Lady Honor Harrington's unflustered soprano went through the bridge like a magic wand of calm confidence. "It seems it's time for us to earn our princely salaries."

• **CHAPTER THIRTY-ONE**

Alexander Thurston crossed to *Conquistador*'s master plot. He folded his hands behind him and stood gazing into its holographic depths with a thoughtful frown, then looked up as Citizen Commissioner Preznikov joined him.

"You have a concern, Citizen Admiral?" Preznikov asked too quietly for anyone else to hear, and Thurston shrugged.

"Not really, Citizen Commissioner. More of a mental side bet."

"Side bet?" Preznikov repeated.

"Yes, Sir. I'm just making a little bet with myself on how soon we see the opposition." The commissioner looked puzzled, and Thurston waved at the plot. "They've known we're here for over thirty minutes, but all we've seen are a few destroyers and a dozen or so cruisers and battlecruisers, and half of them have been positively IDed as Manties. Intelligence says the Graysons alone have more light and medium combatants than that, and I'm fairly confident they left most of them behind to watch their home world when they pulled out their SDs. The question becomes where they are and when we'll see them."

"Ah." Preznikov turned his own gaze on the plot and wished—not for the first time—that he understood the drifting light codes as well as a trained naval officer. He was learning, but he still needed expert assistance to interpret them. At the moment, however, he saw perhaps thirty individual impeller wedges, the slowest of them accelerating at over five hundred gravities as they

sped down converging courses which would intercept
TF Fourteen's vector well short of Grayson, and he felt
his face mirroring Thurston's frown.

"You think their main strength is in Grayson orbit,
don't you?"

"Yes, Sir, I do." Thurston was surprised by how quickly
Preznikov had reached that conclusion. Despite himself,
it showed as he nodded, but the commissioner chose
to be amused rather than offended.

"And the nature of your bet?" he asked dryly.

"How soon they'll move out to join the ships we can
already see."

"Surely they'll do so at a time which permits them
to rendezvous with these other forces?" Preznikov gestured at the moving impeller sources, and Thurston
nodded once more.

"Of course, Citizen Commissioner, but the flight profile they choose to do that should tell us something about
how good the opposing commander is."

"How so?" The commissioner's eyes flickered with
genuine interest, and the citizen vice admiral shrugged.

"We're still over a hundred and ninety million klicks—
about ten-point-seven light-minutes—from Grayson.
That's well within detection range for an impeller drive's
grav signature, but our sensors can't pick up anything
else unless its emissions are extremely powerful, and even
the light-speed signals we *can* detect are almost eleven
minutes old by the time they reach us. We're picking
up some fairly powerful active emissions from their
orbital forts—and there are a few more of them than
Intelligence had predicted, by the way—but we won't
know a thing about whatever starships and/or light attack
craft they have in Grayson orbit until they light off their
drives."

He paused with an eyebrow raised, and Preznikov
nodded to show he was paying attention.

"All right. Now, if our strength estimates are correct,
they don't have anything heavier than a battlecruiser, and
a battlecruiser can pull five hundred to five-twenty gees.

A *DuQuesne*-class SD, on the other hand, can pull a maximum accel of only about four hundred and twenty-five. Intelligence estimates the Manties' new inertial compensators increase their efficiency by two to three percent, which would up that to four thirty-three to four thirty-eight, assuming they've had time to refit with it. Intelligence calls that unlikely, but even if they have, those figures are for maximum military power with no safety margin, and the Manties don't like to do that any more than we do. So figure eighty percent as their normal full power setting, and you get roughly three forty-six to three fifty gees for an SD even with the new compensator. If we see anything in that envelope, it may mean Stalking Horse didn't actually get all their SDs out of the system, and that means we'll have to rethink our entire plan."

Preznikov nodded yet again, and Thurston shrugged. "On the other hand, how soon they head out to meet us will also give me a better read on their commander. It's hard to watch this much firepower coming at you and not start *doing* something, Sir, but a good CO will do just that. The critical factor is for his movements to unite his entire force before we make contact, but the longer he waits, the further committed we become. Given the disparity in force levels we anticipate, that shouldn't make any difference, but it's a matter of professionalism. A good CO will try to make us fully commit whether he figures he can stop us or not, almost by reflex action. And it's axiomatic, especially when you have an emplaced sensor net and the enemy doesn't, that you deny him any chance to gauge your strength—which means waiting to light off the drives we can detect—for as long as possible.

"But an inexperienced commander will want to get his entire force in motion as soon as possible. He'll feel the strain of waiting more, and if he's unsure of himself, he may be looking to react to an enemy's actions rather than initiate his own. In that case, it makes sense to show himself early so he can see what the enemy does and try to take advantage of it . . . but that *also* lets the enemy dictate the conditions of engagement—which, by the way, is a mistake our own Navy's still making against the Manties. So," Thurston turned away from the plot and started back towards his command chair, "a good CO will probably wait until the last moment, then bring his ships out of Grayson orbit under high accel, and a nervous, or tentative CO will probably bring them out sooner, at a *lower* accel. And knowing which sort of commander you're up against, Citizen Commissioner, is half the trick of winning."

"—still coming in at four-point-four KPS squared, My Lady," Commander Bagwell said tautly, and Honor nodded.

She lounged back in her chair, legs crossed and spine curved in a pose of comfortable confidence. Her officers had to know that was a pretense, for she had nothing to be confident about. But what they didn't know (she hoped) was that it was also designed to hide the weary sag of shoulders she lacked the energy to hold erect. *She* knew how exhausted she was, but she had no intention of letting *them* guess.

Now she rubbed the tip of her nose and forced her tired mind to work.

The good news—such as it was—was that the Peeps had nothing bigger than a battleship. At four and a half million tons, a *Triumphant*-class BB—the standard Peep design for the type—was fifty-six percent as massive as her own SDs, but it had no more than forty-five percent of the firepower, and its defenses were little more than a third as effective as her own ships' had been even before refit.

The *bad* news was that they had thirty-six of them, supported by twenty-four battlecruisers, twenty-four heavy cruisers, thirty-eight light cruisers, and forty-two destroyers. *She* had six superdreadnoughts, nineteen battlecruisers (including all those racing in from various other locations to rendezvous with her main force), ten heavy cruisers, forty light cruisers, and nineteen destroyers. There were, in fact, eight more BCs—Mark Brentworth's First Battlecruiser Squadron—and four more CAs in Yeltsin, but none of them could reach her before the Peeps reached Grayson, and she'd used her grav-pulse transmitters to order them to go silent and hold their positions rather than reveal their locations. Mark's battlecruisers had done so even before she ordered it, and she was glad they had, for they'd been at rest relative to Yeltsin and less than eight million klicks from the Peeps when they made transit. The Peeps' higher base velocity would have made it easy to run Mark down if he'd tried to break in-system to join her.

The problem was that her total available force fell well short of the firepower headed for her. She enjoyed the Alliance's usual tech advantage, but that was most effective in a long-range missile duel, and, in this case, the nature of the opposing forces went far towards offsetting it. The armament of Peep battleships was heavily biased in favor of missile tubes—they had little more than fifteen percent of an SD's energy armament but thirty percent of its missile power—precisely because they were supposed to stay out of energy range of true ships of the wall. Sluggish as they might be compared to battlecruisers or lighter units, BBs could pull much higher accelerations than dreadnoughts or superdreadnoughts. These people would be able to avoid Honor's SDs with relative ease, and although battleships were more fragile, the sheer numbers of tubes on the other side would give the Peeps something like an advantage of two to one in missile throw weight in a sustained engagement. She could offset some of that with missile pods, but only in the initial—and longest-ranged—salvos, given the pods' susceptibility to proximity soft kills.

She made herself stop rubbing her nose and folded her hands on her raised right knee. The situation was further complicated by the fact that only a tiny handful of her captains had ever seen action. She had no doubt of their courage or individual skills, but as Admiral Henries had demonstrated, they were still weak in coordination and prone to the mistakes of inexperience. Worse, the Peeps had more total platforms than she. The loss of any one of her SDs would hurt her far more than losing a BB would hurt the Peeps.

Her move to call in the units which could reach her had been an instinct reaction. Their velocity at rendezvous would be low enough that they could still reverse course and stay away from the Peeps, and concentrating them had been an obvious first move. But now that it had been made, she still had to decide what to do with her total force, and her options were unpalatable.

If she stayed where she was, with Grayson's orbital forts in support, the Peep commander would be foolhardy to risk a close action. But though they hadn't launched any yet, the Peeps were bound to probe the space about Grayson with recon drones before they closed. That meant they'd spot the squadron before they entered attack range, and they had the acceleration to crab aside and break past Grayson without ever coming into the forts' range.

Which, unfortunately, would not save Grayson, for neither the planet, its shipyards, its orbital farms, nor its forts could dodge, and immobility was the Achilles' heel of any fixed defenses. The Peeps could break off into the outer system and come back in at as much as eighty percent light-speed, and missiles launched from that velocity against nonevading targets would be deadly. Once their drives burned out, the incoming missiles would be impossible to track on gravitics, and even Manticoran radar had a maximum detection range of little more than a million kilometers against such small targets. Oh, they might get a sniff at as much as two million, given the Peeps' less effective penetration ECM, but they could never localize at more than a million—and if the Peeps launched at $.8\,c$, their birds' drives would boost *them* to $.99\,c$ before burnout. That would give the point defense systems three seconds to lock on, engage, *and* stop them, which brought the old cliché about the snowflake in Hell forcibly to mind.

Almost as bad, the Peeps would be free to do whatever they wanted in the outer system if she held her position in near-Grayson space, and they would undoubtedly demolish Yeltsin's asteroid extraction infrastructure. That, alone, would devastate the system's industrial base, and they'd still be able to turn around and attack Grayson itself whenever they chose. Or, for that matter, they could detach a large enough force to pin her in Yeltsin and send a half dozen battleships to Endicott. The heaviest RMN or GSN ship covering Masada was a battlecruiser, and there were only eighteen of them. They could never stand off an attack with battleship support, yet if they failed to do so—

She shuddered at the thought of the bloodshed which could sweep over Masada and closed her eyes, hiding her desperation behind a calm mask while she fought to find an answer. But she couldn't, and she felt a horrible fear that there *was* one, that only her exhaustion was keeping her from seeing it.

Her mind churned with a frenetic, fatigue-glazed intensity. She understood the attacks on Candor and Minette now, she thought. The Peeps were learning. They'd analyzed Alliance operational patterns and predicted the Allies' probable response perfectly, and their diversionary plans had sucked more than half of Grayson's defensive strength out of position. In fact, the only point on which she could fault their execution was the way they were heading straight for the planet now. They didn't have to do it. They should have made their n-space translation further out, built their speed, and gone straight into long-range missile launch mode—unless those transports tagging along astern of them meant they actually thought they could secure control of the system and wanted to take it intact?

She shook her head mentally. No, they couldn't be that stupid. BBs had the firepower for a smash-and-grab raid, and they probably could have taken out just the forts, but they didn't begin to have the firepower to take out the forts *and* her SDs in a conventional engagement.

Her tired reflections paused. The Peeps didn't have the strength for a conventional engagement, yet their flight profile indicated they were planning just that. If they didn't make turnover to engage Grayson's fortifications, then they'd overfly the planet in little more than two hours at under forty-two thousand KPS, and that would buy them the worst of both worlds. They couldn't use a ballistic missile attack, because the maximum velocity for their birds would be on the order of barely a hundred thousand KPS at a launch range so short her gravitic sensors could hand directly off to radar. Even without her ships, the forts had more than enough point defense capacity to deal with any broadsides a force this size could throw. Some of it would get through, but very little, and the combined firepower of her ships and the forts would rip the guts out of them as they passed. That meant they had to be planning a turnover, which was stupid.

But what if it was? Their RDs would still see her squadron soon enough for them to break off, so why was her battered, aching mind insisting that their approach profile was so important? It didn't make—

And then it hit her.

"They don't know we're here," she said softly.

Commander Bagwell frowned and shot a tense, questioning look at Mercedes Brigham, but the chief of staff held up a silencing hand. Honor's relaxed pose hadn't fooled Mercedes, for the captain knew her too well, just as she knew what Honor had been through in the past fifty-six hours. And as Honor had sat silent in her command chair without speaking, without issuing a single order, Mercedes Brigham had felt her heart sink within her, for that passivity was total unlike the Honor Harrington she knew. But now—

Honor said nothing more for several seconds, and, finally, Mercedes cleared her throat.

"I beg your pardon, Milady. Were you speaking to us?"

"Um?" Honor looked up at the polite question, then shook her head in frustration with her own slowness. She made herself slide upright in her chair, laying her hands along its arms and fighting for a grip on her rubbery thoughts, then nodded.

"I suppose I was, Mercedes. What I meant was, judging from the way they're coming in, they don't know the squadron is here."

"But . . . but they *must*, My Lady," Bagwell protested. "They have to know—from neutral press accounts, if nothing else—that Admiral White Haven turned his prizes over to us after Third Yeltsin. That means they *know* the GSN has eleven SDs." He looked at Commander Paxton. "Don't they?"

"I'm sure they do," the intelligence officer replied, but his eyes were on Honor, not Bagwell, and they were very intent.

"But they don't think they're in Yeltsin." Honor saw only confusion on her staff's faces, except, perhaps, on Paxton's, then dropped her eyes to her com link to *Terrible*'s command deck. Alfredo Yu looked back at her from its screen, and she smiled—with absolutely no idea how heartbreakingly exhausted that smile looked. "Candor and Minette, Alfredo," she said simply, and saw the sudden understanding in his eyes.

"Of course, My Lady. This was their objective the whole time, wasn't it?"

"I think so. I hope so, at any rate, because it may just give us a chance. Not a good one, but a chance."

"My Lady, I still don't understand," Bagwell protested.

"They hit Candor and Minette to draw our SDs out of Yeltsin, Fred," Honor said, "and they think they've succeeded. That's the only reason for them to head in for a normal engagement with the forts. They think they can take them out, and those 'freighters' are probably transports with an occupation force to take over the shipyards after they knock out the defenses. They can't hope to hold onto them, but they can certainly destroy them, and if they've brought along the right tech teams, they could learn an awful lot about our latest systems for their own use."

"It makes sense, My Lady," Paxton said with a sharp nod. "We've been Manticore's most visible ally since the war started. If they can take us out, wreck our infrastructure, then they've proved they can raid any of the Kingdom's *other* allies. What that could do to the Alliance's long-term stability would be well worth the risk of a few battleships to them, even without the possibility of raiding our tech base."

Honor saw the same thoughts racing through the rest of her staff. One by one, they began to nod, but then, predictably, Bagwell stopped.

"You may be right, My Lady. But how does it give us a chance?"

"They don't expect anything heavier than a battlecruiser, Commander," Yu said from his com screen. "When they realize they *haven't* drawn all the SDs out of the system, it's going to be a nasty surprise for them."

"More to the point," Honor said more briskly, "the fact that they're not expecting to see any ships of the wall may just let us get close enough to do some real damage before they break off."

There was a moment of silence, and then Bagwell cleared his throat.

"You're going *out* to meet them, My Lady?" he asked very carefully. "Without the support of the forts?"

"We don't have a choice, Fred. They'll probably spot us in time to stay outside the forts' engagement envelope even if we don't go to meet them, and in that case they can use cee-fractional missile strikes to take us all out. No, we have to get close—clear into energy range, if we can—and kick their guts out before they know we're here."

"But, My Lady, while we 'kick *their* guts out,' that many battleships will destroy *us*, as well," Bagwell pointed out quietly.

"Maybe they will, and maybe they won't," Honor made herself sound far more confident than she felt, "but it's still our best chance. Especially if we can sneak in close enough." Bagwell looked frightened—less, Honor knew, by the prospect of dying than of losing so much of the Grayson Navy—but she held his eyes until, almost against his will, he nodded.

"All right, then, people," she said, leaning forward in her command chair, "here's what I want to do."

• CHAPTER THIRTY-TWO

"Well, there they are, Citizen Commissioner." Thurston sounded disgusted, Preznikov noted, and looked a question at him. "Oh, I'm not complaining," the citizen vice admiral said. "But remember what I said about how when they decided to come out would indicate how good they were? Well, it looks like the answer is not too good."

He shook his head and gazed thoughtfully into the plot. Almost exactly seventy minutes had passed since the task force's arrival, and its units were up to 20,403 KPS. So far they'd covered over forty-six and a half million kilometers, and for a while he'd thought the Graysons were going to fight smart. Destroyers and dispatch boats had shot out in all directions, no doubt carrying word of his attack to nearby systems and screaming for help, but whatever they'd had in Grayson orbit had sat tight. The fact that one of those courier vessels had headed out on a least-time course to Endicott was irritating, since it meant the forces covering that system would be alerted to make whatever preparations they could before he detached Theisman and Chernov, but he'd known from the outset that that was likely to happen. He couldn't divide his own forces until he'd *confirmed* that there were no ships of the wall in Yeltsin, and every minute the Grayson commander had sat tight, denying him that confirmation, was one more minute he'd had to hold onto Theisman and TG 14.2's battleships and battlecruisers.

But now the enemy had come out of hiding, and his timing was execrable. The largest units Thurston's sensors could see were battlecruisers, but the Allied force's

acceleration was 458 g, which was stupid. It was higher
than a Manty BC's "normal maximum" of four hundred
gravities at eighty percent power, so they'd obviously
redlined their drives. Yet that was still over forty gravities
lower than the maximum they *could* have pulled, which
indicated that they had some of their damnable missile
pods on tow. The extra launchers those things provided
in the opening salvos had worried Thurston when he
first conceived Dagger, but the battlecruisers coming at
him couldn't be towing more than one or at most two
pods each, or their accel would have been still lower.

That was what made their movements so stupid. If
Grayson's defenders were going to come out at less than
max accel they should have started even sooner, with
an even lower acceleration, which would have let them
tow more pods. The small number their BCs could have
available at *this* accel would make no difference against
battleship point defense, so all they'd accomplished by
bringing them along was to cost themselves about a half
KPS^2 and give Thurston an earlier look at their numbers and formation than they had to.

If, he thought, you could *call* that a formation. The
untidy gaggle of starships moved towards him in awkward clumps and knots, and he shook his head again.
There were Manty ships in that mess, but its CO had
to be a Grayson, because no Manty admiral would let
himself fuck up this way. Thurston recognized the courage his enemy was displaying, but *Lord* was he dumb!

"Numbers?" he asked.

"Plotting makes it twenty-five battlecruisers, ten heavy
cruisers, forty-odd light cruisers, and sixteen to twenty
destroyers, Citizen Admiral," his ops officer responded.
"We're not positive about the count on the light units
because of their formation. They're not only getting in
each other's way, but some of them are grouped so tight
it's all but impossible to get a close look at their wedges."

"RDs?"

"Not much point at this range, Citizen Admiral," his
senior tracking officer replied. "We can't send drones

in ballistic the way their formation's all tangled up—we'd need to bring them in under power and steer them into location. If we do that, their point defense will have so much tracking and solution time they'll pick them off in droves. Given our vectors, the missile envelope should be about thirteen million klicks, though. We could probably bury the drones in our missile fire then and sneak 'em past, but—"

"But by that time, we'll have plenty of direct observation without them," Thurston agreed. He rocked on his heels for a moment, then shrugged. "Do your best to refine your data."

He walked back to his command chair, and Preznikov accompanied him.

"Does it really matter exactly how many light units they have, Citizen Admiral?"

Thurston wondered if the question reflected honest curiosity, an attempt to jab him into something more "energetic," or simply a probe to see how he'd react to what *might* be a jab. Best to treat it as the first possibility, he decided.

"Frankly, no, Citizen Commissioner. But we've got plenty of time before we come into range, and I'd just as soon get a hard count if I can before I detach the other two task groups."

"You *are* planning to detach them, then?"

"I'm certainly considering it, Sir. We know they've already sent a courier off to Endicott. The closer on its heels Theisman and Chernov arrive, the less time Endicott'll have to set up any sort of defense, but I'm not turning them loose until I'm sure I won't need them here."

Honor sat back in her command chair, holding Nimitz in her lap, and stroked his ears while her ships accelerated towards the enemy. She'd have to resecure his safety harness before they got into range, but there was no need to worry about that yet, and she knew he could feel her anxiety.

The small plot on her console showed less detail than the holo sphere behind her, but her traitor legs had nearly collapsed the last time she'd started to stand. She thought she'd recovered quickly enough to hide it from her staff and bridge crew, yet there was no way she could fool them if she went staggering around like a drunk.

Now she gazed at the plot and wondered what the Peep CO made of her formation. It was certainly the sloppiest one she'd ever assembled, but there was a method to her madness. One she hoped wouldn't occur to him.

There were limits to even a Grayson-refitted SD's EW capabilities. *Terrible* could do a lot to make her impeller wedge look weaker, yet it was so powerful that the deception was unlikely to hold if someone got a good, hard look at it. Which was why she'd "disarranged" her formation and put at least three other ships in front of each SD. With their wedges directly between the superdreadnoughts and the Peeps' sensors, interference should mask the greater power of the SDs' drives. Coupled with the heavier ships' EW activity, that *should* keep the Peeps from realizing what they were truly up against . . . unless they got a recon drone close enough for a good look.

The trick, of course, was to dissuade them from trying to do just that. The chance of getting a big, relatively slow RD past her point defense was low, but it *was* possible, especially if the Peep commander should feel uneasy enough to expend the huge numbers of RDs needed to swamp her defenses.

So what she needed to do was to make the Peeps so confident of what they saw that they felt no need to confirm it, and she'd taken a risky step to do just that. She was running her superdreadnoughts flat out at full military power and zero safety margin, which gave the squadron about a three percent chance of *someone* suffering a compensator failure—with fatal consequences for whoever it happened to. But it also let them pull an acceleration of over 4.5 KPS^2, far higher than any "normal" SD could manage, and she hoped Peep intelligence hadn't yet figured out that the new compensators had increased Alliance acceleration rates by over six percent virtually across the board. If they hadn't, her accel should look too high to be an SD's.

Her eyes moved across the plot to the ships racing towards her from other points in the system. They were decelerating to match vectors now, bringing the formation together well short of the Peeps, and, so far, things seemed to be working. She hoped.

She took her hand from Nimitz's ears long enough to pinch the bridge of her nose hard, but it didn't really help. Her exhaustion actually seemed to be making her mind work faster, not slower, yet it was an undisciplined speed, one that tried to race off in too many directions at once. Would her accel convince the Peeps she had no SDs? Or would it actually make the Peep CO *more* suspicious with its proof that her BCs couldn't be towing enough missile pods to make a practical difference? For that matter, what if his sensor crews had already seen past her EW and figured out exactly what she had? Or—

She lowered her hand and gritted her teeth, then leaned back in the support of her contoured chair while she prayed her fatigue hadn't already drawn her into a fatal mistake she was just too tired to recognize.

"Anything more?" Thurston asked his ops officer.

"Not really, Citizen Admiral. We've positively IDed one more light cruiser, but the mutual impeller interference is still too bad to say anything more certain than that."

"Understood," Thurston grunted, and looked at Preznikov. "With your permission, Citizen Commissioner, I think we can detach the other task groups now. We've got reasonably good reads on their units, and the biggest we've seen are battlecruisers. Admiral Chavez's group can come within one unit of matching them ship-for-ship with battle*ships*, and she's got six BCs of her own for good measure. We can handle them without Citizen Admiral Theisman."

"Very well, Citizen Admiral, I agree."

"Communications," Thurston looked over his shoulder, "signal *Conquérant* to execute Alpha-Three."

"Signal from Flag, Citizen Admiral. Execute Alpha-Three."

Thomas Theisman nodded, but also made a disgruntled sound, and Citizen Commissioner LePic glanced at him.

"A problem, Citizen Admiral?"

"Um?" Theisman grimaced at the commissioner, then shook his head. "No, not really. I've expected it for five minutes now, given the strength coming at us. I just—"

He chopped himself off, and LePic cocked his head.

"You just what, Citizen Admiral?" he asked, and Theisman sighed.

"I just wouldn't have done it yet," he said. "I don't mean that as a criticism of Citizen Admiral Thurston, but it's not actually going to save us that much time against Endicott. Under the circumstances, if I were him, I'd have preferred to stay concentrated until after I'd blown away the opposition here."

"You think he may be unable to destroy them?" LePic looked surprised, and Theisman laughed harshly.

"Twenty-four battleships destroy twenty-five battle-*cruisers?* Oh, no, he'll take them out. It's just a matter of technique, I suppose. My own inclination would be to start decelerating now to hold the range open longer. Given the disparity in tonnages, *we've* got the missile advantage for a change, and I'd like to chop them up before closing to energy range to finish them off." The citizen rear admiral paused, then smiled almost sheepishly. "I suppose part of it's that I've been on the receiving end of Manty missiles too often, Citizen Commissioner. I haven't enjoyed any of those experiences, and I'd like the chance to give them a bit of their own back."

"Well, you should have that opportunity shortly in Endicott, Citizen Admiral," LePic said encouragingly, and Theisman nodded.

*   *   *

"Status change!"

Honor twitched in her chair and jerked her eyes open, shocked to discover she'd actually dozed off at action stations. She shook herself and blinked, then peered at her plot.

"My Lady," Bagwell began, "the enemy—"

"I see it, Fred," she said quietly, and her aching eyes narrowed in disbelief as the Peep formation changed. A full third of their battleships—and *two*-thirds of their battlecruisers!—had just begun decelerating at 470 g. That must be running the BBs' compensators close to redline, although *they* didn't have missile pods to complicate their lives, of course, and she frowned. The larger group continued onward at a steady 450 g, still heading for its eventual turnover, which meant the gap between it and the smaller force was growing at over nine KPS^2.

She reached out to punch numbers into her plot, but she'd never been a confident mathematician, and fatigue seemed to have put extra joints in the middles of her fingers. She fumbled at the keypad, then grimaced in frustration with her own clumsiness and looked at Bagwell.

"Have CIC designate the lead formation as Force Alpha and the trailer as Force Zulu, Fred."

"Aye, aye, My Lady."

"Allen," she turned to her astrogator, "assume all accelerations remain constant to Force Alpha's projected turnover and that Alpha decelerates at four-point-four KPS squared thereafter. What will the range to Zulu be when we're nine million klicks from Alpha?"

"Nine million?" Commander Sewell repeated, and bent over his own console at her nod. His fingers moved with the brisk assurance which had evaded her own, and he looked back up in mere seconds. "Under the assumptions you specified, My Lady, the range to Force Zulu at that point will be approximately six-seven-point-six-eight-eight million kilometers."

"And Zulu's distance from the hyper limit?"

Sewell tapped keys once more, then looked up at her. "Approximately seven-eight-point-two million klicks, My Lady."

"Thank you," she said. She glanced down at her com screen to Alfredo Yu, and for the first time, there was a sharp, predatory edge to her exhausted smile. Her flag captain returned it, and she turned back to her own plot. *Oh, yes, people,* she thought silently at the enemy light codes on her display. *You just go right on putting distance between yourselves.*

"Coming up on turnover, Citizen Admiral," Thurston's astrogator announced, and the citizen vice admiral nodded without even looking up. Meredith Chavez's battleships had five times the tonnage—and thirty times the firepower—of the battlecruisers coming at him. All he had to do was blow straight through them, then decelerate to engage the orbital forts, and he'd control the entire star system in time for a late dinner, he told himself, and smiled at the thought.

"Turnover on Force Alpha, My Lady," Bagwell reported, and Honor nodded, then rubbed her eyes yet again and turned to Allen Sewell once more.

"Time to Point Luck, Allen?"

"Approximately three-three-point-six minutes, My Lady." The astrogator replied so instantly she smiled, then looked down at her com link to *Terrible's* command deck, still rubbing Nimitz's ears.

"Begin shifting formation in five minutes, Alfredo," she said.

"Why aren't they decelerating, Citizen Admiral?" Preznikov asked. Thurston gave him a look of surprise, and the citizen commissioner gestured at the plot. "Their velocity's almost ten thousand kilometers per second, and ours is almost thirty thousand. Surely they don't want to let us past them to attack their planet!"

"They aren't decelerating, Citizen Commissioner," Thurston replied, "because they're battlecruisers and we're battleships. They can't fight us head-on, so they're trying to break past us, hopefully without getting hurt too badly in the process, to 'trap' us between them and Grayson."

"Trap us?" Preznikov looked puzzled, and Thurston nodded.

"As I say, those ships can't fight us, Sir—not and live— but they can pull a much higher acceleration once they get rid of their missile pods. They can overfly us, then use their decel advantage to get back into range of us before we hit the planet, and what they'd like is for us to be so worried by the possibility of their hitting us in the back that we decline to engage their orbital forts for fear they'll attack us from two directions at once." The citizen vice admiral shook his head. "It won't work, of course. We've got the firepower to deal with their forts and fend off their entire mobile force if we have to, but we won't. Most of them will be dead before they pass us, even with the closing velocity we'll have then."

"You sound very sure of that, Citizen Admiral."

"I am, Citizen Commissioner. Oh, fluke things can happen—and usually do—in battle, but the odds against them are just too high for it to work."

"If that's so obvious to you, then why are they trying it? Why isn't it equally obvious to *them*?"

"It *is* obvious to them." Thurston turned to gaze at the commissioner. "They understand the odds just as well as we do, Citizen Commissioner." He knew his voice was dangerously patient, but at the moment he didn't really care. "They've got a losing hand here, Sir, but it's the only hand they've got, and that planet—" he pointed at the green light code of Grayson "—is their home world. Their families are down there. Their children. They don't expect to live through this, but they'll play it out to the bitter end and hope somewhere, somehow, a break goes their way when they need it."

The citizen vice admiral shook his head, eyes once

more on the crimson beads of the battlecruisers sweeping towards his formation, and sighed.

"They've got guts, Citizen Commissioner," he said quietly, "but they're not going to get that break. Not this time."

"Something funny going on here, Skip."

"'Funny'? What d'you mean 'funny'?" Citizen Commander Caslet demanded. TG 14.1 sped straight towards the enemy at a combined closing velocity of over forty-six thousand KPS, which meant maximum effective missile range would be just over thirteen million kilometers. They'd enter that range in less than five more minutes, and he was more anxious than he wanted to reveal. *Vaubon* was only a light cruiser, hardly a high-priority target with battleships to shoot at, but there were light units on the *other* side, as well, and they might well choose to engage *Vaubon* simply because she was small enough they might actually get through her defenses.

"It's just—" Citizen Lieutenant Foraker leaned back, rubbing the tip of her nose, then grimaced. "Let me show you, Skip," she said, and switched her own tactical readouts to Caslet's tertiary display. "Watch this motion," she said, and he gazed intently at the display as the raggedy-assed enemy formation bobbed and swirled. There'd been some movement in it all along, but it had become more pronounced as the range dropped—a fact he'd put down to nerves.

"I don't—" he began, but Foraker was tapping commands into her console, and Caslet's mouth closed with a snap as the same movement replayed itself. The only difference was that *this* time a half-dozen or so of the dots left little worms of light behind, charting their paths, and the "formation" they'd dropped into. . . .

"What *is* that?" he asked slowly, and this time there was more than a trace of worry in his techno-nerd tactical officer's reply.

"Skip, if I didn't know better—and I *don't* know

better—I'd say six of those battlecruisers just slid into a modified vertical wall of battle."

"That's crazy, Shannon," Caslet's astrogator said. "Battlecruisers don't form wall against battleships! That'd be suicide!"

"Yep," Foraker agreed. "That's exactly what it would be—for battlecruisers."

Caslet stared at the glowing light worms and felt his stomach drop clear out of the universe. It wasn't possible. And even if it *were* possible, *surely* one of the battlecruisers or battleships with their better sensors and more powerful computers would have seen it before a light cruiser did!

But those battlecruisers and battleships didn't have his resident tac witch a cold, clear voice said in his brain.

"Communications! Get me a priority link to the Flag—*now!*"

"He says *what?*"

Thurston wheeled his command chair around to face his ops officer with a glare. The enemy formation had begun to put out decoys and brought its jammers online, which was making it even harder to keep track of anything in that mishmash formation. His own ships were doing the same things, of course, but the Manties had obviously provided their Grayson allies with first-line EW equipment. First-line *Manty* EW equipment, he amended sourly. The range had fallen to just under thirteen million kilometers, well within theoretical missile range, but those decoys and jammers cut the *effective* range to seventy percent of theoretical, max. He had perhaps four-and-a-half minutes before both sides began to fire, and he didn't have *time* for last-minute nonsense.

"Citizen Commander Caslet says a half-dozen of their BCs have dropped into a modified wall of battle, Citizen Admiral," his com officer repeated. The ops officer was bent too intently over an auxiliary plot watching something play out to respond, and Thurston glowered at his back. Then the man straightened and met his CO's eyes.

"Caslet . . . may have something, Citizen Admiral. Watch your plot."

Thurston swung back to his own display and opened his mouth impatiently, then paused. Six Alliance battlecruisers were now highlighted in a darker red, and they formed—indisputably, they formed—what might just possibly be a formal wall of battle. It was an unorthodox one, like a huge "V" laid on its side in space, but the intervals were unmistakable. The confusion of the rest of their formation had hidden it from him, but now that those individual units had been highlighted, the spacing virtually leapt out of the display at him. Yet there was something wrong with it. . . .

Citizen Vice Admiral Alexander Thurston punched a query into his console, and his face went pale as dispassionate computers answered it. No, that interval was all wrong for a wall of battlecruisers—but it was just right for one of *superdreadnoughts*. . . .

"All right, people." All of Honor's divisional commanders looked out from her subdivided com screen as they neared the point in space she'd named "Point Luck," and she gave them a smile she hoped looked more confident than exhausted. "I think we're about ready. Captain Yu," as in the RMN, so in the Grayson Navy, an admiral's flag captain was her tactical deputy, and Yu was far fresher than she, less likely to make a mistake through simple, molasses-minded fatigue, "the task force will rotate and engage on your signal."

"Aye, aye, My Lady," Alfredo Yu said quietly, then raised his voice to the other commanders. "The screen will scatter on my Alpha Mark; the squadron will rotate on my Beta Mark," he said crisply, and Honor sat back, waiting like every other officer in her task force, while her flag captain watched a digital timer tick downward.

"Twenty seconds," he said. "Ten. Five. *Alpha Mark!*"

• CHAPTER THIRTY-THREE

Alexander Thurston was still staring at his plot when the highlighted "battlecruisers" swung through ninety degrees, presenting their broadsides to his ships. And as they unmasked their batteries and the lighter units which had obscured them accelerated aside, his sensors showed him what they truly were at last.

He sat motionless, awareness of the trap into which he'd walked tolling through his mind, while TG 14.1 began its own preplanned deployment. There was no point trying to change the original plan at this late date, he thought almost calmly. There was no way to avoid action, and last-minute order changes would only confuse things and make bad worse. So he watched, saying nothing, as Meredith Chavez's battleships turned to open their own broadsides, exactly as he'd specified. *But you expected to engage* battlecruisers, *didn't you?* a voice said in his brain. He'd expected *his* ships to have a massive individual superiority. Every accepted convention said it was as suicidal for battleships to engage superdreadnoughts as it was for battlecruisers to engage battleships . . . and he had no choice at all.

"Citizen Admiral?" It was Preznikov, staring at him, still trying to understand what had become so fatally obvious to Thurston, and then the SDs he'd allowed into missile range fired.

Honor's battlecruisers had only two missile pods apiece. That was all they could tow without massive degradation of their acceleration rates. But superdreadnoughts were big enough they could actually tractor

the pods *inside* their wedges, where they had no effect
at all on acceleration, and now each of her ships of the
wall deployed a lumpy, ungainly tail of no less than ten
pods. They were ugly, clumsy, and fragile, those pods—
but each of them also mounted ten box launchers loaded
with missiles even larger and more powerful than a
superdreadnought's missile tubes could fire.

The last Grayson destroyer skittered out of the way
as the range fell to nine million kilometers, and then
Battle Squadron One, Grayson Space Navy, fired its first
broadside in anger.

"Jesus Christ!" Shannon Foraker gasped, and a small,
numb corner of Citizen Commander Caslet's brain
observed that she'd just spoken for him. One instant, the
situation had been well in hand; five minutes later, fourteen *hundred* missiles erupted from the Allied "battlecruisers." Havenite missiles answered almost instantly, but
all twenty-four battleships between them could produce
only seven hundred missiles in reply, and, unlike the
Allies, they'd spread their first, preprogrammed broadside's fire over all twenty-five of the "battlecruisers" in
the opposing task force. The Allies hadn't done that.
They'd concentrated twice as much fire on just twelve
battleships—less than half as many targets—and taken
the Peep point defense crews totally by surprise, to boot.

At least, Caslet thought with that same numb detachment, they weren't wasting any of it on a mere light
cruiser.

Honor peered into her plot. She'd let Yu time the
actual attack because she was too fatigued to trust her
own judgment, but the plan behind it was hers, and there
would be no time for Yu or anyone else to fix anything
she'd done wrong.

The two formations slid broadside towards one another
at just under forty thousand kilometers per second while
the missiles went out with an acceleration of eighty-five
thousand gravities. At their closure rate, the two

formations had only two hundred and twenty-six seconds before they interpenetrated. Not *passed* one another, but *interpenetrated*, for Honor had deliberately turned directly across TG 14.1's base course to give her energy weapons the best possible field of fire for the bare twelve seconds it would take the Peeps to shoot clear across their effective range envelope. So great was their closing speed that flight time was barely over a minute and a half, despite the range, and both sides had seeded their broadsides with EW missiles packed with penetration aids to make their birds still harder to track.

Which meant most of those missiles would survive to attack their targets . . . and that, even more than usual, it was up to the passive defenses. Decoys and jammers and fire confusion systems fought to deny the enemy valid targets, because it was for damn sure they weren't going to stop many of the incoming birds with active defenses.

They were concentrating on the heart of his own wall. Thurston's brain whirred with the precision of a fine chronometer, buffered against panic by the sheer shock of what had happened. He understood the reasoning behind the Manty admiral's targeting—and, despite his earlier thoughts, that *had* to be a Manty over there, after all. Standard PN doctrine put the task force commander at the center of his wall of battle, where light-speed communication lags were minimized and the wall's interlocking point defense was maximized. But in this sort of minimum-range shootout, point defense was largely irrelevant, and the Manties were going for Task Force Fourteen's brain. *Alexander Thurston's* brain.

"Recompute firing pattern." He gave what he knew would be his final order almost calmly. "Ignore the battlecruisers. Go for the SDs."

BatRon One and its screen went to maximum rate fire with their very first broadsides. The superdreadnoughts retained their original Havenite launchers, with a cycle time of approximately twenty seconds; the lighter Grayson units carried the Mod 7b Manticoran launcher, and the GSN's battlecruisers mounted the Mod 19, both with a cycle time of only seventeen seconds.

But two hundred and twenty-six seconds would allow BatRon One's SDs only eleven broadsides and the lighter ships only thirteen, and there was no time to observe the results of one broadside before the next was fired. The initial fire plans had been locked into the computers, and human reflexes were hopelessly inadequate to modify them in the time they had.

BatRon One's first broadside went in with horrific effect. It was the heaviest and most concentrated one the engagement would see, and Honor's fire control officers had calculated its targeting setup with exquisite care, then run constant updates the whole time the two fleets advanced to meet one another. Despite the short flight time, the Peeps' point defense crews managed to knock down almost thirty percent of the incoming fire. Decoys and jammers threw another ten percent off track, and desperate captains—abandoning formation discipline in last-ditch efforts to save their ships—sprawled out of their wall of battle, frantically rolling in attempts to interpose the impenetrable roofs or floors of their impeller wedges against the incoming fire. Their reckless maneuvers brought PNS *Theban Warrior* and PNS *Saracen* too near one another—their wedges physically collided, and the collision blew alpha and beta nodes in a frenzy of wild energy that half-vaporized both battleships—but their sister ships managed to take yet another twenty-two percent of BatRon One's missiles against their wedges.

Yet for all their frantic maneuvers, thirty-eight percent of Honor's birds got through . . . spread between a mere twelve targets. Five hundred and thirty-two laser warheads—warheads of a size and power only ships of the wall, or RMN missile pods, could throw—detonated almost as one. Bomb-pumped lasers gouged and tore at the sidewalls covering the open flanks of their targets' wedges, and some of them—perhaps as many as twenty percent—detonated directly ahead or astern of their targets, where there *were* no sidewalls.

Battle steel was no match for that tsunami of X-ray lasers. Alloy blew apart in glowing splinters as energy bled into it. Atmosphere streamed from shattered hulls, drive nodes flared and died like prespace flashbulbs, weapons bays exploded in ruin, and the sun-bright boil of failing fusion bottles blossomed in the heart of the Peep formation like gaps in the ramparts of Hell.

No one could ever reconstruct exactly what happened. Not even the surviving Allied computers could sort it all out afterward, but five seconds after BatRon One's first laser head detonated, eleven Havenite battleships—including PNS *Conquistador*—no longer existed, and a twelfth was a broken, dying wreck tumbling uselessly through space.

But then, of course, it was the *Peeps'* turn. Thurston's retargeting order had cost his command a thirty-one second delay between its first and second broadsides, but even the ships who died in that first holocaust had had time to get off three broadsides before the Grayson missiles arrived.

The Peeps' opening salvo was almost uniformly distributed among all twenty-five of the "battlecruisers" they'd been tracking. Had those targets, in fact, all *been* battlecruisers, it would have been an effective fire plan, for it also spread the Allies' defenses thin. Some, at least, of those missiles would have gotten through against every target, and successive broadsides would have finished the cripples. But Honor's orders for her screen to scatter freed her real battlecruisers to maneuver independently against the fire directed at them, and the "confusion" the Peeps had seen in her formation had been nothing of the sort. She'd deliberately broken the screening units down into their own point defense nets, independent of her SDs and freed of any responsibility for covering her wall. Combined with their more effective decoys and jammers, that tremendously degraded the accuracy of the fire directed upon them.

Which meant that "only" six of her nineteen battle-cruisers—and fifteen thousand of her people—died in the first broadside.

She stared at her plot, her face a mask of stone, as the fireballs claimed her people, and the fact that it was a miraculously low loss rate didn't matter at all. Her hands were white-knuckled on her command chair arm-rests, and then *Terrible* shuddered and lurched as Peep lasers blasted through her own sidewalls and into her armor. Flag Bridge wasn't tied directly into Damage Central, and it was very quiet despite the carnage raging about and within the huge ship's hull. Honor couldn't hear the howl of alarms, the battle chatter, the screams of hurt and dying people, but she'd heard those sounds before. She knew what other people were hearing and seeing and feeling, and there was nothing at all she could do but wait and pray.

In direct contravention of most battles, the first broadsides were the most effective ones for both sides. Normally, fire got more effective, not less, as tactical officers adjusted for their enemies' ECM and concentrated succeeding broadsides on more vulnerable targets. This time, there was simply too little time between salvos to adjust fire; half of each side's follow-up broadsides were already in space before the first ones even struck home. Over a third of the birds in BatRon One's second and third salvos wasted themselves on targets which were already destroyed, but the ones that didn't tore in on the surviving Peep BBs, and the Peeps had wasted thirty-one seconds retargeting their fire.

Yet they *had* retargeted, and their new patterns ignored Honor's battlecruisers and heavy cruisers. Every surviving Peep ship poured fire into her SDs, and not even a superdreadnought could shake off that hurricane of fire. *Terrible* faltered as three of her after beta nodes were blasted away. More lasers ripped into her port broadside and blew a quarter of her close-grouped missile tubes into wreckage. Simultaneous hits on Gravitic Array Three and Graser Nine sent a power surge through her systems which not even her circuit breakers could handle, and Fusion Two, hidden away at the very heart of her enormous, massively armored hull, went into emergency shutdown barely in time. The huge ship staggered as her power levels fluctuated, but her other plants took the load, and she shook off the damage, holding her place in the wall as the distance to her enemies fell below missile range to energy range.

GNS *Glorious* was less fortunate. She and *Manticore's Gift*, her division mate, were the center of Honor's unorthodox wall, and just as *she* had targeted the center of the Peeps' wall, the Peeps had targeted hers. She had no idea how many laser heads had battered *Glorious*, but one moment she was eight million tons of starship, thundering broadsides at her foes; the next she and six thousand more human beings were an expanding cloud of gas and plasma.

Honor clung to her command chair, eyes on her display, watching the computers execute the plan she'd locked into them, and the holocaust of those three-point-seven minutes was simply beyond comprehension. Formalism had become the rule for fleet engagements over the centuries, and ships of the wall had not engaged in such point-blank mutual slaughter in over seventy T-years. The losing side in a battle knew when to cut and run, when to break off, and admirals *never* closed on a course which *wouldn't* let them break off at need. But Alexander Thurston had believed there were no ships of the wall to face him, and Honor had had no choice but to come to meet him. And now, as the last missile salvos roared out, her five surviving SDs completed their final turn and brought their energy batteries to bear.

Only seven Peep battleships remained, all but one of them damaged, and their crews knew as well as Honor that they could never survive an energy-range engagement with superdreadnoughts. Yet there was no way they could avoid it, either. Their own wall had completely disintegrated as the units which composed it died, and they maneuvered independently, twisting in desperate, despairing efforts to interpose their wedges. But this was the moment for which Honor had stacked her line vertically rather than horizontally. The sharp angle in its middle meant at least one of her SDs would have a shot at each battleship's sidewalls, however it might twist or turn. There was no time for a neat, formal distribution of fire from the flagship, but Honor had known there wouldn't be. Each superdreadnought's computers had been assigned targeting criteria, and it was all up to them to find and kill their targets in the instant the Peeps' velocity carried them helplessly through Honor's wall.

Five superdreadnoughts of the Grayson Navy fired almost as one, their massive energy batteries blazing away like God's own fury at ranges as low as three thousand kilometers, and five more Peep battleships and two battlecruisers blew apart under their pounding. A sixth battleship coasted out of the carnage, her drives dead, half her hull blown to wreckage while small craft and life pods spilled from her splintered flanks and desperate parties of courageous men and women fought to pull trapped and wounded comrades out of her broken compartments while there was still time.

PNS *Vindicator*, the seventh—and last—battleship of TG 14.1, actually broke past BatRon One completely undamaged and streaked away at forty thousand KPS. A few missiles raced after her, but now she was running away from them rather than into them, and BatRon One had not emerged unscathed from that crushing, short-range slaughter. *Glorious* had already died, now *Manticore's Gift* fell out of formation with her entire forward impeller ring—and both sidewalls forward of frame eight-fifty—shot away.

Damage and casualty reports began to flood in, and Honor's heart twisted within her. One of her superdreadnoughts and six battlecruisers—over thirteen *million* tons of shipping—had been totally destroyed. *Manticore's*

Gift was a wreck, and Walter Brentworth's flagship, *Magnificent*, was little better, though at least she still had most of her drive. Admiral Trailman had been killed by a direct hit on *Manticore's Gift*'s flag bridge, Brentworth's communications were practically nonexistent after the pounding *Magnificent* had taken, and *Furious* had lost over half her weapons. Of Battle Squadron One's original six ships, only Judah Yanakov's *Courageous* and her own *Terrible* remained truly combat effective, and even they would require months of yard time to make good their damages.

Yet five of her six ships had survived—a testimonial, she thought with infinite bitterness, to the engineers who'd designed and built them, not to the fool who'd led them to the slaughter. But they'd done the job, she told herself. She'd lost thirteen million tons of shipping and twenty thousand people; the Peeps had lost over a *hundred* million tons, and their butcher's bill didn't even bear thinking on. She'd just destroyed an entire peacetime navy in less than five minutes of actual combat. The remnants of Force Alpha were fleeing for their lives, and Force Zulu was already headed for the hyper limit. No doubt both of them would go right on running, licking their wounds and mourning their dead. The Fourth Battle of Yeltsin, she already knew, would go down—in the words of an ancient poem she'd read many, many years ago—as "a great and famous victory" . . . so why did she feel like a cold-blooded murderer instead of a victorious hero?

She felt Nimitz on the back of her chair. The bright glitter of adrenaline and the aftershock of the combatlashed emotional tornado which had whipped at him from *Terrible*'s crew still flickered and danced in their link, yet his fierce denial of her cruel self-condemnation came to her clearly. And she knew, in the part of her brain that could still think, that he was right. That, in time, she would come to remember the courage of her crews, the way they'd risen above their rough edges and how magnificently they'd performed for her. In time, she would actually come to remember this ghastly, blood-soaked day with pride . . . and the knowledge that she would, however much her people *deserved* to be remembered with pride, sickened her.

She closed her eyes once more and drew a deep, deep breath, then shoved herself back in her command chair. She turned her head and saw her staff looking at her, and their faces were white and strained. She knew they were as shocked and horrified as she, and she turned her chair to face them and made herself smile, made herself look confident and determined while her heart wept within her.

She opened her mouth to speak, but someone else beat her to it.

"My Lady," Commander Frederick Bagwell said quietly, "Force Zulu has just cut its acceleration towards the hyper limit to zero." He looked up and met her eyes. "They've stopped running, My Lady."

• CHAPTER THIRTY-FOUR

It was very quiet on PNS *Conquérant*'s flag bridge.

It had taken three and a half minutes for their light-speed systems to give them the details of the brief, terrible destruction sixty-three million kilometers behind them, but the disappearance of TG 14.1's impeller signatures had already told them what those details would be. One battleship, Thomas Theisman thought numbly. Only *one* battleship had survived!

He knew who was in command back there—who it had to be. Intelligence had been wrong about how quickly Grayson could refit captured SDs, but it had been right about where Honor Harrington was, for that brutally professional slaughter bore all the hallmarks of her touch. She'd done it to the People's Navy again, he thought. Smashed them with consummate skill—made it look easy.

He wanted to hate her, but he couldn't. Hate what she'd done to his navy, yes, and long to smash her in return, but he'd met the woman behind the name. He'd seen what it cost her to kill her enemies and lose her own people, and somehow that kept him from hating her.

He knew he should break off. Operation Dagger had just been blown out of space with the man who'd conceived it and God alone knew how many thousands of others. Harrington had enough overtake to catch him millions of kilometers short of the hyper limit on his present course, but his smaller battleships had the acceleration edge over even *her* SDs. If he altered course by ninety degrees, her overtake advantage wouldn't matter; he'd be generating an entirely new side vector, one she could never catch him on, and that was precisely what he should be doing, but—

He ignored his staff's shocked silence, ignored the white-faced citizen commissioner in the chair beside his, and punched a command into his console. He watched the computers obediently reconstruct what they could of the brief, savage battle astern of *Conquérant*, and his eyes narrowed.

"Kill our deceleration, Megan."

His ops officer stared at him for one second, then swallowed.

"Aye, Citizen Admiral," she replied, and he heard her passing the orders to the rest of the task group.

"What are you *doing?*" Dennis LePic hissed in his ear, and he turned his head to regard the citizen commissioner much more calmly than he felt.

"I'm thinking instead of simply reacting, Sir."

"*Thinking?*" LePic gasped, and Theisman nodded.

"Exactly. I'm thinking that running away may not be our best option." LePic stared at him in total disbelief, and Theisman smiled thinly. "That's Honor Harrington back there," he said conversationally. "Intelligence said she was here, and she's the only 'Grayson' officer with the guts *and* savvy to pull that off, but she's not a god, Citizen Commissioner. She got hurt, probably badly. Probably badly enough that we can still take her."

"*Take* her?" LePic's horror at the devastation of Meredith Chavez's task group was plain on his face. "Are you insane? You saw what she just did to *twenty-four* battleships, and we only have twelve!"

"That's correct, Citizen Commissioner—twelve *undamaged* battleships which now know what they're really up against."

"But she's got *superdreadnoughts!*"

"Yes, she does. But one of them was totally destroyed, a second's suffered obviously heavy damage, and the other four have almost certainly been hurt as well. And she's exhausted her missile pods. She can't swamp us like she did Citizen Admiral Chavez and Citizen Admiral

Thurston. No, Sir," he shook his head, "the odds aren't as bad as you may think. Not nearly as bad."

LePic swallowed again, but the shock was fading in his eyes as he made himself consider what Theisman had said.

"Are you serious, Citizen Admiral?" he asked quietly.

"I am." Theisman turned his head to look at his ops officer. "Megan, what's your analysis?"

"Citizen Admiral, I can't *give* you one—not from this range. Our data's too poor."

"Based on what you have," Theisman pressed. He cut his eyes briefly sideways at LePic, and Megan Hathaway recognized the warning in that glance. She drew a deep breath and made herself speak slowly and deliberately, forcing any hint of panic out of her tone for the civilian's benefit.

"Well," she said, "you're right that they've lost an SD, and from what we can see from here, it looks like a second one's suffered enough drive damage that it's having trouble staying with the rest of her formation. She's lost six battlecruisers, as well, and more of them must be damaged." She paused and frowned, twisting a lock of hair around her right index finger, and she sounded almost surprised when she resumed. "You may be right, Citizen Admiral. Certainly her other SDs must've taken *some* damage. The question is how much."

"My own thought, exactly." He turned back to LePic. "Citizen Commissioner, we don't dare execute our part of Dagger with combat effective ships of the wall behind us. If we pull out for Endicott and they follow us, they can trap us between themselves and whatever ships are already picketing the system. But if they've taken as much damage as I suspect they have—if, in fact, they *aren't* combat effective anymore—we can engage and destroy them. And if we do that, then we can still achieve *all* of Dagger's objectives, because there won't be anything heavy enough to stop us."

"And just how do you propose to find out if they're combat effective, Citizen Admiral?"

"There's only one way to do that, Sir," Thomas Theisman said quietly.

"My Lady, Force Zulu has now reversed acceleration," Commander Bagwell said. "They're coming back in."

Honor felt her lips tighten. She gazed at Bagwell for a moment, then nodded and looked at Mercedes Brigham.

"What's our status, Mercedes?"

"Not good, Milady," Mercedes said frankly. "*Glorious* is gone, and the *Gift*'s accel is less than a hundred gees—right on point-nine-six KPS squared. *Magnificent* can make about two fifty gees; *Terrible* and *Courageous* have impeller damage of their own, but they're both good for about three sixty. I wouldn't push them harder than that with so many shot-up nodes unbalancing their wedges, Milady." Honor nodded, and Mercedes rocked back in her chair. "*Furious'* drive is actually in the best shape, but she took a real pounding in that last exchange. She's lost half her energy weapons and three-quarters of her missile tubes, and Captain Gates says his starboard sidewall is 'iffy.'" Her lips twitched at Gates' choice of adjective, then she shrugged. "For all intents and purposes, Milady, *Terrible* and *Courageous* are all we've got, and neither of them is what I'd call healthy."

"Analysis, Fred?" Honor asked, switching her gaze back to Bagwell.

"My Lady, they can take us," he said flatly. "They're faster, they're undamaged, and they've got the force advantage. We can probably destroy six or seven of their battleships; the other four or five will destroy us while we're doing it, and that assumes we can get to energy range. We've lost so many tubes a missile engagement would be suicide."

"Recommendation?"

"We'll have to avoid action, My Lady." Bagwell didn't like saying that, yet he seemed surprised she even had to ask. "If we fall back to Grayson orbit now, they don't have the firepower to take us *and* the forts."

"I see." Honor turned her chair back to her console, hiding her face from her staff, and let her own desperate weariness and fear show for just a minute. Nimitz unhooked himself from his safety harness and slid down into her lap, then rose on his true-feet and turned to press his muzzle against her cheek. He purred to her, and she slipped an arm around him and hugged him close while she wondered who was in command of those Peep ships. Who'd kept his wits about himself well enough to realize what Bagwell had just so succinctly summed up? What officer had watched the brutal destruction of twice his own strength, yet had the courage to realize he could still reverse the verdict and win?

She bit her own lip and forced her exhausted brain to work. She *could* avoid action, but only if she started immediately, and even then she couldn't save *Manticore's Gift*. The battered SD lacked the acceleration to evade the incoming Peeps, so Honor would have no choice but to write her off. She might have to abandon *Magnificent*, as well, but Fred was right about *Terrible*, *Courageous*, and *Furious*. They could still avoid the enemy and reach the cover of the forts, and that would save half the squadron.

Yet would it? *Would* it save them? If that Peep CO was confident enough to come back in at all, he wouldn't give up. He could still retreat to the outer system, still send missiles in on ballistic courses. For that matter . . .

She inhaled deeply and squared her shoulders, then turned back to face her staff.

"I'm afraid that won't work, Fred," she said, and the ops officer stared at her. "If we break off, we lose the *Gift* and, probably, *Magnificent*. That's bad enough. But if we fall back, then whoever's in command out there will know—not just suspect, but *know*—we can't fight him. If he wants to, he can carry out a long-range cee-fractional bombardment of Grayson, and we can't stop him. I don't *think* he'd be crazy enough to go for the planet itself, but he could take out the forts, the shipyards . . . the farms."

She saw the stark understanding on the faces of her Grayson staff of what losing two-thirds of their world's food sources would mean, and nodded.

"Nor is that the only consideration," she went on. "There's those freighters and transports. If they were here to take apart our shipyards, they would have come in with Force Alpha, but they were *detached* as part of Zulu. That suggests they were intended to go somewhere else from the outset, and the only place I can think of is Endicott."

"Endicott, My Lady?" Sewell asked, and she nodded again.

"Suppose those ships carry Marines, Allen, or even just a cargo of modern weapons. The Endicott picket doesn't have anything heavier than a battlecruiser; they couldn't stop Zulu from breaking through to Masada, taking out the orbital bases, and landing whatever the transports are carrying. And if the Faithful get their hands on modern weaponry—"

She broke off as Greg Paxton winced in understanding, then went on in a soft, almost regretful tone.

"We don't have a choice, people. If they decide we're too battered to interfere with them, they can do whatever they want outside the reach of Grayson's orbital weapons even if they decide against bombarding the forts from deep space. They can take out our asteroid industry, wreck all the orbital infrastructure in Endicott, turn Masada into a bloodbath. . . . We can't let any of those things happen."

"But how can we *stop* it, My Lady?" Bagwell asked.

"There's only one way *I* know." She looked at her com officer. "Howard, contact *Magnificent*. Find out what her maximum safe acceleration is."

"Aye, aye, My Lady," Lieutenant Commander Brannigan replied, and Honor turned back to Sewell.

"Once we have Captain Edwards' max accel, plot a squadron course to intercept Force Zulu at her best speed, Allen."

"But—" Bagwell started, then drew a deep breath. "My

Lady, I understand your logic, but we don't have the firepower for it. Not anymore."

"I think we can at least cripple their battleship element," Honor replied in that same soft voice. "We can do enough damage to make it unlikely they'll take on the light forces we have left here and in Endicott."

"And while we're doing that, My Lady," Bagwell said very, very quietly, "they'll completely destroy this squadron."

Honor regarded him for a moment. The fussy, detail-minded ops officer looked back without personal fear, but she understood the deeper fear in his eyes. More than that, she knew he was right. But sometimes the price which had to be paid was just as fearsome as the people who had to pay it feared it would be, she thought, and held his gaze for another ten seconds, then lowered her eyes to her com screen to *Terrible*'s bridge.

"Captain Yu," she asked with a small, tired smile, "do you concur with Commander Bagwell's analysis?"

"Yes, My Lady, I do," Yu said, meeting her gaze levelly.

"I see. Tell me, Alfredo, did you ever read Clauzewitz?"

"*On War*, My Lady?" Yu sounded surprised. She nodded, and he frowned for an instant, then nodded back. "Yes, My Lady, I have."

"Then perhaps you remember the passage in which he said 'War is fought by human beings'?"

He gazed at her for another long moment, his eyes almost as opaque as they'd been the day she discovered he was her new flag captain, and then he nodded a second time.

"Yes, My Lady, I do," he said in a rather different tone.

"Well, it's time to find out if he's still right, Captain. As soon as Commander Sewell has that course for you, get us moving along it."

"Citizen Admiral, the enemy is changing course."

Citizen Rear Admiral Theisman held up one hand at

his com screen, breaking off an earnest, hurried conversation with Citizen Rear Admiral Chernov, at Megan
Hathaway's announcement. He looked sharply at her, and
the ops officer studied her console for a moment. Then
she raised her head, a puzzled crease between her eyebrows.

"They seem to be settling down on a rough heading
of oh-seven-three, oh-oh-eight true, Citizen Admiral.
Acceleration approximately two-point-four-five KPS
squared—call it two-five-oh gravities."

Theisman frowned, then strode over to *Conquérant*'s
master plot and glowered down into its depths. That low
an acceleration suggested Harrington's ships had to be
as heavily damaged as he thought they were, but his
frown deepened as he watched CIC's projection of her
course stretch out across the plot. It wasn't the head-
on intercept she'd sought against TG 14.1, yet her new
heading would bring her force across his own line of
advance in little more than forty-seven minutes. And the
fact that she would cross it rather than come in on a
reciprocal meant she'd have far more time—at least
twenty-six minutes of it, CIC estimated—in which to
engage before he crossed her range envelope.

His eyes hardened, and he bit his lip gently. If she
had four healthy superdreadnoughts over there, or even
four that were only moderately damaged, supported by
nine battlecruisers, his twelve battleships and sixteen
battlecruisers were unlikely to last twenty-six minutes
against them. But she *couldn't* have healthy ships—not
after the pounding she and Thurston had just given one
another! Only if she *didn't*, then why was she on a heading like that? She wasn't simply accepting battle, she was
courting it!

"Punch in a same-plane evasive course change to port
at four-seven-oh gees and set for continuous update,"
he said quietly. His astrogator spoke quietly to CIC, and
the plot changed once more. A new course projection
speared out from *Conquérant*'s own light code, and
Theisman tapped an order of his own into the plot. A

broad-based, shaded cone of green blinked alight, spreading out to port, and a digital time display appeared beside it. *Conquérant* was the apex of the cone, and a three-quarters sphere of amber light stretched out ahead of it. The time display ticked downward, and as it did, the cone shrank and the amber both filled in about it and moved steadily aft. Theisman gazed down at the plot, humming softly under his breath, then turned his head as he felt a presence at his elbow.

"What is it, Citizen Admiral?" Dennis LePic's eyes were calm, and if perspiration beaded his forehead, Thomas Theisman didn't hold that against him.

"Lady Harrington has decided not to wait for us, Sir," the citizen rear admiral said. "She's coming out to meet us."

"Out to meet us?" LePic repeated more sharply. "I thought you said her ships were too damaged to fight us?"

"What I said, Citizen Commissioner, is that I *believed* them to be too badly damaged to fight us and *win*, and I still believe that."

"Then why isn't she trying to avoid us?" LePic asked tautly.

"An excellent question," Theisman admitted, then gave a frosty smile. "It's always possible she disagrees with my own evaluation, I suppose."

LePic started to say something, then paused, and his lower lip whitened under the pressure of his teeth as he stared down into the plot. Seconds trickled past, and then he cleared his throat.

"What does this indicate, Citizen Admiral?" He gestured at the green and amber lights and time display, and Theisman chuckled without humor.

"That, Citizen Commissioner, is the space we have to dodge in. If we alter course to any heading which lies within the bounds of the amber zone, we'll pass within missile range of Lady Harrington but remain outside her energy range. If we alter course to stay within the *green* zone, she'll be unable to bring us to action at all."

"And if we stay within neither of them?"

"Then, Citizen Commissioner, we'll have no choice but to pass through her energy envelope at some point."

"I see." LePic watched the time display tick downward from 12:00 to 11:59 and swallowed.

"If they don't change course in the next twelve minutes, My Lady, they won't change it at all," Mercedes Brigham observed quietly, and Honor nodded without looking up from her own display. Damage reports were still coming in, and they were even worse than Mercedes' original estimate. Their chance of inflicting decisive damage on the Peeps, if it came to that, was already lower than she'd hoped, and it was shrinking steadily. She pinched the bridge of her nose again, harder this time, hoping the self-inflicted pain would somehow pierce her fatigue. There had to be something else she could do, some other way she could turn up the pressure, *something* . . . but what?

LePic was dabbing at his forehead now as sweat trickled into his eyes and he stood hunched over the plot, watching the green cone shrink. The amber zone was slowly, inexorably shrinking as well, and Thomas Theisman felt an urge to wipe his own forehead as he stood beside the commissioner.

Damn it, he *knew* he was right! By now, his long-range scans had confirmed the atmosphere and water vapor trailing Harrington's SDs in clear proof of heavy hull breaching. The range remained impossibly long for any sort of visual examination of her units, but he didn't really need that, did he? Her drive strength was down, her ships were bleeding air, her active sensor emissions had changed as she brought secondary systems on-line to replace shot-up primaries . . . *all* of it pointed to ships with massive damage.

And yet, damage or no, she was still coming—coming when she had to know defeat would cost her the total destruction of all four of her SDs. Why? Why was she *doing* it when she *knew* as well as he that he could take her?

He wanted to pace, but such obvious worry on his part would only finish off the resolution to which LePic clung so painfully, and so he settled for rocking slowly up and down on his heels. He'd studied Harrington's record with care since Operation Jericho's dismal failure. Intelligence had done the same thing, of course, and with far better information access, but he had a personal motivation they lacked. She'd beaten him, captured his ship—captured *him*—and that gave him a special insight, a special desire and need to understand her. And as his mind ran back over all he'd read and heard about her, he remembered the final phases of the Second Battle of Yeltsin. Remembered how Honor Harrington had taken a crippled heavy cruiser on a death-ride straight into the broadside of a battlecruiser, *knowing* it would destroy her . . . because she'd believed that before her ship died, it could inflict enough damage to prevent its enemy from carrying on to attack Grayson.

His eyes went very still for a moment, and he fought an urge to swallow. Was that what this was? Second Yeltsin on a grander scale? Was she actually willing to sacrifice four SDs and another twenty-four thousand people in a fight to the death simply to *cripple* TG 14.2's battleships?

His mind ticked harder, faster, considering the possibilities. If she took out his battleships, the rest of Task Force Fourteen's survivors would be unable to take Yeltsin or Endicott away from their other defenders. But she couldn't *do* it, a corner of his brain insisted stubbornly. She couldn't have the firepower over there to pull it off! He was certain she didn't!

But—

He clenched his fists behind him and swore silently. As he himself had told LePic, Harrington wasn't a god. Not even she could do the impossible. But she *was* Honor Harrington, and if *she* thought she could pull it off . . .

*   *   *

"Seven minutes, My Lady."

Honor nodded again. She didn't need the quiet reminder, and part of her wanted to snap at Mercedes for inflicting it on her brutally strained nerves, but it was a chief of staff's job. Besides, Mercedes had to be feeling the strain, too, and if an occasional unneeded reminder was all the sign of it she gave, then she was doing a better job of hiding it than most.

Honor looked around her flag bridge. Mercedes sat calmly at her own console, watching her plot, inputting an occasional update as her earbug whispered reports from other units of the squadron to her. Fred Bagwell sat very still and straight, face blank, shoulders slightly hunched, and rested his motionless hands on his tactical console. He'd already set up the best fire plan his crippled missile tubes and energy batteries permitted; now all he could do was wait, and a drop of sweat trickled down his right cheek.

Allen Sewell had his command chair shock frame unlatched so that he could lounge back and cross his legs. His elbows rested on the chair arms, his hands steepled across his stomach while he whistled silently, and Honor felt her own mouth quirk in wry amusement. Did Allen even begin to realize how his obvious "relaxation" shouted out the tension which had produced it?

She glanced at Howard Brannigan. The sandy-haired com officer was as quietly busy as Mercedes, monitoring the communications nets, but he seemed to feel Honor's eyes upon him. He looked up and met her gaze for a moment, then nodded with a brief smile and bent back to his duties.

Gregory Paxton was at his own work station, and a steadily lengthening block of alphanumeric characters crawled up his display. He was actually jotting down notes, Honor thought, and wondered if he was recording his personal impressions or updating the official post-battle report he was so unlikely to survive to present.

Neither Stephen Matthews nor Abraham Jackson were

present. Her logistics officer had taken over in Damage Central to free *Terrible*'s surviving engineering officers to lead repair parties, and her chaplain was busy with his own grim duty to the dead and dying in *Terrible*'s sickbay.

Her officers, Honor thought wearily. A microcosm of the entire squadron. People she'd come to know and care for directly, as individuals, and she was taking all of them to their deaths, and she couldn't think of a single other option. If only there were some way to bring just a little more pressure to bear on the Peeps. *They* had to be sweating it, as well, and, unlike her, *they* could break off and run away. But—

And then her exhausted eyes sharpened and she shoved herself upright in her command chair.

"Howard!"

"Yes, My Lady?" Brannigan turned from his com console, startled by the sharp energy of her voice.

"Warm up the pulse transmitter for an FTL Flash Priority transmission to *Courvosier*."

"*Courvosier*, Milady?" Mercedes Brigham looked up with a frown. Mark Brentworth's *Raoul Courvosier* was way the hell and gone out-system—almost on the hyper limit, over a hundred million klicks *behind* Force Zulu. The enemy had accelerated right past her and the rest of her squadron on his way in while they hid under a total emissions shut down, but even if the eight of them had been powerful enough to threaten the Peeps, they were hopelessly out of range.

"*Courvosier*," Honor repeated. "I've got a little job for Captain Brentworth," she said, and Mercedes blinked at the sudden, almost mischievous twinkle in her tired eyes.

"Status change!" Megan Hathaway snapped, and Theisman whipped around as a warning buzzer sounded. He stared back down into the plot, and, for just a moment, his heart seemed to stop.

Superdreadnoughts. Eight more *Gryphon*-class SDs

of the Royal Manticoran Navy, the most powerful ships
of the wall any navy had yet built, had just blinked into
existence on the plot. They were a hundred and seven
million kilometers astern of TG 14.2, but they were
accelerating hard. Eight Grayson battlecruisers spread
out to screen them as they closed, and an icy chill ran
through his blood. That force changed everything. Even
if he somehow managed to beat Harrington with no
losses at all, that many fresh ships of the wall would
make mincemeat of what was left of TF Fourteen,
and—

His panicky thoughts stopped suddenly, and his brows
knit. Yes, that many SDs could smash everything he had,
but where had they *been* all this time? They were behind him, coming down his track, but his sensors would
have detected their hyper footprint if they'd just translated into n-space. Of course, Manty stealth systems were
good. They were 5.9 light-minutes back, and the Manties
had proven in the fighting around Nightingale and
Trevor's Star that they could hide low-powered impeller wedges from the PN's sensors at as little as six light-
minutes. That meant it was *possible* they'd been here
all along, creeping in under cover of their EW in an
effort to ambush him as he ran into their arms on his
way out, away from Harrington after TG 14.1's destruction. And the timing was about right for Harrington to
have sent a light-speed message calling them in openly
as soon as she realized he wasn't going to break off and
let them ambush him after all.

All of that was *possible* . . . but he didn't believe it
for a moment. If those were real SDs, Harrington would
already have broken off. She wouldn't *need* to close with
him, even as a bluff, for their mere presence would have
been enough to force him to run for it. No, he thought
coldly. The *battlecruisers* were probably real enough, but
they were "screening" EW drones set to mimic SDs, not
real ships of the wall.

He started to say so, then stopped. The flag deck
recorders had taken down everything he'd said to LePic,

every word of his confident explanation of how he could defeat the surviving Grayson ships of the wall, and any board of inquiry which reviewed those recordings would know he'd been right. But he'd said those things before Harrington headed out to meet him. Before he was faced with the certainty that she *was* going to fight, and that even after he'd won, most of his battleships would still have been pounded to scrap. Now—

"What is it, Citizen Admiral?" LePic asked urgently.

"It would appear to be a squadron of Manty super-dreadnoughts, Citizen Commissioner," Theisman heard himself say calmly.

"*Superdreadnoughts?*" LePic stared at him in horror. "What— Where— *How* can they *be* here?"

"Manty stealth systems are better than ours, Sir," Theisman replied in that same calm, dispassionate tone while his own eyes dropped to the steadily narrowing green cone in *Conquérant's* master plot. "It's possible they've been there all along. If they were too far out-system to rendezvous with Harrington before she came out to ambush Citizen Admiral Thurston—and, given their current positions, that would have to have been the case—they could have been coming in under stealth to catch us if we'd run straight back to the hyper limit on a reciprocal of our original entry vector."

"But—" LePic clamped his jaws together and scrubbed sweat from his forehead, blinking furiously, and Theisman watched him dispassionately. "This changes the situation, doesn't it, Citizen Admiral?" the commissioner said after a moment in the tone of a man fighting desperately for calm. "I mean, even if you completely destroy this force—" he pointed to the light codes of Harrington's oncoming ships "—*this* one—" he pointed at the new-comers "—will still prevent us from carrying out the rest of Operation Dagger, won't they?"

"Eight *Gryphon*-class superdreadnoughts?" Theisman snorted. "They certainly would, Citizen Commissioner!"

"But you still think you can destroy Harrington?"

"I'm certain of it," Theisman said firmly.

"But you couldn't carry out Dagger afterwards?" LePic pressed.

"Not against a full squadron of Manty SDs," Theisman admitted.

"I see." LePic inhaled deeply, and then, suddenly, he seemed to calm. "Well, Citizen Admiral, I can only say that I'm impressed by your determination and courage, especially after what's already happened here, but your ships are too valuable to throw away in a hopeless cause. If we can't carry through with Operation Dagger even if you defeat Harrington, then I see no way to justify the losses we'd take from her in reply. Speaking for the Committee of Public Safety, I instruct you to break off."

Theisman glanced back into the plot. There were still a couple of minutes to go before the green cone disappeared, he noted, and let an edge of mulish obstinacy into his expression.

"Citizen Commissioner, even if we lose every battleship in the task group, the loss of four superdreadnoughts to the Alliance would—"

"I admire your determination," LePic said even more firmly, "but it's not just the battleships. There are also the transports and the freighters, not to mention the units of your screen." The commissioner shook his head. "No, Citizen Admiral. We've lost today—through no fault of yours, but we've lost—so let's not throw good money after bad. Break off, Citizen Admiral. That's an order."

"As you wish, Citizen Commissioner." Theisman sighed with manifest unwillingness, and looked at his ops officer. "You heard the citizen commissioner, Megan. Bring us hard to port and go to maximum acceleration."

"Aye, Citizen Admiral." Hathaway managed to keep the relief out of her voice, but she shot her admiral a look of approving admiration when LePic couldn't see it, and Theisman turned away with a hidden smile of wry regret.

You've done it to me again, My Lady, he thought at the oncoming, damaged superdreadnoughts. *I could still have you—we both know that, don't we?—but I'm afraid*

I'm not quite as eager to die today as you are. Another time, Lady Harrington.

"They're breaking off!" Bagwell said sharply. "My Lady, they're breaking off!"

"Are they?" Honor leaned back in her command chair and felt a deep, painful shudder of relief go through her very bones. She hadn't really expected her threadbare bluff to work, but she had no intention of complaining, and she gazed down at her com link to Alfredo Yu. "It seems wars *are* still fought by human beings, Alfredo," she murmured.

"Indeed they are, My Lady," Yu replied with a smile, "and some of them aren't quite as good at calling the cards as others are."

"You knew," Bagwell said softly. Honor turned to look at him, and the fussy ops officer's brown eyes positively glowed as he stared at her. "You *knew* they'd break off, My Lady."

Honor started to reply, then stopped herself with a tiny headshake. *Let him keep his illusions,* she thought, and shoved up out of her command chair. She gathered Nimitz up and crossed to the master plot with slow, careful steps, mindful of her unreliable knees, and gazed down into it. The Peeps were running flat out for the hyper limit at right angles to their original course, and already Mark Brentworth and *Courvosier* were turning to pursue, though there was absolutely no chance of overhauling them. She could trust Mark to rotate replacement decoy drones into place smoothly enough for no one to notice when the new ones took over from the old, and with eight "superdreadnoughts" in pursuit, the Peeps wouldn't stop running now that they'd started.

Despite all she could do, her knees started to go, and she caught her weight on one hand, leaning against the plot for several seconds, then forced herself back upright once more.

"I believe I'll go to my quarters, Mercedes," she said. "Of course, My Lady. I'll buzz you if we need you," her chief of staff replied quietly. Honor nodded gratefully to her, then made her way to the flag bridge lift. Simon Mattingly followed her without a word, and she felt the admiring gazes of her staff and felt dishonest for not telling them the truth, not admitting how desperate—how frightened—she'd been. But she didn't, for that wasn't how the game was played.

She stepped into the lift and made herself stand upright until the doors closed, then sagged heavily against the bulkhead. Simon stood close beside her, ready to support her if she needed it, and she felt nothing but gratitude, unflawed by any trace of resentment or shame, for his attentiveness.

The lift stopped, and somehow she managed the short, rubbery-legged walk down the passage to her quarters. Mattingly peeled off to take his place beside the hatch, and she staggered across her cabin to the huge, comfortable couch and let herself collapse across it, cradling Nimitz to her chest.

Just a few minutes, she thought drunkenly. *I'll just sit here a few minutes, only a few. Just a few minutes.*

Five minutes later, James MacGuiness walked soundlessly into the cabin, and Admiral Lady Dame Honor Harrington didn't even stir as he eased her down to lie flat on the couch and tucked a pillow under her head.

• EPILOGUE

"—own casualties until we receive Lady Harrington's final report, My Lords," Chancellor Prestwick said. "They appear to be severe, if far lower than we might have anticipated. But we *do* know the enemy's losses were many times our own and that, with the Tester's help, Lady Harrington has once more decisively defeated a Havenite attempt to seize our star system."

A roar of approval went up from the gathered stead-holders, and Samuel Mueller was the first to stand. He clapped his hands loudly, slowly, as was the Grayson way, and other Keys rose to join him. Their hands found the rhythm he'd set, copied it, clapped with him, and Mueller beamed with pleasure at the news while the percussive beat echoed from the Chamber walls and his mind spewed silent curses.

Damn the woman! Burdette must have been right about her after all, the idiot. Only Satan himself could have arranged this! They'd had her, he thought almost despairingly. They'd *had* her, actually managed to turn the people of Grayson against her—and now this! Damn it to Hell, she *must* be the very spawn of Satan! How else could she have survived the dome collapse, being shot out of the sky, a *second* assassination attempt at point-blank range, a duel with one of Grayson's fifty best fencers, and then defeated yet *another* invasion of Yeltsin? She wasn't *human*!

But she'd done it, he told himself grimly while the applause reached its thunderous crescendo. And the fact that she'd come back from public disgrace to accomplish it all in the space of three bare days only made the mindless public love her even more. It would be suicide to attempt anything further against her—or Benjamin Mayhew—now. Especially until he was certain he'd covered all traces of his connections to Burdette and Marchant.

A hint of true satisfaction crept into his assumed smile of pleasure at that thought. His "insurance policy" had already accounted for twenty-six of its thirty targets, including both Marchant and Harding, the only ones he was certain could have testified against him. It was fortunate Mayhew had delayed any move against them until after Harrington had been given her chance to confront Burdette—not that he'd had much choice. Planetary Security had to notify any steadholder before they made arrests in his steading, and Mayhew could scarcely have notified Burdette of his plans to arrest Marchant and his cousin without warning the Steadholder. But unlike Mayhew's men, Mueller's had already been in Burdette, and they'd acted with skill and dispatch. Indeed, Mueller thought with a grim chuckle, they'd made Marchant's death look like the vengeance of outraged private citizens, while Harding had "thrown himself to his death" from a tenth story window.

So he was safe—probably. And it was time to begin playing the compassionate elder statesman, determined to bind up Grayson's wounds, to make sure he stayed that way.

The thundering ovation died at last, and Mueller raised his right hand to attract the Speaker's attention. The Speaker pointed to him, yielding him the floor, and Mueller turned to his fellow steadholders.

"My Lords, our world and people have been the victims of a disgusting and cowardly plot against a person our Protector so rightly called a good and a godly woman. To my own shame, I, too, believed the initial reports. I actually held Grayson Sky Domes—and Lady Harrington—responsible for the deaths of my steaders, and in my anger, I did and said things which I now deeply regret."

He spoke quietly, sincerely, bending his head to acknowledge his fault, and the other Keys gazed at him in silent understanding and compassion.

"My Lords," he resumed after a moment, "I, as many of us, have done grievous damage to Sky Domes by canceling contracts and initiating litigation against them. For my own part, and on behalf of the Steading of Mueller, I now publicly renounce that litigation. I invite Sky Domes to resume construction of the Mueller Middle School Dome, and I pledge the privy purse of Mueller to cover any reasonable expense in clearing the site so that work may begin anew."

"Hear, hear!" someone cried.

"Well said, Mueller!" another shouted.

"In addition, My Lords, and in view of the guilt of one of our own members in organizing this despicable plot, I hereby request this Conclave to consider the rectitude—no, our moral responsibility—to reimburse Grayson Sky Domes and Lady Harrington for all legal costs stemming from any litigation arising from the false panic generated against them."

"I second the motion!" Lord Surtees said loudly, but Mueller raised a hand, for he wasn't quite done yet.

"And finally, My Lords," he said quietly, "in light of the way she has yet again saved our star system and our planet, I move that this Conclave, as the formal representative of the people of Grayson, steadholder and steader alike, vote Lady Honor Harrington, Steadholder Harrington, our thanks as a Hero—" he paused, then shook his head "—no, My Lords, as a Hero*ine* of Grayson, and petition our Protector to append the Crossed Swords to her Star of Grayson!"

There was a moment of silence—this time a profoundly uncomfortable one—and then Lord Mackenzie rose. Mackenzie had been shaken to the bone by the proof of Burdette's treachery, Mueller knew. It had forced him to examine his own feelings towards Honor Harrington, and he didn't seem to like what he'd found when he did. Well, John Mackenzie had always been a bit too noble for Mueller's taste, but the man was held in the highest regard by his fellow Keys, and Mueller bowed to him, temporarily yielding the floor without betraying by so much as a smile that he'd hoped Mackenzie would seek it.

"My Lords," Mackenzie said quietly, "I find this motion a wise and a proper one. It is always fitting that we honor those who have met the Test of Life, and surely no one in our history has ever met—and surpassed—her Test more fully than Lady Harrington. My Lords of Grayson, I second Lord Mueller's motions in full, and ask the Conclave to adopt them by acclamation."

There was another moment of intense silence. Only one other individual had ever received the Crossed Swords to indicate a second award of Grayson's highest decoration for valor . . . and that man had been Isaiah Mackenzie, Benjamin the Great's captain general in the Civil War. For six hundred years, the tradition had been that no one else would *ever* receive the Swords to the Star, but Isaiah Mackenzie had been John Mackenzie's ancestor, in direct line, and if John Mackenzie felt—

A chair scuffed softly as a steadholder rose at the far end of the horseshoe and, as Mueller himself had done only moments before, began to clap. And then another steadholder stood, and another, one by one, until every man in the Chamber was on his feet and clapping.

The roar of sound rolled around the Chamber, then died as the Speaker rose, and Samuel Mueller beamed, his face alight with approval for the woman he hated, as the sharp, crisp blows of the Speaker's gavel announced the Keys of Grayson's unanimous commendation of Lady Honor Harrington.

• AUTHOR'S NOTE

I completed this manuscript in October 1994. At that time, I'd structured the events which occur in Chapter Nineteen because I could think of no more loathsome, despicable, and cowardly act any individual or group of individuals could commit. It is my belief that the sentence "The end justifies the means"—that suppression, repression, and/or murder become somehow acceptable if committed in the name of a "cause" or belief which reduces individuals to expendable pawns— is the vilest of human poisons, and that terrorism, regardless of the terrorist's "cause," is the ultimate act of dehumanization. I did not expect that between the time I wrote this novel and the time it was published a United States citizen would demonstrate an even worse contempt for human life and the fundamental values of his own society or prove capable of an act even more despicable than my fictional villains. That some human beings are capable of such atrocities is an inescapable lesson of history. That we cannot allow those acts to go unpunished or extend to those who commit them any shred of respect, whatever the "cause" which motivated them, is a lesson the civilized human community must teach itself.